Crossing OVER

Crossing OVER

ANNA KENDALL

VIKING

An Imprint of Penguin Group (USA) Inc.

VIKING
Published by Penguin Group
Penguin Group (USA) Inc., 345 Hudson Street, New York, New York 10014, U.S.A.
Penguin Group (Canada), 90 Eglinton Avenue East, Suite 700, Toronto, Ontario, Canada M4P 2Y3
(a division of Pearson Penguin Canada Inc.)
Penguin Books Ltd., 80 Strand, London WC2R 0RL, England
Penguin Ireland, 25 St. Stephen's Green, Dublin 2, Ireland (a division of Penguin Books Ltd.)
Penguin Group (Australia), 250 Camberwell Road, Camberwell, Victoria 3124, Australia
(a division of Pearson Australia Group Pty Ltd.)
Penguin Books India Pvt Ltd., 11 Community Centre, Panchsheel Park, New Delhi–110 017, India
Penguin Group (NZ), 67 Apollo Drive, Rosedale, North Shore 0632, New Zealand
(a division of Pearson New Zealand Ltd.)
Penguin Books (South Africa) (Pty) Ltd, 24 Sturdee Avenue, Rosebank, Johannesburg 2196, South Africa

Penguin Books Ltd., Registered Offices: 80 Strand, London WC2R 0RL, England

First published in the United States in 2010 by Viking, a member of Penguin Group (USA) Inc.

1   3   5   7   9   10   8   6   4   2

Copyright © Anna Kendall, 2010
All rights reserved

LIBRARY OF CONGRESS CATALOGING-IN-PUBLICATION DATA IS AVAILABLE
ISBN: 978-0-670-01246-6

Printed in U.S.A.   Set in Perpetua and Requiem   Book design by Jim Hoover

The city, characters, and events to be found in these pages are fictitious.
Any resemblance to actual persons living or dead is purely coincidental.

To Jack

1

THE FIRST TIME I ever crossed over, it was market day and I was a little boy, barely six years old. I had spilled goat's milk on the linsey-woolsey that Aunt Jo had spent weeks weaving, the linsey-woolsey that she was going to sell at market. Hartah beat me unconscious, and I crossed over.

No. That is not true. I must have crossed over earlier, in dreams. There must have been times when my infant self lay asleep, restless and feverish from some childish illness, pain in my head or belly or throat. That's what is required—letting go, as in sleep, plus pain. Not great pain, but Hartah doesn't believe that. Or maybe he just likes beating me.

That first time, eight years ago—the milk staining the bright green wool, my aunt's gasp, her husband raising his head from the table with that look in his eyes, and I—

"Roger," he said now, "you will cross over today." Again

Hartah raised his head, this time looking at me over the rim of his mug of sour ale.

My neck and spine turned cold.

It was barely dawn. We sat alone in the taproom of an inn somewhere on the Stonegreen Road. It wasn't much of an inn. Three trestle tables of rough wood on the cobbled floor, two ladders leading to "rooms" above that were no more than lofts with dirty straw as pallets. The beams overhead were so blackened and ill cared for that soot dropped onto the tables. Still, last night my heart had surged with gladness when our wagon pulled into the stable yard. During the summer we almost never slept indoors. But now the first leaves had begun to turn color and the air smelled of rain. Hartah must have hidden a few pennies, or stolen them, to pay the innkeeper.

"Today is the Stonegreen harvest faire," Hartah said. "You will cross over." Before he could say more, the inn door opened and four men entered. They were loud, laughing and joking, but no louder than the clamor in my head.

I can't, I can't, I can't, I won't—

But I knew I would.

"Brought your ram, then, Farlowe?" said one of the men. "Puny beast—no prize for you, I wager!"

"Seventeen stone if he's a pound!"

"Pound of sagging skin and weak bones!"

Rough male laughter and cries of "Ale! Ale before the faire!"

The innkeeper's wife came from the kitchen, Aunt Jo trailing meekly behind with Hartah's breakfast. She didn't meet my eyes. She knew, then, what Hartah would make me do this day, and how he would make me do it.

"Ale! Ale before the faire!"

"You shall have it, then," the innkeeper's wife said, a frothy mug in each hand and two more balanced on her meaty fore-arms. "And breakfast, too, if you're with money, you scurri-lous lot! Good morrow, Tom, Philip, Jack . . . Henry, where's that pretty new wife of yours? When I was her age, I was never left alone in bed of a faire morning. Or did you wear her out before dawn?"

The youngest man blushed and looked proud. The oth-ers roared and teased him while the woman set down the ale. She was broad, red-faced, merry— everything my aunt was not. Aunt Jo set a wooden trencher of bread and cheese—no meat—in front of Hartah and backed quickly away. So cowed was she that she didn't even realize he would hardly strike her here, in front of men whom he hoped to be selling to later in the day. Her thin body shuddered.

I felt no pity. Never once had she protected me from him. Never once. And there was no bread and cheese for me. Prob-ably Hartah's stolen coins were only enough for one.

The oldest of the laughing men glanced at me. Casually he flipped a penny onto the table. "Here, boy, water my horse and his burden, the ones with yellow ribbons, there's a good lad."

The penny landed midway between Hartah and me. I saw the muscles of his great shoulders shift, as if he meant to reach for it. But the older man watched us, and so Hartah merely nodded, as if giving permission. As if he were some sort of gracious lord—Hartah! Hatred burned behind my eyes. I snatched the penny and went outside.

The day was soft and clear, traces of the gold-and-orange sunrise still in the sky and the rough grass smelling of last night's rain. I fetched water from the stable yard well both for the horse and for the ram tethered in the cart, its horns bright with yellow ribbons. More wagons pulled up to the inn, farmers arriving for the faire. Their cartwheels groaned under loads of vegetables, sheep, baskets, children. "The caravan comes! I saw it!" a child shrieked, leaning so far over the side of his wagon that he nearly fell out. "I saw it!"

"Hush your noise," his young mother said fondly. She wore a lavender dress and lavender ribbons in her hair, and her hand strayed to stroke her little lad's soft curls.

Bitterness ran through me like vomit.

Hartah would make me do it. He would make me cross over, lying concealed in the back of our worn and faded faire booth. That was why we had come here. And to make it happen, he would beat me first, as he had all the other times.

I was no longer six years old. I was fourteen, and as tall as Hartah. But I was skinny—how could I be otherwise, when I got so little to eat?—and narrow shouldered. Hartah could lift a cask of new ale on each shoulder and not even sweat. But now I had a penny. Could I run away on that? On a single penny and the memory of my dead mother in her lavender dress?

No. I could not. Where would I go?

And yet I dreamed of escape. Sometimes I gazed at Hartah and was frightened by the violence of my desire to do him violence. But Hartah had told me and Aunt Jo of finding the bodies of lone travelers on the roads of The Queendom, set upon by highwaymen, robbed and gutted. After such stories, I huddled in my thin blanket and went nowhere.

My stomach rumbled. I took the penny round back to the

kitchen and exchanged it for breakfast, which I gobbled standing up in the stable yard.

A girl leaned against the well. There were other girls here now, climbing down from wagons or trailing behind their families into the inn. They wore their best outfits, wool skirts dyed green or red or blue, hiked up over striped petticoats, black stomachers laced tight over embroidered white smocks, ribbons in their hair. This one was no prettier, no more bright-eyed, no better dressed than the others, although she wore black lace mitts on her hands. But she watched me. The rest of the girls looked through me, as if I were a patch of air, or else their eyes narrowed and their pink lips turned down in disgust. *Dirty. Weak. Homeless.*

But this girl watched me thoughtfully, her heavy bucket of water dangling from one hand and weighing down her shoulder. Something bright and terrifying raced through me. *She knew.*

But of course that was nonsense. Nobody knew about me except my aunt and the bastard she had married, and sometimes I think even my aunt doubted. He can do *what*? Does he merely pretend? But Aunt Jo said so little, serving Hartah in such cringing silence, that it was impossible to tell what she thought except that she wished I had not come to her on her sister's death. That wish was evident every moment of every day, but even so, she didn't wish it as fervently as I.

However, there had been nowhere else for me to go. My mother dead, my father vanished before I had any memory of him. Aunt Jo would never talk of either, no matter how much I begged. And now, all these years later, still nowhere else for me to go.

The girl nodded at me and walked off with her heavy bucket. Her long black braids swung from side to side. Her pretty figure grew smaller as she walked away from me, so that it almost seemed as if she were disappearing, dissolving into the soft morning light. "There you are," Hartah's voice said behind me. "Getting breakfast, are you? Good. You'll need your strength this afternoon."

I turned. He smiled. A mouth full of broken teeth, and eyes full of pleasure at what would come later. Slowly, almost as gentle as a woman, he reached out one thick finger and wiped a crumb of bread from beside my lips.

BY NOON THE faire was in full whirl. Stonegreen was bigger than I had realized. The inn where we had slept was five miles back down the road, and there was a much better inn beside the village green, along with a blacksmith shop, a cobbler, and the large, moss-covered boulder that gave Stonegreen its name. The boulder reached as high as my shoulder, and someone had planted love-in-a-mist all around it. A placid river, bordered by trees, meandered by half-timbered cottages thatched with straw. The straw, too, had grown green with moss and lichens. Around the cottages grew hollyhocks, delphinium, roses, ivy, cherry and apple trees. Behind were neat herb gardens, well houses, chicken yards, and smokehouses—all the sources of good things that exist when women hold sway over prosperous households. I smelled bread baking and the sweet-sour odor of mulled ale.

The faire was held in a field at the other end of town from the green. There were booths and tents where local people sold crops, livestock, meat pies, jellies, cloth woven by wives and daughters, ale and ribbons, and carved wooden toys. In other booths, merchants from as far away as Glory, the capital of The Queendom, offered pewter plate, farm tools, buttons. A third group, neither local nor from Glory, had come in a caravan of red-and-blue-painted wagons that traveled all summer to country faires. I had seen the caravans before. There would be a fire-eater, puppet players, jugglers, fiddlers, a show of trained fleas, an illusionist, a wrestler offering to take on all comers. Children ran among the booths, and couples strolled arm in arm. Fiddlers and drummers played, boothmen bawled out their wares, animals for sale bleated or lowed or clucked. I saw no soldiers, which, of course, was a good thing.

"Here," said Hartah, and my aunt and I began unloading the tent from his wagon.

Our booth, unlike most others, was completely closed. The stained and faded canvas displayed only a small group of stars, arranged in the constellation of the Weeping Woman. Sometimes people entered thinking we were some sort of chapel, but Hartah was good at spotting those and sending them away none the wiser. Others, recognizing the ancient pattern of stars and their hidden meaning, entered alone, one by one. They conferred with Hartah and, later, came back for their answer, also alone. Hartah could neither read nor cipher. But he was not stupid, he took care, and it had been a long time since we had been denounced as witches. These were prosperous days in The Queendom, and even I at fourteen knew that prosperity lessens suspicion of witchcraft. People were not desperate. It is the poor and desperate, so accustomed to danger, who most fear what they cannot see.

Although, of course, we were not even witches.

As I tugged on the heavy canvas, I thought again about running away. I could do it. Boys my age did it—didn't they? They found work as farmhands or stable boys or beggars. But I knew nothing of farming, not much about horses, and I was afraid not only of highwaymen but of starvation. And in a few months winter would be here. Where did beggars go in winter?

The truth is, I was a coward.

"Look lively, Roger!" Hartah growled. "Your aunt works faster than you!"

And she did. Aunt Jo scurried around like a scrawny whirlwind, afraid of Hartah's fists.

When the tent was up, he shoved me inside it. A rough table was set in the corner and draped with a rug that fell to the ground. Under this, unseen but hearing all, I would crouch for several hours, as the faire-goers came with their requests. We would not get the happy men, women, and children carrying their fairings, drinking their ale, winning prizes for their seventeen-stone rams. We would get the other people found in every village, every city, in every queendom. The people that the happy ones tried not to notice, lest it ruin their pleasure at the faire. The ones who were beset, grieving, afraid. My people.

And so it would begin again.

The first time I ever crossed over, I was six years old. Now I was fourteen and it was the same, ever the same, always the same.

All morning I lay cramped beneath my table, listening. Then, at noon, when the sun beat hot on the heavy canvas, the tent flap was fastened close and Hartah pulled me out. He smiled. "You ready, boy?"

"Hartah . . ." I hated that my voice quavered, that I brought my hand feebly to guard my face, hated that I was too frightened of him to fight back. His fist smashed into my belly. All the air left me, and I gasped with pain. He hit me again, in the chest, the groin, all places covered by clothing where my bruises would not show. The sounds of the fiddles and the drums and the shrieking children hid my cries. I was not an infant now, crossing over in an infant's mindless letting go; I had to choose this. Pain plus choice. I willed it so, and even as my body fell to the ground, it happened.

Darkness—

Cold—

Dirt choking my mouth—

Worms in my eyes—

Earth imprisoning my fleshless arms and legs—

But only for a moment. I was not, after all, actually dead. The taste of death lasted only for the brief moment of crossing, the plunge through the barrier that no one else could penetrate, not even the Dead themselves. A heavy barrier, solid and large as Earth itself, and just as impossible to bore all the way through. Except, for reasons I did not understand, for me.

I tried again to cry out and could not for the dirt clogging my mouth. I tried to flail my arms and could not for the lack of muscle and flesh over my naked bones. Then it was over. The dirt gone, my bones restored, and I had crossed over into the country of the Dead.

A few of the Dead sat on the ground, doing what the Dead do. I ignored them as I took my bearings. There, in the near distance, the gleam of water . . . It might be the river beside Stonegreen.

The country of the Dead is like our country, but weirdly stretched out and sometimes distorted. A few steps in Stonegreen might be half a mile here, or two miles, or five. Or it might be the same. Sometimes our rivers and forests and hills exist here, but sometimes not. The country of the Dead is vaster than ours and I think it changes over time, just as ours does, but not in the same way. It is our shadow made solid. Like a shadow, it shrinks and grows, but from some unseen influence that is not the sun. There is no sun here.

There *is* light, an even subdued glow, as on a cloudy day. The sky is always a low, featureless gray. The air is quiet, and I could again breathe easily, all hurt gone from my chest. Pain does not follow me when I cross over. It is merely the price of passage.

In the cool, calm light I walked toward the gleam of water. Before I reached it, I came to the big, moss-covered boulder that on the other side had marked the village green. The boulder looked exactly the same, although without Stonegreen's surrounding cottages and shops and fields. Without the road, as well. There are no roads here, just untrammeled grass of an everlasting summer. The steps of the Dead leave no marks.

Five of them sat cross-legged beside the stone, holding hands in a circle. They like to do that. It's always hard for me to get the attention of the Dead, but when they're in one of their circles, it's impossible. They sit for long stretches of time—days, years—never talking, and on each of their faces is the calm, absorbed look of men aiming an arrow, or of women bent over a difficult piece of needlework. I passed them by and continued on toward the river.

An old woman sat there, alone under a great overhanging tree, her bare toes dangling in the water. She wore a rough brown dress and a white apron, her gray hair tucked under an old-fashioned cap with long white lappets. The old are the only Dead who will—or perhaps can—talk to me, and most often it is the old women who are good talkers. I sat beside her on the bank and said, "Good morrow, mistress."

Nothing. She didn't yet realize I was there. What do the Dead see when they see me? A wisp, a shimmer in the air? I don't really know. I squeezed her arm hard, just above the elbow, and shouted, "Good morrow, mistress!"

Slowly she turned her head, squinted her sunken blue eyes, and said, "Who's there?"

"I am Roger Kilbourne. At your service."

That tickled her. She gave a cackling laugh. "And what service d'you think you could render me, then? You've crossed over to bother us, have you not?"

"Yes, mistress."

"What the devil do you want now? Go back, lad, it is not your time. Not yet."

"I know," I said humbly. "But I would ask you some questions, my lady."

She cackled again. "'Lady'! I was never no lady. Mrs. Ann Humphries, lad."

This was a piece of luck. Not an hour ago—if hours were the same here, which I doubted—I had lain under the table while another woman of that name had sobbed in Hartah's tent.

"My mother . . . taken from us just this last winter . . . her lungs . . . I know it's wicked to be doing this but I miss her so much . . . the only one who ever really cared what becomes of me or my children . . . my no-good husband . . . drink and debt and . . . my mother my mother my mother—"

My mother, in a lavender dress. But I would never find my own mother here. The Dead didn't wander far from where they crossed over. And neither Hartah nor Aunt Jo would tell me where my mother died, nor how. Of my father, my aunt would not speak at all. I have given up asking.

I said, "Mrs. Humphries, today I met your daughter and namesake, Ann."

"Oh?" she said, swishing her shriveled feet to make the water roil. "Look at the white stones under the water. See how they seem to shift shape."

This is what the living do not understand about the Dead, and what I must never tell them. The Dead, unless they are very freshly crossed over, do not care about those they have left behind.

They remember the living, yes. Memory crosses over intact. The Dead know whom they have left, know who they themselves are. They perfectly recall life; it just no longer interests them. It's as if life was a story they heard once about the acquaintance of an acquaintance, a tale that unaccountably stayed in memory but without any personal connection. Without passion.

What does interest the Dead? For all my crossings, I still don't know. Of course, I'm never here for very long, and only the elderly will talk to me. Yet I have the impression that the Dead are absorbed in something of which they never speak, not even to each other—unless words like Mrs. Humphries's mean more than they seem. *"Look at the white stones under the water. See how they seem to shift shape."*

The Dead will stare at stones for years. At trees, at flowers, at a single blade of grass. What is shifting in their minds, under what unimaginable waters?

Mrs. Humphries had forgotten me. I pinched her hard. If I went back to Hartah without information, my second beating would be worse than my first. My pinch didn't hurt Mrs. Humphries—nothing hurts the Dead—but it did remind her that I was there.

She snapped, "What now, boy?"

"Tell me about when you were a girl." And I held my breath.

Childhood is the one thing that will sometimes get the elderly Dead to talk. Their adult selves, their long lives, the families they left behind—these mean nothing to them now. But themselves as small children: that will sometimes animate them. Sometimes, anyway. Perhaps it is because little children, in their simplicity, are closer to what the Dead are now. I don't know. None of the actual children here has ever talked to me, or even seemed to see me.

Mrs. Humphries gave her little cackle and her old eyes brightened. "I was a rapscallion, I was! You would scarcely credit it, boy, but I was a pretty child, with hair like new-minted gold. But I wanted black hair, like my friend Catherine Littlejohn, so I—"

A family story, undoubtedly told and retold many times. It led to other stories. A prize chicken had been stolen from the Littlejohns and slaughtered for the Feast of the Winter Solstice. A nobleman, one Lord William Digby, had once ridden through Stonegreen and given Ann, that pretty child, a coin as gold as her hair. I listened carefully, watching the stones shift shape under the water.

And all the while, rage built in my heart that Hartah made me do this thing, come to this place, note with such desperation these trivialities from a woman months in her grave. A woman I would never see again. A woman who was dead, when I was not. I only felt that I was. Here, and there.

3

I DELAYED CROSSING back over for as long as I could. Always I feared the dirt in my mouth, the flesh gone from my bones, the maggots and the cold and the darkness. What if one time, they didn't pass? What if I became trapped in that terrible moment between life and death, forever awake in my rotting grave?

And I did not want to return to Hartah.

So I loitered by the mossy green boulder, and watched the Dead, and tried to get another one of them to talk with me. None would. They sat holding hands in their circles, or they sat alone, gazing at a blade of grass. One of them, a gentleman or even a lord in his velvet breeches and doublet, a short sword on his hip, lay full length on the grass. He stared straight up at the gray, featureless sky. He never even blinked. I wanted to kick him, but what if this should be the one time when a kick aroused a younger Dead? That sword was as real and solid as everything else here.

Some of the Dead wear strange dress, clothing I have never seen on my travels with Hartah. Crude fur tunics. Armor with red plumes on odd-shaped helmets. Long white robes. The old ones speak languages I don't know, when they speak at all. But wherever or whenever their lost lives, they all behave the same.

Listening.

Watching.

Waiting with unimaginable patience. I don't know what they wait for, what their calm gazes see. And they do not, or cannot, tell me.

When I had lingered as long as I dared, I took a sharp stone from my pocket. I rested my left hand against the Stonegreen boulder and drove the stone as hard as I could into my hand, harder than necessary. It does not take nearly as much pain to leave here as to come. But I wanted to inflict pain, and I could not inflict it on Hartah, so I cut my hand and crossed back over into the land of the living.

". . . and dyed her hair black, like her friend Catherine Little-john's," Hartah finished. The woman in the tent burst into tears.

Again I lay under my table, but I already knew that this time I was not needed. The woman sobbed, "Oh, it *was* my mother! No one else could know those things, not all those details, not like that—oh! And she said she's safe and happy. . . ."

"Yes. And that she loves you very much," said Hartah.

For these occasions he used a voice that Aunt Jo and I seldom heard: low, slow, completely scrubbed of his usual snarl. He sat far away from the women—our customers were usually women—both to not make them uneasy with his great bulk and to give himself an air of mystery. Hatred of him filled my mouth like rancid meat.

"My good mother! Oh, thank you, good sir, I can never thank you enough, you have given me a gift beyond price!"

But of course there was a price. Hartah exacted it, plus a promise of silence, from Mrs. Ann Littlejohn, born Humphries. He did the same with Catherine Carter, born Littlejohn, and with Joan St. Clare and her young cousin Geoffrey Morton. They had all lived in Stonegreen their entire lives, the Humphries and Carters and Littlejohns and St. Clares, as had their parents and grandparents before them. Their family secrets were shared secrets, and the dead Mrs. Humphries had known them all.

"A good day's work," Hartah said to me after the last customer had left the tent. He meant his work, not mine. Already he had forgotten the beating he'd given me this morning, blotted from his mind as completely as the grave blotted love from the minds of the Dead.

"May I go?" I tried to keep anger and fear from my voice.

"Yes, yes, go, who needs you now?"

Outside, long shadows fell across the faire field. Dusk gathered on the horizon, soft and blue and smelling of the night to come. Farmers drove their wagons, lighter by what they'd sold and heavier by what they'd bought, down the Stonegreen Road toward home. The cottagers of Stonegreen lingered at the remaining booths and at the ale tent, not wanting their brief holiday to end. Several, men and women alike, were drunk. They staggered about, singing and laughing, their merriment echoing from group to group. I found my aunt sitting in the shade of Hartah's wagon. With no money to enjoy the faire, she had probably sat there most of the day. Wordlessly she raised her eyes to mine.

"A good take," I said. "We will eat."

She didn't smile; all smiles had left her years ago. But she laced her hands together on her skinny belly, as if in thanksgiving prayer. I couldn't stand to watch. Grateful prayer, for a crust of bread and slice of cheese! I stalked away, to the river, and found myself standing under the same great overhanging tree where I had sat with Mrs. Humphries in the country of the Dead.

Under the tree, staring at the dappled shadows on the river, stood the girl from the inn yard this morning. The girl with the long black braids. "You're back," she said, and I froze.

"Where did you go all day?" she continued. "I didn't see you anywhere at the faire."

She had looked for me. *She* had looked for *me*. And she didn't know where I'd been. So why had she looked for me? I couldn't think of anything to say, and so stood there, wordless, like the oaf that I am.

"Oh!" she cried suddenly. "What's wrong with your hand?"

The bruise where I had hit myself with the sharp stone. It had bled a little, the blood had crusted over, and around the angry wound my flesh was puffy and red, rapidly turning purple. Foolishly I covered it with my other hand, clasping both in front of me. Then I realized that the gesture was exactly what my aunt had done, and I scowled ferociously.

The girl didn't notice. She'd darted toward me, picked up my clasped hands, pulled them apart. She had removed the black lace mitts she'd worn in the morning, and the long white sleeves of her smock fell back over her arms.

"Did you cut yourself on—oh!" Immediately she put her left hand behind her back. But I had seen.

"Don't tell," she whispered softly, childishly, and the fear in her eyes loosened my tongue as nothing else could. I understood fear.

"I won't," I said. "I won't tell, I never would. But you should be more careful. Not that it signifies—I assure you, it doesn't! Not to me! It means nothing!"

She nodded unhappily, tears in her eyes. The eyes were deep brown. Brown eyes, black hair—she should have looked drab, like a painting without color, but she did not. She burned bright in my gaze, a beautiful girl with one tiny flaw that signified nothing. Or, to some, everything.

I babbled on, trying to find words that would reassure her. "Only the superstitious say it matters. Only the ignorant. Why, I've heard tell that Queen Caroline has the same thing! And she is the queen!"

"The queen is a whore," the girl said flatly, and I blinked. This girl spoke her mind freely. Spoke her mind, did not take enough trouble to hide the tiny sixth finger on her left hand, the same mark rumored of Queen Caroline. The mark of a witch.

"Be more careful!" I blurted, and looked around to see who else had heard her call the queen a whore. No one was near. "Take better care, my lady!"

"I am no lady," she said, giving me the same smile as Mrs. Humphries when I'd called her a lady. Would all women, then, react with the same pleased amusement to my honoring them so? But I didn't want to honor all women. Only this one, standing here with my injured hand still in her own small white one. She said, "My name is Catherine Starling. Cat."

"I'm Roger Kilbourne."

"My father farms at Garraghan."

I didn't know what or where Garraghan was, and I had no information I wanted to offer about my aunt or Hartah. But I didn't need to speak. With a toss of her black braids, Cat said, "I don't believe in witches, anyway!"

"You must be careful who you say that to."

"I know. I am careful. I can trust you, I knew that right off this morning. You don't believe in witches either, do you, Roger? All that foolishness —putting curses on people and sickening cattle and talking to the dead! Faugh!"

I said nothing.

She brought her left hand from behind her back and joined it to her right, still holding mine. "I'll tell you what I do believe in, Roger," she said with that luscious smile. "I believe in stars and flowers and sweetmeats and my doll!"

I saw it then. Her beauty had misled me, as had her pretty voice. She didn't stumble over her words like the poor creature Hartah had kicked in the last town; her head was not too large nor her eyes blank. But her wits were not all present, and the mind in her head was younger than her near-woman's body. It didn't make me think less of her. It made me want to protect her, keep her safe from those who would make her childish tongue and sixth finger into excuses to hurt her. The warmth of her hands felt like the best thing that had come to me all summer.

Before I could answer, another voice, high with fear,

called, "Cat! Where are you!" An older woman burst through the trees to the riverbank. "There you are! You know you are not supposed to—she wandered off, sir, I hope she has not troubled you—" At the sight of my hand in Cat's, the woman stopped cold.

She was Cat's mother: the same brown eyes, black hair, pretty features, although this woman's hair was tucked up under a cap and her face was tense with worry. I hastened to reassure her.

"No trouble, mistress, none at all. We were just talking. She is fine."

Mrs. Starling looked from me to her daughter, trying to assess the situation. I saw her take in my old clothes, too small for me at ankle and sleeve; my dirty hair; the hole in one boot. I saw her decide that whatever I had seen, I could have no influence anywhere, and so was no threat. But she was kind.

"Thank you, sir. Cat must go now; we start for home. Come, daughter."

"Bye, Roger," Cat said. "See you again!"

That would not happen, I knew. Not only because Cat was obviously the child of a prosperous farmer, but because she was beloved by at least one parent, who would do everything to keep her safe. I watched her go away, and in my breast warred a strange and bitter mix of regret, jealousy, and desire. I wanted Cat to stay. I wanted to go with her. I wanted to be her, sixth finger and all.

A sixth finger and impaired wits would be lesser afflictions than what I bore.

Slowly I left the leafy riverbank and went back to Hartah's wagon.

4

WE SPENT THE NIGHT at the same rough inn five miles from Stonegreen, and for once there was dinner for all three of us. I gobbled the bread and cheese, not knowing when I would get more. Even Aunt Jo ate well, sitting on the wooden bench as far away from Hartah as she could, her eyes cast down. Firelight turned one cheek rosy, which looked grotesque on her thin, lined face. Would my mother, had she lived, look like this? No. My mother, in my childish memory of her, had been beautiful.

Why, I thought at Aunt Jo, *won't you tell me where and how my mother died, you pitiful woman?* Aunt Jo raised her head. For an instant her gaze met mine. She looked away.

"Good food," Hartah grunted, and belched.

In the morning the air had turned much colder. In another few weeks there would be frost on the grass. Hartah, to my surprise, turned the wagon south. As the sun warmed the day, he seemed in a very good mood indeed, whistling tunelessly. I rode in the back of the jostling wagon, sitting on the folded faire tent, and watched a fly crawl across the back of Hartah's neck. After several hours of wordless travel, I risked a question addressed to his and my aunt's back.

"Where are we going?"

"To the sea." He laughed. "I have a desire for sea bathing."

He barely bathed at all. I could smell him every time the wind shifted.

Over the next few days, there were fewer villages the farther south we went, and so fewer chances for harvest faires. The land grew wilder, less fertile. Fields of harvested crops gave way to pastures for sheep and then, as the ground became rockier and steeper still, to goats. After several days in the slow, creaky wagon, we turned east. For the last time we spent the night at an inn, a rough place full of rough men who did not look like farmers or herders. There were no women. Hartah paid the last of his money for a tiny room up under the eaves and left Aunt Jo and me there.

"Bar the door," he said, "and don't open it until you are sure it's me." He went back downstairs and did not return for hours. My aunt slept restlessly on the sagging bed. Rolled in my blanket on the floor, I could hear her light sighs, see her body twitch in starlight from the tiny window. Did she dream, even as I did?

Let there be no dreams tonight.

There were none, and the next morning Hartah was cheerful. "A good place for information!"

Aunt Jo looked at him, and then away.

After that, there were no inns, and we slept in or under the wagon, eating provisions Hartah had bought in Stonegreen. His good mood subsided, replaced by a restless tension I didn't understand. But he didn't hit me or Aunt Jo. He barely noticed us, until one night, over a campfire built beside a rocky landslide that hardly blocked the cold wind, Hartah looked at me directly. His eyes flickered red and gold with reflection from the flames, like a beast. "How'd ye like to be rich, Roger?"

For some reason, I thought immediately of Cat Starling, back on her prosperous farm, of her clean black braids, her carefully ironed petticoat. I said nothing.

"Scared ye, have I?" Hartah jeered. "So much the better. There's fearful work for all of us ahead, and all of us will share the spoils. That's only right. You're a great one for right, ain't ye, Roger?"

Anything I said might provoke him. I stared at the fire. Hartah took another swig of the brandy he'd brought from Stonegreen.

"That's good, stay silent, boy. Silence is what'll be needed, mark my words. But you'll stay silent or swing with the rest of us, eh? You'll see that. I know."

I had no idea what he was talking about, nor did I care. As long as he left me alone, as long as he kept his fists on the brandy and not on me. When he again raised the bottle, I slipped down into my blanket and prepared to sleep.

But then I glimpsed Aunt Jo's face, her eyes wide and horrified, her withered lips parted in a silent scream.

⌛ ⌛ ⌛ ⌛

The next day I could smell the sea on the wind, although I couldn't yet see it. We left the main road and climbed a muddy track upward into hills even wilder, cut with deep ravines and falls of rock. The horse, old to begin with, faltered and strained. I thought the poor beast might drop dead in her traces, but still Hartah urged her on. The wagon wheels groaned, even though the load now consisted only of its driver. Aunt Jo and I walked behind. All of our provisions were gone except a half loaf of hard bread, and Hartah had dumped the ragged faire tent into a ravine. When I dared to ask him why, he laughed and said, "Rich men don't need such sorry lodgings!"

We reached the top of the track with the horse still alive, pulling the wagon into a thick wood of old oak and wind-bent pine. Here the tang of salt air was strong. In a clearing beside a swift hillside stream sat a crude wooden cabin, its log roof sealed with pitch.

"Hallooooo!" Hartah called. Two men came out of the cabin, one young and one about Hartah's age. The older leaned on a wooden staff, one of his legs bent and useless. He hobbled toward us.

"So you've come."

"We have," Hartah said.

"Is this your boy?"

"Yes."

"Well, see that he does his share of the work."

"He will."

The younger man stared at me, scowling. He looked about seventeen or eighteen, wide-shouldered and handsome, with yellow hair falling over bright blue eyes. I found myself wondering if Cat Starling would have liked him, would have kissed him.

"Then come," the older man said.

"Are the others——"

"Soon."

Hartah said to Aunt Jo, "Make camp. There, under the trees by the creek. Don't come near the cabin, or you'll wish you hadn't. You too, boy." He and the yellow-haired youth strode into the cabin, the lamed man limping after them.

My aunt and I drew the wagon under the trees, tethered and watered the horse, made a fire. There was nothing to cook. As I gnawed on my share of the bread, hard and moldy, these men were noticed in the clearing. None had families with them. They disappeared into the cabin.

My aunt handed me her piece of bread. She had not touched it. When I looked at her in surprise, I gasped. Never had I seen a face like that. Whiter than frost and her eyes just as frozen, wide open and fixed in terror.

"Aunt . . . what . . ."

Abruptly she turned her head and vomited into the weeds. Thin strings of brownish green bile retched from her mouth. In truth, I was surprised anything came up at all, we had eaten so little. Even more surprising, vomiting seemed to hearten her, or at least to return her voice.

"Go, Roger. Go now. What they plan . . . you must not . . . run!"

I stared at her across the dying fire. Never once had she told me to escape Hartah, or tried to protect me from him. I said, "What are they planning? What's going to happen?"

"Go. Go. Go." She was moaning now, like an animal in a trap, as she rocked back and forth by the fire on her skinny haunches. How could I go, leaving her like this? She was my aunt, my mother's sister, and I could not leave her here alone with whatever she feared so much. . . .

No. That was not true. The truth was harsher, more shaming: I was afraid to run. To go off into that wild country, without weapons or money or food . . . and Hartah had threatened to . . . if he came after me and caught me. . . .

I felt shamed by my own cowardice, and shame turned me angry. "You've lost your wits! I can't go! Be quiet or I'll—" I stopped, appalled. I sounded like Hartah.

Aunt Jo stopped, too. No more moaning, no more rocking. She sank onto her blanket, her face turned away from me, and lay quietly. But one more sentence came from her side of the fire, and it was clear and cold as sea air.

"Your mother died at Hygryll, on Soulvine Moor."

I went still. It seemed the whole world had gone still: leaves didn't rustle, wind didn't blow, embers didn't snap in the ashes of the fire. *At Hygryll, on Soulvine Moor.* After years of refusing to tell me anything of my parents. *My mother.*

"Where is Soulvine Moor?" I demanded. "And how? How did she die?"

Aunt Jo said nothing, rigid as stone.

"*How?* And what of my father Aunt Jo!"

But Aunt Jo would say no more. She lay down, as stiff and unresponsive as if it were she and not her sister who had died at that unknown place. Unknown now, but I would find it. Now that I had a name, I would find it. And for the first time ever, I would cross over with gladness.

My mother, in her lavender dress . . .

It was a long time before I could sleep. I watched the stars between the branches of the trees. I watched the clouds drift in and cover them. Toward morning, it began to rain. I crept under the wagon. The cold rain didn't matter; tomorrow I would go. My aunt had told me to run, and now I had a reason, a place to run to. Tomorrow I would go, and I would find the place my mother had died, and I would cross over and find her.

But toward morning Hartah woke me, and everything came crashing down.

"Boy! Get up, curse you, get up now!"

I started awake, sitting up and had that I hit my head on the bottom of the wagon, a sharp crack that sent spears of light through my brain. Hartah seized me by one arm and pulled me from beneath the wagon.

The little clearing was bedlam. Men ran around cursing, hitching Hartah's old horse to a wagon that must have arrived in the last few hours. The rain still fell, a slow, cold drizzle that soaked through my wool tunic as if boring inward. Through the gray curtains of rain the men's lanterns gleamed fitfully, illuminating now a clenched face, now the load upon the wagon bed, which was unseen beneath a tarp.

"Come!" Hartah roared, dragging me with him.

Someone else yelled, amid a row of curses hot enough to blister rock, "She be too early! She be too early!"

We ran behind the cabin and then kept going. There was a second track here, leading steeply downward. As Hartah and I descended in the darkness, I tried to keep my feet on the muddy ground, desperately watching by the light of Hartah's swinging lantern for firm footing amid the streaming water. The smell of salt grew sharper. I could hear a wagon close behind me, the horse led by someone. We left the trees, and the wind hit me so hard I almost fell. All at once I could hear the sea surging below.

At the bottom of the track we reached a tiny, pebbled beach. The sky was pitch-black, but as lanterns came down with the men, I saw that the beach lay between steep cliffs and the sea. The pebbles were dotted with large rocks, and even larger ones jutted from a wild sea. Dark waves rose and crashed on the boulders, some sending spray inland to dash against the cliffs. Rain fell steadily.

"There!"

"Hurry, damn you!"

"She be too early! Too early!"

"We can still do it. . . ."

Do *what*? The yellow-haired youth pushed me out of the way, so hard that I fell on the rocks. I staggered up, dazed; no bones seemed to be broken, but I shrank back against the cliff, peering desperately around. No way back up to the cabin except by the one track, and men stood there, swinging their lanterns.

Yellow Hair pulled the tarp from the wagon and tipped it. Such strength! A load of dry firewood spilled onto the beach in an enormous pile. Someone lit a brand soaked in oil and tossed it onto the wood, which flared instantly. Dry, cured, oiled— someone had prepared the wood with great care. The flames mounted high into the windy sky, a great bonfire.

And all at once I saw a light far out on the surging dark sea.

She be too early! We can still do it—

No. No. They were going to—

I had heard of such things. I hadn't wanted to believe them. It was like witches or like sick-curses, too monstrous to be believed. But here, here and now, my uncle—

Three lights flashed in rapid succession out on the dark sea, and the men on the beach shouted.

"She sees us!"

"She's coming in—"

"Get ready!"

The ship out there thought the bonfire was a guide-light, the kind made to lead vessels toward safe harbor. She was sailing blind, and she-- in the wild storm, and that fire would lure her toward the rocks. How far out did the rocks extend from the beach . . . how soon would the captain realize what was happening . . . ?

I didn't know. I had never been on a ship. And there was nothing I could do.

Time passed. I don't know how much time. The rain lashed me as I huddled against the cliff, and out there on the sea, the ship fought the storm. Her lights seemed to come closer, then to recede. In the rain and darkness I couldn't judge distances. I couldn't judge anything.

But enough time passed for the clouds to lighten in the east, over the top of one cliff, and hope seized me. If it got light soon enough for the ship to see the danger . . .

It did not. Even over the hammering waves I heard the crash as the ship ran into the rocks and splintered. Her lights bobbed wildly. A few moments later they went out.

The men on the beach screamed in joy.

Dawn approached. As the invisible sun rose behind the angry clouds, the entire horrifying scene came into view. The ship lay on her side about a quarter mile out, breaking up as the sea pounded her again and again. Figures struggled in the surf, trying to get ashore. Some disappeared beneath the chaotic water and didn't reappear. Others reached the beach, dripping and exhausted and bruised, their clothes torn ragged by the rocks. And my uncle's men rushed to meet them.

I saw the yellow-haired youth grab a sailor by the neck, push him down, and drive a knife square into his back.

It was no contest. For every survivor from the wreck, there was a killer on the beach. Blood streamed along with the rain, turning tide pools red. The men moved in a frenzy, silent now but all the more terrible for that, flashing their knives in and out of living flesh.

After a while, no more figures staggered ashore.

Cargo began to wash up then, great casks and wooden boxes, dashed against the rocks in their passage. The men dropped their weapons—knives and swords and spears would have endangered them in that slippery sea—and waded out to grab the casks before they could split open. Stumbling, cursing, gripping the slippery rocks for balance whenever possible, the wreckers retrieved what they could, half carrying and half floating the cargo ashore. The sun rose higher behind the clouds, and I could see sticky red on the discarded blades.

"You!" Hartah roared at me. "Help! Fetch in cargo!"

A box was abruptly tossed up by the waves, coming down on a rock just yards from the beach. The wood splintered and broke. Cloth spilled from the box, immediately sodden with salt water. Red, gold, blue—the rich silks and velvets and brocades swirled in the water or clung to rocks even as my clothes clung to my body. The dyes began to run, staining the water colors that no sea ever was: red . . . yellow . . . blue . . . *lavender* . . . . I stumbled toward the shore until a hand on my arm stopped me.

"Roger! Go!"

My aunt Jo had materialized on the beach. She must have come down the muddy track, come after everybody else had left the cabin, come to tell me where my mother was. . . . I couldn't think. My back to the cliff, I stared at her, dumb, amid the wreck and the rain and the cloth dyeing pebbles fantastic colors.

"Go!" She thrust something at me, and without thought, I took it. Hartah's knife, plucked from the bloody sand. She wanted me to take it, to run away while there was still a chance. A chance to find my mother's death place, to cross over and see her again—

My feet finally moved.

A huge cry, and Hartah loomed before us. Some of the ruined cloth from the wreck clung to him, dripping blue velvet draped lopsided over his shoulders like a mockery of a cape. In his hands he held a metal-bound wooden box. From somewhere behind me, someone cried, "Soldiers! Run!"

Rage blossomed on Hartah's face. His head jerked upward, searching the cliff for soldiers. Rain streamed down his red nose, across a bruise on one cheek. Always, rage must go somewhere. He screamed at Aunt Jo, "I told you to stay above!" He raised the wooden box and brought it down hard upon her skull.

Her slight body crumpled onto the rocks.

Without thought, I slid Hartah's knife between his ribs and twisted it.

His big body went rigid. One arm raised to grab me, and I stepped backward, pulling out the knife. Instantly blood gushed from his side—so much blood! It pooled among the rocks, mingled with the rain, splashed when Hartah fell to his knees and then, after a long terrible moment when time itself seemed to stop, onto his face beside Aunt Jo.

The knife dropped from my slack fingers.

"Soldiers!" someone screamed again, and then they were pouring down the track, slipping in the mud, dozens of them in the rainy dawn. There was no other way off the beach except out to sea, where the ship broke up even more with each crashing surge of the waves. Some of the wreckers fought back, but it was hopeless. Only two of us were taken prisoner, me and the youth with the yellow hair, and there was no way Cat Starling would ever, ever have kissed either one of us.

5

I LAY FACEDOWN on the ground in the clearing above the beach, bound hands and feet, my mouth shoved against the wet dirt. The yellow-haired wrecker lay beside me, similarly bound. The rain had slowed. Soldiers dressed in rain-sodden blue milled around, and shouts sounded continuously as horses, Hartah's old nag among them, hauled wagons up from the beach. Every so often a boot kicked me in the leg or the belly, and painfully I brought my bound arms up to shield my head as best I could.

What would these soldiers of the queen do to me?

All my life Hartah had told tales of soldiers torturing prisoners, but even in my fear I knew I would not be tortured here. The soldiers didn't need to force a confession. They would hang us on the evidence of their eyes.

"A priest!" the yellow-haired man cried. "It is my right to see a priest before I die!"

Two pairs of boots stopped on the muddy ground, inches from my head. "He's right," said a voice. "It's the law."

"And did they have law in their minds when they wrecked the *Frances Ormund?*" demanded another voice, rougher than the first. "Sir."

The *Frances Ormund.* That must be the name of the ship. Again I saw the bodies on the beach, the tide pools red with blood, Hartah and the others shouting in triumph as they snagged the cargo washing ashore. The killings. And I had killed, too. The knife sliding so easily between Hartah's ribs, like butter into good cheese . . . And just before, the heavy wooden box, smashing down onto my aunt's head . . .

My mind shuddered away from both images, and from the knowledge that I was a murderer. And yet I did not regret killing him. The thought astonished me. I, who had shrunk from killing a rat that had crawled into the wagon, a snake in the house, when we had a house. But it was true. I should have killed Hartah long ago. And I should have no fear of death now. After all, I—of all people!—knew that both he and I would continue on across the grave, in the peaceful country of the Dead.

But I did not want to go there. Not like this, not forever. What had Mrs. Humphries said to me? *It is not your time. Not yet.*

The first soldier said, "Nonetheless, Enfield, I am bound by the law."

"Sir, these scum don't deserve the law! Begging your pardon, sir . . . but ten hands dead, with only two survivors! And a woman aboard, the captain's own wife!"

"I demand a priest!" the yellow-haired youth screamed. A boot kicked him hard in the side. He gasped and writhed on the ground.

"Enfield," the other voice said, but without warning. All at once I was seized by the arm and hauled to my feet.

"Sir, let him at least see what he's done before he hangs! Let him face the survivors!"

The officer made no objection. Enfield dragged me to the cabin. As we went, one soldier spat in my face. Over a high limb of a great oak, two more soldiers threw a pair of nooses.

The inside of the cabin was dark, lit only by a single lantern on a small table. Two people sat in wet, bloody clothes. One had a crude bandage wrapped around his temples; he sat with his head in his hands, moaning. The other was a woman.

She was neither young nor old, with gray streaking the salt-crusted hair that dripped onto her torn gown. Her face was swollen, either from her battering in the sea or from tears. Grief dulled her eyes. Enfield thrust me before her on my knees.

"This, Mistress Conyers, is what killed your husband and wrecked the *Frances Ormund*—this!"

She looked at me. I steeled myself for the blow. Instead she said with a kind of hopeless wonder, "But he's just a boy."

"Worked with the wreckers, mistress. The foulest vermin there is . . . He'll hang with the other."

Her brow furrowed painfully. I could see that she hadn't taken it in yet: the wreck, her husband's death, her own freakish survival. She was like those newly arrived in the country of the Dead, bewildered by where she found herself, unable as yet to make sense of this new terrain.

She said, "How old are you, boy?"

All at once I found my voice. I wanted to live. Two nooses swung outside, and I was not yet ready to dwell in that other country. And I looked—so skinny, so underfed—younger than I was, despite my height. I fell to my knees.

"Eleven, mistress. And I did not wreck the ship! My uncle brought me there—he made me come—I didn't know—I didn't know!"

Enfield snarled, "A blubbering coward, as well as a wrecker." He seized me, but I tore myself from his grasp and stayed on my knees.

"Please, mistress, I swear to you—*I did not know!* And my aunt was there, too, my uncle killed her as well—look for the body! It's skinny and frail. . . . She didn't enter the sea, she wasn't killed by anyone coming ashore—she was my mother's sister!"

Again Enfield grabbed me, this time much harder. But the dazed, grieving widow raised her hand. "No, wait, please . . . please."

"Mistress, he'll say anything to get himself off! He's lying!"

"Was . . . was . . ." It seemed hard for her to weave her thoughts. "Was there a woman's body on the beach?"

I thought Enfield would lie, but somewhere amid the vengeance in him also lay truth. As it did in my story, if he but knew it. After a long pause, he said, "There was."

"Murdered?"

"Her head was bashed in," Enfield said reluctantly. "But this bastard might have done it himself!"

"No," I said. "Aunt Jo was the only one ever kind to me."

And now, when she was dead, I saw that this, too, was true. My aunt had never protected me from Hartah, no. But she had shared with me what food she had. She had told me to run from this very clearing. She had lost her life coming down to the beach to tell me, yet again, to run. *"Roger! Go! Go now!"*

And I had treated her with rage, with contempt, because I was too afraid of Hartah to direct those feelings at him.

Tears pricked my eyes. For Aunt Jo, for my lost mother, for myself. Then shame flooded me—fourteen was too old to cry! *Eleven* would have been too old to cry. All I could do was hang my head, but I knew both Enfield and Mistress Conyers had seen.

She said wearily, "Let him live. He's just a child."

"He is not! This is an act and he a coward, a lying—"

"Let him live. It is my right."

Enfield bellowed, pulled me upright, and dragged me outside. He was not going to listen to her; he was going to hang me. But all he did was hold me fiercely and force me to face the great oak.

One noose dangled, empty, from a high tree. The other lay around the neck of the yellow-haired youth. His whole body trembled and his eyes rolled wildly. He shouted something, but the words made no sense. Three men on the other end of the rope pulled, and the young wrecker was jerked off his feet into the air.

He went on jerking for what seemed forever, kicking desperately. The men knotted the far end of the rope around another trunk. The rope chafed the tree bark as the hanging man struggled for air, his face distorted as he swung, kicking and kicking and kicking. . . .

Eventually the kicking stopped.

Enfield drew his knife and cut my bonds. He shoved me to the ground, where I lay looking up at him.

"Now go," he said. "Run. It *is* her right."

But the dead man had had the right to a priest, and they had hung him without any priest. Looking at Enfield's face, I knew I would not get twenty feet into the woods before he, or one of the others, spitted me on a sword. Or worse. Mistress Conyers would never know.

Her gown, bedraggled and drenched and torn though it was, had been made of richly embroidered velvet.

She had been the wife of a ship's captain.

Enfield obeyed her, as long as he was in her sight.

I got to my feet. But instead of running into the woods or toward the track from the clearing, I ran back into the cabin and threw myself again at Mistress Conyers's feet.

"My lady! Please—if I go, the soldiers will kill me! Take me with you!"

Outrage finally brought some color to her face. "How dare you—my husband—"

I said, "I can bring you news of him from the country of the Dead!"

"Guards! *Guards!*"

I did the only thing I could. I threw myself against the corner of the table, hard, aiming so that the corner would hit my forehead. Pain shot through me like fire, great sharp lightning bolts of pain piercing my head, and the room went dark.

I crossed over.

I STOOD IN the same clearing, although the
cabin was gone. Nine of the Dead sat cross-legged in a circle,
holding hands, and I had appeared in the middle of their circle.
They ignored me, or didn't see me, or didn't care. I stepped
over them and started through the clearing toward the track
down to the beach.

There was no track.

The sea lay below me, calm and gray beneath the eternally
calm sky. I stood at the top of a steep cliff, much steeper than it
had been in the land of the living. There was no way down. Far
below, tiny figures moved on the rocky beach, although there
was no sign of a ship, either afloat or wrecked on rocks.

Was one of those figures Hartah? Was another Aunt Jo?

I pushed the thought aside; otherwise I could not act. I
had to get down to the beach *soon*. Always the newly Dead had

a period of disorientation when they could be talked to and would answer—but that period was very brief. I had to get to the beach while the Dead from the *Frances Ormund* were still bewildered, still not reconciled to their new home. Otherwise there was no chance that any of them—who were young sailors, not gossipy old women—would notice me at all. Frantically I thrashed my way through the woods at the edge of the cliff. No paths down. The beach disappeared from my view, and I stumbled back to the clearing.

The hanging tree stood before me, its leaves unmoving in the quiet air. I shuddered. *"Where is the track down?"* I screamed at the circle of Dead. None of them as much as glanced up.

I ran back to the cliff edge. Two of the newly Dead had waded out to rocks and sat cross-legged on them, quietly contemplating the water.

Time was running short. If I threw myself off the cliff, I would surely die—that is, if I *could* die here! But if I didn't get down there soon, Enfield would just as surely kill me in the land of the living.

I cried out, a great echoing howl of despair. One of the tiny figures on the beach looked up, shading his face with his hand. The next moment he flew through the air to stand beside me at the top of the cliff.

I don't know who was more surprised, he or I. A rough sailor, he wore a brown jerkin with a leather belt and torn pantaloons. Salt water dripped from his clothing, his untrimmed beard, his greasy hair. He screamed, drew a knife from his belt, and charged toward me.

"Stop!" I shouted, before I knew I was going to say anything. And he did.

"How did ye do that? How did you bring me to ye?" he sputtered. "And where be I?"

He didn't yet realize that he was dead. Was that why he had been able to soar through the air and up the cliffside? I had never seen any other Dead do anything like that—what else could they do?

My mind raced faster than it had ever done before. This was my chance, probably my only chance. He repeated, "Where be I?"

I said, "You are in my queendom!"

He eyed me, fear and doubt warring in his eyes. "Ye don't look like no prince!"

My clothing was as poor as his, and not much drier. I said, "No, of course not. This is the queendom of . . . of Witchland, and I am an apprentice witch. How else could I have flown you up the cliff?"

Fear routed doubt. The sailor threw himself at my feet in the weeds and rocks. "Witchland! Oh, spare me, sir . . . uh, my lord . . . spare me!"

"I will spare you if you tell me all you know of the ship that brought you here, its voyage, and its captain."

The sailor, still on his belly, peered up at me with the expression of a dog that expects to be beaten. I realized then what I should have seen at first. His beard had hidden most of his face, but his flat nose and big head, the slur in his voice, his confusion at being asked three questions at once—this man was like Cat Starling, but without her beauty. His was the mind of a child, and it was as a child that he could not grasp where he was, what had happened to the ship, or why the murderous seas had turned calm in the space of a heartbeat.

"Rise," I said as lordly as I could manage. "Good. Now, tell me—what was the name of your ship?"

"The *Frances Ormund*." He turned his eyes toward the sea and grimaced in bewilderment—where had the ship gone?

I did not want him thinking, remembering, realizing. "Look at me. No, directly at me . . . good. Now, who was her captain?"

"Cap'n James Conyers."

"Good. Where was she bound?"

"For Carlyle Bay." It seemed to steady him to have only one short question at a time, questions he could answer with certainty. The fear had not left his misshapen face, nor the knife his hand, but I sensed that as long as I kept his attention focused on me, he would not panic. The knife had a curved blade, wickedly sharp, and a wooden handle carved like an openmouthed fish.

I said, "How many hands aboard the ship?"

"Eleven, and the cap'n, and Mistress Conyers."

"What was your cargo—no, don't look down—what was your cargo?"

"Gold from Benilles and cloth from . . . I forget." He hung his head.

"It's all right that you forgot," I said. Cloth and gold— a rich cargo, a small ship, a light crew. A good choice for wreckers.

"Oh!" he said, brightening. "And we brung a man from Benilles—someone important, he was! With medals on his chest!"

The man, his medals, and his importance had all been devoured by the hungry sea. "What is your name?"

"Bat."

"No other name?"

"No, sir. Bat be all I carry."

"And what kind of captain was James Conyers to you, Bat? A fair master?"

This question was too complicated. Bat looked at me hopelessly.

"Did Captain Conyers ever have you flogged?"

"When I fouled the line. The cap'n, he give me three lashes. But they was light. He tell me that I . . . I be trying as hard as I can, and that be true."

"Did he—"

But Bat had found his tongue. "The cap'n have the bosun flogged for stealing, and we put him ashore at Yantaga, we did. No pay, neither, and lucky he warn't sent to no gaol. The cap'n, he stood on deck when the big storm came, and he won't let no man leave his post, and then afterwards he said—"

I heard all of what the captain said, what the captain did, what the captain was. This simple-witted man stood before me, salt drying on his ruined clothes, and painted the picture of an idol, a man such as I, at least, had never known. Fair. Kind. Intelligent. Capable of doing anything. How much was true, and how much blind devotion?

Bat finished with, "But where be the cap'n now? I can't leave my post!" Panic took him. "Did you witch my cap'n?" The curved knife in his hand twitched.

"I did not." More figures had emerged from the sea to wander the beach below. One might even be Captain Conyers. "Bat, come with me." I tried to make my voice as full of authority as I could—I, a skinny and fearful murderer fighting for his very life. Which, in this country, hardly even existed. But Bat followed me.

I led him to a stump halfway between the cliff and the clearing. "Sit there. Wait for me or the captain or the first mate. One of us will come."

"Aye, sir." He sat. I had no doubt that he would wait there until the end of time, if necessary. I left him.

Behind thick bushes, I tried to make myself fly through the air, as Bat had done. I willed it, I jumped, I closed my eyes and tried to command myself. Nothing. Apparently it was not enough to merely be here; one had to also be dead.

I bit my tongue, enough pain for a return, and crossed over.

"He's reviving," a woman's voice said. I lay on the floor of the cabin. Mistress Conyers's face, weary and grieving and disgusted, sagged above me. "Guards, take him outside and set him free."

"No, wait!" Beyond shame, I clutched the sodden hem of her velvet gown. "Listen to me! I—"

"Out!" Her voice rose to a shriek. She was not, I sensed, a woman giving to shrieking, but here and now . . . Her husband lay dead in the roiling sea, his ship wrecked on the rocks, her life in ruins. A soldier seized me, not gently.

I blurted, "Captain Conyers bought you roses in Yantaga! When you put into port to put the bosun ashore for theft . . . yellow roses, masses and masses of yellow roses!"

The soldier had me halfway out the door. Mistress Conyers said, "Wait."

"Mistress——"

"*Wait*." And to me: "What do you know of yellow roses at Yantaga?"

I knew what Bat had told me, no more. But her face had gone white, and so, of course, there was more. With women, there is always more. I stabbed wildly around in my mind for something to say, to give her, something that might preserve my life.

"The roses were a . . . an offering. Between you two. For something important."

Her eyes filled with tears. To the soldier she said, "Leave us."

"Mistress, it may not be safe to——"

"Leave us!" And there it was, the tone of authority I had tried for with Bat and could never, not in this land nor that other, achieve as she did. She was born to that voice. The soldier dropped me and stalked out the door.

"Who are you?" she said. "How do you know these things?"

We stared at each other across the dim space, lit by only one lantern and the gray light from the small window. The other survivor moaned in a corner. The cabin smelled of male sweat, of rodent droppings, of my fear. But I had no choice.

"My name is Roger Kilbourne. I know these things because your husband just told me, while I lay unconscious. Mistress, please believe me, please let me convince you. I can tell you more of your voyage on the *Frances Ormund*, much more . . . No, please hear me out! I am not lying or conniving or trying to play on your grief. I don't know why I am this way, and I want nothing from you except my life. Please listen to me. I can . . ."

I had never said it aloud to anyone except Hartah and my aunt, and then only when I was a child, too young to know that some things are better left unsaid.

"I can travel to the land of the Dead."

7

SHE BELIEVED ME. Hartah had always said that only country folk believed in my ability, never the city-bred nor those above us, and I had found that true. But Mistress Conyers was a rare creature, one of those few who look squarely at the evidence before them, who weigh it, who can accept even that which is distasteful or frightening if it also seems true. After I told her all I had learned from Bat, Mistress Conyers accepted that I could cross over. She also accepted that if I was not to be killed, she must take me away from the soldiers filled with lust for revenge over the *Frances Ormund*. She believed me, she took me with her, and then she disliked me intensely for both those things.

Witchcraft.

Child of ship wreckers.

We left late in the afternoon. The rain had stopped and

the sea had gone from raging to grumbling. Those bodies that could be recovered lay under wet blankets in the backs of wagons, along with such cargo as could be fished from the waters. Mistress Conyers and I rode in a different wagon from the corpses, and I stuck close to her. Soldiers in rain-soaked blue glared at me with murder in their eyes. The body of Captain Conyers had not been found. His widow and I did not talk.

We stayed close to the coast, heading always downhill, away from the mountains. In the early dusk of autumn we reached a large inn on the coast. A rider had been sent ahead, and we were met at the inn by a large party of men who had ridden hard and fast to arrive just as we did. These, it turned out, came from Captain Conyers's brother's estate, somewhere farther inland. The queen's Blues left us then, perhaps to make their own camp for the night. With them they took the other survivor from the *Frances Ormund*. With relief, I watched the soldiers ride away. These new men were armed and booted like the others, but they had no reason to hate me. Not unless Mistress Conyers should give them a reason.

Should I slip off now, disappear into the gathering night? To go where, to eat what, to live how? Here I was being well fed, for the first time in a long time. My head still hurt where I had thrown myself against the table in the cabin, but I had a clean bandage for the wound. And I remembered all too well Hartah's stories of highwaymen, robbers, lone travelers gutted and left to die.

So I stood in a dim corner of the stable yard, a place where the wooden side of the inn met a high fieldstone wall, and watched the commotion. Men carried chests from the *Frances Ormund* into the stable; I had no doubt they would be well guarded tonight. The corpses stayed on the wagons, which were drawn behind the inn. Among the new arrivals a woman dismounted, having ridden as hard as the men. She carried a cloth bag into the same door where Mistress Conyers had been taken. All the horses trembled with hard use, lathered with sweat. They were watered, rubbed down, fed, and housed either in the stables or, when there was no more room, in a paddock. The well winch creaked continuously as bucket after bucket was drawn. Inn servants rushed about, calling to each other. No one noticed me.

Eventually good smells of cooking wafted on the soggy air. By now it was full dark. I made my way to the kitchen, stood behind a table, and bent my knees to look shorter.

"What d'ye want?" a harried servant snarled at me.

"I am Mistress Conyers's page," I said with as much dignity as I could manage. Certainly my clothing looked no worse than the widow's: just as torn, just as covered with dried salt.

Instantly the woman's expression changed. "Oh, I'm so sorry, sir, I didn't know—won't you step into the taproom? Matty will bring ye something to—Matty!" A bellow that could startle rocks.

"I prefer to eat here," I said loftily, "away from the soldiers."

"Yes, of course, just as you like, sir." She dropped me a curtsy. Pages in rich houses usually came from quality. The woman scurried to set a small table by the fire. On it she put a meal such as I had not had since . . . No. I had never had such a meal.

Thick soup with little meatballs floating in it. Warm bread with new butter. Golden ale. And an apple tart, the crust rich and flaky, the apples sweetened with honey and spices. I ate it all. When I finished, my belly felt full and my blood swift in my veins.

"Sir," the serving woman said timidly, "if ye've finished, perhaps ye'd like to take your mistress's dinner up to her? It's ready, finally. Matty will light the way." Another curtsy.

I took the heavy tray, and saw that my own dinner, which I had thought so wonderful, wasn't a button on Mistress Conyers's. Roasted goose, the skin crisp and the scent so rich I could barely notice the currant jam, the red wine, the dozen other dishes, most of which I could not even name. It didn't matter; I had had mine.

I followed Matty, who held a lantern high through dark corridors and up stairs. At a heavy door with an unsmiling man in armor seated outside, Matty knocked. The door was opened from within by the serving woman I had seen riding in with Conyers's men.

Mistress Conyers sat in a carved oak chair beside the fire. She wore dry garments, a plain gown of dull black and a black cap: mourning clothes. She had been crying but now her face looked set and grim. When she saw who carried her dinner, she said, "You!"

"The cook asked me to carry this to you, mistress," I said. It was impossible to bow with the tray; I might drop it. "As your page."

"You are not my page!" she said, so fiercely that the serving woman started. Mistress Conyers said, "Leave us, Alice."

The woman went swiftly, closing the door behind her. The room was spare but clean, and the wide bed looked comfortable, its hangings fresh and colorful. A table, two chairs, and a bright fire in the hearth, banishing damp and chill. I had no idea where I would sleep tonight. I set the tray on the table and then stood awkwardly, my hands dangling at my sides, not sure what to do next. I needn't have worried; Mistress Conyers took charge of the situation.

"I don't know what you are," she said, "witch or charlatan or scoundrel. I don't know how you know the things you said about my husband, or why you were with those men who wrecked . . . who wrecked . . ."

She turned her face away, but in a moment had regained control of herself. "I don't know if you talked to my dead James or not. He—"

"I did talk with him! And he said he loves you very much!"

I was no better than Hartah, exploiting her grief.

She continued as if I hadn't spoken. "—was a good man, the best of men, and I don't need you to tell me either that he loved me or that his soul resides now in a better place than this. I want you to go, boy. Innocent or guilty, witch or not, I want you out of my sight. I cannot stand to look at you. Go."

"Where will I go? I have no family, and I'm only eleven years—"

"You are not." She stared at my chin, with its downy covering of hair, and at my Adam's apple—things she had not seen in the dim light of the cabin. My lie had come back to prove me a liar.

I cried, "But I have no place to go! No people, no trade, no money—"

"Is that what you want from me? Money?"

Mistake, mistake.

"I'll give you money," she said contemptuously. "Then go."

"If you give me money, mistress, it will be stolen from me at the first inn I stop at, or by the first ruffians who pass me alone on the road. And what will I do when it's gone? Please, mistress, from compassion—"

"The same compassion you showed my husband and his crew?"

"It was not me!"

She studied me. Perhaps she thought my desperation, too, was an act. But always before, I had had the protection of Hartah's big fists, even if they were sometimes turned against me. I had had his ready knife, his connections with other scoundrels like him, his knowledge of cheating and lying, counterfeiting and stealing. This pampered lady with her superior virtue— what did she know of the life I'd been forced to lead? Her money and her birth kept her safe. At that moment, I almost hated her.

She said, "I do believe it was not you who wrecked our ship, and with it our fortunes. But nonetheless, I still don't want to look at you."

"Then find me a job on one of your estates, some humble job where you will never see me!"

She laughed, a sound so bitter that I was startled. "You don't listen, do you, Roger? Your uncle's wreckers have taken everything I have. If I am not careful, I will be as poor as you. There is no estate."

"But . . . I don't understand . . ."

She rose, poured herself a glass of wine from the tray, and retreated to stand with her back to the fire. It threw her face into shadow. Her fair hair, washed now and curling under her cap, made a halo around her unseen features.

"You are very young," she said, her voice quiet now, and weary. "And I can see that you have not lived much in the great world. My husband is—was—the fourth son of a minor baron. His brothers inherited such 'estates' as there were. James had his own way to make in the world, and he invested everything he had in the *Frances Ormund*. Our cargo from Benilles and Tenwarthanal, plus the passage money from a nobleman we were carrying to The Queendom, would have let us rent a house somewhere, buy another ship, finance another voyage. Now I am ruined."

"But the cargo . . . I saw the chests carried in . . ."

"A little gold, enough to pay what we owe. The rest was cloth and spices, all spoiled by the sea."

"But your family—"

"Cast me off when I married James against their wishes, ten years ago. And my brother, now head of the family, will help me only grudgingly and meanly. He belongs to the old queen. Now do you understand what devastation your uncle created? And why I cannot stand the sight of you?"

A long silence. Finally I whispered, "Yes."

She came closer to me, then. As her features came clear, I saw the sad bewilderment on them, and something else as well, the same thing I had seen about her in the inn. This woman, whatever her personal sorrows, was incapable of unfairness. In the flickering light she studied me carefully.

Finally she said, "Can you really cross over to the land of the Dead?"

"Yes."

"You could be burned for that, as a witch."

"Yes." My heart began to pound.

"Burning is a terrible death. Much worse than drowning."

"Yes."

Another long pause. Then, "I'll tell you what I will do. A courier leaves from here tomorrow for court, because all shipwrecks must be reported to the royal advisors and recorded with the Office of Maritime Records. I will send you with him, with a letter of introduction to an old servant of mine. She is neither important nor influential, but perhaps she can find something for you to do at court. If you are wise, you will tell no one of your 'ability,' nor attempt to use it there. That is all I can do."

"Thank you, mistress!" I was overwhelmed. No one had ever shown me this much kindness. Clumsily—I had never done it before—I fell to one knee in an attempt at a courtly bow.

"Oh, get up," she said tiredly. "You make as bad a courtier as you do a prisoner. I'm going to write the letter now, so that I never have to lay eyes on you again. Ask Alice to send downstairs for pen and ink."

I opened the massive door. Alice waited patiently on the other side. As she scurried down the stairs, I wondered what would become of her if Mistress Conyers had really lost all she claimed. How poor was a person who could still send a servant running for pen and ink? Mistress Conyers's poor was not my poor.

Seated at the table, Alice again sent from the room, Mistress Conyers abruptly stopped scratching her pen across the paper and looked up at me. "Can you read?"

"No, mistress."

"Can you cipher?"

"Only a little, in my head."

"Can you do *anything* of practical use?"

If I said no, she might withdraw her offer of help. Wildly I sought for something plausible, unskilled but needing muscle. "I . . . I can do laundry, my lady."

"*Laundry*? A boy?"

"Yes."

"Very well." She finished her letter and, having no seal, folded it tight. "My old servant is named Emma Cartwright. She's serving woman to one of Queen Caroline's ladies." Her lips curved into a sad half smile at some sweet, lost memory. "I have not told her anything about you except that you are willing, biddable, and strong." She gazed at me doubtfully.

"I am strong, even though I don't look it!"

"Yes. Well. At court, you would do well to stay clear of the royal family, in the unlikely chance that your paths should ever cross. There are many strange things at court these days. Many there would consider you a witch. Say nothing to anyone, including the courier who will take you there. His name is Kit Beale."

"How will I find him?"

"Sleep in the stable. He will find you."

"I thank you, mistress, for all you're doing for—"

"I don't want your thanks. What I want is to never see you again. Now go."

"Yes, mistress. Where . . . where will *you* go?"

She turned away, gazing into the fire. "I don't yet know. And at any rate, it's none of your concern."

"No, mistress. It's just that . . . that I wish you well."

"Go!"

This time there was no mistaking her tone. I went, clutching the paper I could not read, the paper that would keep me from aimless begging on dangerous roads, the paper that would save my life.

Or so I thought then.

I SLEPT IN the stables, as instructed, along with
a dozen Conyers servants. We lay in the hayloft, atop and beside thick mounds of hay fresh from harvest. Below, the horses
stamped, adding their own scent to those of hay, wool, leather,
and male sweat. I would have liked a place beside the sloping
loft wall, but those were taken. So I lay in the middle of the
men and listened to their somber chatter.

"Be turned off now, most likely. Master had promised me
to Cap'n Conyers when he made shore."

"Where will ye go?"

"Where will *she* go?"

"My cousin at an inn at——"

"My father, who might take ye on——"

"The *Frances Ormund*——"

"The wreck——"

"My sister's husband, he farms near Garraghan—"

"The *Frances Ormund*—"

I sat up straight, trying to see in the gloom who had mentioned Garraghan. Cat Starling's father farmed at Garraghan. But in the dimness of the loft I could not tell which man had spoken, and even if I knew, what good would it do me? Cat Starling could not help me, even if the man took me to her, which he would not do. And the man "promised to Cap'n Conyers" was now bereft of his future master and his expected livelihood, thanks to Hartah and his wreckers.

I lay down again, beset by thoughts of Hartah, of Aunt Jo, of the sailor Bat who did not know he was dead, of what I did know—that I had murdered. But exhaustion wrung my body, and eventually I slept—only to wake to the man next to me shaking my shoulder and others cursing in the darkness.

"What? What?" Dazed, I put up my hand to shield my face from Hartah's blow.

"Ye cried out in yer sleep," the man said, disgusted. "Get away from me, boy, I need my rest! Go!"

Others also yelled at me. *Go, go, go*—from my aunt, from Mistress Conyers, now from these men. There was no one on this Earth—or that other—who wanted me nearby. I groped for the ladder until I found it, and lowered myself over the edge of the loft. The men, grumbling, settled back onto the hay. At the top of the ladder I whispered to the man who'd woken me, "What did I say?"

"'Bat.' Ye were afraid of a bat. Now go and let me sleep!"

Bat. I had cried out the dead sailor's name, perhaps in some dream. Never before had I called out at night; Hartah would have beaten me for disturbing him. Did my sleeping mind feel more freedom now that Hartah was dead? Or did more things haunt my dreams since the wreck? What else might I call out another time—and who might hear me?

I made my way to the bottom of the ladder. During the night the clouds had cleared and a nearly full moon shone through the open stable door. The air was cold and sharp, the silence broken only by the restless stamping of horses. I curled up in a corner, on a pile of not-too-clean straw, but no more sleep came.

At dawn a man entered the stable from the inn and stood over me. "Are you Roger Kilbourne?"

"I am."

He thrust a hunk of bread and meat at me. "Then eat breakfast. We start for court shortly. Faugh, lad, you smell! Wash at the well or you don't ride with me."

"Yes, sir."

I did as he told me and hurried back to the stable yard. The courier had just finished saddling his horse. "At least you'll ride light, lad. There's naught to you but bones and eyes. Here, put this on. You can't go to court in those bloody and torn clothes, what ails you?"

It was a tunic of green wool, clean and whole, and I guessed it was his own. He was just as thin as I, but four or five inches shorter. The tunic was too short but fit everywhere else. Almost overcome by this simple kindness, I stammered, "Thank you, sir."

"I'm not 'sir,' I'm a courier. My name is Christopher Beale—call me Kit. By damn, you know nothing of court life, do you?"

"No, sir . . . *Kit.*"

"Then the skies alone know what will happen to you there. Come on."

He swung easily onto the saddle, then reached down a hand to me. The truth was that I had never before ridden a horse. But I sensed that I would now have to do many things I had never before done, so I grasped his hand and half climbed, was half pulled up behind him. I almost gasped; we were so *high*.

Kit twisted in the saddle to look at me. "You've never ridden pillion before?"

"N-no." The height was dizzying; I clutched his waist.

"And what is it you're going to be at court?"

"A l-laundress."

He stared at me a moment longer, shook his head, and we cantered off. I hung on for my life. But after a few minutes the rocking of the animal between my thighs came to seem more natural, and I lost some—not all—of my fear of falling off.

We rode all day before coming to a wide river. There was a fishing village here, large and prosperous, but we didn't stop. Kit turned the horse west, on a wide, well-used road along the river. Just beyond the village, we stopped and dismounted to let the horse drink. My knees bowed outward, and when I tried to walk, I nearly fell. Kit grinned.

"You'll get used to it. Or maybe not. A laundress, did you say?"

"Yes. Does . . . does the court lie along the coast?" I knew it did not, but I wanted to get Kit Beale talking, so that I might learn from him as much as possible. He shook his head and gave me a superior smile.

And yet I could tell you things about the country of the Dead, and then you *would be the ignorant one.*

Kit said, not unkindly, "No, lad, no. Don't you know the lay of The Queendom, your own homeland? Look here." He drew his sword and began to sketch in the dust of the road. "See, here is the coast. We came up from the south, the wild coast, from just before the border with the Unclaimed Lands. This river here"—he drew it with the tip of his sword—"is the River Thymar. The palace is in the capital city, Glory, on a large island far upriver, just before the Lynmar joins the Thymar. The Queendom is one huge valley. We're surrounded by mountains to the south and west, hills to the north, and the sea to the east. The valley we're in is all flat, fertile land. Easy riding."

"Where is Hygryll?"

"Hygryll? I don't know it, but the name sounds like the south. Maybe in the mountains of the Unclaimed Lands."

"It's on Soulvine Moor."

All at once his eyes grew cold. "What business could *you* have with Soulvine Moor?"

"Nothing. I just heard the name once."

"You'd do better to never have heard it. That's no place for men to go, lad."

"Why?"

Kit shoved his sword back in its sheath. "We go now. We've tarried too long already."

"Why is Soulvine—"

"Be quiet," he snapped, and I was.

He said nothing to me that night, nor the following day's ride to the capital. Not one single word. I had closed off my only source of information.

Although I knew that Glory, the capital of The Queendom, lay inland, that did not mean that I could ever have imagined the city itself. Hartah had kept us to villages, small and isolated, where there was less chance of encountering soldiers. And yet as Kit and I first approached the capital, it looked to me almost like a village, a vast village of thatched huts and numerous greens, all set between fields now busily being harvested of their crops. I saw no shops of any kind. As Kit had sketched in the dust, the whole was ringed in the far distance, south and west, by mountains, those in the west sharply high against the blue sky and those in the south hidden in soft haze. To the north, the country rose gradually in gentle hills.

In fact, The Queendom was a series of rings nestled inside each other. The widest was the distant, three-sided curve of mountains and hills. Then came a vast ring of plains, fields, pastures, and—although I could not see them now—the smaller villages through which Hartah had wandered. Closer in was this sprawling web of connected villages, curiously devoid of shops or alehouses, which circled an island in the wide River Thymar. And on the island was the capital city of Glory.

The entire island was ringed by a high, thick stone wall that came right to the water's edge. Soldiers patrolled the ramparts. Huge iron gates, now all raised, were set into the wall. Wide, high stone bridges connected the riverbanks to the island. Other gates had no bridges but instead docks, to which barges came and went on the placid waters of the river. In some places, the circling island wall seemed to project out *over* the river, which I didn't understand.

The only thing visible beyond the city wall was a single slender tower, soaring several stories high and dotted with narrow, slitted windows. An open section near the top held immense bells. Above that was a flat roof surrounded by a parapet.

"Don't gape like a fool," Kit said. "You're not even inside yet."

We were stopped at the land side of a bridge, where a guard dressed in blue read a paper that Kit handed him. The guard glared at Kit's green tunic, then at his face, and Kit glared back. As the horse clattered over the stone bridge, I glanced back over my shoulder. The guard in blue made a gesture at us, one so filthy that in any farming village it would have started a fight to the death.

The Blues and the Greens. Even in the countryside we knew of this, the scandalized talk of every faire and alehouse. I said, "Kit, what—" but my words were drowned out by the pealing of the bells in the tower. They sang a sweet song—but it was *loud*. When the clamor stopped, we had passed under the iron gate and I forgot my question in astonishment at Glory.

Never had I imagined such a place.

Another ring, but nothing like the villages outside. Stone walls ran crazily through the city, carving it into small spaces crammed with tents. The tents held people, shops, livestock, alehouses—everything I had ever seen in the world, all crammed into spaces too small to hold them, all yelling and reeking. Children shrieked, running among the legs of adults. Chickens cackled. Songbirds in painted cages trilled, adults cried out to each other, a fiddler played, with a wooden box at his feet to receive coins. Everything seemed for sale—food and copper work and live ducks and cloth and chamber pots and leather goods and ale—and at least half of it smelled.

"Red pea soup! Good red pea soup, made fresh this morning!"

"Chickens! Live chickens!"

"Lemme go, Gregory, it's not your turn!"

"Lavender and herbs!"

"That was my pot, you oaf! Mine!"

"Empty your chamber pot *here*, will you!"

"Grain for bread!"

"I saw it first!"

"Red pea soup!"

My senses reeled. Kit smiled.

"Flooded your brain, has it, lad? We'll be inside soon."

Inside *what*? "Is it all like this?"

"Everything outside the palace. The law says no trade for three leagues around Glory except within the city itself. There's not much room left on the island, and the old queen decreed that no stone or wood structures are allowed here. Except the palace, of course."

That explained all the tents. I saw now that the stone walls, which probably surrounded the palace, were all connected, a single vast structure with sections that shot out in all directions like a huge, rigid, gray plant sprouting stone branches. Some of these branches were short and wide, some long and narrow, some curled gracefully back on themselves like tendrils of stone, some led to other structures, round or boxy or triangular—there was no pattern to it, no plan. And no windows, anywhere. Not one. The palace was another ring, although irregular in the extreme, within the circle of the city. What must it be like inside, at the heart of all these rings?

Kit shouldered his way through the crowded, narrow

streets, leading the horse, which barely fit but seemed accustomed to the close, smelly din. People shouted at Kit and he shouted back. Over his shoulder he called to me, "Much of this rabble goes home off the island at night!" I said nothing, stunned by the noise and reek and lack of space to move.

We edged our way toward a wooden gate set into the palace wall. Kit showed his papers to yet another guard, this one dressed in green. The gate was opened, and we stepped inside the palace.

I blinked. Everything was different.

WE STOOD IN a large stableyard, open to the sky, very clean and very quiet. The thick wooden gate shut out all noise from the city. The very cobblestones seemed to have been scrubbed of normal dirt. A stable boy rushed forward to take Kit's horse and lead it into a closed stable at one side of the stable yard. Kit and I walked to the other side of the yard, the crunch of our boots on stone the only sound, and through a second, less fortified gate.

Another courtyard, planted with bushes and boxed in by stone walls with many wooden doors, all painted green. Servants went in and out of the doors. I said timidly, "I have a letter of introduction to one Emma Cartwright, a serving woman to—"

"You go nowhere until you've bathed," Kit said with disgust. "You *are* a savage, aren't you? There, to the left—that's the laborers' baths. I'll be here when you're done." He strode through doors on the right. Almost I ran after him—what would I do if I were left alone in this strange place? But I did as I was told and went through one of the doors on the left.

More strangeness! The room—perhaps more than one room—had been built out over the river, and the floor removed except for a wide ledge around all four walls. A new floor, wooden on stone pilings, had been built two feet under the water, so that the Thymar flowed right through the room. A few men bathed, naked, in the clean water. I remembered that we had passed a section of the Thymar down river where it had abruptly turned reeking and foul; the city's sewage must be sent there. Here, upriver, the water was clean for bathing, and perhaps farther upriver, cleaner yet for drinking. It was an ingenious system.

I removed my clothing and piled it on a shelf against the wall. Other shelves held bars of strong soap. I scrubbed myself clean, pulled back on the tunic Kit had given me, and cleaned my boots in the water. Since I couldn't bear to put on my smelly small clothes, I wadded them up and left them in a corner, going without underclothes. There was also nothing I could do about my filthy trousers, but the tunic hung to my hips, hiding the worst. Having no comb, I ran my fingers over and again through my wet hair until it held no tangles.

Kit waited in the courtyard, wearing fresh clothes. No riding clothes, these, but a tunic of green velvet, white silk hose, and green shoes. His dark hair gleamed and he had a silver earring in his left ear. I saw that despite his slight stature, he was handsome: a manly little man.

He looked me over and sighed. "I suppose you'll have to do. Come."

More courtyards, and my astonishment grew until I thought my eyes, my brain, could take in no more.

Each courtyard was more sumptuous than the last. Wide, quiet, bright with trees and late summer flowers, ringed with buildings of painted gray stone. Then buildings faced with smooth white marble. Finally buildings faced with mosaics of pearl and quartz, all in subtle shades of ivory and cream, all in subtle patterns that changed as the light moved over them. Small fountains appeared, falling in graceful, tinkling arcs. All was subdued, quiet, with a balanced and graceful beauty I had not known existed in the whole wide world. Even the people we passed, dressed in fine green clothing, moved with quiet grace. A few nodded to Kit.

Kit said, "Close your mouth, Roger." He seemed to grow more and more tense the closer we got to . . . wherever we were going.

Almost I wished I were back with Hartah, with Aunt Jo, jostling along in our wagon. This was too strange, too different. I could never belong here.

Kit said, "Here I leave you. The quarters for Queen Caroline's ladies are over there, through that gate. Present your letter of introduction to the guard. I must report the wreck of the *Frances Ormund* to the Office of Maritime Records and give the news of the hanging of the one surviving wrecker. May all their souls burn forever."

I could have told him they were not. I could have told him that the wreckers, along with their victims, sat on the beach and the rocks, contemplating the quiet sea. I could have told him his educated belief, that souls burn or else go to paradise, was much farther from the mark than was the countryside belief that they endure in their own land. I told him nothing.

"Worse luck that it had to be me," Kit said gloomily. "Never a Blue courier about when you need one."

That was his only reference to the peculiar situation that I—that the entire queendom!—knew existed at court. Kit Beale walked away. With Mistress Conyers's letter in my sweaty hand, I moved toward the bored guard to meet the unknown Emma Cartwright, she who held my fate in her hands.

She was much older than Mistress Conyers, stout and wrinkled, just as clearly born a servant as the other had been born a lady. Emma Cartwright wore a plain gown of dull green, her hair in neat gray braids wound around her head. But her eyes were piercing. "Did you read this letter, boy?"

"I can't read, mistress."

"Ah. And Mistress Conyers thinks you should work in the court laundry."

"Yes."

"A boy. As a laundress."

I said nothing, because what could I say? And was I supposed to kneel? Kit had laughed at me for trying to kneel to him—was this the same? My ignorance shamed me.

We stood in a small, cheerful chamber hung with a tapestry of noblemen on a hunt. Unlit wood was stacked neatly in the fireplace. A pretty carved table held a bottle of wine, several pewter goblets, and a bouquet of flowers. Embroidery, rather badly worked, lay tossed on a three-legged stool. A polished door led to a bedchamber beyond; I could see that in one corner someone had dropped a painted fan behind a brass water bucket.

Mistress Cartwright sighed. "Very well. I'll ask Joan Campford, who runs the Green laundry. Although why Lettice should mix herself in your affairs——"

I was startled to hear this servant use what must be Mistress Conyers's given name: *Lettice*. Then all at once I grasped the situation. Emma Cartwright must have known Mistress Conyers when she was quite small; perhaps she'd even been little Lettice's nursemaid. That was why Mistress Conyers trusted her. And so——

The door burst open and a girl rushed in. "Emma—you must help me!"

For a long moment I stood frozen, and then I dropped to my knees. No doubt here—*this* was a lady. She was also the most beautiful girl I had ever seen.

She was small, with long brown hair, its color mingled cinnamon and copper and nutmeg and bronze—more gleaming shades than I could count. The hair flowed loose from beneath a little jeweled cap that framed huge eyes of bright green. The skirts of her gown, green silk with a low bodice and full sleeves, were held up in both hands; she'd been running. Her pointed little chin quivered. She ignored me.

"What is it, my lady?" Emma said.

"The prince! I—oh, here he comes! Tell him I'm ill, dead, anything!" She dashed through the door to the bedchamber and slammed it, seconds before a youth appeared in the outer doorway. Emma sank into a low curtsy.

"Mistress Cartwright, summon Cecilia, please."

I disliked him immediately. His peremptory tone, his rich clothing, his handsome and sulky face. He looked not that many years older than I but was much more filled out. Well, why not—he ate well every day of his life, the bastard!

Then I realized I was silently cursing a *prince*, and the blood rushed to my face. How did I dare? I bent my head even lower, but I needn't have worried. The prince no more noticed me than he would a piece of furniture.

Mistress Cartwright said, "Your Highness, I would summon her except that she is ill and vomiting in her chamber."

His scowl deepened. "Vomiting? I saw her just moments ago and she was fine!"

"Yes, Your Highness. It came on quite suddenly, and she rushed away lest she disgrace herself in front of you. I'm afraid she ate too eagerly of the roast swan at dinner. Lady Cecilia has a delicate digestion."

I peered sideways at the prince. He looked uncertain.

Mistress Cartwright said, "If Your Highness would like to wait until I get her cleaned up, her soiled gown changed, and her mouth washed with—"

"Oh, leave it! Let her rest. But tell her I shall expect her at the masque tonight!" He turned and stomped off. Mistress Cartwright closed the door softly behind him. Instantly the inner door opened and Lady Cecilia ran to her serving woman, hugging her. "Thank you, thank you!"

"What happened?" Mistress Cartwright looked grim.

Lady Cecilia laughed, a high sparkly laugh that went on a bit too long. "He tried to kiss me again. And I slapped him and ran away!"

"Did you encourage him before that, my lady? Were you flirting again?"

"Maybe a little." She smiled, the most enchanting smile I had ever seen. It tilted the corners of her green eyes, showed off her small white teeth. Her skin looked soft as swansdown, and as white. I felt light-headed, which must have caused some slight motion because all at once she noticed me. "And who is this?"

"A new servant. My lady, this is a dangerous game you're playing with Prince Rupert, I have *told* you that. You cannot—"

"Oh, Emma, I can manage myself, and the prince, too. It's all in fun. He knows he must leave on his wedding trip in the spring, and he knows I serve his sister the queen. He would never try more than a kiss, nor I a slap." She giggled, still smiling down at me. "Rise, new servant. Do you have a name? And what will you do here at court?"

"Roger Kilbourne, my lady. I'm to be a laundress."

"A laundress! How funny!"

Standing, I was much taller than she. All at once I was grateful that the tunic Kit gave me came at least over my hips. My member felt hard as stone. And for a lady born! The light-headedness increased.

"You ears are the most interesting shade of red, Roger," she said. "Are you blushing? You would look well in a doublet of that shade."

It was incredible. She was *flirting* with me, as she must have flirted with the prince. Did she flirt with every man, then? Apparently so. I was not used to being a man anyone flirted with. I was not used to being a man. I was not used to any of this—I,

Hartah's unwilling and underfed slave. Her eyes sparkled like diamonds—no, like emeralds—no, like—

Mistress Cartwright said, "That's enough, my lady. Go inside and rest, you are supposed to be sick from eating too much roasted swan. Roger, I will take you now to Joan Campford."

"Good-bye, Roger of the Red Ears," Lady Cecilia said.

I would never see her again. Or if I caught a glimpse of her, it would be at a distance, riding or dancing or feasting with the queen's ladies, flirting with the prince. And she would not remember my name.

Wordlessly I followed Emma Cartwright to the palace laundry, where my new life was supposed to begin.

10

HEAT FROM THE constant fires, three of
them going day and night, and from the pressing irons. Steam
choking the air. Soap so harsh it rose blisters on my hands
and arms up to the elbow, to join the skin burns from every
careless error with a hot iron. A perpetual ache in my shoulders from hauling cold water from the river. Cold and heat,
strong soap and stronger stains, fire and water. This particular
laundry—there were others in the palace—dyed and cleaned
the clothing and bedding of soldiers, servants, and couriers. Queen Caroline, like her mother, insisted on cleanliness
throughout her palace. They were both famous for that.

At the end of the first day, I thought I could not stand the
work. By the end of the second day, I knew I could stand it but
didn't want to. By the end of the second week, I had accepted
my fate. It was not all bad here. Joan Campford, although she

ran her laundry like a captain of the guard, was not unkind. I had three good meals every day in the servants' kitchen, nourishing food such as I had seldom enjoyed before. The other laundresses, all older women, made endless jokes about the boy doing women's work, but no one beat me. So I became resigned. That's what hard and ceaseless work is designed to do: require all your energy so that none is left over to think of another life.

Except that I did think of other lives. As I hauled water and boiled sweat-soaked tunics and pressed clothing, I thought constantly of Harrald, of Aunt Jo, of the farmer Ormund, of what I had done on the rocky little beach, of Lady Cecilia, of my mother among the Dead "at Hygryll on Soulvine Moor." Worse, I dreamed of them all. And in my dreams, as I had done in the hayloft of the inn, I called out.

"Wake up! Wake up, curse you!"

The boy who slept on the next pallet in the apprentice chamber shook me roughly awake.

"That's the second time tonight! Who can sleep with you caterwauling like that!"

"Not me," said another voice, equally annoyed. "I am sick of hearing about Frances Ormund! Who is she, your sweetheart? Go lie with her and not with me!"

Frances Ormund. Fright took me. What had I said, and what might I blurt next in my sleep, perhaps alongside someone who understood what he heard? Blindly I groped my way from the apprentice chamber to find somewhere else to sleep. The best I could do was the servants' kitchen, under one of the long trestle tables where we took our meals.

A few hours' fitful sleep, and another hand shook my

shoulder. "What are you doing here? You can't sleep here!"

Groggy still, I half opened my eyes. A girl crouched under the table beside me. From some dream, or some madness, I thought she was Cat Starling. Before I knew what I was about, I had pulled her to me and kissed her.

She punched me hard in the nose.

"How dare you use me like that! Who are you? Guard! Guard!"

"No, wait—please!" My nose was on fire, the agony bringing tears to my eyes. "I'm Roger Kilbourne the laundress! Please, don't call the guard!"

She paused, a safe distance from me. "A boy laundress?"

"Yes, I—I'm sorry I kissed you, I was dreaming and—I'm sorry!"

But I was not. It was the first time I had ever kissed a girl, and despite the pain in my nose—had she broken it?—I could still feel her soft lips under mine. She was Cat Starling, she was Lady Cecilia, she was a kitchen maid in a dark green gown and white apron, in the pearly dawn. Again my member was stiff. Was this going to go on the rest of my life, this madness about girls? How was I going to bear it?

"What are you doing here?" the girl demanded. "If you're a laundress, why aren't you sleeping in the apprentice chamber?"

"I was. They made me leave. I . . . I cry out in my sleep and it disturbs them. I meant you no harm!"

Severely she studied me. There was about her none of Cat Starling's simplicity of mind, none of Lady Cecilia's flirtatiousness. This was a girl used to hard work, with no nonsense about her. Well enough to look at but not beautiful, her fair hair bundled into a knot, her eyes a light, judgmental gray. Small burns and cuts covered her hands: kitchen injuries.

"I believe you," she said. "Now leave."

"I will. But my nose . . . I think you may have broken it. . . ."

"You deserved it. Oh, all right, sit there and be still."

She brought me a cloth dampened with cool water. I held it to my nose, watching her as she fed the fire and began to knead bread left to rise overnight in the warmth of the banked fire. Other servants arrived, glanced at me, and ignored me. A few men drifted in from the stables and sat at the other end of the table, chatting idly and teasing the women, a full hour before breakfast. I realized that the palace held life beyond the laundry chambers.

"I'm new here," I said to the girl. Her strong arms, bare to the elbow, kneaded the bread. "I'm Roger Kilbourne."

"So you said."

"Who are you?"

"Why should you care?"

"So I will know to tell the queen who broke my nose. I understand she keeps careful record of all crimes."

The girl stopped kneading, stared at me, and laughed reluctantly. I was astonished at myself. Where had the courage come from to tease this girl, to tease any girls? With Cat Starling I had felt protectiveness, with Lady Cecilia I had been tongue-tied and oafish. The only quick wit I had ever shown was in dealings with the Dead.

She said, "What do you know of the queen?"

"I have never seen her." I knew only what everyone knew, plus too much about the orderliness required by this exacting monarch. Endless clean linen from the laundry, to match the washed cobblestones, the spotless rooms, the careful record of shipwrecks. Endless clean clothing: green for the young queen's household, blue for the old, brown for the stable, gray for those who gardened anywhere in the palace.

The girl said, "May Her Grace live long," and something moved behind her eyes, something that gave the commonplace words a meaning I did not understand. "Now let me work."

"All right—but will you tell me something first?"

"Maybe."

"What is your name?"

"Maggie Hawthorne. Now go away!"

Yet another person telling me to go away.

"Maggie Hawthorne, if I sleep here under the table at night, will anyone beat me?"

She gazed at me in surprise. "No, of course not. But I am first here in the morning, and if you misbehave again, *I* will beat you."

I didn't doubt she could do it. I nodded gratefully, nursing my painful nose. And since she didn't tell me a third time to go away, I stayed and waited for breakfast.

The palace housed two rival queens.

Not, of course, that I ever saw either of them. Queen Eleanor, the old queen, should have relinquished her throne to her daughter when the princess reached thirty-five. So had the custom always been in The Queendom. No one monarch should rule too long, lest power become too entrenched and so corrupt. Queens always abdicated when the heiress to the throne reached thirty-five.

But Queen Eleanor had refused. Princess Caroline was not fit to rule, she said. The queen's duty to her country made it impossible to pass the Crown of Glory to a daughter who was—what?

Unstable in her mind, said some rumors.

A witch, whispered others.

A poisoner, said still others. The princess's consort, dead right after the birth of her youngest child and heir, and he died so suddenly in the bloom of health . . . a poisoner and a witch.

No, said those loyal to Caroline. *It's all the old queen's vanity and love of power. She merely seeks excuses to hold the throne longer.*

And so she had, since the army had backed her against her daughter. Queen Eleanor controlled the Blues. That had not stopped the princess from having herself crowned, although not with the Crown of Glory, which her mother kept in her own possession. The old queen could have had Queen Caroline removed from the palace, but she had not. And so both queens lived in separate areas of the vast structure, each with her own guards and servants and loyal courtiers.

Rumors continued to fly, and in the inns and taverns and farmhouses across The Queendom, the common people argued, or snickered, or just waited, shocked and fascinated to learn what might happen next. *As good as a masque*, said the irreverent and bold. The harvest had been good for several years, the land at peace, barns and larders and still rooms crammed with stores for the winter. Who ruled in Glory mattered little compared to a full belly and snug cottage and warm fire. Let the two queens skirmish over who sat on which elaborately carved chair.

But within the palace, it meant everything.

"You here again?" Maggie said, as she said every morning.

"Why did you wake me?" I crawled, frowsy and irritable, from under the trestle table in the kitchen.

"You cried out in your sleep, Roger. You were afraid of a bat."

Bat. The simpleminded sailor who did not realize he was dead, whom I had left to wait for his lost captain at the top of the cliff above the sea. Again I felt the terror of that night, saw the yellow-haired youth die in his noose, choking and kicking the air. Saw my aunt's skull crack open as Hartah hit her with the brassbound wooden chest. Felt the knife slide into Hartah's flesh, easy as a bird wing slicing the air.

"What is it, Roger? You look . . . I don't know."

"It's nothing."

"You *always* say that. Bats can't hurt you, you know. You needn't be afraid."

"I'm not afraid of bats!"

"But you said—"

"Don't you have work to do?"

"I was doing it," she pointed out, "until you called 'Bat! Bat!' like some half-wit."

"Can this half-wit have some breakfast?"

She brought me bread, hot and crusty from the oven, with

new butter and stewed apples, and I lingered as long as I could in the fragrant warmth of the kitchen.

In the laundry the backbreaking work went on, but I saw that my body was filling out, getting stronger and bulkier. The good food and hard work added muscle and bone. Joan Campford, kind under her slave-driving severity, made me new trousers and small clothes. I never saw Lady Cecilia, nor any of the nobility, in my round of laundry chambers, servants' kitchen, servants' baths. I was on an endless narrow track, like a donkey treading his small circle to turn a millstone.

Maggie and I became friends, talking and laughing in the early morning kitchen. She told me of her older sister, married and sharp-tongued and bitter, and of her brother, Richard, a soldier with the Blues. I said, "But you are with Queen Caroline and the Green—"

"Hush," Maggie said, glancing quickly around. However much the rival queens were discussed in the countryside, people were more discreet within the palace. I could easily imagine that each camp informed on the other. Maggie continued, "I was glad to get any place in the palace. Otherwise I must have lived with my sister."

"Can I have more cheese, Maggie?"

"You're always so hungry."

"True enough," I said humbly. "But it's partly because you make such good cheese."

"Katherine made this cheese."

"But yours is better."

"I don't make cheese. Don't you know the difference between a cook and a dairymaid?" But she was smiling, and she brought me a meat pie, rich and spicy, which I devoured in four bites.

But the other side of Maggie's friendship was her intense desire to know everything I did, thought, was.

"Who is Mistress Conyers?" she asked one morning.

"No one."

"Everyone is someone, Roger. You called her name in your sleep. Who is she?"

"A woman of quality who was kind to me once."

"A woman of quality? Were you born on her lands?"

"No, no. She has no lands."

Maggie eyed me suspiciously. "Quality without lands?"

"They were lost."

"How? When?"

"You ask too many questions."

She flared. "Who usually talks to me first? Almost every single morning?"

"I do, Maggie," I said humbly. "But I can't help what I say in my sleep. All I can do is ask you to not tell anyone else."

She said slowly, "Sometimes, Roger, I think you are not what you seem to be."

To that I had no answer.

So I said the one thing I probably shouldn't, but the question had been on my lips a dozen times these past weeks. "Maggie, what is Soulvine Moor?"

Quickly her gaze raked the kitchen. The other servants, busy with their work, paid us no attention. "Don't say that aloud here! What's wrong with you?"

"I—"

"Be quiet!"

I had never seen Maggie frightened before. Always she was calm, competent, relentlessly in charge. I whispered, "I'm sorry. I'm so ignorant. But please tell me . . . I need to know!"

"Why?"

"My mother died there."

Maggie went stiff, and then her whole body shuddered, a long spasm from her neck clear down her spine. She gazed at me with horror in which was mixed a kind of sadness.

"Roger—never ever tell anyone that. You did not say it to me, I did not hear it."

"But—"

"I did not hear it!"

She turned and walked away from me, leaving her bread half kneaded on the table—Maggie, who never left a task without finishing it. I caught her arm. "Maggie, don't go!"

She jerked her arm free and glared at me but said nothing.

"You have to talk to me!"

"I don't have to do anything."

People were starting to look at us. Again Maggie turned away, but something brought her back. Her tone didn't soften, but a strange note crept into it. "Roger, you can't help your ignorance, I know that. You can't even read, can you? Just try to stay silent and do your work."

My work. Pressing irons, dye vats, buckets and buckets and buckets of water. That's all she thought I was: Roger the laundress. All at once I couldn't bear Maggie's low opinion of me. She was my only friend in the palace, and to her I was an oafish laundress, my hands often green with dye. And she would not tell me what I needed to know about Soulvine Moor. I *had* to make her tell me more. Anger, shame, desperate craving to make her talk all churned in my mind, turning it to mush, the mush flavored with my instinct that Maggie could be trusted.

I moved very close and whispered in her ear. "I can cross over into the country of the Dead."

Maggie jerked away from me. She stared, incredulous, and then disgust settled over her features. She shook her head.

"I had not figured you, Roger, for a liar. Ignorant, but not a liar."

Again she shook her head, and walked away from me, her back very straight. The rest of the day she stayed away from me, and when she entered the kitchen the next morning, she had another maid with her. And all the mornings after.

I was more alone than ever before, alone in the palace nested inside the teeming city nested inside the vast village nested inside the circle of fields and plain and hills and mountains. Winter gave way to the sharp freshness of early spring. I had been at court for six months, scrubbing and boiling and ironing and dyeing and hauling. And I might have gone on like that forever, except that the prince's wedding, once again, changed all.

11

"MORE WATER! More water, boy!"

I had hauled water since dawn, until my shoulders felt as if they would fall off, and it was now almost dusk, and still Joan Campford wanted more water. The open courtyard of the laundry chambers seemed a solid mass of rushing women, skirts hiked up to keep them off the wet stone floor.

"More water! We need more water!"

Pots boiled, cloths flapped in a fitful wind, and I had never been so tired in my life. To make it all worse, spring had given way to a sudden, unseasonably late cold. Water I hauled from the river to the boiling vats was near freezing, the courtyard fiery near the boiling pots, and the roofed ironing chambers steaming like wet wood on a new fire. I was always too cold, too hot, too achingly weary.

"More water!"

"I can't bring any more water!"

Words I hadn't even known I was going to say: anguished words. Joan Campford stopped and looked at me, really looked. Her broad red face softened. "Aye, ye've done good work, boy. Did ye get anything to eat today?"

"No."

"Go to the hall and eat. We can manage without ye for a bit."

"Thank you!"

I stumbled through the corridors to the servants' hall, which was even more frenzied than the laundry.

Prince Rupert's bride, Princess Isabelle, had arrived two days ago from her own queendom beyond the northern mountains. She brought with her an enormous train of soldiers, servants, courtiers, ladies. They all must be fed, housed, waited on, and their cloth—bed linen, towels, garments, horse blankets—kept clean. Naturally, I had seen none of the strangers, who did not visit the laundry. But all meals for our own servants had been suspended as all the kitchens raced to keep up with feeding Princess Isabelle's retinue and entertaining her court. Everyone else snatched scraps of food as we could, and kept working. Nor had I been able to sleep in the servants' kitchen. I'd lain on my old pallet with the apprentices, and hoped I was too exhausted for dreams that might make me cry out in what passed for sleep.

By now, I wished the royal couple in the country of the Dead.

But this madness would go on only two days more. Tomorrow was the wedding, and the next day Princess Isabelle would take her new consort back to her own queendom. The laundresses gossiped that the princess's mother was dying, and very soon Princess Isabelle would be Queen Isabelle. It was a good alliance for Prince Rupert, even if his bride was a full six years older than he. Meanwhile, tonight was a great masque, which had required that endless bolts of cloth not only be ironed but also that they be dyed yellow, the color of the princess's court. That had proved a messy business. My hands, face, hair were streaked with yellow. Even my feet had ended up bright yellow.

The servants' kitchen was frantic with dinner preparations. Maggie, her fair hair greasy and falling around a face smudged with flour, scowled at me. "Roger! Why are you here?"

"I'm starving."

"Why are you *yellow*?"

"Dye."

"Why are you swaying like that?"

"I'm exhausted."

"We're all exhausted." But her tone softened, sounding almost as she had in the days before I had mentioned Soulvine Moor and so lost her prickly friendship. She snatched a meat pie from a table and thrust it at me. "Here. Don't tell—these are for Her Plainness's table."

"Is the princess very plain, then?"

"I didn't say that—no, I *didn't*. Now go away, can't you see we have enough people here already?"

It looked like half the palace was here; the rushing, shouting cooks and maids and serving men were packed as thick as chickens in a crate, and just as agitated. It reminded me of my own brief glimpse of the city outside the palace walls, in the summer. How long ago that seemed.

I gobbled my pie, too tired to savor the exquisite taste, and fell asleep in a corner piled with empty crates smelling of vegetables.

Music woke me. I leapt to my feet and for a long moment I thought I must be dreaming. This did not happen in servants' halls!

Lords and ladies streamed into the hall, accompanied by their musicians. All save the musicians were masked, their faces covered with fantastic devisings of feathers, silver, jewels, cloth of gold, beads, and fur. Laughing, calling, dancing, staggering—they were clearly drunk. The few servants sitting at tables, eating dishes left over from dinner—what time was it? How long had I slept?—leapt to their feet and then sank into curtsies and bows.

"So this is where that vile tart came from!" someone screamed. More calls, derision, laughter. Their bright silks and velvets and satins filled the hall with green. All green—this was the young queen's household, then. A courtier seized one of the serving maids and swung her, terrified, into a dance to fiddle and flute.

"Have you never seen a kitchen before, Hal?"

"Hal sees only bedchambers!"

"I have never seen a kitchen. I thought food grew . . . grew . . ." The man turned aside, tore off his mask, and vomited over a table piled high with fresh bread.

"Ugh!"

"Put him in one of those crates!"

"Put him in the stew pot!"

But that drunken remark, which I did not understand,

silenced a few of the courtiers, and all of the servants. The servants' faces twisted with disgust, or fear, and then immediately stiffened again. No one, not even the kitchen steward, knew what we should do. The fiddling and dancing and laughter and shouting went on.

"Give Hal some more ale!"

"Give him a kitchen wench!"

"Ale! Ale!"

"The queen!"

Instantly the musicians stopped playing. Courtiers and servants alike sank to their knees. Silence descended like a hard rain, and the old queen came into the hall.

She was alone, save for her personal guard of two Blues. Queen Eleanor, sixty years old, had ruled for forty-one years, since the death of her mother in a hunting accident. She wore a gown of pale blue silk embroidered with darker blue at the hem. The gown, like her simple silver crown, was austere and quiet and expensive. Her face was deeply lined, her hair white as an egret's wing. But she stood straight and tall, and power emanated from her like steady heat.

No one moved or spoke.

When the old queen did so, it was in a low voice that carried into every corner of the hall, into every apprehensive ear. Her gaze swept over the courtiers. "None of you belongs here."

I realized then that I was still standing, frozen beside the vegetable crates. I tried to sink to the floor without calling attention to myself.

The queen's voice rang out imperiously. "Caroline."

The rustle of skirts moving forward; this lady had not knelt. She removed her mask of green feathers over cloth of gold. "Yes."

So this was the young queen!

Her mother said, "You especially do not belong here."

"This is my palace. And this is my merriment, before my brother must leave us."

Queen Caroline, thirty-seven years old, was beautiful. Also dangerous, in some way I could feel but not understand. Her body curved lusciously under a tight green bodice, but so did many others among the ladies. The difference lay in her eyes, black with silver glints, as if something shining were submerged in dark water. The difference lay in the set of her white shoulders, the thrust of her lovely breasts, the very intricacy of her coiffure, black as her eyes, braided and puffed and set with jewels in contrast to the old queen's smooth white hair.

The two women stared at each other. I could see both their faces clearly. The old monarch stared at her daughter. Although neither queen grimaced, hatred crackled between them. And neither lowered her chin nor blinked.

Queen Eleanor said icily, "A strange merriment, to terrorize the kitchen servants on the eve of your brother's wedding."

"It is my choice," the young queen said, "and mine to make."

"It is not. Rupert!"

The prince unmasked and came forward. He wore green, not blue, perhaps to go unnoticed among Queen Caroline's household. But even I knew that to wear his older sister's colors and not his mother's was a deadly insult. He looked just as handsome as when I had seen him chase Lady Cecilia, all those long months ago. He stood, sullen, beside his sister, one hand upon her shoulder.

The old queen said, "Rupert, return to your bride, who awaits you upstairs. Your manners are deplorable."

"Yes, mother," he muttered. This was not the imperious prince who kissed ladies-in-waiting. This was a pouting boy, ordered by his mother to behave or else take the consequences. What consequences? I could not imagine.

Prince Rupert skulked from the hall, followed by the old queen and her ladies. When they had gone, Queen Caroline said to the silent company, "Unmask."

Everyone obeyed, but still no one spoke, not even those who were most drunk. They had seen their young queen reprimanded in front of her court and the palace servants. No one dared say anything until she had spoken.

Queen Caroline's black eyes glittered. But she did not flinch. In a strong clear voice she said, "My mother has never been able to recognize merriment—just think what a gloomy time my father must have had while getting me upon her!" And she laughed.

The court, too, exploded into bawdy laughter. She had disarmed the old queen's haughtiness, somehow turning Queen Eleanor into a comically prissy old woman. Courtiers guffawed and chattered. The young queen stood amid them, smiling. She was not far from me, and despite myself I looked for her famed sixth finger. Yes, it was there on her left hand, not a whole finger but just the stump of one, held bent inward to hide it as much as possible, and it seemed as if—

Among the unmasked throng I glimpsed Lady Cecilia.

The sight of her struck me like a blow. I stood, took a step toward her. My arm was caught from below and Maggie pulled me back down to my knees. "What are you *doing*? She has not given us leave to rise!"

Where had Maggie come from? She must have worked her way, on her knees, through the kneeling servants and over to my vegetable crates. But this thought, and Maggie's presence, only flitted across my mind, which was turned to mush by the sight of Lady Cecilia.

She, too, wore green, soft silk billowing into stiffer, elaborately embroidered skirts. Her shining brown hair was braided and puffed as elaborately as Queen Caroline's, and her bodice cut as low. A fancy mask of green-dyed feathers dangled from one little hand. But whereas the queen looked mature, luscious as a ripe pear, Cecilia was a little green berry. Her slim waist and small breasts started my heart thumping. Her face somber, she leaned against a courtier, a good-looking youth whom I instantly hated. Her eyes swept across me without recognition.

But in all the milling nobility, another pair of eyes found mine. Queen Caroline moved across the kitchen floor and stood before me. "Rise," she said.

Confused motion among the servants on their knees—were they all supposed to rise, or just me? A few staggered to their feet, the rest did not. The queen ignored them all.

"Boy, why are you yellow?"

My throat would not produce sounds.

"Yellow is the color of the Princess Isabelle. You are of my household, not hers. So why are your face and hands yellow?"

"I . . . I . . ."

"Are you trying to insult me, boy, by wearing the color of another royal?"

"No, Your Grace!"

"Then are you a fool?"

"I . . . I work in the laundry! We dyed the cloths for—"

"I think you must be a fool. And so you will be my fool." She beckoned to a courtier, who sprang to her side. "Robin, bring this fool to my rooms at midnight."

"Yes, Your Grace," he said, but he did not look pleased.

"You will find him in the laundry," she said. Clapping her hands, she cried, "Come, let us go now to the dancing! Servants, you may rise, and we thank you for your hospitality. The steward shall give you all Amelian wine to toast my brother's marriage!"

A ragged cheer went up from the younger servants. Amelian wine was the rarest and choicest of vintages, and very expensive. The queen's court swept from the hall.

Maggie said, "Oh, Roger, why does she want you?"

I was too stunned to answer. Only one thought raged in my dazed mind: Maybe Lady Cecilia would be there, too, in the queen's rooms, at midnight.

12

"WHERE IS THE QUEEN'S
new fool?" a voice said loudly in the darkness of the apprentice
chamber. Boys woke and cursed—until they saw who stood in
the doorway, lamp raised high. Then some clambered out of
bed and dropped to one knee, although there is nothing sillier
than a bow made in a nightshirt. Others pretended to be still
asleep. A murmur ran through the room, low as wind in grass
and just as hard to locate: *Lord Robert, the queen's favorite, Lord
Robert . . .*

I scrambled from my pallet, still in my one suit of clothes; I
had not put on the nightshirt that Joan Campford had made for
me from a worn bedsheet. But I had it rolled beside me, along
with my change of small clothes, my wooden comb, and a little
knife for shaving: all that I owned in the world. I didn't know
what to expect from this night, and after I saw Lord Robert, I

knew even less. Why had he come himself instead of sending a page? At least he had known to look for me in the apprentices' chamber and not the laundry as the queen had told him.

"I'm here, my lord!" I called, and the high, squeaky voice did not sound like my own.

"Then come with me." He sounded impatient, and yet there was a note of amusement, too. I didn't see anything amusing. I trailed after him, my little bundle in my hand, and the others watched me go.

By the torchlight in the courtyard, I could see him better. After the queen and her courtiers had left the kitchen, Maggie had told me about Lord Robert Hopewell. In her shock over my summoning, her coolness had vanished. Lord Robert was perhaps forty, tall and well built. He had courted Queen Caroline when they were both young, but she had chosen instead another lord, far less strong, less handsome, less intelligent, as consort. Maggie had not said why, although from the way she pursed her lips, I imagined that she had a theory. Maggie always had theories. The queen's consort had given her two sons, and then a daughter to rule after her, Princess Stephanie, now three years old. Shortly after the heir's birth, the consort had died of the sweating sickness. I had the impression from Maggie that nobody much missed him. But this, too, was not spoken aloud. Since then, Lord Robert had again become the queen's favorite.

He led me from the servants' portion of the sprawling palace through courtyards I remembered from my visit, so many months ago, to Emma Cartwright. Wide, quiet courtyards, their trees and barely budded bushes now white in the cold moonlight, ringed with buildings of painted gray stone.

Then buildings faced with smooth, white marble. Finally, buildings faced with mosaics of pearl and quartz, with small fountains playing among them. On this trip, however, there were no people. And we went farther than the quarters of the ladies-in-waiting—was Lady Cecilia in there, fast asleep under Emma Cartwright's stern guardianship?

We went all the way to the courtyard of the young queen.

It was magnificent: bright with torchlight, tiled with green mosaics, set about with gilded branches of red berries in tall, exquisite green urns. Soldiers dressed in green tunics stood guard. They flung open doors for Lord Robert and we passed through a large, dark room empty save for benches against the wall. Then another large room, also dark, but this one furnished and hung with tapestries. Finally a much smaller room where candles and fire burned brightly, and the queen sat alone at a heavily carved table set with wine and cakes.

She still wore her masquing gown, low cut and sumptuous. Her white breasts gleamed in the firelight. But she had taken down her hair, and it fell in rich dark coils around her face and shoulders.

"I have brought him," Lord Robert said. "Although I still don't believe any of it."

"Thank you, Robin," the queen said. I dropped clumsily to one knee. "Rise," she said. "Are you frightened, boy?"

"Of course he's frightened," Lord Robert said, grinning. "For one thing, he's dyed yellow. No man can be at ease when dyed yellow."

"But he can't help that," she said sweetly. This midnight she was all sweetness, a different woman from the one I had seen crackling with hatred for her regal mother. "He must do whatever work the laundresses demand of him. Is that right, Roger?"

"Y-yes, Your Grace." She knew my name.

"But you have no reason to be nervous here. No one will hurt you."

How many times had I heard that sentence from Hartah, always followed by *"if you do as I say"*? But she had no need to utter the rest of the sentence aloud. She was a queen. Everyone did as she said.

"Well, since he is here, give him some wine," Lord Robert said, pouring himself a goblet.

"No, not yet," she said. "Roger, how old are you?"

"Fourteen, Your Grace."

"Just a little older than my oldest son," Queen Caroline said. "Percy is eleven. Can you read, Roger?"

"No, Your Grace."

"And where is your family?"

"All dead, Your Grace."

"Like the crew of the *Frances Ormund*."

I almost staggered and fell, held upright only by my hand on the corner of the table. She knew. Somehow she knew about the wreck . . . and *what else*?

"You talk in your sleep," she said gently, but her eyes raked my face. "And I have people who report to me everything that happens in my palace. Did you know that, Roger?"

"N-no, Your Grace." I had guessed that she had spies, but not that they would report on lowly laundresses. Maggie? Joan? No, it would have been one of the other apprentices, whose sleep I had disturbed night after night. What else had

I said? Lord Robert lounged in a chair, his expression somewhere between disapproval and amusement.

"Ordinarily, of course, I would not find it interesting that a laundress—even a boy laundress—called out the name of a ship foundered by wreckers. It was a public event, after all, and word spreads. But you have called out other things, too, Roger. 'Soulvine Moor.' 'Hygryll.' 'Lord Digby.'"

Lord Robert looked up sharply from his wine. The amusement disappeared.

"What do you know of Lord Digby, Roger?"

Old Mrs. Humphries, sitting under a tree by a river in the country of the Dead, prattling of her childhood. I said desperately, "Your Grace, I know only that he once rode through the village of Stonegreen and gave a gold coin to a child."

Robin said, "Bruce Digby never gave anything to anyone."

"Lord *William* Digby!" In my agitation I scarcely knew what I said. All sweetness had vanished from the queen's face. She had so many faces, this queen; she was changeable as weather. Now neither firelight nor candlelight brought warmth to her chill marble.

She said, "The grandfather? And how could you know that, Roger? He died long before you were born."

"The child told me! When she was an old lady! It was a family story!"

"And is Soulvine Moor, too, a family story?"

I could only gaze at her in despair.

"I think, Roger, that it was not Lord William Digby whose name you called out, but that of Lord Bruce. And—"

"No, no, it was not!"

"You dare to interrupt me? And I think that calling out

'Soulvine Moor' and '*Frances Ormund*' was not by happenchance, either. Nor was calling out 'my lady Frahyll.'"

I remembered Lady Frahyll. Another talkative old woman, another country faire with Hartah's booth. But that town had boasted a manor house, and the lord's mother had recently died. A harmless, babbling old dame, too old and too dead to preserve the distinctions of rank. She had told me happily about the people of the countryside, and I had saved myself a beating from Hartah.

"Frahyll is not a common name," the queen said. "It bears the tortured syllables of southern names, names from the Unclaimed Lands or even from Soulvine Moor. Names like 'Hygryll.' Like 'Hartah.' You call out 'Hartah' often, Roger. Is he, too, dead?"

I was mute with terror.

"Roger, can you cross over to the country of the Dead?"

Lord Robert said impatiently, "That is impossible. I have told you and told you, Caro—crossing over is a superstition. A belief among the ignorant country folk, who still believe that spitting at frogs at midnight causes thunderstorms."

The queen ignored him. Her gaze, black flecked with submerged silver, never left mine. Terror held me mute. She could torture me, burn me for a witch. . . .

"Think carefully, Roger, before you answer me. I will have the truth, and there are ways of obtaining it. They are not pleasant ways. I don't want to have to use them on you but—"

"For sweet sake, Caro, he's just a boy!"

"—but I will if necessary. I am not a cruel woman, Roger. I am a woman who wants to rule my country well. Who faces obstacles to my rule, obstacles you cannot begin to imagine. Who will do whatever is necessary to rule well, for the greater good and for the sake of my daughter, who must rule after me. Do you understand me?"

"Y-yes."

"Then I will ask you one more time. Answer truthfully, and answer with full awareness of the consequences. You are not stupid. I can see that you are not stupid. Roger, can you cross over to the country of the Dead?"

"Yes," I said.

"Show me."

"Caro——" Lord Robert began.

"Show me now. Here."

I said wildly, "I must have . . ." I couldn't say it, but I had to say it. "I must have pain. I can do it myself."

"Then do so."

I laid my little bundle on the polished table and unwrapped it. Lord Robert, now looking elaborately bored, smiled condescendingly at the plain nightshirt made from a bedsheet. I took my shaving knife and plunged it into my thigh. Pain burned along my nerves. Even as I made the necessary effort of will, I heard the queen cry out as my body toppled, and dimly I felt Lord Robert, cat-fast, catch me as I fell.

Darkness—

Cold—

Dirt in my mouth—

Worms in my eyes—

Earth imprisoning my fleshless arms and legs—

For the first time in half a year, I crossed over.

The palace was gone. Only the river remained, wide and calm as in the land of the living, but the ring of jagged western mountains had vanished; they must be farther away here. Everything had stretched out. The island was so huge I could not see across it, and trees dotted the vast plain on the opposite bank, where there had been farms and fields. Trees and groves and ponds and the Dead.

There were many more of them than there had been in the countryside, but the huge plain didn't seem crowded. Perhaps—and it wasn't the first time I'd had this idea—the ████ ████ ████████ ██ ██████, ██████ ████ ████. More of the Dead were well-dressed than in the villages where Hartah had set up his booth. Silk gowns, burnished armor, old-fashioned farthingales, brocade cloaks and doublets, all alongside strange white robes or crudely stitched clothing of leather and fur. People had lived by this river for a very long time.

No matter what they wore, these Dead behaved like all the others: sitting in circles, gazing at the grass or sky, doing nothing. I tripped over a soldier in peculiar copper-colored armor and went sprawling. He said nothing, just went on staring at the featureless gray clouds. Scrambling to my feet, I saw blood on my hand where I had just cut it on a stone, blood on my leggings from the knife I had thrust into my thigh. I was the only one here who could bleed. And yet I felt no pain. That would not recur until I went back.

Frantically I raced among the silent groups. I needed an old person, preferably a woman, or a newly arrived Dead— someone who would talk to me. *"I will have the truth, and there are ways of obtaining it. They are not pleasant ways. . . ."*

A man suddenly materialized a few yards away. One moment he was not there, and the next moment he was. He wore a long white nightshirt of rich cream-colored linen and a woolen nightcap, and on his shriveled finger was a ring set with three huge rubies in intricately wrought gold. He gazed at me wildly. "Where am I?"

I thought quickly. "You are safe, sir."

"I died! I am dead!"

"Yes, sir. And I am your guide in this place, sent to greet you."

"I am dead!"

"Yes. And I am your guide. You must come with me."

I think it was the strange yellow dye on my face that convinced him. He stared at me, shuddered, and followed.

I led him to a little grove where no one else sat. He looked at his arm, withered but without pain, and said wonderingly, "My illness is gone."

"It's over, sir. And you must answer questions for me."

He nodded, still too bemused to question my completely false authority. That state of mind would not last. I must move quickly.

"What is your name, sir?"

"Lord Joseph Deptford."

"And your position at court?"

"A gentleman of the bedchamber to Prince Percy. Although since I became sick . . . Who are *you*, boy?"

"I told you, sir, I'm your guide in this place. For the sake of being judged fairly, you must answer just a few more questions. What was your last illness?"

"Weakness in the heart. I—"

"Is the young prince difficult to attend?"

"He—now, see here, boy—"

"I cannot take you to my master without this information! Is the prince difficult to attend?"

"He is impossible," the old man said flatly. "He pulls my beard and whispers treason about his grandmother, anything his mother wishes to hear, and—enough! I will answer to your master in person! This impertinence is over!"

I left him among the trees, free now to discover that for him, all impertinence was over. In a moment he would lapse into the tranquility of the Dead. My little knife had been left behind in the queen's chamber, but there were sharp stones enough by the river. I whacked one against a burn on my hand from a boiling laundry pot, and I crossed back over.

I lay on the hearth rug before the fire, the queen sitting on the rug beside me in a puddle of green silk skirts, in all her glorious unbound hair. Lord Robert still lounged at the table, drinking wine.

"That was quick," the queen said. "Did it happen?"

"Yes, Your Grace." I sat up, a little dizzy, and a part of my mind thought how weird it was to be sitting on the floor with a queen, like two children playing at dice.

Playing at death.

"Well, tell me," she said. Then, more ominously, "Convince me."

"I spoke to a Lord Joseph Deptford. He died just now, minutes ago, in a white nightshirt and blue woolen cap. He was a gentleman of the bedchamber to Prince Percy, and he told me"—Was this wise to say? Nothing was wise to say—"that the young prince is difficult to attend. He pulls the old lord's beard."

Lord Robert laughed and said, "True enough. But easy palace gossip, for all that. And even if that old fool Deptford did die tonight, that could be a lucky guess. The whole palace knows he is ill."

"Lord Robert could be correct," the queen said to me. "What else have you?"

"Only . . . only . . ."

"Out with it, Roger!"

To even utter the words might bring me death. To not utter them certainly would. I closed my eyes and said, "He told me that the prince whispers treason about his grandmother. Because it is what he believes that Your Grace would like to hear."

Lord Robert's goblet crashed to the floor, splashing wine onto the queen's skirts. She breathed out slowly—*aaaahhhhhhh*—like a sigh. Then she leaned over and kissed my cheek, and it was a mother's kiss, tender and gentle and terrifying as spring buds.

THE QUEEN GAVE me two new suits
of clothes, both green-and-yellow velvet with green ribbons at
the knees. She gave me a place to sleep, a tiny alcove off her
presence chamber, where no one could hear me cry out. "For I
cannot have you closer, Roger," the queen said. "You're a boy,
but a boy nearing manhood, and I am a widow. I don't want to
give my enemies food for scandal."

I felt my ears burn. But she meant it, despite the whole
court's knowing that Sir Robert was her lover. He went
openly in and out of her privy chamber, a little amused smile
on his face, sometimes snapping his fingers at me or giving me
a whistle, as you might a dog. Yet he was not unkind to me,
not meaningfully.

"You must keep the yellow dye on your face," Queen Caroline said. "It makes you different from other fools. And it's a

splendid joke on that stiff-necked prig my brother was forced to marry. Yellow—the color of her court!"

Her brother, Prince Rupert, and his plain bride had left court the day after the wedding. None of us would likely see them for several years.

"Your Grace," I said desperately, "I haven't wit enough to be a fool!" A fool must stay close to the queen, making sharp and funny comments on the personalities and doings of members of the court. I knew none of the members of the court. I could not make sharp and funny comments. I would fail.

"Of course you have wit enough to be a fool."

"I do not! Could I . . . could I be a page?" A page's duties I thought I could manage.

"Pages are highborn, like my Alroy. They are also ten years old. No, you must be my fool."

"I am not funny enough to—"

"Then become funny," she said sharply. "I need a reason to keep you close by, a reason that no one will question."

"Yes, Your Grace."

I stayed in my alcove, sleeping off my laundress exhaustion, until the day after the wedding. Then, for the first time, and dressed in my new clothes, I accompanied the queen as she received in her presence chamber. I took the place she indicated, to the left and below the queen's tall chair on its raised dais. Sitting at her feet.

"Listen to everything," she whispered to me. "Learn, so that you will better know who to approach and what to ask when I send you to cross over."

"It doesn't happen like that, I can't—" But she didn't want

to hear it. She waved her hand and the guards threw open the great doors.

I was terrified. *Be funny.*

The presence chamber was the first room of the queen's suite, the largest and barest room, furnished with only her throne upon a dais and benches along the walls. Next came the outer chamber, where she was attended by her ladies. This, too, was of a good size, richly furnished with tables, chairs, space for dancing and the presentation of the masques that the court so loved. Then the privy chamber, where I had crossed over for her, with its heavily carved table and privy to it all. Then was the queen's bedchamber, which I would, of course, never see. The presence chamber was where her public events took place, because the palace's real throne room was still in the control of the old queen. To my dazzled eyes, the presence chamber was intimidating enough—what must the throne room be like?

Queen Caroline's advisors entered, a procession of three old men tottering behind Lord Robert. Women, who create life, must rule. But men, who defend life, must advise. Thus is the balance of the world preserved. The queen's green-clad advisors each bowed before her and then stood to the left and right of the throne. None of them so much as glanced at me, crouching at the foot of the steps to the dais in my yellow face dye and green-and-yellow velvets. I was just another piece of furniture, like the steps themselves, but less useful.

The queen said, "Let the petitioners come."

There were not many. I thought that the wedding feast, the masques and dances, had tired everyone so that their business with the queen must have been postponed. Later, I learned that I was wrong. The petitioners were all in the palace throne room with the old queen.

Where the power resided.

Queen Caroline's lips tightened. She barely opened them to say to the first man, "Why do you come before me?"

"Your Grace, I am in land dispute with my neighbor, Mistress Susannah Carville."

"And what is the dispute?"

"We each claim the fields on the right bank of the River Ratten."

I blurted out, "All lands are the queen's, except when they are rotten!"

There was total silence. Then the petitioner said, "The right bank is, of course, Your Grace's as well! But the use of it is in dispute between Mistress Carville and me."

"Continue," the queen said. She shot me a disgusted glance. I had not been funny. I had failed.

Almost I wished myself in the country of the Dead.

Over time, I became a little better at being a fool. Sometimes, someone would laugh at my jest. A very small laugh. The queen, however, became no better at being sought out for anything important. Minor land disputes, minor points of law, minor appropriations of money for minor building. Queen Caroline settled them all with justice and knowledge. This was a side of her I had not seen before, much different from the woman who had threatened me with torture, or the one who each morning asked sweetly how I had slept. She was a just and equitable queen to her subjects beyond the palace.

Nonetheless, it seemed to me that she was hardly a queen at all. The palace teemed with the old queen's Blues. Queen Caroline had her own Green guard, but it was tiny in comparison. And no one ever petitioned her for anything to do with the army. Courtiers' gossip whispered about the new navy—The Queendom's first—being built in Carlyle Bay, at the mouth of the Thymar River. However, in the presence chamber I heard nothing of any ships. I listened and I learned, but the truth is that I did not really care about the ships, or the army, or the endless land disputes

I had enough to eat, enough sleep, sometimes ale or wine to drink.

The queen did not send me on any more journeys to the country of the Dead.

My jests as fool were becoming sharper, more knowing.

But most of all, when the day's work—which did not look like "work" at all to one who had labored for Hartah, had sweated in Joan Campford's laundry—ended, I was with the queen's ladies. With Lady Cecilia.

"Are you here again, Roger? I see that you are. And yellow as ever!" And then her pealing laugh, always brighter and higher than the laughter of the young queen's other ladies. Always Lady Cecilia walked more quickly, danced more animatedly, smiled more widely, played the lute more passionately before tiring of it and tossing it aside. Her very needle, as the ladies sewed, darted faster in and out of the rich cloth, although the results often left much to be desired.

That's how they spent their days of attendance upon the queen: sewing or reading aloud or playing music or following her in walks around the various courtyards within the vast palace. When the queen was about her "business of state" in the presence chamber—the meager amount of business the old queen allowed her—I don't know what the ladies did. I sat at the foot of the queen's throne, making my feeble jokes while the time dragged by.

The nights were another matter entirely.

Then the men, the courtiers in their green silks and velvets and slashed satins studded with jewels, joined the ladies. Queen Caroline was there, too, in the outer chamber lit by candles in great branching candelabra. They all gambled at cards and dice; they danced to lute and pipes and flute; they rehearsed and presented masques. They drank wine and ate sugared cakes. They flirted—how they all flirted! Nominally the ladies were under the charge of Lady Margaret, an older woman with a long, horselike face and sad, intelligent eyes. But Lady Margaret could not keep the bevy of young, pretty, richly dressed girls from their endless romantic gossip. While the queen was sometimes serious, talking alone in a window embrasure or beside a warm fire with Lord Robert or one of the older men, the ladies were never serious. And Lady Cecilia least of all.

"Yes, my lady, I am still yellow." How I longed to appear before her dressed in something other than my fool's cap and crazy green-and-yellow tunic!

"And still a fool?"

"A fool to follow you around, my lady."

"That you are!" She gave her high trill of laughter, only there was something wrong with it. It was too high, too trilling. Her eyes were too bright.

"Is something wrong, my lady?"

"Why should anything be wrong?" she said, her smile vanishing. A second later it was back, too wide. "Don't be impertinent!"

"I'm sorry, my lady."

"You should be!" She tossed her head, her huge green eyes glittering at me, her small chin raised. I knew she wasn't really angry. She was flirting, as she would have flirted with anything male that sat beside her, from a fishmonger to Sir Robert himself. And she was so beautiful! The candlelight flickered over her hair and it shone in so many shades and browns that I couldn't count them: nutmeg, molasses, bronze, cinnamon, almost-but-not-quite gold. But her face was too pale.

"Where is everyone tonight?" Lady Cecilia said impatiently. "The chamber is half empty!"

"I don't know, my lady." I, too, had noticed the room's emptiness. Each week there were fewer courtiers in the queen's rooms. They had gone, I guessed, to the old queen's chambers in that part of the palace I had never seen. Did the deserters dare to attend Queen Eleanor while wearing the young queen's green? Or did they change their clothes with their loyalties?

Cecilia said, "We have barely enough people to dance! I want to dance!"

"But you must wait for the queen to command dancing."

"Of course, of course!" Restlessly she shifted on her stool. It was right after dinner, early in the evening. Bright fires burned in the two great hearths at either end of the chamber. Lady Cecilia and I, with two other of the youngest ladies, Lady Sarah and Lady Jane, sat on cushioned stools close by the fire. The others stood in clumps around the room, talking to the courtiers, waiting for the queen to declare the evening's entertainment. Lady Margaret sat on the other side of the hearth, reading a book. Cecilia stuck out her pink tongue at the heavy volume, slid her eyes sideways to meet mine, and giggled.

The queen sat in a far corner with a sour-looking man I had never seen before. He was dressed well enough, in black velvet with a black satin sash, but his face was weather-battered and his hair unfashionably short. He didn't look like a soldier, nor an advisor, nor a courtier, and I had never seen anyone at court wear black. He and the queen leaned close to each other in earnest conversation. Lord Robert occasionally glanced at them from his own conversation with Lord Dearborn.

Lady Sarah said, "Cecilia, there are other things in life besides dancing."

"I think she knows that," Lady Jane said slyly, and Lady Sarah gave a bark of laughter. I didn't understand the jest, nor Cecilia's sharp reply.

"Hold your foolish tongue, Jane Sedley! And you, too, Sarah!"

"And who shall make me? Your yellow cavalier?"

I said, trying to be witty, "Green wood burns hotter than yellow."

Lady Jane and Lady Sarah looked at each other and burst into more laughter, which grew wilder and wilder. They held their sides and roared. Tears sprang to Cecilia's eyes. She jumped to her feet and rushed off.

She had nowhere to go except to the other side of the room. I followed her, bewildered about what I had said to make the others laugh like that. Cecilia stood in an empty window embrasure, leaning out over the velvet-covered seat, her face pressed to the thick glass. Outside, a few flakes of unseasonably late snow fell into the empty courtyard.

"Lady Cecilia—"

"Oh, leave me alone!"

"If I said something to offend you—"

"Of course not! What do you mean? Why should I be offended?" She whirled so suddenly to face me that I had to step back. "I have no cavalier, green or yellow or bright orange!"

"I know you don't," I said. A memory came to me: Prince Rupert scowling in a doorway, demanding Cecilia's presence.

"Then why did you say I do?"

"I didn't! I was making a jest . . . green wood . . . it was but a jest."

"It wasn't funny."

"I know," I said humbly. "Please forgive me." I started to go down on one knee. She grabbed my hand and pulled me up.

"Stop! You can't kneel to me while the queen is in the room! But you didn't think about that, did you?" She peered at me. "You really are just an ignorant savage."

All at once her mood changed with that quicksilver speed that now, I belatedly realized, had in it something of hysteria. "I know! I shall be your teacher! I shall teach you to be a courtier—to play the lute, and gamble, and . . . oh, all sorts of things! It will be the greatest amusement!"

"My lady . . ."

"And we shall start now! With the lute! Come!"

"We can't now," I said with enormous relief. "The queen is calling for dancing."

Queen Caroline had just raised her hand to the musicians who waited obediently in a corner of the room. "The jereian!"

she called. Ladies began to form one line, gentlemen another facing them. Those not dancing crowded back to the walls, I among them. The queen's fool did not dance; not even Lady Cecilia was mad enough to think that. She skipped away to join the line of ladies, and the dance began.

Like all the court dances, it was slow, stately, sedate. More suited to the old queen than to Queen Caroline. I remembered the drunken masquers tumbling into the kitchen on the eve of the prince's wedding, and knew there was wildness caged among these courtiers, just as there was in Cecilia. It was troubling. But why didn't Queen Caroline introduce other, more vigorous dances? They existed; I had seen them at faires, among villagers exhilarated with holiday, with ale, with a day's freedom from labor.

But I did not understand the queen. She contained mazes, labyrinths. Crafty, kind, passionate, ruthless, just, deceitful— she was all of these. The one thing that never changed was her determination to obtain the throne that should already rightly have been hers. I had no doubt that she would do nearly any-thing to that end—as she had once told me herself.

The queen chose to watch, not dance. She sat on a big, carved chair beside the fire, Lord Robert beside her on the stool that Lady Jane Sedley had vacated. I scurried to take my place at the queen's feet, now that the sour-faced stranger had left the room. From here I could watch Lady Cecilia move her graceful little body in and out of the figures of the dance, weaving slowly forward and back, her slim waist swaying and her green skirts changing color in the flickering firelight. . . .

"Enough," the queen said. She raised her hand and immediately the musicians stopped playing. "I find I do not want dancing, after all. I am weary. Good night."

It was still very early. Courtiers and ladies gazed at each other in bewilderment. The queen turned to walk through her rooms, and the ladies of the bedchamber picked up their skirts to scurry after her. Cecilia was not one of these. She stood with a disappointed pout in the middle of the room. "Could we not dance anyway . . . ?"

But, of course, they could not. Not without the queen. Some courtiers, the older ones, left the room, including a reluctant Lord Robert. I knew he would be back later, much later, alone, to be admitted to the queen's privy chamber. And then Lady Margaret left, one hand on her belly. "If you will excuse me . . . the pork at dinner . . . will not you young ladies retire as well?"

"It's so early," murmured Lady Jane.

"So early . . ." "Not at all tired . . ." "So very early. . . ."

With a sad smile, Lady Margaret walked from the room, her hand still on her aching belly. The younger courtiers' eyes sharpened. They would stay, and without the sharp and intelligent eyes of Lady Margaret upon them. Or the eyes of their queen.

I didn't know what I was supposed to do. Usually the queen retired very late and her ladies at the same time, and I went to my alcove to sleep. But Lady Jane was right—it was far too early to sleep . . . *Should I stay here? What should I do?*

Learn all you can, the queen had told me once. *Nobody notices a fool.*

I would stay. I wanted to stay. Lady Cecilia was here.

"Let us wager!" Lady Jane cried. She seized a pair of dice in a golden cup.

"I'll wager with you, pretty Jane," said Lord Thomas Bradley, "but not for a coin."

"For what then?" Lady Jane asked, widening her eyes with mock innocence. "A kiss?"

"Oh, I think more than a kiss."

"How much more?"

"A game is no good unless the stakes are very high. Such as . . . everything."

Lady Jane smiled at him over her fan. "Everything against what? What do you put up for your side of the wager?"

"My best mare."

"Done, my lord!"

I was shocked. This did not happen in the queen's presence. Queen Caroline liked gambling, and she was good at dice and cards. Nor did she cheat. I had watched Hartah cheat often enough to know it when I saw it. If the queen lost, she smiled and paid up. Nor did she try to keep her ladies from flirting and kissing. But I had been at court long enough to know that an unmarried lady must stay a virgin. It was one thing for the queen to take Lord Robert as a lover; she was a widow, and a queen. But her ladies must remain chaste until marriage, to preclude all doubt about who fathered their husband's eventual heirs. So why was Lady Jane Sedley laughing like that at Lord Thomas and eagerly sitting down to wager with him for "everything"? Or had I misunderstood?

I had not. More pairs of courtier-and-lady formed, sitting opposite each other at different small tables, the dice between them. Those not willing to gamble, or perhaps unchosen, clustered with excited envy around the players.

Lady Cecilia stood in the middle of the floor, her expression tense but otherwise unreadable. She was not one to join watchers, to be left out of whatever amusement presented itself.

Sudden jealousy tore through me like a gale. If she paired with one of these young lords to wager her chastity, if she lost, if she went with him to some secluded chamber . . . I couldn't breathe. All at once I could feel again Hartah's knife in my hand, sliding into his flesh, and I knew I could do the same to any man who wagered with Cecilia for her sweet and untouched body. Stupid, irrational, *insane* . . . who was I to have such thoughts? Yet I had them.

A handsome minor courtier, Lord Dillingham, walked toward Cecilia. His sword gleamed at his hip. He grinned at her but she, for once, did not flirt back. Instead she rushed forward and grabbed me by both hands. "Roger! I shall wager with you! For a silver coin with Her Grace's image stamped upon it! Come!"

Jane Sedley, seated opposite Lord Thomas, looked up and gave a derisive laugh. But before I knew it, Lady Cecilia and I were seated at one of the little tables, people crowding around to watch this new amusement. One of the queen's ladies, wagering with the queen's yellow-faced fool!

But Cecilia faced me quietly, all at once as sedate and sober as Lady Margaret herself, and laid a silver coin upon the table. "The game shall be fifty points," she said. That was an incredibly high number; a single game would last all night. We began, and she stayed sedate, barely talking, her eyes upon only the dice. After a while the watchers, disappointed, drifted to other tables. No flirting, no bawdy jokes, no forbidden crossing of the boundaries of rank. We were too dull.

Bewildered, I threw the dice and counted points, as I was told. What was Cecilia doing? Was she secretly as shocked as I at the licentiousness of these young ladies and gentlemen, and so, choosing this method of preserving her chastity? But surely she could have just announced that she preferred not to play, or even retired for the night? One other lady, besides Lady Margaret, had done that. What was truly happening here?

We played on. Cecilia never looked at me. Finally a great shout arose from one of the other tables; someone had won. Or lost. Under cover of the babble that followed, Cecilia bent her head over the dice and said, "Roger, are you my friend?"

How to answer that? A lady-in-waiting could not be friends with the queen's fool. But I let my heart answer.

"Yes, my lady."

"And friends do favors for each other, do they not?"

"Yes." My stomach grew cold.

"I need a favor from you, Roger."

"I am in attendance on the queen . . ."

"Not always. Not right *now*. Please . . . please. It is very important."

She raised her head and I saw that tears gleamed in her green eyes. Tears, and fear. I would have gone anywhere, done anything, to erase that look from her lovely face.

"Go out the kitchen gate—you came from the kitchens, didn't you? The queen found you that night in the kitchen?" Some private memory twisted her face with grief. "Go into the city. Ask your way to Mother Chilton, it's not far. Tell her you need a milady posset. And you must go masked, and in plain clothes."

I reeled with all these instructions. The only thing I found to say was, "What's a milady posset?"

"Never you mind. It's merely a thing that I need. Oh, Roger, don't fail me now!"

"But you have other friends . . . men with swords . . ."

"I cannot tell any of them! Oh, for sweet sake, smile, Sarah is looking at us—" Cecilia trilled with laughter. She cried loudly, "You have won, you swine!" She pushed the silver coin across the table to me.

Lady Sarah strolled over, smiling maliciously. "So the fool won! A good thing you did not make Jane's wager with him, Cecilia. For now Jane must pay up."

Lady Jane stood and pushed over the table, stamping her foot in its high-heeled slipper. But even I could see that her anger wasn't real. Was she really going to allow her chastity to be won in a dice game? Or was Lord Thomas not the first?

The queen, whatever her own reputation, would not approve of this. Neither of the queens.

The courtiers, making bawdy jests, crowded around Lady Jane and Lord Thomas. Lady Sarah turned to watch. I felt another, larger coin thrust into my hand, and then Cecilia flounced away toward the others, crying, "Jane! I will be your lady of the bedchamber!"

The coin in my hand was gold.

I put both in my pocket and slipped out the door from the outer chamber to the presence chamber. If Cecilia saw me go, she gave no sign. In my alcove I drew the curtain and stood there, shivering in the dark. The tiny space had neither fire nor candle. But usually I was there only when asleep, and Queen

Caroline had given me three warm blankets. I wished I could crawl under them and never come out.

What was I going to do?

I couldn't bear to see Cecilia so unhappy. Was she sick, and the milady posset a cure for some illness? But then why not tell the queen and ask for a physician? Was the posset some herb that brought temporary—if deluded—happiness? Such things existed, I knew. But ale or wine would do the same thing if enough was drunk, and it didn't cost a gold piece. I had never even *seen* a gold piece before.

What was I going to do?

Slowly I took off my green-and-yellow fool's suit. At the same time, I faced the truth. I was afraid to go into the city alone.

Slowly I drew on my old rough trousers and patched boots.

I was a coward.

I pulled on the tunic that Kit Beale had given me.

I had always been a coward. When I stayed under Hartah's beatings, when I begged Lady Conyers to keep me by her, when Queen Caroline threatened me with torture if I didn't do her bidding. A coward.

With my knife I cut off a section of a blanket, cut two holes in it to make a mask, and thrust it into my pocket. I put on my hooded cloak, a gift from the queen.

I was going out into the city. For Cecilia.

14

THE QUEEN'S ROOM emptied
soon enough; the lords and ladies all went to put Lady Jane
and Lord Thomas to bed. That whole business shocked me
still—a lady, allowing herself to be gambled for like a whore!
There was so much different about the court from what I had
vaguely imagined when I arrived here with Kit Beale. Even
Queen Caroline—why had she retired so early? Who was the
sour-faced man in black whose conversation had so upset Her
Grace?

I crept through the darkened presence chamber. Just before my hand touched the doorknob, I realized my mistake.
Green guards stood on the other side. If I, the queen's fool,
walked past them in rough dress, the queen would know it
within minutes. So, I was beginning to realize, would everyone else in the palace, which was a web of spies. If the queen

had me searched, the gold piece would be found. Then what of Cecilia's secrecy?

I went back to my alcove, put my fool's garb back on, tightly rolled my old clothes in my cloak, and walked back through the presence chamber. This time I opened the door.

"Good morning, queen's men!" I said, and kicked up both legs like a frisky colt.

One of the guards smiled. "It is evening, fool."

I looked amazed. "Are you sure? No, it's eight o'clock of a morning! I heard a cock crow!"

"Then you ears are full of candle wax."

"The better for noises to slip inside!"

He laughed and gave me a mock kick, his boot just connecting with my ass. The other guard watched sourly. "Get away from me, fool. I have no liking for half-wits."

"Ah, but I am but a quarter-wit, so you must like me! Shall I bring you breakfast from the kitchen?"

"I mean it, get away with you."

I skipped out of his boot reach in mock fear, pantomimed extreme hunger, and scampered off.

Immediately I was lost in the intricate maze of the palace. I couldn't remember the route by which Kit Beale had brought me, and I had not left the queen's chambers in weeks. Now that I thought of it, neither had she. Did she never go beyond the palace, outside to the city or the countryside? Was that her mother's doing?

By asking servants, I found my way to the kitchens. Now I knew where I was; the laundry was in this part of the palace, as was my old apprentices' chamber. Dinner was long over and only a few kitchen maids remained, scrubbing pots or preparing for tomorrow. Among them, mixing loaves of bread to rise overnight for breakfast, was Maggie.

"Roger!"

"Hello, Maggie."

"You did indeed become the queen's fool! I had heard that." Her tone was not entirely approving. The other girls stared at us, and Maggie snapped at them, "Get back to work!" They did. Maggie was in charge here, just as she had once taken charge of me. Fed me, befriended me, laughed with me. It was good to see her, despite her disapproving look at my yellow face and bizarre clothing

She pushed a lock of hair off her sweaty face. The kitchen was very warm. "What brings you here, Roger?"

I kept my voice low. "I need to go out of the door where the kitchen barges bring food from the farms."

"Why?"

"I just do."

"Is this queen's business?" Her voice, too, was low, but she kept her face calm and her strong arms busy mixing bread.

"Yes, but I cannot say what. And you must not, either."

A pause in mixing, soon over. "Oh, Roger, what have you got yourself involved in now?"

I didn't answer. Let her think my errand was an important matter on behalf of the queen. Maggie would help me all the sooner. Cecilia's sad face filled my mind.

She said, "It's not connected with the navy, is it? Please say you are not involved in that mess!"

What mess? What about the navy? How could a kitchen maid know more than I about matters of state? But I already knew the answer to that. Queen Eleanor kept all military matters away from her daughter's side of the palace. And lords and ladies did not gossip about weighty matters, lest they be overheard and misinterpreted. They could trust no one. Lower servants, however, could gossip about anything, as long as they did so in whispers, because no one in power cared what they said or thought. The palace servants—all except me—often knew everything.

I said, "It is not about the navy. But I must go soon, and I must change first and go unseen."

She sighed. "Wait a short while. Sit there and eat, as if hunger alone had driven you here." She went to the hearth and poured me a bowl of soup left over from the servants' dinner. It had cooled and I was already full, but I ate it with a great show of famine.

When Maggie had dismissed the other girls, I went into the larder and changed into my old clothes. They were far too tight; I had filled out since becoming the queen's fool. I put the piece of blanket over my face, my eyes and mouth at the crude holes. When I emerged from the larder, Maggie made a choking noise somewhere between a scream of laughter and a grunt of exasperation. I pulled my hood up over my head so that it hung over my forehead.

"This way," she said, shaking her head. Another small courtyard open to the sky, this one stacked with empty crates and jars and smelling of old vegetables. After the warm kitchen, its coolness was welcome. Maggie unlocked a door set into the wall and the scent of the river rushed in. The water flowed lazily just a few feet away, and stone stairs led down to poles at which to tie up barges. No barges floated there now. Between the river and the palace wall, a narrow path curved away in both directions.

"You can go either left or right," Maggie said.

"Which way to Mother Chilton?"

She grabbed my arm, pulled me back inside, and slammed the door. "Why are you going to *Mother Chilton*?"

"I cannot tell you that," I said with as much dignity as I could muster, which wasn't much.

"The queen would not have business with that witch!"

"She is a witch?"

"You, No, No, of course not. There is no such thing. Mother Chilton is a healer. But Roger . . . what have you done now?"

"I have done nothing."

"Then who has?"

Her gray eyes looked steadily into mine. I didn't answer. Finally she said, "Turn left. Go three alleys over and turn right. Look for the tent with a picture of two black swans drawn near the bottom. Wait, you'll need a lantern."

When she'd given it to me, I said humbly, "Thank you, Maggie. I could not do this without you."

"I suspect you should not be doing it at all. I'll wait here to let you back in. Don't be long!"

"I won't." How could I promise that? I couldn't know how long I would be. I went out through the open door, holding my lantern.

In the autumn, Kit Beale had told me that the city was mostly deserted at night, the keepers of the shops and booths having gone back home to the surrounding villages. In this cold spring, it seemed completely deserted. Tents provide little shield from cold. But within a few of the cloth buildings, lanterns gleamed, and I heard laughter from what seemed to be an alehouse. Still, I would not like to be here, with the kinds of people who stayed late at night. My teeth chattered as I scurried along, and not with cold. In the third alley, I had to stoop to find the two black swans drawn at the very bottom of a tent. A crude drawing, pretending to be the mischief of a child. Cecilia had blithely assumed that I could easily carry out her wishes, because she was used to people carrying out her wishes. But without Maggie, I would never have found this place. Never.

A bellpull hung outside, and I pulled it. After a few minutes of bone-rattling chill, the tent flap was pushed aside and a voice said, "Come in, then."

I went inside.

An open fire burned in a brazier in the center of the tent, sending its smoke through a hole in the roof and its light flickering on canvas walls. Dozens of poles stood against the walls, their butts jammed into the bare earth, and each pole dripped objects tied with string to big nails. Bottles, plants, feathers, hides, bits of wood, bulging cloth bags of all sizes, things I could not name. Besides the poles, there was room for only the brazier, a pallet of straw and blankets, and a table with a single chair. On the chair sat not the crone I'd expected but a woman neither young nor old, fat nor thin, pretty nor ugly. She wore a gray dress and gray cap. No one would ever glance at her twice; in fact, I had the sensation that I was not really seeing her at all. And yet she was solid enough, sitting there in her unadorned chair, her face pale in the dim light.

"What do you want?" she said, not unkindly.

"I'm looking for Mother Chilton."

"I am Mother Chilton."

"You?"

A faint smile. "Me. What are you after, lad? Unmask."

"I cannot." And then, inanely, "I'm sorry."

She stood and moved close to me. Now the fire was behind her and her face in shadow. With one firm hand she turned my chin to the fire and stared through the blanket holes and into my eyes. Her own eyes were colorless, an even light gleam that seemed to reflect all light, keeping none. Her breath drew in sharply. "Who are you?"

"I told you, I cannot—"

"Do you come from Soulvine Moor?"

The question completely undid me. Soulvine Moor, which Maggie had chided me for even mentioning? Soulvine Moor, where my mother had died? I gasped, "What . . . what of Soulvine Moor?"

"Are they ready, then?"

"Ready for what? Mistress, I come for . . . for a milady posset!"

A long moment, and then she laughed, forced and bitter. "I see. A milady posset." Her hand dropped from my chin and she moved away. "Get out!"

"I can pay!" Desperately I fumbled in my pockets until I found the gold piece. I held it out to her.

"A milady posset," she repeated. "And I asked you—well, why not. All right. Sometimes none of us know where we are. Or who. Sit there."

I did, afraid to disobey. She moved briskly about the tent, taking things from bags, putting vials and bowls upon the table. Her body shielded whatever she was doing. Presently there was a crisp odor, like apples combined with something else, and she handed me a vial stoppered with wax.

"Have her drink this all at once, then eat nothing for a day. She will feel no sickness. And I don't have to tell you, do I, that she should lie with no one for at least a week?"

My ears grew warm. My lady Cecilia did not lie with men; she had proudly refused to play the court's bed-wagering game. Mother Chilton gazed at me with amusement and handed me the vial. But there was speculation in her amusement, and I got out as fast as I could.

Maggie let me back in by the kitchen-barge door and locked it behind her.

"Did you get what you needed?"

"Yes."

"Good. I suppose. Roger—be careful. These are strange times."

She seemed less angry at me than before, less impatient. She was glad I was back safe, which made a little warm fire in my heart. I risked questions. "How are they strange times, Maggie?"

"Wouldn't you know better than I? I only know what I hear of gossip, or am told by my brother, the soldier with the Blues. *You're* the one beside the queen."

I said slowly, "I sit at her feet. I make jokes about matters I don't understand. I hope desperately that my joke will fit its subject, at least a little. And that it will be funny, at least a little. I dye my face yellow. I make inane movements like dancing backward and pretending to fall down. And all the while I'm afraid that I will do something wrong, something that will displease the queen. Always I'm afraid, Maggie. Sometimes I wish I were back here, carrying water in the laundry, sleeping under the trestle table."

She took my hand. Hers was warm, rough with work. "We are the same age, and yet sometimes I think I am much older than you."

She would not think that if she had known the things I had seen and done. The wreck of the *Frances Ormund*, the knife sliding into Hartah's flesh . . . I had not trusted Maggie with my past, however much I trusted her in the present. I said, "I need to know as much as I can learn in order to merely survive, and yet I know nothing. You hear more in the kitchen, from the servants who wait at table and the bargemen who come from outside, than I do among the courtiers. They must guard their tongues around the queen, and I am always around the queen. So please please tell me—how are these strange times?"

"The two rival courts in the palace cannot go on forever," Maggie said, her voice low. "There are whispers . . . well, there always were. But my brother tells me that the rumors grow more intense, both in the army and in the villages. The old rumors."

I remembered Cat Starling's flat words: *The queen is a whore.* "Why do the rumors grow more intense now? Because of Lord Robert?"

"No. Well, maybe a little. Consort Will was much beloved, you know. He was so generous to the poor, and he traveled all about the countryside, listening to people. I was not yet working at court when he died, but I remember villagers whispering that the queen had him poisoned."

"Poisoned? Her own husband? I don't believe it. He was no threat to her rule." I realized all at once that we were talking treason. If anyone overheard . . . But we were two young servants in a cold and deserted kitchen courtyard, beside a pile of vegetable crates and slop buckets, and there was no one else around.

"Some say," Maggie continued, "that she had already taken up again with Lord Robert, and so wished her husband gone."

"Why does she not marry Lord Robert now?"

Maggie shrugged. "Perhaps she does not wish to share power, not even with a consort. Some say she waits for a better alliance through marriage, a foreign prince, after the old queen dies. Some say—" Maggie raised the lantern, looked fearfully around, and put her mouth close to my ear. "Some say she is a witch."

All at once pieces fell into place in my mind, like tumblers clicking into a lock. The queen's readiness to believe that I could cross over, in the face of Lord Robert's amused disbelief. Maggie's horror that time in the kitchen when I asked where Soulvine Moor lay. Mistress Conyers, telling me to avoid the notice of the queen . . . But I knew that there were no witches. I alone knew this with certainty. I had crossed over to the country of the Dead, had talked to the Dead, had even talked to old women burned as witches. They had not been that. But common people believed in witches, and were terrified of them, and an army was made of common soldiers. No one was more superstitious than a soldier—I had seen it again and again at faires. And I knew all too well that a statement need have very little truth in it to be believed.

I said slowly, "Agents of the old queen have put about rumors that Queen Caroline is a witch. Haven't they? Among the army, and in the countryside. Queen Eleanor has fanned the flames of gossip and fear against her own daughter, in order to keep her crown."

"How should I know?" Maggie whispered. "But the army is as close to the old queen as feathers on a chicken."

Now I understood why Queen Caroline had so few petitioners. Such hatred and maneuvering between mother and child! My own mother in her lavender gown, so tender and caring in the few memories I had of her . . .

"Maggie, what's on Soulvine Moor?"

But, despite all she had already said, there were places Maggie would not go. She stared at me mutely, and all at once I realized that the hand holding mine had turned icy and her teeth chattered.

"You're freezing! I'm sorry, come back into the kitchen. I cannot thank you enough for all your help." I led her back inside. "Just one thing more—what is a milady posset?"

Maggie stopped just before the closed door to the kitchen. She flung my hand back at me and screeched, all at once careless of listeners, "A *milady posset*? Is that what you went to Mother Chilton for? A *milady posset*?"

"I—"

"For whom? Look at me when I speak to you—*for whom*?"

"I can't say."

"I'll bet you can't! And to think I trusted you—that I even thought—a milady posset! You're a filthy animal!"

"Maggie, don't—"

"Don't tell me what to do! And get out of my sight! A *mi-lady posset!*"

She flung open the door and darted through to the kitchen, slamming it behind us. Before she could run off, I grabbed her by the shoulder. "What is it for? What?"

"Don't pretend you don't know! Who was she, some whore brought in for you, that you stupidly believed was clean and now take pity on? Were you the only one who had her? And to think I helped you!" Maggie tore herself free of my grasp and ran out of the kitchen, leaving her bread half kneaded on the table.

And I understood.

Lady Cecilia had the crawls. She had bedded with someone, and he had given it to her. Men could carry the disease but did not fall ill of it. Women did. Untreated, the crawls could even make it impossible for women to ever bear children. Bawdy jests overheard at country faires had told me that girls greatly feared the crawls, which turned them red and itching in their . . .

Cecilia. My shining lady.

Who was he?

In the larder I changed back to my court clothing. I stole a kitchen lantern, lit it, and made my way back through the labyrinth of courtyards, scarcely seeing them. Anger and hatred burned in me. For him, who had taken her. For her, who had played me for the fool I was. All the while I adored her, worshipped her, would have given my life for one kiss from her, Cecilia had been lying with one of the courtiers, perhaps allowing herself to be won in a game like Lady Jane. . . .

No. The truth came to me so suddenly that I stopped cold beside a winter-empty planting bed, my feet as rooted to the ground as the tree whose bare branches arched above. It was not some random Lord Tom or Sir Harry. If it had been, Cecilia would have done whatever the other ladies did in such circumstances. It had been someone she could not admit to. It had been the prince.

I saw her again, running to Emma Cartwright the day I had arrived at court, hiding in her room from Prince Rupert. I had thought then that her hiding was genuine, when I didn't yet know her. Cecilia lived for admiration, for being pulled, for love. She had been teasing him, as she teased me, as she teased every man at court. But Prince Rupert had bedded her, and the other ladies knew. (*"Cecilia, there are other things in life besides dancing." "I think she knows that!"* and *"Green wood burns hotter than yellow"*—the prince had favored green to please his sister.) Emma Cartwright had left court shortly after I arrived—dismissed because she knew too much? Did the good Mistress Cartwright know that Prince Rupert carried the crawls, and that he had undoubtedly carried them to his new bride? That knowledge might have canceled his wedding to Princess Isabelle, might have endangered The Queendom's political alliance with the bride's rich realm. No wonder Cecilia had been nearly hysterical. The crawls from a prince, with a royal marriage hanging in the balance and the danger of wrath from two queens.

It was that moment, in the dark of a cold spring night, that for the first time I understood what life at court truly was. I had been a fool; I was a fool still. But now I knew. Nothing was as it seemed. Everything was for sale, and everything was judged by how it affected the web of power.

My new knowledge turned me careful. I extinguished my lantern. In the dark I fumbled toward a flower bed, took Mother Chilton's little cloth bag from my pocket, and buried it. It was an easy matter to rearrange ornamental green stones to disguise the freshly turned earth.

After a long time standing there, thinking, while my toes grew stiff and the hairs in my nose froze, I moved on. I passed the guards with a jest and made my way through the deserted presence chamber to my alcove. I drew back the curtain.

And there, waiting for me in the darkness, stood the queen.

"Where have you been, Roger?" she said.

15

"WHERE HAVE YOU been, Roger?" the queen repeated when I did not—could not—speak.

With the kitchen lantern at the end of my suddenly slack and terrified arm, I could scarcely see her face, only the gleam of light on the green satin of her gown. "I . . . I went to the kitchen . . . I was hungry!"

"So you told the guards. And what else? No, wait, not here. Follow me."

I stumbled after her, wondering if I was to be led to some dungeon, to some instruments of torture that would . . . But the queen led me through the outer chamber to her privy chamber, the room where I'd had my first audience with her. The door to her bedchamber was closed, as ever. In the privy chamber Lord Robert sat beside a bright fire, with a goblet of wine before him on the ornately carved table.

The queen closed the door and leaned back against it. Her face was kindly, her eyes warm. She smiled at me. "Now, Roger, tell me where you have been and whom you have spoken to. And leave no detail out."

How much did she know? I had to protect Maggie, protect Cecilia. . . . Why protect Cecilia? Because I loved her still. And I could no more deliver her to the hands of the queen than I could a butterfly to the pin that would fix it, squirming, on a board.

"I was hungry," I said. "I went to the kitchen to get something to eat. I have a friend there, a kitchen maid, and . . . and we lay together. In the courtyard where the barges bring vegetables to the palace."

The queen stood so that she could see both me and Lord Robert. From the corner of my eye, I saw him give a tiny nod. So he already knew where I'd been, and with whom. Her web of spies—or his—must extend itself even farther than I had guessed. If one of those spies had overheard Maggie and me—

The queen studied me, still with that kindly smile on her beautiful, ruthless face. Finally she said, "I believe you. You have grown taller and fuller since you entered my service, Roger, and I can believe you would lie with a maid. Nonetheless, after I retire, Lord Robert will search you to make sure you carry no messages to anyone. And you will not leave my rooms again without permission, do you understand?"

"Yes, Your Grace." Relief flooded me, so strong that for a shameful moment I thought I might cry.

All at once the queen came toward me, took both my hands in hers. She stared deeply into my eyes, her voice low and soft. "In the coming days I will need you, Roger. No one else can do for me what you can, and your gift makes you a treasure beyond price. The Queendom is in grave danger. I am determined to protect it, and to someday hand the realm intact to my daughter. I will do whatever I must to protect my realm. Do you believe that?"

And I did. Her dark eyes so earnestly searching mine . . . The queen was beautiful, but I knew I was not responding to her beauty. Cecilia filled all that part of my mind. The queen was a skilled actress, but I didn't think she was play-acting about this. She was genuinely concerned about the future of The Queendom she was not being allowed to rule, and she would do whatever was necessary to protect it. She would flay me alive if that would help. She would even do the same to Lord Robert, if she had to. . . . Did he know that?

In one night, my mind had traveled over too far a distance. I was bewildered, frightened, weary. The world was not as I had thought it.

"Yes, Your Grace," I said. "I believe you care for The Queendom."

She dropped my hands. "Good. Robin, give him some wine, search him, and send him to bed. This is a tired lad."

Lord Robert rose. The queen walked toward her bed-chamber, but in the doorway she turned and looked back over her shoulder at me. "Your kitchen maid—was this your first time?"

"Yes," I said, and she smiled at me roguishly and shut the door.

Lord Robert's search was swift, not gentle, and very thorough. Somewhere during its course, I realized that he—a lord of The Queendom, the queen's advisor and lover—was afraid of me, because of what the queen had called "my gift." She was not afraid, but he was.

No, the world was not as I had thought it.

Lord Robert found nothing in my clothing, on my person. "Go to bed," he said roughly, "and don't ever do this again."

The next afternoon Cecilia came with the queen's other ladies to the outer chamber. Queen Caroline had spent the morning closeted in her inner chamber with Lord Robert and a series of couriers, all of whom looked as if they had ridden hard to arrive at the palace. Some of their clothing looked strange, and no one knew where they had come from. She sent word early that her ladies need not attend her and so they had not. Nor did I, and I spent the whole long morning alone in the vast presence chamber or the deserted outer chamber, staring out the open window at the courtyard. Sometime during the night the cold had finally released its grasp, and it was spring. But the soft air and sweet scents didn't move me.

Not even hunger moved me. I didn't dare go to the kitchen for anything to eat—not after the queen's warning—and nothing was brought to me, so my stomach clenched and growled. Breakfast and dinner were carried in to the queen. The smells of roasted meat and steaming soup filled my mouth with hopeless water.

I made myself a vow, during those long hours at the window. I had been uninterested in the larger life at court for too long; I would be so no longer. If I could not choose my fate, I could at least meet it with less ignorant eyes. I would observe, I would ask questions, I would learn.

Finally when the afternoon was nearly gone and the shadows were long in the courtyard, the ladies-in-waiting and their courtiers burst into the outer chamber in a great flock, chattering and tired and happy. "We rode as far as the mountains, Fool!" Cecilia called cheerfully to me. "A wonderful ride!"

"Yes, my lady," I said. She was smiling, her skin warmed from the sun, her hair still damp from a bath. Never had I seen her look more beautiful. Hysteria shone in her green eyes like fever. My stomach rumbled.

"Now we must have music! Music and dancing!"

The others took up the cry: *Music! Dancing! Music!* Only recently had the queen given permission for dancing to occur when she was not present. The ladies and courtiers were young, alive, oblivious to whatever the queen may have been doing all day, although they would leap to her service the second she required them. Although were they really so oblivious, so heedless and carefree as they seemed? All of them—everyone at court—were such skilled actors. Except me.

Musicians were sent for. Under cover of all the bustle, Cecilia said to me, "Roger?"

I said, "It is buried under the tree in the fish-fountain courtyard, on the side of the tree facing the fountain. Organize a game of hide-and-seek or hide-the-coin, and you can easily retrieve it. Drink it all at once, eat nothing for a day, and lie"—my voice faltered—"with no one for a week."

"Oh, I thank you so—"

"Was it Prince Rupert?"

She stiffened beside me, then rose and flounced off, her

satin skirts swishing. But a moment later she was back. Lips so close to my ear that I could smell the scented soap on her damp hair, she whispered, "Don't think less of me, I could not bear it," and again she was gone.

My chest contracted in on itself, held, had to be forced to breathe again. Why should Lady Cecilia care what I, the queen's fool, thought of her?

I watched her move through the slow, sedate figures of the court dance, her restless charm confined to one step forward, two back, a slight dip of the head. Wrong, wrong. The wrong dance for her, the wrong man, the wrong contrast between these courtiers' gaiety and the ominous absence of the queen.

Just as darkness fell, the door to the privy chamber opened and the queen stepped out. Instantly dancers and musicians fell into deep curtsies. The queen gazed at them bleakly. She wore a gown of such deep green it looked almost black, and the dark color turned her skin chalky white. It made her look older, unlike the woman who had questioned me at midnight, let alone the one who had roistered with her court in the kitchens on the day she had found me there. It occurred to me now that never since had I seen her join her courtiers with that same abandon.

Had she come to the kitchen that night only for me?

"Roger?" she said now. "Come, fool."

I rose and moved among the kneeling courtiers, toward the privy chamber.

"Resume dancing, then," Queen Caroline said, smiled at them all, and closed the door. She turned to me. "It occurred to me that you must have eaten nothing, Roger, since yesterday. Sit, eat."

There it was again: kindness in the woman who had threatened me with torture, remembrance of the small amid whatever great concerns consumed her. Lord Robert sat at the other end of the table, now covered with a green-embroidered dinner cloth that hung to the floor, his face as bleak as hers. His fingers curled loosely around the stem of a wine goblet. When he raised the goblet to drink, the green stones of his rings flashed in the firelight.

I loaded a plate—it was a royal order, after all—with meat and fruit and bread and cheese, and devoured it all. I drank two goblets of wine. The queen and Lord Robert talked only of trivial things: the change in the weather, the shoe that his horse had thrown, Lady Margaret's cold, a favorite hunting dog about to whelp. The fire burned low, throwing the room into shadow. After my heavy meal and heavier thoughts, I felt sleepy. When I slumped low in my chair on the far side of the table, the queen said, "Roger, you may go now and—"

The door was flung open with the force of a gale and soldiers burst in.

Blue soldiers, not the queen's Green guard. Their sleeves above the armor were blue, the ribbons on their helmet blue, the arms on their shields . . . their short swords were drawn. Before I knew I was even going to move, I had slid down in the chair and slithered under the table, where the long cloth hid me.

Lord Robert leapt up, his hand going to his sword. But then a woman's voice rang out.

"Caroline."

I knew that icy voice, although I had heard it only once. The old queen. The door slammed shut. Beneath the edge of the cloth I could see the hem of her blue gown, the heavy boots of her soldiers. I felt Lord Robert hesitate. Then he went around the table, between the two queens, and knelt. "Your Highness," he said, giving her not the title of a reigning monarch but of a royal family member.

She ignored him. "Caroline, what have you done?"

"I have done nothing." As much ice as in her mother's voice, and much more rage.

"I think you have," Queen Eleanor said. "Your couriers come and go from the harbor at Carlyle Bay, and other strange couriers ride in from the west. And your lover here"—it was impossible to convey the contempt in those three words—"has called upon the lord high admiral himself."

Queen Caroline said, "I would know what happens in my queendom."

"*My* queendom, Caroline. You are not fit to hold it, and could not hold it if you had it."

"I was crowned well over a year ago!"

"A sham without my presence, and without the Crown of Glory, and you know it. I would give you The Queendom if I thought you could hold it, but you cannot."

"Because you have turned the army against me. You know I could rule, but you want to keep all power for yourself!"

"And so I shall, for the good of The Queendom. I will not see it descend to civil war. And you will keep your fingers—all eleven of them—off my navy. Do I make myself understood?"

The young queen said levelly, "Mother, are you planning to send both the new navy and the army to attack Benilles? To take The Queendom into war?"

Dead silence.

I had heard of Benilles—where? Then it came to me: Bat's

voice in the country of the Dead, about the *Frances Ormund*: *"Gold from Benilles and cloth from . . . I forget where."* Had Captain James Conyers's cargo included information, as well? So perhaps it had not been by mere chance that the old queen's Blues had interrupted Hartah's wreckers. The soldiers had been waiting in that desolate place, for something that did not happen because my uncle's wreckers foundered the ship and Captain Conyers drowned.

Queen Eleanor said, "Caroline, if you interfere in matters that do not concern you, you will regret it."

"If you plunge the Queendom into a war we cannot win, *you* will regret it."

I wondered, cowering under my table, which of the two women had the greater capacity for hatred.

The old queen said, "Keep to your music, daughter, and your wild young court, and your powerless lover. As of tonight, you will receive no visitors except these. I will have guards at the doors of your presence chamber. Since it was not enough to restrict you to the palace, I will also restrict those you may see. I have spoken."

A swish of the blue gown as she turned, a slam of the door behind her soldiers.

The young queen said, "I will——"

"Hush, Caro," Lord Robert said, in a tone that would have silenced an earthquake. "The first thing you will do is dismiss your fool before he hears even more than he has. Roger, go."

I crawled out from under the table, just as I had done so many times in Hartah's faire booth. And, like those times, I held information I did not want. But I made a rapid decision. "Your Grace . . ."

"I said go!" Lord Robert thundered.

"Your Grace, I know something more of Captain Conyers and the *Frances Ormund* and Benilles. I learned it from a sailor of the crew and from the captain's widow."

She stared at me, white-faced, her mouth still twisted with anger at her mother. I knelt before her and told her that Bat had said "somebody important" had been on board the ship, someone "with medals on his chest." Mistress Conyers had mentioned passenger money from a nobleman, suggesting a sum large enough to make a difference to her husband's fortunes. And Queen Eleanor's soldiers, a large number of them, had already been gathered in this remote corner of The Queendom.

When I finished, she said, "Roger."

"Your Grace?"

"Rise and look at me." Lord Robert watched us closely from across the room.

"Do you realize you have just confessed to participating in a deliberate wreck?"

"Yes, Your Grace."

"And that such a crime is punishable by hanging?"

"Yes, Your Grace." I saw the yellow-haired youth choking in the noose, kicking the air.

"Then why have you told me?"

"Because I thought you might wish to know. Because it might . . . might be useful to you to know. And you are my queen."

She was silent. Her black eyes, with their glints of submerged silver, searched mine. Lord Robert said dryly, "And because he knows you value his 'gift' too highly to kill him, and may in the future remember his willingness to aid you."

"That, too," I said, and the queen smiled.

"You did well to tell me," she said. "I won't forget it. Roger, say nothing of what you heard tonight."

"I will not, Your Grace."

"You may go."

In the outer chamber, I was immediately besieged by courtiers and ladies. "What happened in there, fool? What did the old queen say to Her Grace?"

What? What? What? The word echoed in my head, as if from a drum instead of being whispered from a dozen eager throats. They were like a bunch of ravens, feeding on carrion.

I said, "Her mother told Queen Caroline that the expenses of her household were too high."

Lord Thomas said, "The fool is lying."

Then Lady Cecilia cried, "Oh, look, the moon has risen full! Let's all play a game of hide-the-coin among the court-yards! Such fun! Come, all of you, I shall go out and hide the coin first!"

She caught Lord Thomas by one hand, Lady Sarah by the other, and it was true that the moon had risen full. Its light shone through the window, lying silver on her bright face and on the hard, polished stone floor.

16

A WEEK LATER, I sat at the queen's feet in the presence chamber, listening to the few petitioners who came to her and not to her mother. They were all peasants or farmers, allowed in because the Blue guards posted just beyond the door didn't think they were worth keeping out. A peasant's stolen cow, a farmer's field in dispute. One of the queen's advisors had fallen asleep, his beard stirring with his light snores.

In the courtyard beyond, someone screamed. Not a woman, a man.

The queen's own guards leapt in front of the dais, shielding it. But no Blues were attacking; the ones stationed at the door looked as startled as everyone else. Another scream—a woman this time—and a shout. Then running outside, people rushing and calling, and the captain of the Green guard ran into the presence chamber and up to the queen, not even kneeling.

"Are you unharmed, Your Grace?"

"Yes, Captain, I am. What has happened?" She looked toward the door.

More Greens marched into the room and took up posts around the queen. The Blues at the open door looked at each other, clearly mystified and without orders, their hands on their swords.

"I asked you—*what has happened*?"

The captain knelt then, just as yet more Greens closed the doors to the presence chamber, shutting the Blue guards without, and barred it. The captain said, "Your Grace, Queen Eleanor has . . . The queen is dead. Long live the queen!"

"*Dead*?"

"Yes, Your Grace." He did not raise his eyes but I, crouched on the bottom step of the throne and looking up, could see them. I saw no fear—he was a captain of the guards—but I saw doubt. Much terrible doubt.

"Did she—"

"Just now, Your Grace. She was with her advisors and she slumped to the floor and—the physicians are with her now. She—I—" He looked for certainty, and found it in duty. "There is unrest in the palace, Your Grace."

The queen said sharply, "My children?"

"I have already secured the nursery; the princess and her brother are safe. But you must stay here until my men have secured the entire palace. Your privy chamber would be better yet."

For the first time I realized why the privy chamber, and presumably the bedchamber beyond, had no windows.

"I will go to my privy chamber," the queen said, "but only to dress. And as soon as possible, Captain, I will go to the throne room. Clear and secure that first. And if you can spare the men, have them bring to me my ladies of the bedchamber and Lord Robert Hopewell."

"Yes, Your Grace."

"Roger, come with me."

She swept from the presence chamber, leaving behind her the grim-faced guard and the peasants still on their knees. One of them, his back to me, whispered something to his friend. In her privy chamber the queen told me only, "It is not safe for you out there," before vanishing into her bedchamber and closing the door.

I didn't know what to do. I went cold, then hot, then cold again. There was no wine. I sat at the carved table, and then on the floor. I poked the fire, which did not need poking. I could not settle, could not think.

No. That is not true. I could think, but only of one word, the word the peasant had whispered to his friend—had dared to whisper there, in the queen's own presence chamber.

Poison.

The queen is dead, long live the queen!

"I will do whatever I must to protect my queendom." She had said that to me.

The queen is dead, long live—

Finally the door was flung open and Lord Robert entered, at the same time that the queen emerged from her bedchamber. I fell to my knees. She had changed without aid from her ladies, who were . . . what? Delayed? In hiding? Slaughtered by the Blues? *Cecilia—*

"Caro," Lord Robert choked out.

She did not answer. She looked magnificent, dressed in a gown I had not seen before. It was so embroidered with green jewels that the green velvet underneath could scarcely be seen. Her full skirts swept the floor and lengthened to a train behind. Long lace-and-satin sleeves fell almost to her fingertips, hiding the bud of the extra finger. She wore an emerald necklace and earrings and her rich black hair hung loose down her back, her bare head ostentatiously awaiting a crown.

Lord Robert ignored all that. He grabbed her hands, causing the sleeves to fall back over her white arms.

"Caro . . . sweet palace of the heavens, Caro . . . *what have you done?*"

Poison, the peasant had said.

"Please escort me to the throne room, Lord Robert," she said, and at her tone he jerked and then— finally, belatedly— knelt.

"The queen is dead," he said in a voice as rigid as Queen Eleanor's, "long live the queen."

"Roger, you will stay here," she said. "I will need you later. Bar the door and open it to none but myself or Lord Robert. Do you understand?"

"Yes, Your Grace."

"Open the door, Lord Robert."

He did, and he trailed her out, and now I could hear the great bells in the tower begin to toll, as slow and stately as the court dances required by the old queen, sending the news to The Queendom of death, and change, and triumph.

◈ ◈ ◈ ◈

I didn't know how much time I had.

If the Green soldiers could not secure the palace, would the queen return to her privy chamber or wait in her presence chamber? Might she bring her ladies in here for safety, if guards brought them to her? Most important of all, how long had the old queen been dead?

If I was going to do this at all, it must be now. Before I could change my mind, I seized a carving knife from the table and jabbed at my arm. Pain sprang along my nerves, making me drop the knife. I willed myself to cross over.

This time I was close by the river, almost in the water. A large group of soldiers sat together on the grass, all dressed in the same leather armor and crude sandals, as if they had died together. Like the rest of the Dead, they bore no injuries or maiming. The whole group ignored me. From their old-fashioned garb I guessed that they had been there a long time. For all I knew, they might be there forever.

The western mountains had disappeared altogether, as if the valley now stretched larger than in my previous visit, and the river seemed even wider and slower. I was still on the island, however. Running along its banks, in and out of groves of trees, I searched for the old queen. Circles of the Dead, more Dead lying on the grass or gazing at rocks—*where was she?*

I found her wading ashore from the river, sputtering and angry. Water dripped from her blue silk gown and from her crown, the simple silver circlet she favored on her white hair. Even wet, Queen Eleanor had a terrifying dignity. Even furious. Even dead.

I dropped to one knee. "Your Grace!"

"Who are you? Where am I?" And then, a moment later, "I am dead."

No use lying, not to this woman. "Yes, Your Grace."

"And you are . . . you are my daughter's fool! With the stupid yellow dye on your face!"

"Yes, Your Grace."

"What happened, boy? Are you dead, too?"

I thought quickly. "Yes, Your Grace."

"And this is the country of the Dead." She turned thoughtful, then, and I saw it begin: the contemplative remoteness of the Dead. In a few moments I might not be able to reach her at all.

Desperately I said, "Were you poisoned, Your Grace?"

That caught her attention. "What?"

"Were you poisoned by your daughter, Queen Caroline? Did any messenger visit you last night or this morning, was there any strange person in your chambers, did anything happen that might have been poisoning?" I did not know what I was looking for.

"Caroline," she said vaguely, as if trying to remember the name. It was happening, right before my eyes. She was detaching from the living. She was no longer subject to those loves, those hatreds, those ties.

"Your daughter, the new queen! Who may have poisoned you and now has your queendom! Your Grace!"

Gracefully she sat down on the grass and stared at a flower. I had lost her. This was one old woman I could not jar into jolly stories of childhood.

I smacked my fist against my thigh. To have taken this risk for nothing! I must get back, now. I must—

Two soldiers materialized a short way off. They wore Queen Eleanor's blue. My body blocked her from their view, but one cried, "The whore's fool! Seize him!"

He rushed toward me, sword drawn. The other, not so quick in mind, looked around him dazedly. I stepped aside and pointed. "Your queen!"

That stopped the attacking soldier. He fell to his knees and bowed his head. "Your Majesty! Are you safe?"

She, of course, said nothing. Not for a long moment. But then she looked up at me and said simply, "Yes." A moment later she had relapsed into the calm of the Dead.

The second soldier came uncertainly toward me. "What is this place? What . . . they said Queen Eleanor was dead. . . ."

I saw it come to him, then. He looked down at his own belly, as if expecting to find it run through with the sword of a Green, and then looked again at me. I couldn't help but be moved by his bewilderment.

The kneeling soldier sprang up. "None of your fool's talk, boy! Where are we? What witchcraft did the whore use on us?"

Here, then, was my story, handed to me like meat on a golden plate—the same story I had once told Bat. If I could use it to make these soldiers believe I was not Queen Caroline's ally but her victim, they might not harm me. Swiftly I said, "You have caught me out! Yes, the young queen used her sorcery to bring us all here to Witchland—I saw her do it! She crooked her sixth finger and chanted her spells and . . . and flew through the air and brought us all here! Me, too, for daring to say fool's rhymes that displeased her . . . And she has ensorcelled Queen Eleanor! Look, the queen breathes and yet cannot speak, cannot see—"

The soldier cried out in superstitious fear and outraged fury. He waved his drawn sword, but there was no one to run through—until three Green soldiers appeared beside the river.

There must be fighting in the palace. Men were dying. And now there would be fighting here as well.

The two Blues rushed toward the Greens, who drew weapons and counterattacked. And I saw what I had not thought possible: the Dead fighting each other to kill. Only it did not, could not happen. One soldier got the advantage and slashed brutally at another's head. The blade passed right through flesh and skull and bone, and the man stood on his feet still, unharmed.

That stopped them all.

I dared not go closer. I could be harmed, even if they could not. From beside the queen I called, "In Witchland, no one can die. Look how many the witch has brought here! And she can summon us back whenever she chooses. . . . It has been done to me before!"

The Blue soldiers looked wildly around. The three Greens had already retreated out of earshot; soon they would be tranquil and motionless. The Blues didn't understand, but they believed me. In the face of the senseless, men will seize on any belief that promises sense.

The less quick of the Blues said uncertainly, "Ye have been here before, fool?"

"Yes. Come here, to your queen—just you!"

He came. I said to him, very low, "What happened to her? Did she drink or eat anything, or—"

"I don't know. I wasn't there. But my captain, he said she clutched her belly and cried, 'Poison! My daughter!' But ye say it was not poison, it was witchcraft? I don't know——"

"It was witchcraft," I said firmly. "Look at her! She's not dead, she breathes and sits, you walk and talk. . . . You are banished in Witchland until they summon you back. And so are these others." Two more Blues had appeared in the river and were staggering, dripping, to shore. "You must tell them! I hope I don't——" Deliberately I broke off my sentence, bit my tongue hard, and crossed over.

My tongue bled into my mouth. I writhed on the hearth rug and then all at once I was weeping. But was I weeping from pain, or from knowledge?

In truth, I had no certain knowledge. The old queen had cried out that she had been poisoned, but she might have cried that even if her death had come from a failure in her heart. She might have clutched her belly anyway, believing her daughter to have poisoned her no matter what the fact. And the "Yes" that the old queen said to me—the last thing she would ever say to anyone—might have meant anything.

But I believed that Queen Eleanor had been answering my question. *Yes*. Yes, she had been murdered, and Queen Caroline was what rumor had called her: a poisoner.

The queen is dead. Long live the queen.

I don't know how long I lay on the hearth, my thoughts in chaos. Queen Caroline had always roused in me so many contradictory emotions: Fear. Admiration. Anger . . . Respect. Now my feelings toward the queen reduced to only one: a desire to survive her patronage.

Eventually I rose and washed the blood from my mouth

with cooling water. Eventually Lord Robert's voice bellowed on the other side of the door. "Fool! Open!"

I unbarred the door. He and Queen Caroline stood there. Her ladies and courtiers clustered at the other end of the outer chamber, some looking frightened and others triumphant. I fell to my knees as the queen swept through the doorway.

Lord Robert said, "Only a few moments, Your Majesty. This is urgent."

"So is this. Close the door, Robert. Roger, rise. Why is there blood on your chin?"

"I bit my tongue, Your Grace." My words came out thick and garbled.

"Clumsy of you. And on your sleeve?"

"Drippings from my tongue, Your Grace."

She took my face between her hands. I had to force myself to not recoil at her touch. *Poison.*

"I need you to go to the Dead. You must find a man called Osprey, the palace locksmith. A short, squint-eyed man who died this evening. He wears the seal of The Queendom on his breast. You must ask him for the location of the key to the iron safe, where the Crown of Glory is kept. I need that key now, Roger, right this moment. I am going to the throne room and I want to be wearing the crown that my grandmothers have worn since time itself was young."

I gaped at her. "Your Grace, it's impossible, the Dead don't—"

"Don't what?" she said sharply, dropping her hands. "Don't talk to you? You have declared that they do. You have shown me that they do. What is the difficulty?"

"It's . . . it's the *country* of the Dead!" I said desperately.

"It's vast, and . . . and wild, and to find a specific person is so difficult, I probably wouldn't come across this Osprey if I searched for days, and you said you need it now, the Crown of Glory, now——" I was babbling from sheer terror.

She said, "Try."

One word, with so many unspoken words behind it. And in her eyes, everything to justify my terror.

Hartah had told me what instruments of torture look like. What they can do to a helpless body. So for the second time I cut my arm with the queen's jeweled carving knife, crossed over, and—amazingly—found Osprey. Finding him did me no good. He had been dead too long, and he was not old, and I could not rouse him. I shouted in his ear, I shook his shoulder, I lifted him bodily, dragged him to the river and threw him in. He lurched out, lay on the grass, and gazed at the sky. He would say nothing to me.

"It's the queen's fool again," a Blue soldier said. "The witch bounces him back and forth."

"Aye, and she racks his bones with pain," said another. "Poor oaf."

There were more of them now, the dead soldiers. Some of the Blues stood guarding the unknowing old queen at the edge of the island. Others milled about, talked, kept their swords drawn. They did not know they were dead. They had believed me when I said this was Witchland, and they had repeated that belief to newer arrivals all too ready to believe it. Of course the young queen was a witch—hadn't that been rumored for years? Of course she had sent them to Witchland! And that belief kept them animated—as alive as they would ever be again.

What had I done?

"Don't come closer, fool," one soldier said. "I'm sorry, boy, but the witch has you for fair, doesn't she?"

"Yes."

"Then don't come near us!"

I did not. A little ways off, a Green soldier lay tranquil on the ground. The Blue followed my gaze. "You see, fool, how evil is the witch-whore you are forced to serve! She magicks even the corpses of her own to Witchland. She dare not let their relatives find her mark upon their bodies, lest her witch-ury be plain to all ... No, don't touch him, we do not know if this be a trap of poison, or worse."

I did not intend to touch the Green, nor anything else. In despair, I crossed back over and faced Queen Caroline. Blood seeped from my cut arm, sticky on the velvet. "Your Grace, I . . . I'm sorry, I couldn't find Osprey, I . . . It is such a big place! I had no time!"

She stood with her back to the fire and gazed at me from hard eyes. On the other side of the door, Lord Robert called urgently, "Your Grace!" I was near fainting from fear. To be run through with his blade, or burned alive, or . . . I knew there were deaths even worse. And I had failed her.

She said softly, "Did you *really* go there? To the country of the Dead?"

"Yes!" I stabbed about in my mind for something to convince her. "I saw the old queen!"

Swiftly she crossed the room and seized my arm. "What did she say?"

"I . . . nothing that . . ."

"Don't lie to me, Roger! What did the old hag say?"

My life balanced on my next words. Only honesty would convince her—she was so good at detecting evasions—might even implying that she had committed murder be construed as treason? Done if I spoke truth, done if I did not. Despairing, I choked out, "She . . . *she* said you . . . poisoned her. That she felt it in her belly and clutched her belly and died. She cursed you."

The queen laughed, a high hysterical peal that, horribly, reminded me of Lady Cecilia. But this was no Cecilia. In half a moment she had herself back in control, and into another of her lightning changes of mood.

"You *were* there. I am sorry I doubted you. Those are exactly the lies my mother would utter, the old bitch. There, don't look so scared, Roger, no one will hurt you. You did your best, I know, and in the future there will be more for you to do, and you will succeed. There now, little fool, it's all right. Come along, and I shall allow you to see me take back my palace." She gave my arm a quick caress, smiled at me. Then she opened the door to Lord Robert and forgot me.

And so, not daring to do anything else, I followed behind the young queen, who was now the only queen, into the part of the palace where lay the power of the living.

The palace had been secured. There seemed to be more Greens than the queen had commanded formerly, and this puzzled me until I studied their tunics. Some looked very new; others seemed ill-fitting. These soldiers must be former Blues, either recruited secretly ahead of Queen Eleanor's death or else newly turncoat this afternoon.

For the first time, I saw the palace throne room. It was no more lavish than Queen Caroline's former presence chamber, and just as bare. However, it was so much vaster that I wondered how the palace could contain it. This, then, was why the city outside the palace walls had been squeezed into a narrow circle of jammed alleys and temporary tents. This enormous expanse of polished stone floor, vaulted ceiling two stories above us, walls hung with so many candelabra that the windowless room seemed full of light. Despite the change in the weather, the throne room was cold; no fireplaces could warm the chill of such a vast space. The only furnishing was a raised dais at one end, holding a carved throne. The queen, a white fur cape thrown over her dress of jeweled green velvet, sat on the throne and received her new subjects.

Queen Caroline's ladies watched, wide-eyed and pale, from the left of the throne, her courtiers from the right. One by one, the old queen's advisors came before her in the huge empty space, knelt, and removed their blue robes. Each said, "I swear fealty to Queen Caroline, and to her alone, unto death." Then each, shivering with cold, was handed a new robe of green to put on over his undertunic. There were not very many advisors. Those who had refused the oath must have been imprisoned. By tomorrow, I guessed, they would be dead.

At a gesture from the queen, Lord Robert mounted the dais and knelt. She smiled at him, but her face was very pale, and only I overheard the words she whispered to him. "The army?"

"No," he said.

Her face did not change, by what effort of will I could only imagine. Lord Robert resumed his place and the procession of advisors continued.

"I swear fealty to Queen Caroline, and to her alone, unto death."

No loyalty from the Blue army. I realized what that meant. The word the captain had spoken—*poisoner*—was what the army believed of Queen Caroline. The Blues did not see her as the natural successor to Eleanor; they saw her as the unnatural murderer of their queen. And they would fight to avenge that murder. The Greens had been able to secure the palace only because the main part of the old queen's army was housed outside the city. The great gates to both the island and the palace had been shut and bolted and archers set on the ramparts. No one could either enter or leave.

We were at war, and under siege.

The procession seemed endless. After the advisors came Queen Eleanor's ladies and courtiers. These, too, were far fewer than I guessed they had once been. Some seemed to choke on their words. Then the physicians, musicians, stewards, couriers, pages. The boys, some as young as eight, knelt before the queen, who wore on her head only a simple circlet of gold. Tomorrow the safe would be broken open through hours of patient labor and the Crown of Glory claimed, but tonight the oaths went forward without it. Loyalty, like the palace itself, was being secured. And perhaps as precariously.

"I swear fealty to Queen Caroline, and to her alone, unto death."

The serving men, the ladies' maids, the gardeners. How long could the Green guard hold the capital against the entire Blue army? But for tonight the queen sat on the throne and heard everyone in the palace promise to die with her if necessary.

"I swear fealty to Queen Caroline, and to her alone, unto death."

Last came the cooks, the laundresses, the seamstresses, the stable boys and grooms, the kitchen maids, all kneeling in batches to swear. I saw Joan Campford, her rough red hands swollen with winter chilblains. And later it was Maggie, who sank to her knees with a grace and dignity that might almost have matched the queen's own. She did not glance at me. I wondered about her brother Richard, soldier of the Blues, but I could tell nothing from Maggie's face.

"I swear fealty to Queen Caroline, and to her alone, unto death."

And then it was over, and nearly midnight. The queen's court moved their possessions into the rooms beside the throne room, the rooms that had been the old queen's. Everything was bustle and confusion. I found Cecilia in tears as she followed the harassed steward to her new chambers.

"Oh, Roger, it's all so different! I don't know what to do! I wish the old queen hadn't—"

"Hush," I said quickly. "It's all right, my lady."

"Why does your voice sound like that?"

"I bit my tongue."

"I can barely understand you. Oh, what will I do now?"

"You will go where you are told and serve Her Grace as you always have."

"Yes." Her eyes darted wildly around. "I'm to share a room with Jane Sedley. The ladies on . . . on this side of the palace shared, because there were so many. And now we have with us the Blue ladies as well as the Green."

"They are all Green now," I reminded her.

"Yes, of course. Only it's so . . . so strange!"

"My lady," said Cecilia's serving woman, the young and timid girl who had replaced Emma Cartwright. Her arms were full of gowns. "Where shall I put these?"

"I don't care! Roger, what will happen? They say the old queen's army is outside the gates and they will starve us out! Or worse!"

"Go to bed, my lady. Her Grace will need you in the morning."

"I—"

"Good night, my lady."

"Good night." She went, and it was only later that I realized I had been giving orders to a lady. I, the queen's fool.

No one had thought to assign me a place to sleep. I found the queen's new presence chamber, which actually looked small after the throne room. I knew the single guard posted in the room. He looked grim and would answer none of my questions, but he admitted me to the deserted outer chamber. No guard here—I guessed they were needed to defend the palace if the Blues should attack. There was no curtained alcove off these rooms, but a great fire had burned in the fireplace at some point during this terrible day, and the embers still gave off a faint warmth. I curled up beside the ashes. My tongue hurt. My arm hurt. My heart hurt.

It was a long time before I could sleep. When I did, I dreamed I journeyed to Soulvine Moor. It looked exactly like the country of the Dead, and my mother sat there in her lavender dress, silent and unmoving, beside the old, dead queen.

17

"WE WILL RUN out of food."

"The army has seized all the horses."

"They will burn us all at once, in a huge fire, where all the villagers can see."

"The servants will hide the food from us."

"We will have to eat rats. They did that in the old times during sieges."

"They will take the city and burn us as traitors——"

The ladies and courtiers whispered among themselves. Now there was no dancing, no gaming, no flirting. The Blue army was camped along both banks of the river. Or so I was told by those who had climbed the stairs to the windy ramparts atop the city walls. Below, I attended the queen. She spent all morning with her advisors, and all afternoon moving around the palace.

"There is no meat left in the kitchens," the people whispered to each other.

"The servants are hoarding the food somewhere."

"My mother will be desperate for news of me; she's all alone in the country house—"

"My father—"

"My son and his family—"

"Burn us alive—"

"No fruit left—"

Only the queen remained serene. She did not ration the food left in the larders, the wheat stores, the cellars. No barges came to the kitchen docks, and in spring food always ran low, consumed over the winter. By the fifth day of the siege, we ate bread and cheese and ale, but we ate fully. No one understood this, least of all me. Why didn't the queen count and ration the remaining food? We would run out soon enough, because of course the servants must be hiding some of it against starvation. I would have. I hoped Maggie was.

This was when I saw the cellars for the first time, along with everywhere else in the palace. I accompanied her every afternoon. "Keep your eyes open, Roger," the Queen told me. "Remember everything. I don't know what I may need you to do in the future." She had dropped all requirements that I act the fool, or that I make witty comments. This was good, because all wit had deserted me.

Everywhere we went, the queen, magnificently dressed and accompanied by a guard of tall, handsome Greens, smiled at her new subjects and studied them and let them wordlessly know that she ruled here now. To the stillrooms. The laundries. The kitchens. The guardrooms and stables and servants'

halls, of which there were more than I had known. The courtiers' chambers. Despite the siege, masons had been set to work
in the palace, tearing up the blue tiles in the royal courtyards
and replacing them with green. When they ran low on green
tiles, they interspersed them with white or cream, creating
intricate patterns. In the laundries, blue cloth was dyed green:
bed hangings, table linen, livery, cushions, saddle blankets.
Seamstresses worked feverishly to create enough emerald-
colored tunics, gowns, doublets. In the royal dining hall, even
the blue glass plates, imported from some distant land, had
been packed away in straw, replaced by delicate white plates
decorated with graceful green vines. The queen, gracious and
smiling and tireless, oversaw it all, and I went with her.

We also went to the royal nursery, where for the first time
I saw the queen's heir, three-year-old Princess Stephanie, with
her six-year-old brother. The queen's older son, Prince Percy,
had been sent away over the winter to be a page in the house
of a Green noble, as was the custom. The little princess was
thin and pale; she did not look strong. A grave, gray-eyed child
without her mother's beauty, she had her grandmother's long
face and wide jaw. In fact, she looked so much like a sickly,
miniature version of the dead queen that I was startled. What
did Queen Caroline think of that? I couldn't tell. She kissed
her children, held them, played with them, and I could not tell
if it was genuine mother love, or the regard of a master chess
player for her pawns.

I could not tell anything the queen might be thinking. She
was as contradictory as ever: serene in the face of civil war, of
siege, of starvation. Calculation in her eyes as she assessed her
new realm. Kind to everyone in the palace, all those terrified

servitors sinking into deep and reverential bows even as they believed, probably, that she had poisoned their monarch. The one place I did not go with Queen Caroline was the dungeons, if they existed. And if they did not, then where were all the advisors and soldiers who had refused to take the oath of fealty? Were they already in the country of the Dead?

No, I did not understand the queen. Beautiful, cruel, kind, ambitious—and most of all, unruffled. Even as the food ran out and the Blue army lined both banks of the river and the ladies-in-waiting whispered in terror.

"Starve us out—"

"Burn us all—"

"What is she *doing*?"

Then, on the sixth day, Lord Robert found us as we made our afternoon tour. We were crossing an exquisite courtyard, larger than most, with three circular flower beds. Tiny green shoots pushed up through the black soil of the beds. The air was soft and sweet. The queen had left off her furs and I my hooded cloak. My face had been freshly dyed yellow just that morning; my wit was no longer required, but my appearance as the queen's fool still was. Lord Robert was in full armor.

He knelt, straightened, and said simply, "They're here."

She said sharply, "Where?"

"Within sight of the palace, obviously, since the lookout on the tower saw them. How else would I know?"

"Don't speak to me in that tone, my lord!"

"I beg Your Grace's pardon."

Tension crackled between them like heat.

He said, "Your Grace, may I—"

"No. You may not. I need you here."

"Your Grace, I am commander of the army! My place is out there, leading!"

"No one can be 'out there' until the siege is lifted—you know that. And your place is beside me. Go observe from the tower, and bring me report of the battle."

Battle? What battle? What was happening?

Lord Robert bowed stiffly and stalked off.

"Come, Roger," the queen said. "We return to my rooms."

"Your Grace—"

"Yes? What is it?" She walked so swiftly that those we passed barely had time to fall to their knees, collapsing like so much scythed grain.

"You said 'report of the battle'—who is fighting outside the palace?"

She spared me a glance, never breaking stride. "Who do you think is fighting?"

I had begun this conversation; I must finish it. "Not our Greens against the Blues; we have not enough soldiers. So—"

"Yes?" We entered the outer chamber and the queen's ladies sank to the floor in puddles of green silk.

"—so we must have allies to fight with us?"

"You are waking up, Roger. Lucy! Catherine! I want you!"

The ladies of the bedchamber shot to their feet and followed the queen into her privy chamber. As soon as the door closed, the rest of the women seized upon me. Cecilia cried, "Roger! What's happening?"

"There is a battle being fought," I said.

"Is the palace being attacked?" Cecilia's green eyes were

so big there seemed no room in her face for anything else. She looked drawn, even gaunt, and the clutch of her little hand on mine was icy cold.

"Not yet, my lady."

"Cecilia," Lady Margaret said, "come at once. This fool can tell us nothing, and we have our orders."

I said, "What——"

"We are to get dressed in our best gowns and go to the throne room," Cecilia told me as Lady Margaret turned stern with the other young ladies. "A page ran to tell us so but he did not say why. Is the queen going to surrender? Will we all be taken prisoners by the Blues?"

"No, my lady." *Would we?*

"Cecilia! Come!"

They bustled away. The outer chamber was empty, except for two Green guards who looked as uneasy as I. I waited, as I had done so often before. Sometimes my whole life in the palace seemed to consist of either waiting or fear. Or both together.

If the queen did indeed have allies arriving, it could only be the army of her sister-in-law, Queen Isabelle. Isabelle's mother had died shortly after the wedding, and Isabelle had been crowned. How many soldiers would she send? If the Blues defeated them and took the palace, what would happen to me— would they think it worthwhile to hang a fool? And what would they do to the queen? They could murder her and put Princess Stephanie on the throne, with a loyal Blue advisor to rule for the child. If there were any loyal Blue advisors left alive. And what would happen to Lady Cecilia? Surely soldiers wouldn't press charges of treason against a girl as foolish, as innocent, as lovable as my lady. . . . It would be like killing a kitten.

People killed unwanted kittens all the time.

The privy chamber opened. The queen wore the green-jeweled gown she had worn six nights ago to receive the oaths of fealty. But this time she had on her head the Crown of Glory, broken out of Osprey's iron keeping-box. Heavy beaten gold, the crown was set with jewels of every hue, a rainbow of the colors of every queen who had ruled The Queendom. Emeralds, sapphires, rubies, amethysts, diamonds. Onyx, beryl, opal, topaz. Jewels I could not name, neither the stone nor the color. How could the queen's slender neck even hold up such heaviness? But it did, and she swept past me, her ladies scrambling to hold up her long velvet train, her guard falling into step before and after her. She looked as if neither defeat nor surrender could ever be possible.

"Come, Roger," she threw at me over her shoulder. "It won't be long now."

We waited in the throne room, and from the faces it was clear who knew what we waited for, and who only conjectured.

The advisors knew. They stood in their long green robes to the right of the throne, a group of old men with carefully blank faces and apprehensive eyes. The courtiers and ladies did not know. Grouped at the left, the young men and women in all their finery looked like a flock of alert peacocks. Loveliest among them was Cecilia, in a robe of green silk that exposed most of her small firm breasts. She shivered, but not with cold. The vast throne room was chill as ever, but braziers must have been lit under the dais. Heat radiated from the throne as if the queen herself had fire within her. She sat straight-backed, head held high, and waited.

And waited.

And waited.

I grew stiff, crouched on the dais steps. Cecilia's gown rustled and swayed; she was shifting from one small foot to the other. Finally the door was flung open and Lord Robert, in full armor, strode into the room. The armor, like Lord Robert himself, looked clean and unused, not at all as if he had been fighting a battle. It seemed to take him forever to cross that vast floor. His boots rang on the stone, the only sound. Queen Caroline half rose, then lowered herself again to her throne, regal and imperious. Lord Robert knelt.

"Rise."

"Your Grace . . . it is as you predicted. The countryside around the island is ours. The Blues gave way with only a brief fight, and the others stand at the west bridge."

She didn't move or speak, but something flashed from her, like unseen lightning.

"It is my duty as commander," Lord Robert continued, "to tell you that this Blue retreat is only temporary. Their army is startled and confused, and they lost soldiers in skirmishes at the bridges. But the main portion of the Blue army was not there, and they will regroup and continue the siege. To bring the others inside—"

"Bring them in," she said. "Open the west gates to the city and the palace."

Lord Robert snapped his fingers. A courier set off at an all-out run—running from a throne room, with his back to the queen! She said nothing, however, and her eyes gleamed as bright as her crown. Lord Robert moved to stand with the advisors. He looked odd there, an armored soldier in the strength of his prime amid the old men in their green robes. I saw his big, hard hands clench into fists.

I was confused—the west gate? Queen Isabelle's army would have marched down from the north. To the west lay only inland villages rising to high, jagged mountains. If there were queendoms beyond those mountains, I had never so much as heard their names. But I remembered all the strangers that had come and gone from Queen Caroline's former rooms, in the long weeks before the old queen died. They'd all had the look of hard riding, even though a few—clearly couriers— had been barely more than boys.

It was a boy who first entered the throne room.

No older than I, he walked alone across that vast expanse of floor, his head held high. No one spoke or moved or, it seemed, even breathed, and the only sound was the boy's boots ringing on the stone. Heavy boots, with strange metal caps on the toes. He wore no coat—unless he had left it outside the room— but only tunic and breeches of rough brown cloth and, on his head, a wreath of dead twigs, like the mockery of the flower wreath a girl might wear at midsummer. No sword or other weapon. As he approached the throne, we could all see that his forehead bore strange markings of red dye.

He came right to the foot of the throne steps, and *did not kneel*.

A murmur ran over the courtiers, like wind in a field. The boy turned toward them. Lady Cecilia, standing closest to him, shrank back, and I felt my muscles tense, ready to spring if he touched her. But instead he turned, walked to the left of the dais, and faced away from the throne. He began to sing.

His voice filled the entire chamber. Powerful, sweet and

yet guttural, the song seemed to swell to the vaulted ceiling with strange words:

> *Ay-la ay-la mechel ah!*
> *Ay-la ay-la mechel ah!*
> *Bee-la kor-so tarel ah!*
> *Ay-la ay-la mechel ah!*

Now two more figures appeared in the doorway, and these were not boys but men. Warriors. They wore tunics of some shaggy fur, metal-capped boots, and helmets topped with twigs. Each man carried a cudgel, thick around as my leg, and each had a strange metal stick slung across his shoulder. Knives at their leather belts, but no swords. The pair advanced, singing along with the boy in deep, unmusical voices, and beating their cudgels upon the floor as they advanced.

> *Ay-la ay-la mechel ah!*
> *Ay-la ay-la mechel ah!*
> *Bee-la kor-so tarel ah!*
> *Ay-la ay-la mechel ah!*

Halfway down the room, the two warriors parted and one marched to and along the left wall, the other the right, stopping several feet from the dais. Two more marched behind them, and two more behind those, and yet two more. All of them sang the guttural song, and pounded their cudgels upon the floor, and stood to line the walls. And still they came, more and more and more, until the entire length of the huge room was lined with warriors. And still more came.

And more.

And more.

They formed double lines down the room, triple lines, four abreast. The noise was deafening. The queen's advisors glanced sideways at each other. And still they came.

> *Ay-la ay-la mechel ah!*
> *Ay-la ay-la mechel ah!*
> *Bee-la kor-so tarel ah!*
> *Ay-la ay-la mechel ah!*

Now the room was full of men pounding their cudgels on the floor, singing their wild rough song. Only an aisle remained, stretching from throne to door, and down it came six more boys with crowns of twigs and red-tattooed foreheads. Three beat drums and three played string instruments that sounded like cats being strangled. Behind them walked more men, two abreast, with short capes made of gray feathers. These wore their knives in elaborately beaded belts, with more beads braided into their long hair. The musicians—if you could call them that—joined the singer beside the queen's courtiers, and the warrior captains parted to join their men. The singing grew in intensity, the cat-strangling lutes were plucked faster, the cudgels beat in double time on the stone.

> *Ay-la ay-la mechel ah!*
> *Ay-la ay-la mechel ah!*
> *Sol-ek see-ma taryn ah!*
> *Ay-la ay-la mechel ah!*

A single figure appeared in the doorway and walked toward the throne. As he advanced, the warriors fell to one knee before him, as they had not knelt to the queen. Lord Robert's face darkened and his hand moved toward his sword. The chieftain was huge, a giant with sun-leathered skin and dark hair going gray, his braids twined with beads. His cape was made of feathers of every possible bird, of all possible colors. At the exact moment that the chieftain reached the dais, all noise stopped.

He gazed at the queen and went down on one knee. But he did not bow his head, and his gaze met hers with a proud vitality. He had the bluest eyes I had ever seen, as if pieces of sky had been beaded into his head. I couldn't look away from that fierce blue, and for a long moment, neither could she. Whole rivers flowed between them.

Then he had risen and was saying something in his guttural language. A man stepped from behind the throne. I recognized him: the small, sour-faced man in black velvet that had come to the queen all those weeks ago. He was no less sour-faced now. He knelt, rose, and said, "Your Grace, Solek, son of Taryn, comes to your court, as agreed, to offer the services of his army, for the payment agreed."

Queen Caroline said, "Tell him he is welcome to the court of The Queendom."

The small man translated.

She continued, "Lord Solek is—"

"They do not use that title, Your Grace," the small man said.

He had interrupted the queen. One never interrupted the queen. But she let it pass, her eyes still locked with the stranger's. "He is in my queendom now, with the title I choose to give him. Tell him that I will have rooms prepared for him and his captains in the palace, but that I deeply regret we are unable to house his entire army."

After the translation, the stranger gave a great shout of laughter, as startling in that formal room as a rampaging bear, followed by a short speech.

The translator said, "The Chieftain says that, of course, his men will camp beyond the island, and he with them."

I thought of the villages that surrounded the island, each with its own neat cottages, its little green, its sheep and chickens and pretty girls. These savage warriors—so many of them! and perhaps even more outside—were the roughest-looking men I had ever seen. They scarcely looked like men at all, with their shaggy fur tunics, huge cudgels pounding like hoofs on the floor, feathered capes, and twig-topped helmets. And what were those metal sticks each man wore on his shoulder?

The queen said, her voice now lowered so that even I, closer than anyone except Lord Robert, had to strain to hear. "Eammons . . . is there a polite way to tell him that the village cottages—and the village women—are not available to his men?"

"No," Eammons said sourly. "There is no way. It would be a gross insult."

Lord Robert said to the translator, "These savages will be of no use to us if they defeat the Blues but turn the queen's own subjects against us!" His voice held a strange satisfaction, which in turn angered the queen.

She rose from her throne and descended the steps. Immediately all of us—but none of the savages—fell to both knees. She stood beside the chieftain in her green gown, its train spreading up the steps behind her, as the translator hissed, "Don't take his hand, Your Grace! For the sake of heaven, do not touch him!"

She did not. Beside him, she looked tiny, although she was not a small woman. In a low, intimate voice she said, "Translate what I say exactly, Eammons. *Exactly*, word by word. 'Lord Solek, I will speak frankly. Please forgive my ignorance of your customs. Your soldiers are manly and strong. My villagers are gentle. Do your soldiers' discipline and restraint match their strength and their ability in war?'"

"Your Grace—"

"Translate!"

He did. Lord Solek's blue eyes darkened and his face went hard. I took a step backward, away from that look. Lord Robert's hand went to his sword, but the queen did not flinch. Instead she looked up at him with a look I had never seen on her face—helpless, naked, feminine appeal. And then she curtsied.

A gasp went up from the advisors, the courtiers. Lord Robert put out one hand, as if to yank her upward from obeisance to anyone—she, the queen! But she had already straightened, her curtsy done but her beseeching look going on, eyes fastened onto Lord Solek, until he threw back his head and again gave that huge, rough laugh. He turned to his captains and gave a long speech. When he was done, each captain raised his left fist aloft for a moment before letting it drop.

"He said," Eammons reported, "that his men will stay away from your villages."

Lord Solek had said a great deal more than that. The promise of punishments if his savages did not obey? Of rewards if they did? And what had Queen Caroline promised in order to bring Lord Solek's army here in the first place?

She said, "Tell Lord Solek that he is bid to come to dinner in my rooms at sunset. With whatever of his chiefs it is customary to bring. We have much to discuss."

And still her dark eyes held his blue ones, and neither looked away.

18

THE BUSTLE OVER the dinner was enormous. It turned out that before the siege began, the queen had planned ahead and ordered certain foodstuffs sequestered for this entertainment. But it was only the beginning of spring and there were no fresh vegetables or fruit, only dried. No fresh meat, only salted or smoked. And the appalled cooks had only a few hours to prepare. "What do they even eat?" one wailed. "They are savages!"

"I heard they eat roasted rocks," quavered a frightened kitchen maid, and the cook slapped her.

The queen had sent me to the kitchens on an errand. She was closeted in her privy chamber with Lord Robert and her three most important advisors, none of whom looked happy. Lord Solek had marched out with his men, singing and pounding cudgels on the floor as when they marched in. The pages had all been commandeered by the frantic steward, who was trying to have tables set up, entertainments arranged, and precedence established in the same few hours that upset the cooks. Ladies, courtiers, and musicians went from victims of siege to performers in a masque that must be instantly created. The palace seethed with hectic activity and with terrified conjecture about the "savages." And I had been sent to the kitchens to tell the head cook that the translator, Eammons, had a delicate stomach and could eat only a few slices of chicken and a little thrice-ground bread.

"Chicken! There are no chickens left, boy! And where am I to get thrice-ground bread?" She reached out to cuff me, presumably because she could not cuff Eammons. I danced away from her and went to find Maggie.

She was frantically pouring wine over dried apples while kneading biscuits with her other hand. "How am I to make a dessert without sugar?"

"You'll manage. Did—"

"Go away, Roger, I haven't time for you. No, wait—what news? No, wait, why are these apples so *mealy*?"

I knew more about girls than I once had. Lady Cecilia was responsible for that. Deftly I elbowed Maggie aside and began kneading the bread myself, freeing her to concentrate on adding spices to the apples. I said, "The savages are camped on the north bank of the river, in Fairfield and beyond. All the villagers have left Fairfield, the soldiers on the ramparts saw them flee. So far the savages have not harmed anyone. The Blues are camped on the plain beyond Darton Ford, they can barely be seen from even the top of the tower, and nobody thinks there will be any more fighting until tomorrow morning at the earliest. What of your brother?"

"With the Blue army."

"Have you heard any more than I just said?"

"Don't knead so hard, Roger, it's bread not stone! I heard only that the first 'battle' hardly deserved the name. The savages marched in and when the Blue archers let loose their arrows, the savages used their fire-sticks and—"

"Their what?"

"Don't stop kneading! Have you never before made bread? The savages have new weapons. Fire comes from the end of their metal sticks—fire and small fast projectiles they call 'bullets.' A few men died and then the Blues ran away."

I had never heard of such weapons. From her face, neither had Maggie. She whipped sweet cream as if it had sinned, her face pulled taut with wonder and fear. But, being Maggie, she kept talking.

"The Blues will regroup, everyone says so. Now, you tell me—what has the queen promised the savages in return for their help in securing The Queendom?"

"I don't know."

She looked at me straight. Her fair hair straggled down her face, and her gray eyes were serious. She looked pretty. Not as beautiful as my Cecilia, of course, but still . . .

What was I doing thinking about girlish beauty *now*? I said, "I really don't know what the queen promised. But I'm to be at the dinner, and perhaps I'll find out then."

She stared at me. "You're to be at the dinner? The dinner for the savage lords?"

"Yes." And then it was all between us again, what I had told her about crossing over, about my mother dying on Soulvine Moor. She did not trust me. I could feel her withdrawal, sure as a swift tide.

"I have work to do, Roger."

"I'm going," I said coldly. Damn her—I was doing the best I could. And now I knew why Queen Caroline had looked so serene all the days of the siege. She knew what powerful new weapons her savage allies would bring. I wanted to go up on the ramparts, or even climb the bell tower, to see the situation for myself, but I didn't dare. I still must go only where the queen sent me. I was still the queen's fool.

The dinner for Lord Solek and his captains took place in the queen's new presence chamber, which had been transformed. Gone were the cool blues and grays of Queen Eleanor. The stewards, rushing around shouting and cursing all afternoon, had remade the royal chambers. Green cloth hung on the walls, where cloth had never been before, gathered into draperies and festoons tied with jeweled green ribbons. Lest the place look too feminine, shields hung between the velvets and satins. The high table was draped in green damask, and at it sat the queen, Lord Robert, her three most trusted advisors, Lord Solek and three of his chieftains, and a translator. Also, to my surprise, three-year-old Princess Stephanie. Purple was the princess's color and her gown was a miniature of her mother's, but with a much higher neckline. She sat pale and grave, and on her lank hair was a small golden circlet set with a single amethyst.

The rest of the court sat at lower tables in the chamber,

all below a hastily constructed platform on which the masque would occur. I, with the Green guard, stood behind the high table, reconciled to being unfed. "I shall want you tonight," the queen had said. "Listen to everything."

As it happened, there was little information to listen to. The queen and her advisors began by offering the usual compliments to the visitors, all through Eammons, but compliments seemed to make Lord Solek and his chiefs uncomfortable, and no compliments were offered in return. So instead the queen fell into a game, asking the names of things in the savage language, repeating them prettily, and teaching Lord Solek our words.

"And what do you call this, my lord?" She pointed to the wine in her goblet, turning the stem slightly to make the wine swish and the candlelight flash fire from her jeweled rings. The bud of her sixth finger she kept curled under, hidden in her palm.

"*Kekl.*" It was like the grunt of a boar, and just as wild. Lord Solek had eaten and drunk prodigiously, but he did not seem affected by the wine.

"*Kekl.*" From her, it was music. He gave his great laugh. The advisors smiled, with strain. Lord Robert did not smile. He had not smiled all evening.

"And this?" A soft hand fingering the goblet suggestively.

"*Vlak.*"

"*Vlak,*" she repeated. "*Kekl in vlak.*"

He was charmed, almost against his will. The heat that I had felt between them from the first glance had been no more than that, the heat of man and woman. But now he gazed at her, almost puzzled, and I wondered what the women of his own country were like, in that unknown place far to the west across the distant mountains.

Lord Robert drank more.

"Wine," Lord Solek repeated, making the word guttural. "Queen Caroline."

"Yes," she said, and their eyes locked, watched by her uneasy advisors and his wary chieftains. It was a relief when the entertainment began.

Lady Cecilia was in it, and it was shocking. Not to the visitors, who would had in polite incomprehension, but to the court. Gone were the stately dances that the old queen had insisted on. Cecilia, Lady Jane, Lady Sarah, my lords Thomas and George and Christopher—all of them performed *village dances*, as if they were peasants. They sashayed and roistered and kicked jeweled slippers and polished boots. The women swished their skirts with abandon so that ankles and even knees were revealed, and the men swung the girls so high their feet left the floor. The musicians played the lively village tunes, although without the bawdy lyrics. There was supposed to be a masque, too, but the players never got to it because after the second shocking dance, Lord Solek leapt from the high table to the floor below and bellowed something.

Eammons choked out, "He says he will . . . will dance with Your Grace."

Dead silence.

No one asked the queen to dance; it was her prerogative to do the choosing. Not even Lord Robert could transgress that rule. But that had been the old dances, the old court. And the savage chieftain stood on the polished stone floor, his hand outstretched toward the dais, his brilliant blue eyes both an invitation and a challenge.

Queen Caroline gathered her train over her arm and descended to the floor. To the musicians she said, "Play."

They were almost too shocked to obey. The piper's lips were stiff with horror; they could barely curve around his instrument. But somehow a tune was started and taken up. The queen and the savage danced.

He was quick, with an athlete's grace, and the peasant dances were, of course, much simpler than the endless complicated figures of court dances. Lord Solek did not do too badly. She flowed like water around him, looking small next to his bulk even in her high-heeled slippers, and when he swung her high at the end of the dance she seemed to float toward the ceiling. Then she was sliding down against his body until her feet were again on the floor, and again there was silence. No one dared move or speak.

"All dance," the queen said.

Panic, but controlled panic. More courtiers and ladies scrambled up from the tables, down from the masque platform. The savage's three chieftains leapt up and each seized a lady, all of whom looked terrified. Lady Cecilia cowered in Lord Thomas's arms, as far away from the savages as she could get. And so they danced.

It went on for an hour. The little princess was taken away to bed by her nurse. The stewards brought more wine, more ale. The savage captains performed a "dance" together from their own country, a brutal leaping toward one another, knives drawn, in a three-way mock combat that I thought any moment would become the real thing. This was dancing? But when it was over, they laughed and clasped hands and knelt before Lord Solek, who cut each of them lightly on the left cheek with his own knife. Drops of blood dripped into their beards. All three laughed again, and the queen smiled. And not even I, who had studied her day after day, month after month, who had done for her what no one else in The Queendom could do, could tell if the smile was emotion or calculation. Or both.

Then the entertainment was over. The savages left the palace. Courtiers, ladies, advisors retired, and the servants began to clean the debris from the feast. Green guards admitted me to the queen's outer chamber, where I still slept on the hearth. I crept cautiously through the dark room, holding my candle aloft. But a sliver of light came also from the privy chamber beyond. The door was open a crack, and within Lord Robert was shouting.

"—bad enough that you promised him the princess for his barbaric son, but to also   "

"That is not your business."

"—promise the ships and their captains, and—"

"I am doing what is best for The Queendom!"

"You are selling him The Queendom! Do you really think you can control him, after he defeats the Blues? We'll be left with nothing but his army of savages, which *he* controls! Those damn *guns*—"

It was a strange word; I had never heard it before. But I had heard the queen's tone before, and I knew that Lord Robert ignored it at his own peril.

"I will not let anyone else control *my* queendom, Lord Robert."

"And how do you think you can stop him? By taking him to your bed?"

"How dare you!"

"You were sniffing at him like a bitch after hound spoor!"

The sharp crack of hand on flesh; she must have slapped him. Appalled, I crept quietly back toward the far door, extinguishing my lantern. In the dark I deliberately overturned a stool, cursing loudly.

"Who's there?" Lord Robert called. He flung open the privy-chamber door and peered, backlit, into the outer chamber.

"It's Roger the fool, my lord! I tripped while coming in. . . ."

The queen called, "Come, Roger!"

I groped my way across the room and into the privy chamber, rubbing my shin and looking as foolish and unknowing as I could. Lord Robert glared at me. The queen looked composed, all her fury hidden. She said coldly, "You are dismissed, Lord Robert."

He had mastered himself, or her slap had mastered him. But he was not the actress she was, and the color was high in his face as he made his bow and left. The queen smiled.

"What did you hear? Don't lie, Roger. Not to me."

"I heard angry voices, but no words. And then I tripped over the stool."

She studied me, and I could not tell if she believed me, or if she were just stowing away my lie for her own use in her own time. But all she said was, "I have work for you now."

"Yes, Your Grace."

From the table she picked up small jeweled scissors, an

elegant trifle for snipping thread. "You will cross over and find one of the savage warriors dead from today's battle with the Blues. Only two were killed, both slain with lucky arrows from Blue archers before the Blues fled. From one of them you will find out two things. First, you will say, *'Solek mechel-ah nafyn ga?'* And they will answer either *'ven'* or *'ka.'* Listen while I say it again, and then say it back to me."

Eammons must have taught her the words. How many words? Had the exchange of language with Solek at dinner been no more than pretty feminine play? It might be that she clearly understood much of what he said. Or not. We went over and over the words until the queen was sure I had them correct.

"Good, Roger. Second—"

"Your Grace, whatever those words mean . . . common soldiers . . ."

"Common soldiers know everything," she said calmly. "Just as kitchen maids do."

Was that a reference to Maggie—even a threat? I couldn't tell. With the queen, I could never tell. But I did not forget that this woman had poisoned her mother.

"Second, I want you to learn the secrets of that fire-powder in the warriors' guns. How is it made? What must the tubes from which the projectiles fly be made of, and how?"

"Your *Grace*—"

She put her hand on my shoulder. "This is important, Roger. The most important thing I have ever asked you to do. The fate of The Queendom may depend upon it. In a few more days, more help will arrive for us, but meanwhile this will help me so much now. Can I rely on you?"

This was the queen at her warmest, her most persuasive. The threat and the warmth, all mixed together. I nodded, too frightened to find words. But she went on gazing at me, and so words were necessary. I tried to say, "Yes, Your Grace," but what came out was, "What other help?"

She frowned, withdrew her hand, and then laughed. "Why not? It isn't really a secret. I'm sure conjectures are rife about the court. My brother's bride, Queen Isabelle, sends troops to reinforce Lord Solek's army. They are on their way already."

Queen Isabelle. I had been right after all, or at least partially right. Queen Caroline had remained so calm during the siege because she had not one but two armies to oppose the Blues rising against her. And then I saw something else. Queen Isabelle's army, loyal to Queen Caroline through the marriage tie, would also ensure that Lord Solek could not take the throne for himself. She was not trusting in Lord Solek completely; she had other insurance. The Queendom did not really depend upon my report from the country of the Dead. However, she did not believe that either the savage chieftain—who, after all, did not know our language—or I would realize this.

It was the first time that I had ever thought, for so much as a second, that I had the upper hand with her.

"Are you ready, Roger? Then go now."

She handed me the jeweled scissors. I thrust it into my soft underarm, just above the yellow velvet of my parti-colored sleeve, and I crossed over.

Dirt in my mouth—
Worms in my eyes—
Earth imprisoning my fleshless arms and legs—
Then I was over, and something was very wrong.

AS EVER, THE DEAD still sat, or lay, gazing at nothing. But the *ground* was wrong. I was used to the way the country of the Dead stretched or shrank, so that what was close by in the land of the living might here be miles off. But always the ground was the same, covered with low, dense grass. Always the sky was an even, featureless gray. Always the river meandered placidly, flat and slow.

Not now. The grass stood in uneven patches: some places high weeds, some low grass, some bare ground. The river had rocks in it and the water, flowing faster, eddied around the rocks in tiny bursts of white foam. The sky seemed darker. And beneath my feet, the ground rumbled softly. What was happening in this place, where nothing ever happened?

Dazed, I began walking along the river. I saw no one I recognized. After a while the trees grew denser, making small groves and then patches of woods. The land grew wilder and I had to veer away from the water. I could not find the two dead savage warriors, and even if I had, they would have been sitting tranquilly, as unreachable as the rest of the Dead. In the land of the living, the queen waited for my answer. What was I going to do?

All at once, a man jumped out at me from behind a thicket of bushes. I hit out at him and he hit back, his blow landing on my jaw, not hard enough to break it but hard enough to knock me down. It was a Blue soldier. As I lay panting for breath, he grabbed me by the arm and hauled me over to another soldier, who recognized me.

"Boy! Did the witch-queen, that whore, send you back here again?"

It was the same soldier I'd spoken to on my last crossing. I stammered, "Y-yes. She told me . . . she told me to see how all goes in Witchland, until she herself can return."

He spat, and his saliva made a little wet spot in the dirt. Had the Dead always been able to do that? But clearly this man still did not believe he was dead. The country of the Dead was filling up with people who, like Bat, did not believe they inhabited it. And the landscape began to turn stormy when the Blue soldiers did not behave like the Dead. The rumbling of the ground, the wind and lightning and darkening of the sky—all increased as the number of Blue soldiers increased from battle on the other side. *I had caused this.* I, Roger Kilbourne, with the lies I had told about "Witchland."

"All here goes slow," the Blue captain said to me. "We have found no way to go back to The Queendom. Queen Eleanor remains under a spell, not eating nor sleeping nor talking. But there are more of us now, sent by the magic fire-sticks."

"Fire-sticks?"

"Weapons that belched fire along with their magic, wielded by an army of male witches chanting foul spells." He shuddered and spat again. "It was a battle outside the city walls, won by darkest magic."

The *guns*. Today's skirmish had been small; Lord Robert had said the major battle would take place tomorrow morning. And when those additional Blue soldiers died and arrived here, they too would be told this was Witchland. And so the number would grow, of men who did not behave like the Dead because they did not know that they were.

"But we caught one of the witches," the Blue said grimly. "Just a while ago. And we will burn her."

"You caught a witch?"

"Yes. Tell *that* to the witch-queen when she snatches you back!" His face took on a strange expression, both horrified and sly. "Does she strip you naked for her ensorcelling? And herself, too?"

"No. Yes. No." I scarcely knew what I was saying. They had caught a witch here, a woman, and were going to burn her? How? Who?

"Did the whore-queen—"

"Can I see the witch?" I said. "I could . . . I could report back to the . . . the whore-queen that she does not have the control over Witchland that she thinks she does!"

He considered, nodded. The ground rumbled under my feet. "Come then, boy."

I followed him across the plain, away from the river, to another patch of woods. The leaves blew in a restless breeze, where there had never been a breeze before. On the far side of the little woods were three dozen Blues, some standing and some sitting, none of them behaving like the Dead. A captain held a writhing girl by the arms. It was Cat Starling.

"Let me go!" she shrieked. "Let me go!"

Beside her was a great pile of dry wood, with a tall stake in the center.

"Help!" Cat cried as I stood there, dumb. "Help me, whoever you are! I've done nothing wrong! I—want—my—mother!"

"Tie her," one of the Blues ordered.

The soldier dragged Cat, still screaming piteously for her mother, toward the stake. Another handed him two long strips of red wool. They had been torn from her skirt.

The Blue with me said, "She has the sixth finger. Just like the witch-queen who controls you. You'll enjoy this, boy."

I found what brain I had left. "Wait! I must talk with her first!"

The soldier scowled. "Why?"

"To . . . to . . ." All at once country lore, heard at so many faires with Hartah, came back to me. And I thought, too, of Bat, from the *Frances Ormund*. "To take the amulet from her! She will not burn so long as she has the amulet."

"Aye, that's true," said a Blue seated on the ground. "My granny always said that. Their magic amulets protect witches from fire."

"You're a brave man," the soldier beside me said. He stepped back respectfully, and I walked to Cat.

"Give her to me."

The captain did, and I wrapped one arm around her waist.

She flailed and struck at me, but she was no fighter and I found I could hold her, although not without difficulty. That made her flail and shriek more. Under cover of her noise I spoke into her ear with all the urgency and authority I could.

"Cat Starling, a message from your mother—think of the river at Stonegreen. Think hard and wish yourself there. Do it *now!*"

She seemed to have not heard me. The soldiers looked at each other—was that suspicion on that face there? I was supposed to be looking for an amulet. . . . I thrust one hand into her blouse, between her breasts.

At the touch of her skin, I got an immediate and enormous erection. My member leapt like a startled dog. The effect on Cat was different. She brought up her nails and raked them across my face, crying "Mama!" The next moment she was flying through the air, faster than a bird, toward that distant place where Stonegreen should be.

The soldiers all cried out and fell on their faces. To tell the truth, I shivered myself. Cat *looked* like a witch, flying away from us, even though I knew she was only a girl too simple-minded to know she was dead. Like Bat, who had flown up the cliff face because he wanted to. How much else could the Dead do? And when would these Blues discover it? One thing they could not do was kill each other again, but Cat hadn't known that. Her body would not really have burned. But I had at least spared her more terror.

How had she died, back there among the living? Burned there, too, as a witch?

A Blue rose cautiously from the ground. "Did you get the amulet, boy?"

"No. She was too quick for me."

"Witches are," another said grimly. He looked at my bleeding arm, my bruised jaw. "Does the whore-queen hurt you, boy?"

"Sometimes. I—oh, she calls!" I put on the expression of a brave man suffering without noise, bit my tongue, and crossed back over, just as the uneasy sky flashed with sudden, shocking lightning.

The queen sat at the carved table, holding a goblet of wine, her green-jeweled skirts spreading inches from where I lay on the floor. Unlike all my other returns, this time she seemed hesitant to touch me. She said, "I watched, Roger, and all at once these long scratches appeared on your cheek."

I put my hand to my Cat's scratches. My fingers came away bloody. So that was how it worked. Never before had anyone watched me while I sustained injury in that other country.

The queen said, "Do you . . . do you want some wine?"

"Yes, please, Your Grace."

I sat up slowly. My jaw ached where the Blue had hit me and the touch of the goblet on my mouth hurt. But I drank all of the wine.

"Now tell me." Her uncertainty had vanished, along with any concern for me. She was again the queen. "What did the savages say to your question, 'ven' or 'ka'?"

I had listened carefully at dinner. "*Ven*" was yes, "*ka*" was no. I thought I knew what answer she wanted, and I gave it to her. "They said '*ven*,' Your Grace. Lord Solek does . . . he *does* seek your throne."

Instantly she stiffened. "How did you know that's what the words meant?"

Mistake, mistake. Muddled by the wine, by the pain in my jaw, by seeing Cat Starling again—I hadn't meant to reveal that I knew what Queen Caroline had wanted to ask the savage Dead, any more than I would reveal that I was making up the answer. But there was no help for it now.

"Your Grace . . . at dinner with Lord Solek . . . you named the word for 'throne' to teach him, and he told you their word for 'want' when he desired more ale. . . . I'm sorry, I was standing so close, "

"You have a good ear," she said disapprovingly. "I will remember that, Roger."

"Yes, Your Grace."

"And their answer to my question was *'ven.'* You are certain."

"Yes, Your Grace." My lies were multiplying like ants in spring. Once, I would have been afraid to lie to the queen. But I didn't think this lie, warning her of danger from Lord Solek, would do me harm. She must anticipate that already. To say *"ka"* would have been even worse. And she would not have believed me.

"And my second question? How is the fire-powder made?"

"Your Grace, how could they tell me that? I pointed to their *guns*—"

"They have them still, over there?" It was the first time she had ever asked me anything about the country of the Dead except information about the land of the living. But her curiosity didn't last. It was a byway, and the queen's ambition kept her on the main road, always.

"They have their *guns*, yes," I said. "And they pointed to them and mimed for me that they do not make them, nor the fire-powder. There are special craftsmen who do that, just as we have special craftsmen to do blacksmithing or to build ships."

"That makes sense," she said thoughtfully, and I breathed again. My jaw throbbed; I could feel it swell. Cat's scratches burned on my cheek.

All at once the queen stood in a swirl of green silk. "You've done well, Roger. Thank you. Here is a token of my appreciation." She tugged a ring off her finger, a gold ring set with small emeralds, and gave it to me.

"Your Grace—"

"For you. Now go to bed. It's past midnight; you were gone longer than usual. The battle may begin as early as dawn, and I want you to watch it with me."

"Me?"

"Who knows what you will learn? You are quicker than even I knew. Perhaps you aspire to take Eammons's place as translator."

"No, no . . . of course not . . ."

"A joke, Roger." But she was not smiling. Her dark eyes, with their flashes of submerged silver, measured me even as I stumbled from the room, one hand clutching the ring she had given me, my jaw bloating painfully with the blow I had taken in the country of the Dead. I was vulnerable there. I was vulnerable here.

I shut the door to the privy chamber quietly behind me, and went to another sleepless night beside the ashes.

20

THE QUEEN SPOKE TRULY.

The battle began just before dawn.

I stood wrapped in my cloak on the palace tower. This was the only place on the island city taller than two stories, and it was nothing more than the flat roof of the bell tower. The space was no larger than a small bedchamber, circled by a low stone parapet. A wooden trapdoor, now raised, covered the spiral stairs that led through the bell cavern and on down to the palace below. I stood jammed into the small area with Queen Caroline, a few advisors, and the queen's personal guard of Greens.

No one spoke. A light breeze blew. The unrisen sun streaked the east with red, as if blood already flowed.

From here I could see the whole of the palace spread below, as I had never seen it before. Finally I saw that the shadowy maze of courtyards and buildings, so bewildering to walk through unguided, made symmetrical patterns. The whole was far larger than I had imagined, a vast and beautiful stone rose with too many petals to count. Every courtyard was now empty, the fountains stilled, the new green buds washed gray in the pale light. Soldiers of the Green stood atop the wall that enclosed the palace, with more soldiers on the ramparts circling the very edge of the island itself. Between lay the narrow ring of the tent city, as deserted as the courtyards. The great city gates were closed, soldiers posted at their bridges. Was Mother Chilton somewhere in one of those tents? Was Maggie in the kitchen, kneading bread for a victory feast if Lord Solek's army defeated the old queen's Blues?

And if the savage warriors did not win—

I could not think about that. My mind refused it. We who were closest to the queen would surely die, but I could not bear to think how. My mind could not keep its grasp on the possibilities, just as it was unable to grasp what lay beyond the stars now fading from the sky.

The last stars disappeared and the sun rose.

The Blue army stood massed on the northern plain, foot soldiers in the center and archers to either side. The officers, on horseback, were scattered behind their cadres. A drum sounded a code I did not understand but which turned my blood to water: *Boom boom BOOM BOOM boom.*

The savages had crossed the river from Fairfield sometime during the night. They now stood on the Thymar's northern bank, directly below the city. Yesterday I had thought them so many, filling the throne hall with their chanting numbers and pounding their cudgels on the floor, but today they looked a pitifully small number compared to the Blues. They weren't massed in orderly rows, either, but stood in uneven clumps, and as I squinted in the rising light, it seemed that many were *laughing*. Was that possible? Did men laugh at the start of battle? I had no way to know, but it seemed strange.

There was one group of Greens among the savages, Lord Robert's troops. He had left the rest of the Greens inside the palace, where they would make a last stand to defend the queen if necessary. Lord Robert sat astride a huge black horse, a magnificent animal with green jewels on its bridle and the queen's emblem on its armor. His Greens stood behind him, silent and grim, their shields raised.

Lord Solek was there too, at the forefront of his own savages. Neither he nor they wore any more body armor than before, although they carried shields. The butt end of each man's *gun* rested lightly on the ground. To the left of the small army, I was surprised to see, stood the musicians from yesterday, including the boy with twigs braided into his hair and two other young singers. As the sun streaked the sky with red that matched the paint on his face, he began to sing, and the musicians to play.

The weird instruments wailed away. The boys' powerful voices floated up on the dawn air. The savages chanted, marching forward in ragged lines, their guns held loosely in their hands. Across the plain, the drum changed rhythm—*BOOM BOOM BOOM*—and the Blues also marched forward.

The queen put both hands on the stone of the parapet, leaned forward, and said something under her breath. A prayer? A curse? A threat?

The two armies marched toward each other.

When they were barely within bow range, the Blue archers fitted their arrows and let fly. A few struck savage soldiers, who went down. Lord Robert rose in his stirrups and waved his sword. I could not see Lord Solek marching at the forefront of his men, but all at once a huge noise came, such a noise as had never rung on that plain. *Crack crack crack* . . . the savages were making explosions with their *guns*.

Fire leapt from the end of each metal stick. Many rang on the Blues' shields, hard enough to knock them down. As they scrambled back to their feet, a second wave of savages flowed to the front of the line and fired. I heard men screaming. Most did not get up. Smoke rose from the *guns*, forming a pall over the battlefield.

Now the savages broke ranks. A third wave parted, flowed to each side, and fired on the archers. The first wave of men had been doing something to their *guns*. Now they ran to the fore and fired again while the second group stood behind them and also did something to their weapons. Many of the archers went down. Many of the savages dropped to one knee as they fired. And all the while, the shouting and yelling came from them, not all at once but from whoever was not firing guns, and the horrible music played beneath the island walls, and the savage boys sang as if to fill the world with harsh syllables.

The Blues broke. Whether it was by order or from fear, those left standing turned and ran. Their drums ceased. The savages pursued them—the big men were so fast!—and caught many. Knives flashed in the sun. Screams echoed across the plain, and the ground ran red.

I turned away. I, who could see, talk with, touch the Dead, was sickened by all this dying. I knew pain and fear, and I could easily imagine myself one of those on the battlefield.

The queen leaned farther over the parapet and watched it all, a tiny smile at the corners of her red lips.

The battle was quick. No, the battle went on forever. Time itself was maimed and twisted, and still I could neither look closely nor stay turned away. When the fighting was finally over, with some Blues escaped but more lying dead upon the ground, the savages marched back to the palace. They carried their own dead—so many fewer than the Blues!—at their rear. Lord Solek marched in front, chanting. Way off to the side, Lord Robert marched with his Greens in pursuit of the fleeing Blues. On the battlefield, the bodies lay like abandoned dolls.

Finally—finally!—the boys stopped singing, the absence of their hoarse voices stilling the musicians as well. But nothing could silence the chanting soldiers.

"Come," the queen said, standing very tall. "My lords, come. To the throne room, to greet our victors."

She had not named me, but I knew better than not to follow her. Still, I lingered as long as I could on the tower roof. The Blues were defeated. The great northern gate was already being raised to admit Solek's army. And in the distance, on the plain, the first of the villagers were running from their hiding places toward the fallen, who were their husbands and brothers and fathers. I could hear the cries of the grieving women, desperate and frantic, like birds lost far out at sea.

Inside the palace, there was a repeat of yesterday's ceremony, gone terrible and bloody. Ladies, courtiers, advisors massed beside the dais. The queen sat tall on her throne. Lord Solek's army marched in, chanting, led by a chieftain negligently holding his broken arm. When Solek himself arrived, Eammons translated Solek's words, delivered as simply as if he had been announcing that water is wet: "We have won."

But this time he did not kneel, and so Queen Caroline could not tell him to rise. Their eyes, one silver under black water and the other blue as sky, locked so fiercely that I had to look away.

"You have The Queendom's deepest thanks," the queen said. "And mine."

I could take no more. No matter what it cost me, I could not listen to her words dance around her calculations, which must be paid for in other people's blood. Solek's army to defeat the Blues, and Queen Isabelle's army to defeat Solek's if he did not march her line. To gain Solek's help, the tiny Princess Stephanie sold into marriage before she turned four. And on the plain, hundreds of Queen Caroline's own subjects dead or dying.

For the first time ever, I slipped away from the queen without her permission, sidling back along the edge of the dais until I was behind the crowd of courtiers, all eagerly pressing forward to watch the ceremony. I would watch it no longer, would help the queen no longer, would accept no more kindnesses from her, except when I must do these things to survive.

The wall behind the throne was hung with a tapestry of heavy embroidered silk. Noiselessly I slipped behind it, where a doorless arch gave servants access to the throne room. Someone followed me through, to the narrow stone passage beyond the tapestry.

"Lady Cecilia!" I whispered. "You should not be here!"

She caught my arm. "What will happen now, Roger! Please tell me!"

"Nothing that will harm you, my lady," I said. The light was dim, coming only from an alcove farther on. In the gloom I saw that Cecilia's face was ashen. Her teeth chattered, from either cold or fear.

"How can you know that? Will the savages take us all? All the women, I mean? Are we to be prizes for them?"

"No, no," I said. "The queen made Lord Solek promise that his men would leave our women alone."

"That was the village girls. I mean us, the queen's ladies—are we to be marriage prizes? Like the princess?"

This had not occurred to me. Before I could answer, Cecilia sobbed, "Oh, Roger, I am so afraid!" She threw herself into my arms.

All thought fled my mind. She was so soft, so small, and she smelled so sweet. My arms were around her, her crying eyes pressed to my chest, and I held her. Just that: held her, and I wanted the moment to never end. Without knowing what I did, I lifted her face and pressed my lips to hers.

A moment of shocked stillness, and she pulled away. "Roger!"

"My lady, oh, forgive me—" She could have me whipped, have me sent away from court—

But she was smiling. Tearfully, but still my kiss had wakened the coquette enough for her to mock me through tears. "Really, I had no idea I was so irresistible."

"I love you, my lady. I have loved you since the first moment I saw you." It was true; never in my life had I meant anything more. I was dizzy with her, intoxicated with her.

Cecilia laughed. But a moment later she leaned close to me and whispered, "Then if a savage comes for me, will you hide me? Will you, Roger? You must know all the palace hiding places."

Would that I did! Were there hiding places, secret corridors? Of course there were, although I had never thought of this before. But this was a palace of secrets, of things hidden. Perhaps one reason the queen had kept me so close beside her was to keep me from discovering those hidden passageways, hidey-holes, escapes.

"I will serve you always, my lady!"

"How funny! You sounded almost like a courtier when you said that! You with that funny yellow paint on your face . . . Hide me now, Roger. Show me where I can go to be safe from the savages!"

I would have given my left eye to be able to do that now. But I could not. So instead I tried to look important, and ended up merely feeling stupid. "I . . . I have an errand for the queen. I can't delay! But you will be safe, my lady, I promise you that! If it takes my life, I will keep you safe!"

She cocked her head to one side. "I believe you, Roger."

"Thank you, my lady!"

Why was I thanking her? I didn't know what I meant. Her nearness addled my brain. I blundered away down the corridor, toward the kitchens.

Maggie sat at the trestle table, her head in her hands. Only a few other servants remained in the kitchen. The fire was nearly out; nothing had been done about dinner. I stood beside her. "Maggie?"

She looked up. No tears, but a depth of quiet suffering that Cecilia's hysteria could never match. That thought came, and was banished. "Maggie?"

"My brother, Richard," she said. "With the Blues."

"I'm sorry. Maybe he escaped to—"

"Maybe. The others have already gone out onto the field, all the servants, to find their dead. In a minute I must . . . I thought that first I should . . . What do you want?"

I didn't know what I wanted, why I had come here, had come to her. Before I could summon a fresh set of lies for yet another girl, Maggie's eyes grew wide at something behind me, and she leapt to her feet. I turned.

The boy with red twigs in his hair, the first singer, stood in the doorway. Unarmed, he nonetheless stood without fear. The few servants in the hall stiffened, and a middle-aged cook hissed loudly.

The boy walked to Maggie, who was closest. He said in a heavy guttural accent, "Food. For Solek and queen."

"We have nothing. No food," Maggie said. And, indeed, the kitchen looked as bare as if overrun by ravenous rats. The siege, plus yesterday's feast, had all but emptied the larders. Yet I guessed there was some food left in hoarded stores. Queen Caroline planned too carefully to let her capital starve.

"Food," the boy repeated, but not demandingly. Up close, he was extraordinarily handsome under the red paint on his forehead and cheeks. Dark hair, eyes as blue as Lord Solek's. He was taller than I, and broader. Did Maggie notice that?

"No food," she said. How did she dare?

The blue eyes searched her face, which had gone white with defiance. His hand reached inside the shaggy fur tunic to draw out something, which he held out to her. "You eat," he said gently.

It seemed to be a kind of dried meat mixed with berries. The thing actually smelled good. Maggie stared at him.

"No food," he said. "You eat, girl."

Something pounded behind my eyes. "She doesn't want your stinking savage rations!"

His gaze measured me, and I saw the moment he dismissed me. Laying the food on the table beside Maggie, he raised his voice loud enough for the rest of the frozen servants to hear. "No food? We bring food. You eat." He looked again at Maggie, then strode from the hall.

A man ran in from the opposite side, from the courtyard where the barges docked. "The savages are letting us take our dead for burial. Walter . . . I didn't find him. Maybe he got away!"

A middle-aged cook who'd just entered the hall spat, "He was avenging Queen Eleanor, the true queen, and yet now he must run! Shame scars this day!"

Another woman shushed her, with a quick glance at me. Of course. The servants had all taken the oath of fealty to Queen Caroline, but not all of them had meant it. Some of the former Blues were blue still, despite their green tunics, and even some of Queen Caroline's most loyal servants had relatives among the Blues. Like this man, like Maggie.

The cook snapped, "Begin work, all of you! Before long the queen will send someone for her dinner, and here the fire is nearly out! Bestir yourselves!"

I went out of the kitchen, leaving Maggie to her grief. I

could do nothing to ease it. But I did not want to return to the queen, who had caused that grief. So I spent the entire afternoon prowling the palace, trying to discover secret passageways or hiding places. But, of course, if they were that easy to discover, they wouldn't be secrets. I found nothing.

But I learned much.

I wore my cloak, hood pulled low over the yellow dye on my face, and sat quietly in alcoves, pretending to wait for someone. In courtyards, pretending to weed spring beds. At docks, where barges held downriver by the siege were once again arriving with their loads of goods for the palace. In the guardroom of the Green army. Even in the laundry, where Joan Campford gave me more yellow dye and treated me with a confused deference that upset us both. "I never thought my laundress boy would be fool to the queen," she said, shaking her head. "Now get away with ye."

At dusk, as the lanterns and candles were being lit in the palace, I made my way back to the queen's rooms, bracing myself for punishment for absenting myself. That was when I learned the most astonishing thing of all: There would be no punishment. The queen had not called for me, had not asked after me, had not even missed me. The presence chamber was empty except for the guards. In the outer chamber were no courtiers, only a little knot of the queen's ladies, sewing with a sobriety and earnestness totally foreign to all of them except Lady Margaret. With her sat Lady Sarah Morton, Lady Jane Sedley, two others. And Lady Cecilia, who did not greet me, but whose eyes had lost none of their fright since this morning. No such fright, however, twisted the face of the wanton

Lady Jane. She wore a small, sly smile as she stitched away on a chair cushion, or what was supposed to be a chair cushion. Lady Jane, like Cecilia, was no needlewoman.

"Fool," Lady Sarah said to me, "what news?"

"It is nightfall," I said in my role as fool.

"I know that, idiot!"

"Then if you know, you don't need 'new.'"

"No silly wordplay! Are the savage soldiers still in the palace or have they gone back to their camp?"

"Well, one is certainly here," Lady Jane breathed, and rolled her eyes at the closed door to the privy chamber.

I said, "Savage is as savage says."

"He knows nothing," said Lady Jane, her voice full of disgust. "He's a *fool*, Sarah."

Lady Margaret said, "That's enough nasty chatter." The others ignored her.

Lady Sarah said, "The fool has eyes! And while we're stuck here, on guard—"

"Aye," I said, "I have I's, and you have you's, and they have theirs! Alas!"

"He knows nothing," Lady Jane repeated, and turned her back on me.

She was wrong. I had learned much in my afternoon of prowling. No secret passages, but much else. I knew that Lord Solek's younger and handsomer soldiers had walked through the castle, learning it well but also making themselves agreeable. They had given away food—of which their army, on the move, could not have had very much. They had offered help. They had gestured admiration for much, and looted nothing. In the narrow ring of the city, to which shopkeepers were returning, the savages had bought items, paying in gold. Outside the palace, savages had helped carry the Blue dead to burial grounds, whenever grieving kin had permitted them to do so.

"Well, they aren't so bad," reported the villagers and merchants loyal to Queen Caroline. "Not as bad as some."

"Their gold's as good as any."

"They can *fight*," said a young Green guard, not without admiration.

"Good discipline."

"Fair dealing, at least so far."

I saw a serving woman gaze after a tall young savage, and her admiration was not for his fighting or his gold.

But the queen's ladies, stuck all afternoon in the outer chamber, knew nothing of all this. They sewed and they speculated, equally badly. Cecilia's eyes were round with fright. When the outer door swung open, she jumped, gave a little cry, and pricked her finger.

Lord Robert strode in, dirt and sweat and blood on his clothing. His boots rang on the stone floor as he made straight for the privy chamber.

Lady Margaret, the ranking lady-in-waiting, leapt up and said, "Lord Robert!"

He neither looked at her nor broke stride.

"My lord!" she said desperately. "You cannot see the queen just now!"

He stopped then, turning on her a look that made Cecilia shrink against the back of her chair. *I* would not have liked to face that black temper. Lady Margaret, usually so composed and acerbic, paled.

Lord Robert said, "And who are you to tell me when I can or cannot see the queen?"

"She . . . she left orders. That no one is to disturb her."

"Really." He took a step closer to Lady Margaret. She stood her ground beside the frozen group of seated women, the hem of her green skirt trembling on the floor. Lady Margaret, trembling!

Lord Robert said, "And what is the queen doing that she does not desire to be disturbed?"

"I . . . she did not tell me, my lord."

"And whatever it is, is Her Grace doing it alone?"

Lady Margaret conquered her trembling. She looked straight at Lord Robert and said, "Her Grace is not obligated to tell me what she does." The unspoken half of her statement was clear: *Nor tell you, either.*

Lord Robert said, "The queen will see *me*," and started toward the door.

I called out, "Lord Robert! She is with Lord Solek!"

Slowly he turned to face me. The ladies all stared, aghast. I said, "She told me, too, that they must not be disturbed. They are settling the future of my lord's army. It is a . . . a delicate negotiation."

He sneered, "And what does a fool know of negotiations?"

"Nothing, my lord. I only repeat what I was told. They are discussing the army."

It was the wrong thing to say. Lord Robert was, supposedly, the head of the queen's army. In three strides he was at the door and yanking on the handle. The door was barred from within.

Lord Robert's hand flashed to his sword. But a sword is no good against heavy oak. He kicked the door and bellowed, "Caroline!"

I said in a low voice to the five women, "Get out. Quickly. She will never forgive you for witnessing this, if she knows."

Lady Margaret, oldest and quickest-witted, said, "Yes! Come *now*." She had to pull Cecilia to her feet, but the last of their green skirts disappeared through the door to the presence chamber, with Lady Margaret closing it behind them, a scant moment before the queen flung open the door on the opposite side of the room.

Her gaze swept quickly around the room, found only me, and rasped, "Go."

I did not have to be told twice. I scampered from the room, hunched over, trying to look as much as possible like some small animal, harmless and mute. In the presence chamber, the queen's ladies huddled against the far door, too afraid of the savages to risk the open courtyard beyond. As I approached, Lady Margaret said sharply, "Well?"

What to say? "She . . . sent me away."

Lady Jane said, "Was Lord Solek there?"

"Of course he was there," Lady Sarah said. "We already knew that. Only—why didn't Lord Robert challenge him? No, wait—Lord Solek must have already left the queen."

"We would have seen him go," Lady Jane argued. "Unless . . . Oh! There must be a secret passage from the queen's bedchamber!"

"*Enough*," Lady Margaret said, and not even those two dared disobey her tone. Lady Margaret looked at me with new, reluctant respect. "You did well, fool."

Lady Sarah said, "But did you *see* him? Will the savage and Lord Robert fight over her . . . later, I mean?"

I said, "Lord Solek and the queen had matters of The Queendom to discuss."

Lady Jane snorted with delicate lewdness.

Lady Margaret said, "The fool is right. Lord Solek had to discuss the army with the queen, and that is what we will say to anyone who asks. Do you all understand that? *Do you?*"

One by one they agreed. Lord Solek was there on affairs of state. It was a meeting of negotiation, to which Lord Robert arrived late because he had been pursuing the retreating enemy. The three of them had discussed matters of The Queendom, such as the princess's betrothal to Lord Solek's son. The meeting among the three was about important affairs of The Queendom. Lady Margaret rehearsed them over and over.

But it was Cecilia who knew what really to ask. As the ladies finally dispersed, under heavy guard, to their chambers until next sent for, Cecilia caught my arm. "Roger—what was the queen wearing when she opened the door?"

"Go to your chamber, my lady," I said. She pouted and flounced off, escorted by two Greens.

The queen, barefoot, had been wearing nothing but a short shift, and her dark hair had tumbled loose around her bare shoulders.

The next day Lord Robert rode from the palace on his magnificent black charger, gone to his estate in the country, and did not return. He had gone, Queen Caroline announced to her court, at her behest, on an important mission of state.

"ROGER, I HAVE work for you," the queen said.

That could mean only one thing. My spine froze.

Weeks had passed since the battle. Spring flowed into early summer, with roses budding in courtyards and crops pale green in fields. Lord Solek's savage soldiers were everywhere—how could so few of them seem like so many? They directed the Green guards, they marched through the spider-net of villages around the palace and secured them for the queen, they supervised the barges arriving at the palace, they controlled everything that happened in Glory. A few had learned some words of our language, but most managed with gestures and demonstrations of what they wanted. They were tireless, superbly disciplined, courteous in their rough way. They were— always, everyplace—*there*.

The queen kept me close by her, except when she was in

her privy chamber with Lord Solek. She never mentioned what I had seen the night of the battle. She didn't have to mention it; we both knew it was worth my life to stay silent about the scene between her and Lord Robert. Much of the time, as Lord Solek received reports from his captains and directed his growing power over the capital, the queen sat with her ladies as they sewed or sang or gambled or danced. She said little, and did not join them in their forced revels. They had to be cheerful and amusing, for her sake; she did not have to cheer or amuse them, and she didn't. She sat quiet, thoughtful. Sometimes she didn't hear when Lady Margaret spoke to her.

Queen Caroline's beautiful face showed nothing, but I could sense her growing fear. This had not been part of her plan. Lord Solek was swiftly, surely, securing power over The Queendom. The queen had defeated her mother's forces only to fall before those of her lover.

"Will she marry him?" Cecilia whispered to me as she sat in a window embrasure, supposedly sewing. Her cushion cover was a tangled mess; I could have set neater stitches myself.

"Marry him?"

She giggled. "Well, they bed together, don't they?"

"I am never in the queen's bedchamber. Hush, my lady." Quickly I glanced around. Cecilia had no discretion, and sometimes I thought she had no memory. Both Lady Margaret and I had warned her again not to speak of the queen and Lord Solek. But she was like a kitten: curious, wide-eyed, playful, completely adorable. The scent of her made my head float and my eyes blur.

"Maybe she *should* marry him," Cecilia said. "He's very handsome. Those blue eyes."

"Lady Cecilia . . . *please!*"

"Well, he is. And Princess Stephanie is not strong. The queen is old but not that old—he could maybe give her another daughter in case—oh, all right, Roger. You cautious old thing." She patted my shoulder. Her touch was like wine. "It's all right now, don't you see? We're at peace again and everything's all right. The queen—oh, she wants us now!"

"Stay, she wants me," I said, and rose to follow the queen to the high roof where we had watched the battle. Three or four times a day we did this, climbing the steep stone steps through the bell tower, just she and I and two Green guards, the same two I often saw drinking ale in the guardroom with one of Lord Solek's captains. That savage captain had a good ear for words; he was among the best with our language. *"I like to gaze at my queendom at peace,"* the queen said to explain her frequent trips to the tower. I knew better.

Now she leaned on the stone parapet and called me to her. Her Green guard stood by the trapdoor to the staircase, a respectful distance away and out of earshot of whispers. She knew as well as I that her guards were Lord Solek's spies. The queen's hands gripped the stone hard. Wind pulled at her hair, her gown. She had lost weight, and there was a fierce desperation in her dark eyes. She said, "Roger, I have work for you."

"Y-yes, Your Grace."

"You will cross over and see if the country of the Dead contains a new arrival, a messenger from my brother's bride."

"Your Grace—I have tried to tell you . . . the country of the Dead is such a big place, to find one person—"

"Nonetheless, you will find him. He will be small, in order to ride fast, and he will be wearing yellow, the color of

Isabelle's court. You will ask him when her army will arrive here."

"Your Grace . . . you are presuming that such a messenger was not only sent but also is now dead. . . ."

"He must be dead, or he would be here. Or Isabelle's army would."

And she needed them. Her need was in every line of her taut figure, her tense face. Only an army that she commanded could counterbalance the one led by Lord Solek, the bedmate who was usurping her queendom. Queen Isabelle's army, bound to Queen Caroline through Prince Rupert's marriage, would not have the *guns* of Lord Solek's men, but the Yellows had a reputation as the best soldiers in the world. If Queen Isabelle bore a daughter, that princess would be second in line for the Crown of Glory, after the sickly Princess Stephanie. Queen Caroline had a strong claim on her sister-in-law's army, in addition to the affection of her brother. And she had sent for the Yellow army much earlier, had carefully timed their probable arrival as part of her grand design. So where were they?

Her situation was clear to me. Mine, as always, was not to her. To find one messenger in the country of the Dead—if he was even there!—would be impossible. I had lied to the queen before and gotten away with it—but what if another lie caught me out?

"You will cross over now, right here," the queen said to me. "Not in my privy chamber—right here on the tower. I have already told my lord Solek that my fool is given to fits."

Fits? And she did not trust her own privy chamber—were there spy holes? In her bedchamber, as well? Things were even worse for her than I had guessed.

As if to confirm my fear, the queen said in a low voice that seemed torn from her against her will, "He seeks to send Princess Stephanie to his barbaric country until her marriage. Roger—*men* rule there!"

My eyes grew so wide that the wind on the tower made them water. Men did not rule; they could not create life, only defend it. I—everyone at court—had assumed that Lord Solek acted on behalf of some unknown barbarian queen. But if *men* ruled . . . And for a future queen to be sent away—unthinkable! A princess or queen left her queendom only once, on her marriage journey, to inspect in person the dowry her husband brought her. After that, her place was in her own palace, always. Princess Stephanie was only three; she would grow up not even knowing The Queendom that she must one day rule. Her loyalty would be to the savage realm, not her own. She might even forget her mother tongue.

"I cannot make Lord Solek understand," the queen said, still in that same low voice, although we both knew that Lord Solek understood only too well. "Go now, Roger, and find Isabelle's messenger. Have a fit right here, right now."

Have a fit! How did one have a fit? I had never even seen a fit. The queen's hand brushed mine; her fingers left me with a piece of gold. What good was gold to bring on a fit? All at once I was angry, furious, at the way I was used. I was a tool, no more than her spoon or her goblet. A tool—just as she was to the savage who shared her bed and wanted her queendom.

There was no choice but to do as I was told.

I screamed and jumped up on the stone railing. The Green guards rushed forward, swords drawn, and pulled the queen away from me. I tossed the gold coin in the air, cried, "I buy the sky! Why why why!" and jumped back down from the parapet to writhe on the stone floor. My hand felt in my pocket to work my little shaving blade free of its sheath, and viciously I cut my palm. Blood filmed my hand, and I crossed over.

I did not know where I was.

I stood among huge boulders, an outcrop such as I had never seen anywhere near Glory. Among the boulders grew scrub bushes, leafless and misshapen things that sent out twisted twigs from twisted stems. I blundered into one. Its sharp thorns pricked my already bloody palm. The ground shook under my feet and the dark sky raced with clouds. My gut twisted. I had caused this devastation.

Noise came from my left. Careful to avoid the thorny bushes, I picked my way among the boulders until I emerged onto the plain beside the river, but a plain changed and misshapen as the bushes. Rocks were strewn everywhere, some small enough to kick, some as big as I was. More of the scrub bushes spiked the ground, which rumbled under my feet. Amid this chaos the Dead sat or lay in their usual oblivion—but not all of them.

The noise came from two sources. The river ran more swiftly now, breaking and swirling against new rocks, sending up spray and sound. But most of the noise came from across the river. Blue soldiers, hundreds of them, dead in the recent battle with the savage warriors. The Blues were being drilled by their captains. They marched, shouted, brandished swords, stamped their boots. None of them acted even remotely as if he was Dead. One of them caught sight of me across the water. He cupped his hand to shout across the river.

"Witched fool! What news, boy?"

I could not have answered to save my life. When I stood, dumb as one of the inexplicable boulders, he yelled even louder. "*What news?*"

When I still did not answer, the soldier and the man next to him stepped onto the river and walked across its surface to the other side.

Dizziness took me and everything swirled and swooped. When I could see again, one of them had hold of my arm

"His wits are returning, Lucius," his friend said. "Boy, ye be all right?"

"Of course he not be all right, he's witched, you idiot!"

"No worse than us, stuck here in Witchland. . . . Fool? Ye be all right?"

"Y-yes." Their boots were not even wet.

Lucius said, "What news, then? Does the whore-queen still hold the palace?"

"Y-yes." I fought to master myself. "But Lord Solek—"

Lucius let loose with a string of violent oaths. I had not heard such language since Hartah. "The savage holds the palace for her?"

"Yes." The truth was too complicated to explain, even if I had wanted to.

Lucius shook my arm, not gently. "What, then? How do we escape from Witchland? Have you nothing good to tell us?"

"Leave off, Lucius," his friend said. "Don't shake the fool like that. He's on our side. He tried to get the young witch's amulet for us, remember?"

Cat Starling. What had happened to her after I left? I said, "Have you taken the amulet from her since I was last witched here?"

"No one has so much as seen her. Is that what will send us back—the amulet?"

"I don't know yet," I said. "But the . . . the witch-queen keeps me close, and I hope to learn how to undo my own ensorcellment, and so yours. I work for that night and day. Meanwhile . . ." I tried to fake a sob, and discovered it was not fake. There are many kinds of witching.

"Don't cry, fool," Lucius said with disgust. "You're nearly a man."

"He's not crying—are you, boy? What can we do meantimes? We drill, you see, to prepare for the battle. When we go back, that savage will not beat us, no matter how many firesticks he brings against us, nor how the witch-queen deforms Witchland to frighten us. We will defeat her and her savages. We fight for The Queendom."

They all believed still that they were in Witchland, all the Blues whom Lord Solek's army had killed. I had said so to the first ones, who told the others as they arrived, and so none at all believed that he was dead.

The second soldier grew impatient. "I asked you, fool, what can we do to aid our own freedom from Witchland?"

"You can . . . you can continue to prepare for battle." They expected more from me. Lucius's eyes darkened with anger. At the same moment, the sky rumbled and lightning flashed from one glowering cloud to another. I invented wildly: "And you can make amulets that will be useful on your return. Each amulet should consist of five of the thorns on the new bushes that have appeared—you have noticed the new bushes?"

They nodded, listening carefully, anxious to miss nothing that might save them. My stomach clenched, but I went on. "Wrap the five thorns—and they must be five perfect thorns, not blemished—in a bit of cloth and wear it around your neck. The thorns will not hurt you in this place"—truer words were never spoken, since nothing could hurt them in this place— "but once out of Witchland, they will impart a little of the witch-power to each of you. This have I learned by stealth, and as a result of my own ensorcellment."

Lucius nodded. "I will tell the captain, I thank you, boy. We are in your debt."

"Then you can help me now. I seek a messenger from Queen Isabelle, who married our Prince Rupert. The messenger was . . . was witched here. He will be a small man, a rider, dressed in yellow. He may be under the same spell as Queen Eleanor. Have you seen him?"

Both soldiers shook their heads. They thanked me again, and I watched as they walked on the surface of the water back across the swift river. Then I set out to find the messenger in yellow.

It was hopeless. The land had become so much more difficult to walk across, let alone to scan. Boulders, thorn scrub, groves of trees thicker than before, and somehow menacing. Beneath my feet, the ground rumbled. I scrambled away from the riverbank and toward the north, the direction of Queen Isabelle's queendom, frantically searching. I looked for a long time, becoming dirty and exhausted. Although even if he were here, I didn't see how I could find the messenger.

Instead, a dead Blue found me. He jumped out from behind a boulder several yards away. Unlike the other Blues I had seen here, he had lost the discipline of soldiers. His eyes were crazed and wild. He shouted something incoherent. Thinking himself in Witchland had unsettled his wits, perhaps never strong to begin with. Or perhaps dying had deranged him. He carried what he must have brought with him, seized from the enemy in battle: a *gun*.

He shrieked again, raised the thing, and fired at me.

Something hard and hot—so hot!—struck my left arm, sending me falling backward against the rocks. The sky gave a great *crack!* of lightning. I screamed; the pain was pure agony, searing my flesh like flames.

And then I lay on the stone roof of the tower, it was night, and I had other questions to torment me. I already knew I could be hurt in the country of the Dead, by the Dead. But what would happen to me if I were killed there? Would I return to my body in the land of the living, or would I lapse into the unknowing tranquility of the Dead?

Now I had not one but two places where I could die.

The pain continued. It was too dark to see my arm, but when I made myself flex it, I could tell that the bones were not broken. This was a flesh wound only, but I had seen men die of flesh wounds that turned black and rancid. And the pain did not diminish, burning like acid along skin and nerves.

Cradling my left arm in my right, I forced myself to my feet. Where was the queen, her guard, anyone at all? How much time had passed? My eyes adjusted to the night, and I peered over the parapet. Most, although not all, of the courtyards were dark. So was most, but not all, of the narrow ring of the tent city. Above, the stars shone brightly, without a moon. Summer had barely begun; the night air was cold and sharp.

I tried the trapdoor that led from the tower roof. It was bolted from below.

Something must be happening in the palace, something that had drawn the queen away from the tower. She had forgotten me before, but never while I was on a mission for her to the country of the Dead. What if she had been murdered, as she had murdered her mother? What if no one came to the tower before morning? The courtyard was many stories below, too far to jump. I didn't think I would freeze to death here, but I needed to clean the wound in my arm, bandage it . . .

Why did everyone always abandon me?

I leaned over the parapet and screamed, "I'm here! I'm here!"

And then, "I'm here, you bastards! I AM HERE!"

Nothing.

I don't know how long I stood there, clinging to the stone railing, shivering and cursing, my arm pure agony. Stars moved overhead, I know that. I grew light-headed, maybe feverish. And then, on a rooftop below the tower, two figures emerged. It was forbidden to all but soldiers to go onto the roofs at night. These were not Greens. In the starlight I could see their silhouettes clearly: a soldier of the savages and a woman. They embraced.

My voice was hoarse, but I called down, "Help me, please! I am Roger, the queen's fool, and I am trapped on the tower by mistake! Please, send for help!"

Instantly the woman vanished, perhaps unwilling to be identified. The savage came to the edge of his roof, peering upward at me. He looked a tiny figure, no more dangerous than a small pet dog that stands on two legs. Distance deceives, promising safety where there is none.

The savage called something that I of course did not understand, and then disappeared from the roof. Several minutes later—it seemed like hours—the door to the tower roof opened and a man emerged.

Lord Solek himself.

Behind him was Eammons, the translator, who said, "What are you doing here?"

"I was forgotten! The queen—" I gasped as a wave of dizziness hit me.

Eammons said sharply, "What about the queen? What did she say to you?"

There was something wrong with his tone. It held not only sharpness but fear. Of what? Something was wrong here, very wrong. With every last shred of strength in me, I summoned what wits I had. They were all that had kept me alive until now. They counseled caution, counseled evasion, counseled lies.

"Nothing. I . . . Her Grace left and . . . I wanted . . . I wanted to be alone. So I came here. But I fell asleep and the tower was locked at dusk; I guess that is the usual way. And by now the queen must be looking for me. . . ." I tried to look befuddled, foolish, out of my depth. It was not hard.

Lord Solek said something, and Eammons replied. Translating my words, I guessed. The savage chieftain gazed at me from cold blue eyes. Up close, he was even more terrifying: huge, hard, full of suppressed energy, like an enormous boulder about to fall and crush me. Then he shrugged, turned, and strode off.

"Go back to where you belong," Eammons said irritably.

"If you do this again you will be flogged, queen's fool or no. If she doesn't order it, I will."

He will? Did Eammons, who now trailed Lord Solek and not the queen, have that much power? It was clear that Solek did; he now kept as close a watch throughout the palace as Queen Caroline had once done.

I, on the other hand, had no power, not even to stay upright. I staggered down the tower steps, far behind Eammons, who had hurried after his master. Every few steps I stopped and rested against the stone wall. Then, at the bottom, I collapsed.

Sometime later—that same night?—a page bent over me, shaking my good shoulder. "Fool? Fool? Are you ill?"

"Mag . . . Mag . . ." I couldn't get the word out for the chattering of my teeth: *Maggie.* She was the only one I could think of who might help me, cure me, care what happened to me. But, of course, the page didn't know Maggie. He was only nine or ten, a scared little boy in royal service to a palace gone mad.

He said, "Who?"

"Mag . . ."

"I'll get her!" And he was off, running into the courtyard, bringing the only person he knew who served the queen and had a name like what he thought he had heard. When next I opened my eyes, Lady Margaret bent over me, a green velvet cloak over her nightdress.

"Fool? Are you sick?"

"H-hurt," I managed, and then I fainted, and knew no more.

22

I WOKE ON a nest of blankets on the floor beside a strange hearth. A fire burned brightly. The room was small but richly decorated in green and warm brown, with a table between me and the door. Sunshine streamed in the one window through a curtain of light silk. On the window cushion sat an elderly serving woman, mending a petticoat.

"Where . . . ?"

She rose, looked me over, and said a single word: "Wait." She left the room.

I sat up. I felt light-headed, but the pain in my arm was gone. It had been bandaged, and the bandages smelled of some faintly vinegary ointment. Carefully I got to my feet, trying to puzzle out where I was. A second door, ajar, led to a bedchamber. I glimpsed a narrow bed and a plain, highly polished chest. Three books were stacked neatly on top, beside some needlework. The other door opened.

"Roger!"

The serving woman had returned, and with her was Lady Margaret. Some part of my mind realized that this was the first time she had ever used my name instead of calling me "Fool." Clumsily I fell to my knees.

"Rise," she said impatiently. "How do you feel?"

"Better, my lady. Did you bring me here and—"

Lady Margaret interrupted me to speak to the serving woman. "Leave us, Martha.

"Yes, my lady."

When she had gone, Lady Margaret said, "Eat first. You've had nothing for two days. Sit there, and eat that."

As soon as she said this, I was ravenous. Nothing existed except the bread, cheese, and wine on the table. I gobbled like a boar. Then, when my belly was full, Lady Margaret existed again, looking haggard. She was ten or fifteen years older than the other ladies, and still in the queen's service because no one had married her, and she had never been a beauty. Still, I had not thought it possible that her long face could look this gaunt and drawn, and there were violet shadows beneath her eyes. I said, "The queen . . ."

"Knows where you are. I told her that you had fallen ill from being locked all night outside on the tower during a fit, and that I would have you cared for. She sends her good wishes."

But no regrets for having locked me out during my "fit." Nor any reasons for having left me there, where I might have died. I said dryly, "The queen is well?"

"Don't be insolent, Roger."

Lady Margaret was much shrewder than Cecilia; I needed to remember that. I bowed my head in repentance. Also to hide my anger. But her next words made my head jerk upward to stare at her.

"I did not tell the queen that you were injured as well as ill, nor that the injury came from a savage's *gun*. Fortunately, it was but a flesh wound. But how did that happen while you were locked on top of the tower, Roger the Fool?"

We gazed at each other. I chose honesty, partly because I didn't think I could get away with anything else. Not with her. "I cannot tell you, my lady. On the queen's orders."

"There is much that cannot be told, these days."

"Yes."

She leaned close to me and lowered her voice to a whisper. "You have been ill for two days," she said, "and so you don't know what has happened. I'm going to tell you, Roger, but only because I think it important that you know the truth and not the rumors swirling around the palace. And because I think you already know more about the truth of Lady Cecilia than does anyone else."

"Lady Cecilia?" Now I was truly bewildered. I thought we had been talking about the queen.

"You were on the tower roof helping the queen look for the messenger from Queen Isabelle, weren't you?"

"Yes."

"He arrived while you were in your fit."

"He arrived? He's here?" Not among the Dead.

"He was here, but no longer. Nor is Isabelle's army, which will never come to the queen's aid."

I was staggered. Queen Isabelle *must* come to the aid of her sister-in-law; that's what queens did. There was a marriage pact. And any daughter of Isabelle and Rupert would be second in line for the Crown of Glory. Queen Isabelle could not have refused to send her army.

"Why?" The word burst from me like the explosion from a savage's *gun*. And Lady Margaret had mentioned Cecilia. . . .

All at once I knew, and the world turned sick around me.

"Yes," Lady Margaret said, looking at my face. "Queen Isabelle had a bout of the crawls. Her physicians say it has scarred her inside, so that she may never bear a child. She caught the crawls from Prince Rupert, who said he caught it from Cecilia."

"It was the other way around! Cecilia caught the disease from him!"

"That is not what Queen Isabelle believes," Lady Margaret said wearily, "nor Queen Caroline, either. Rupert is her brother. She believes as she wishes—and so do you, Roger. You believe Cecilia, that foolish child, because you want her to be the victim. But the truth is more complex than that."

"As if anyone here cared for truth!"

"Everyone here cares for truth," Lady Margaret said, "just not the same truth. And yours is this: You helped Cecilia obtain medicine for the crawls early in her infection, and she sent you for the milady posset because she knew what she was experiencing. Queen Isabelle did not know, and waited too long, and has paid the terrible price. There will be no heir to her throne. Queen Caroline will gain no help from her, and is practically a prisoner in her own palace. The messenger with the news arrived while you were in your fit, and the queen rushed away from the tower. Somehow the door must have become locked behind you."

"And Lady Cecilia . . ." I could barely get out the words. All those men who had refused to swear fealty to the queen, vanished to who-knew-where, dead, tortured . . .

"Cecilia escaped."

"*Escaped*? How?"

"I don't know. No one knows. Someone warned her, just before the queen sent for her. I was with Her Grace; her other attendants had been sent to bed. I was there when the messenger arrived and the queen received him. She had only minutes before Lord Solek was alerted and joined us, and in those minutes the queen . . . I have never seen her that bad," Lady Margaret finished simply.

I had. I could picture the scene: the queen raging, Lady Margaret trying to calm her, the messenger terrified for his life. Then Lord Solek striding into the room, so that the two women and the messenger must pretend that all was well, that this was a routine message from her brother. And as soon as possible, the queen would have given the order to arrest Cecilia, and take her . . . where? To what punishment? I shuddered.

"My lady, did *you* warn Lady Cecilia?"

"No. I remained with the queen. So did Lord Solek, for some hours. Whoever warned Cecilia had time to do so. Cecilia has so many admirers; it could have been any misguided Sam Slip-Lip."

"But who else would have known what the messenger said?"

"I don't know. But I think you understand what the palace is. Spies, spy holes—still, it *is* strange that someone knew to warn Cecilia. There has always been something strange about Cecilia. But it is the queen I am afraid for. As are we all, with our supposed savior as the gaoler. The savages have their fire-sticks, their poison-tipped knives, their brutality. I am afraid for the queen, and I cannot forgive him his treachery."

I didn't care what she could or could not forgive him, nor that Lady Margaret remained loyal to her queen, still. She was one of those who, having given her allegiance, would never change it. I cared only about Cecilia. "But . . . how could Lady Cecilia have escaped the palace that night? The gates were barred!"

"I don't know. And neither do I greatly care. Cecilia brought this on herself, on all of us, and she deserves whatever she gets. But you should know the truth because it will help you to better serve Her Grace."

Lady Margaret actually thought I was going to do that. I was not. But I bowed my head again and said, with sincerity, "Thank you for nursing me, my lady."

"I didn't do it for your sake," she said irritably, rising from the table. "In truth, I didn't do it at all. The nursing was done by my woman and by your friend from the kitchen, a Maggie Someone."

"*Maggie?*"

"You called for her so insistently that I finally sent a page for her. She nursed you like a sister. But now you seem well enough, and I am glad to have both of you out of my rooms. The queen has been asking for you. Go serve her, fool, with whatever it is you do."

"Yes, my lady." I rose, fortified by the good food, and left the ladies' chambers. But not to go to the queen.

I knew where Cecilia had gone, and where she might still be found.

The mid-morning kitchens bustled as if this were a normal day, a normal year. Stews bubbled in great pots over the fires. Bread baked in brick ovens. Chickens and rabbits turned on spits, dripping fat into the hot embers. No matter who held power, or who imprisoned whom, or who bedded whom, courtiers and soldiers and servants must be fed.

No one looked surprised to see me, who had so often been sent by the queen with orders for where and when food should be served. Only Maggie, trimming vegetables at one end of the long trestle table, raised glad eyes. "Roger! Are you feeling better? You're wobbling a little."

"I'm fine. Thank you for nursing me. Lady Margaret said that no true sister could have been more devoted."

Maggie scowled at me; some people cannot stand praise. She snapped, "You need more yellow dye for your face. It faded while you were sick."

"All right. Maggie—I need more of your help." I said it in a whisper, but not the keenest of the queen's spies, or Lord Solek's spies, or anybody's spies could have heard us over the din of the kitchen. "I need to get out of the palace."

"Out?" She looked blank for a moment, and then began wielding her little peeling knife as if it were a sword and carrots were the direst of enemies. "You're going after that titled little bitch!"

I was shocked at her language, her look. "Lady Cecilia is not—"

"Everyone knows she disappeared two days ago! Ran off with some man in heat, probably, and you're going to—oh, why are men so stupid!" And she burst into tears.

Now people *were* looking at us. I was dumbfounded. Did Maggie, like Lady Margaret, know that Cecilia was the reason Queen Isabelle's army would not arrive in The Queendom? There was no way Maggie could know that. But she was clearly in distress, and I put my hand on her arm. She shook it off so violently that I, still weak from my illness, staggered against the edge of the table.

"Don't touch me!"

"All right, I will not, if that's what you want. But I need to get out of the palace tonight without being seen, and you are my only—"

"No!"

"Maggie—"

"I won't do it! It's too dangerous! Go to her if that's what you want, but leave me out of it!"

All at once anger swept me. No one but me cared that without help Cecilia could be captured, tortured, killed. My lady, so playful and lighthearted and laughing . . . unlike Maggie! I stalked out of the kitchen to the laundry, where amid the clouds of steam from the wash pots I stole a small packet of dye.

In the courtyard outside the ladies' chambers I pretended to collapse again. Two Greens picked me up, not very gently: "You take his arms and I'll take his legs—damn but the fool's grown almost as heavy as a real man!" They dumped me back in Lady Margaret's chamber, where her serving woman sighed, remade the nest of blankets by the hearth, and sent word to the queen that I was still unwell. I stayed there all day, pretending to sleep.

In the evening, while the ladies were attending the queen and Lord Solek at whatever revels he chose, I painted my face with the red dye I had stolen from the laundry. Into my hair I braided the twigs I had broken from the tree in the courtyard where I collapsed. From Lady Margaret's chest I took a green velvet cloak lined in fur, and a white nightdress. I put them on, the nightdress fitting over my own fool's outfit only because it was so billowy. I pulled the cloak tight around me, put up the hood, and made my way through the palace to the west gate. Two Greens guarded the gate. They had been Blues, had sworn the oath of fealty to Queen Caroline, and now served Lord Solek. They were the kind of men who would serve anyone for enough coins and enough ale. Unlike Solek's savages, who were kept under such strict discipline that no girl of The Queendom had been molested by any of them, these two were avoided by every serving woman in the palace. That's how I knew about them. Women talk, and ever since the night that Cecilia had sent me to Mother Chilton, I had been listening.

"Well, what comes *here?*" said the Green with the bristly beard.

The other nudged him, elbow hard in the ribs, and said uncertainly, "My lady—"

But Bristle Beard's eyes were sharper. "Not a lady, Dick— look at them boots!" He grabbed for me and I danced away. I let the hood of my cloak fall back, then snatched it back up.

"It's one of them fancy savage singers! In a shift!" Bristle whooped and grabbed for me again.

I said, trying to speak in a high-pitched version of the savages' guttural accent, "I be—"

"We know what you be," Bristle Beard said. Dick had abandoned his initial caution; he made kissing sounds in the air and grabbed me. To these rough idiots, all the savage singers looked alike, and I had used the red dye liberally. Dick pretended to kiss me, went "Faughhh!" and pushed me to the ground.

"Sing for us, boy!"

"Sing a pretty girl's song or we'll treat you like a girl!"

"You, but not me, I don't fancy male meat." He kicked me.

I cried, "I be go for Solek!"

That sobered them. Bristle Beard said, "Let me see your pass."

I shook my head as if I didn't understand and repeated, "I be go for Solek."

Bristle Beard said, "He's supposed to have a pass."

Dick was quicker. "Yeah, but if he's dressed like *that* for Solek . . . who knows what those savages do when they be by themselves? Those singers are all flower-boys anyway. I don't want no part of this."

"So we—"

"Go," Dick said to me, scowling. "You can understand that, can't you, you sick dog? *Go.*" He unbarred and opened the gate. I scuttled through into the city.

It was dark and cool, although summer wound through the night air like embroidery through cloth. I was nowhere near the kitchens, where the food barges drew up to deliver and Maggie had let me out of the palace once before. But if I stuck close to the palace wall and circled to the right, I thought

I would arrive there. This proved to be harder than I expected. The alleys lined with tents twisted and turned, sometimes away from the wall, sometimes toward it. Also, many of the tents had been torn down, replaced with wooden structures in various stages of construction. It was the old queen who had decreed that, on the island of Glory, only the palace should be a permanent dwelling. Queen Caroline must have done away with that law, perhaps in an attempt to win her subjects' favor. My way was frequently blocked by piles of lumber and brick, by raw-wood houses lighted from within, once by a sty full of nasty-looking boars that snorted at me in the darkness and bared their teeth.

I felt weak from illness and ridiculous in my green velvet cloak and lady's nightdress. But I kept the hood drawn well down over my face, and few people were out on the streets to see me. Perhaps in the night my dark green cloak looked brown or black. No one stopped me, not even when I encountered two of Lord Solek's savages. They passed me without a glance and went into an ale tent. As they drew aside the flap, warmth and light and laughter spilled out. The queen might be a virtual prisoner in her own palace, her throne all but usurped, but for the common people, there was peace and liberality.

Eventually I found the dim alley, and the tent with the picture of two black swans at its hem. I knocked on the doorjamb, did not wait for an answer, and pushed my way inside.

Mother Chilton sat in the same chair. It was as if she had not moved in all these long weeks since I came here last. The same fire burned in the brazier in the center of the tent, sending its smoke through the hole in the roof and its light flickering on the canvas walls. The same poles hung with the same bottles, plants, feathers, hides, bits of wood, cloth bags.

This time, Mother Chilton rose as I entered. My disguise did not deceive her for a moment; she did not even comment on it.

"You've grown, lad. You're nearly a man."

"I've come for—"

"I know why you've come." She moved closer to me, and it seemed that as she moved, all the objects hanging from the poles moved too, yearning toward her. In her eyes swam strange colors, lights. "You seek the Lady Cecilia, who sent you here to find."

"Yes. Is she safe? Is she here?"

"She was here. Here and gone. And she will never be safe."

My breath stopped in my throat. "Never? Why? And where has she gone? Did you help her escape from the capital?"

Mother Chilton did not answer me directly. Seen up close, her face was smooth cheeks, wrinkled forehead, and those eyes that were no color at all. She said, "So they are not yet ready in Soulvine."

Once before she had mentioned Soulvine to me—"*Do you come from Soulvine Moor? Are they ready, then?*" That visit, I had been shocked that she would connect me with what no one else would even name. This time, I didn't care. I cared only about finding Cecilia and protecting her.

"Where is Lady Cecilia? Did you help her?"

"I did, lad. But you don't know why. You know much, even more than you think, but you don't know what Cecilia is."

"What is she?"

"A pretty, empty-headed tinderbox that will ignite all."

I said with as much dignity as I could manage, "I know she

is not a great wit, but she is not empty-headed. And yes, she has 'ignited' me, and I am not shamed by that."

Mother Chilton did not laugh. She closed her eyes and an expression of great pain crossed her face, as if I had turned a knife in her bowels. I sprang forward to catch her if she fell, but she didn't so much as sway on her feet. But I think I swayed at her next words.

"I have sent Cecilia into the Unclaimed Lands. It is the only place the queen cannot reach her. Caroline studied the soul arts but she has no talent. Still, it is why the queen recognized *you*. I told Cecilia to go into the Unclaimed Lands but not to enter Soulvine Moor, not for any reason. It may be she can find some goatherd or scrub farmer to marry her, pretty little kitten that she is, and keep her safe. But you can't go after her, lad. I thought once that you came from Soulvine. You do not, and you've already caused enough disturbance in the country of the Dead."

"You . . . *you* can cross over to the country of the Dead?"

"No," she said without explanation.

I seized on what mattered. "You sent Cecilia south to the Unclaimed Lands *alone*?"

"She is not alone." Mother Chilton put her hand on my arm, and a strange thing happened: my vision blurred. Almost, something formed in front of my eyes, some picture— but no. It was gone. Mother Chilton withdrew her hand.

"You are not ready," she said sadly. "Lad, don't go after that girl. She was born on Soulvine Moor, and although Caroline brought her to Glory as a child, she is still a Soulviner. Do not go after her."

"I must," I said simply.

"You're a fool," she said with equal simplicity, and I didn't know if she referred to my character, my post with the queen, or both. For a long moment neither of us spoke. The fire crackled in the brazier. Finally Mother Chilton said, "Don't try to go about in daylight as either a girl or a savage bard. You can't even sing. Take off that ridiculous nightdress and scrub your face with this cloth. I will give you a cloak."

I said sullenly, tired of being ordered like a child when I was on a hero's mission to rescue my love, "The red dye won't wash away. It must wear off."

She mounted and attacked my face with the cloth. It came away red with dye. She dragged the twigs, not gently, from my hair. I put off the green velvet cloak and pulled Lady Margaret's nightdress over my head. Mother Chilton slapped a poultice on my wounded arm, yanking back my sleeve to do so. Instantly, cool strength flooded through my arm. She took my court cloak and handed me a thick hooded cloak of brown wool lined with brown rabbit, by far the nicest I had ever owned.

"I . . . I cannot pay you. . . ."

She said sharply, "Give me that gold piece in your pocket."

How had she known? Before I could ask, she added, "And give me Caroline's ring, too. How stupid are you, to carry markers like those around with you? Give them to me."

Markers? I put my hand in my pocket and clutched both my gold piece and the little ring set with tiny emeralds. I had planned to use both to bargain my way to Cecilia. If she took—

Of its own will, and without mine, my hand drew out of my pocket and laid both ring and gold piece on the table.

"How did you—"

"Here, lad." She gave me a handful of silver pieces; I was too dazed to count them.

"How did you—"

"Hush. Go to the alehouse by the east gate and drink there all night. In the morning, when the worthless alehouse louts stagger out of the city to do what they call 'work' in the fields, go out with them."

"But how—"

"I said to hush!"

But I could not, even though I could barely get out my next words. "I never . . . never believed in witches. Are you . . . a witch, mistress?"

"Get out before I kick you out, lad. Your stupidity shames us all."

"But I—"

"Get out!"

"Will you tell me just one more thing? How did Cecilia know about you in the first place, for the milady posset I mean, and why are you now helping her to—"

"Such stupidity will destroy us all yet," she said despairingly, and then all at once I stood in the dark alley, and the tent door was laced tightly shut behind me. I blinked, and a shudder ran over me. So it was true and I had never known it; witches existed in the world. Or maybe Mother Chilton had merely babbled, and I had walked myself from her tent. Or maybe—

"Hello, Roger," said a voice behind me in the darkness. I whirled around. There, wrapped in a gray cloak and somehow sounding scared and furious and determined all at once, stood Maggie.

23

"WHAT ARE *YOU* doing here?" It came out harsh and accusing, my tone born of my own fear, my own unsettling doubts about what I was doing here.

"I'm going with you," Maggie said in an un-Maggie voice, humble and beseeching. Nothing was as it should be.

"You're not. Go back inside the palace."

"I can't let you go lurching around the countryside alone. You're too ignorant," she said, and *that* sounded more like Maggie. But she was the second woman in two minutes to tell me how stupid I was, and I lost what remained of my temper.

"I have 'lurched around the countryside' since I was six years old! With people you couldn't imagine, doing things you couldn't imagine! Damn it all, Maggie, leave me alone!"

She started to cry.

Her tears were not like Cecilia's, stormy and clutching,

tears a man could comfort. She stood there in the starlight with her hands hanging limply at her sides, tears sliding silently down her face. Her nose began to run. But she didn't move, didn't go back to the palace.

"Maggie . . . I can't take you."

Finally she said, "You understand nothing." Which was not true, and certainly didn't help. She added, "I mean, nothing about me."

"What don't I understand?"

"Anything!"

I stalked off, toward the alehouse by the east gate. I could feel Maggie following me. There was a pocket in my new cloak, and I put my hand into it and fingered the coins Mother Chilton had given me. Ten silvers—more than I had ever seen together in my life. Five hundred pennies! I was a little afraid of so much money. Just before we reached the alehouse, I bent over and under cover of my cloak, I slipped nine of the silvers into my boot.

The alehouse was half tent, half newly constructed wood. A brazier burned brightly in the center, warming all but the farthest corners. Queen Caroline had undone her mother's edict that tradesmen must leave the city at night, and the two long tables on either side of the brazier were full of people drinking and talking and laughing. Maggie and I took one of the small, cold, corner tables. Keeping my cloak and hood on, I laid my silver coin on the table, and the serving woman looked hungrily at it and so not at us. She brought two mugs of ale, two bronze coins, and seven pennies.

Maggie said in a low voice, "Where did you get the money, Roger?"

"That's my concern."

"Then where do you think Lady Cecilia has gone?"

"I don't know."

"Then how will you—"

"Maggie, you've been very good to me. Helping me, feeding me, nursing me. But I must do this alone."

"No," she said simply.

"Who are you to—"

"I'm coming with you. I'm dressed as a boy, Roger, under my cloak. I have cut my hair. I'm coming with you."

A ˈˈˈˈˈˈˈˈ thought ˈˈˈˈˈˈˈˈˈˈ Appalled at myself, I said, "Maggie, are you a spy for the queen?"

She stared at me, her face a mottled maroon. But she didn't attack me. She said only, "I told you that you were stupid. Don't you know how much I hate the queen?"

I hadn't known. "Why?"

"Because Richard was a Blue who died for his loyalty and bravery."

So her unaccustomed tears had not been for me, after all, but for her brother. The thought was welcome. I said gently, "You know now for certain that Richard is dead?"

"Yes." Maggie had control of herself now, "I finally heard. But that's not the only reason I hate the queen. She beds the savage lord who killed so many of us in The Queendom. She murdered her own mother—everyone says so. And she has treated you like a dog—no, less than a dog. Like a *thing*. You could have died up there on the tower roof. She is a monster, and I hate her. I cannot stay and serve a monster. Not any longer, now that I know what she really is. Queen Eleanor was right, her daughter is not fit to rule. I was serving the wrong queen." She took a sip of her ale, her eyes anguished.

I realized then what made Maggie different from most people I had ever known: She could name hard truths. Not even Mother Chilton, with her anguished evasions, had done that. Maggie was domineering, stubborn, and meddlesome, but she could name truth. Like Mistress Conyers. Like—perhaps—Queen Caroline herself.

I made one more attempt. "You have a sister in a village somewhere—you told me once. You could go to her."

"I also told you that my sister is a miserly, grasping fishwife who screams at everyone, including her husband. I am not going there. I am coming with you."

An unwelcome suspicion formed in my mind. I was willing to risk everything for Cecilia. Was Maggie then willing to risk everything for me because . . . "Maggie," I choked out, "do you . . . are you . . ." I could not say the words: *in love with me.*

A long silence spun itself out, fragile as cobwebs.

Maggie finally answered. Her voice held great carefulness. "You are my friend, Roger. My brother is dead, my sister a shrew, and I can no longer serve a queen I despise. If I stay in the palace one night longer, I will go mad. I have nowhere else to go except with you."

Nowhere else to go. I well understood that! Relief crept through me, warming as the ale. Maggie was my friend, she had nowhere else to go, and it had been deeply vain of me to suspect anything else. I would not entertain such vain thoughts again. Who was I, fool and murderer and homeless wanderer, that anyone should love me?

Still, I made one more attempt to dissuade Maggie from

coming with me. "You said in the kitchen that leaving the palace was too dangerous for you to—"

"I meant danger to *you*, idiot!"

"That's my concern, not yours!"

"It's mine now," she retorted, sounding again like the Maggie I knew: competent and scornful.

"Well, come on, then," I said ungraciously, and after that neither of us spoke again. We sat, drinking slowly, while the alehouse emptied as the night wore on. I spent sixteen more pennies, the last ten for the serving woman to let us sleep beside the dying brazier. In the early morning we joined the laborers streaming over the east bridge, the men and women who would work for daily hire, planting and weeding the fields, then spend all they earned in the alehouses and cook shops of the city when night came. No one noticed us. We walked to the farthest of the village fields, where a cottage woman sold us as much bread, cheese, and dried meat as we could carry, plus a goatskin water bag, in exchange for a silver. Then we took the southeast road toward the coast.

It was the same road I had ridden with Kit Beale, nearly nine months ago. Then it had been autumn and now it was early summer, and Maggie plodded beside me. Now, as then, I didn't know what I was going toward, or what would happen to me. But all else was different. I was different. And every step of every mile, Cecilia filled my heart. With worry, with fear, with pain. With love, which was all three.

My arm hurt only a little. Whatever Mother Chilton had done to it, the *gun* wound seemed to be healing more rapidly than it had under Lady Margaret's nursing. I was still weak from my illness, and sometimes I had to stop and rest. Maggie had more strength than I. Still, I rested less than expected, and for that, too, Mother Chilton's poultice may or may not have been responsible.

Maggie had said little all that first day. But when we had made our camp in a thicket well off the road, when we had eaten our bread and cheese and meat, she faced me across the glowing coals. It was cold after the sun set, and both of us wrapped our cloaks tight around our bodies. The moon was a thin crescent in the east, barely visible, and the stars shone high and clear.

"Roger, what will you do if you find Lady Cecilia?"

I didn't want to discuss Cecilia, not with Maggie. I said brusquely, "Serve her."

"As her fool?"

"No!"

"As what?"

"You cannot ever let anything rest, can you?" I said angrily. "Lady Cecilia is in the Unclaimed Lands. She is not alone, but whoever is with her is only one person. Mother Chilton did not tell me who it is. Cecilia will need servitors, guards, a court."

"You are neither a servitor nor a guard," Maggie said, "and you are certainly not a courtier." She stared straight into the fire, scowling.

"She trusts me. And anyway, you're going to need a home, too, Maggie. You wanted to escape the palace, and you have. But what now? Lady Cecilia could maybe give you a place as her serving woman, or—"

"Be quiet!" Maggie said with such fierce pain that I was astonished. It did not seem to me a fall in rank to go from cook to lady's maid, but I questioned her no further. I didn't want any more arguments. Maggie lay down and rolled herself into a ball with her back to me.

I dreamed, that night by the fire, that I was back in the laundry at the palace. I was dying cloth green, but then—in the manner of dreams—I was dying people, and not green but yellow. All the people were female, and all of them were naked: the queen, Cecilia, Cat Starling, Maggie. "There," I said, "now you are all fools." I woke with such a powerful bodily response that there was nothing to do but creep off into the bushes and hope Maggie did not wake.

All fools. Including me.

Maggie and I walked for several days while talking but little. She was sullen, seldom even looking at me. The Queendom was in soft spring, filled with new light and tender green, but the nights were still cold. The moon grew steadily until it was a full round circle, shedding a silvery glow over all beneath. The land around us became wilder, less fertile. Fields of new plantings gave way to pastures for sheep and then, as the ground became rockier and steeper still, to goats. Hills turned to mountains, with deep ravines and abrupt cliffs. Whenever anyone rode down the road from either direction, Maggie and I hid. But I realized that Hartah, with his gruesome stories of highwaymen and robbers and dangers to lone travelers, had lied to me. I saw no corpses gutted and rotting by the road. And each day, fewer and fewer riders appeared. We had reached the edge of the Unclaimed Lands.

"Our food is almost gone," Maggie said.

"There's an inn up ahead. We can get provisions there, and ask for information."

"An inn? How do you know?"

"I know," I said. And so we came to the last inn where I had ever stayed with Hartah and Aunt Jo. It looked the same, a rough place for rough people. Somewhere to the east lay the sea, and I noticed, as I had been too naive to notice before, the sheltered creek that would be so convenient for smugglers. Dense woods behind the inn would let a traveler approach or leave unseen from the road. *"A good place for information,"* Hartah had said. I took another of Mother Chilton's silvers out of my boot and put it in my pocket.

"Maggie, you must do exactly as I say while we are inside this inn."

She said reasonably, "What are you going to tell me to do?"

"Say nothing. You can maybe pass for a boy if you keep your hood up, with all that dirt on your face, but not if you speak. And when we take a room upstairs, you must stay there with the door barred until you're sure the person knocking is me." I hated that I was giving her the same instructions Hartah had once given me, but there was no help for it. In this, at least, Hartah had been right. This was no place for a woman. Aunt Jo had been old and shriveled, but Maggie was young and, if not exactly pretty—no one was pretty next to Cecilia—would still be in danger. And I, with my small shaving knife, could not defend her.

Who was defending Cecilia? It should have been me.

Maggie nodded. She pulled her cloak far over her face. I said, "Part the cloak at the waist so they can see your boots and breeches. They must think we are two boys." She nodded again and did as I directed—a first.

Two men sat drinking in the taproom, with another carrying in mugs of ale from a room beyond. They studied us with cold eyes.

"We need a room for the night," I said, holding out my palm with a silver coin on it. "My brother has fallen and hurt his leg."

Maggie began to limp.

The innkeeper looked from my coin to my face to my thick, fur-lined cloak. His voice was genial and oily. Aye, lad, I've a fine room for ye, upstairs. My best. And mayhap a bit of supper?"

"No, thank you."

"As ye wish. This way."

I followed him upstairs. The same tiny room under the eaves, the same sagging bed. Maggie limped behind me. The innkeeper said, "Thirty pennies for the night."

That was outrageous, but I nodded. "Fine. My brother must rest his leg, but I'll come down with you and have a mug of ale."

His greasy smile broadened. "As ye say, sir."

Maggie, looking frightened, hobbled into the room. I heard her bolt the door. I followed the innkeeper to the taproom, let him bring me a mug of ale from the back room, let him charge me a ridiculous three pennies. The remaining seventeen lay on the table beside my mug. The other two men sat across from me, saying nothing. They were neither young nor old, dressed in patched brown wool, and neither had washed in a very long time. Their smell would have been even worse, except that the room was cold. Wind off the sea whistled between chinks in the walls, turning the small fire fitful. We all wore cloaks.

They would make their move soon—robbery at best, murder at worst—and I must make mine first. "Warm in here, is it not?" I said.

No answer.

"Very warm." I made a great show of wiping my forehead and neck. And I waited.

Finally one growled, "Where ye bound, boy?" His teeth were broken, brown as his cloak.

"I'm looking for my lady mistress."

That got both their attention, and the innkeeper's as well.

"She fled her father's estate a few days ago, and forgot to tell me where to meet her."

"Forgot? What d'ye mean, boy? Speak plain!"

"I am speaking plain." I opened my eyes wide, looking as guileless as I could, and then clutched my stomach.

"You sick?"

"No, no, just something bad that I ate . . . Yes, she forgot. And she never forgets me. I'm her musician, you see, and she is very musical. Shall I sing for you?"

"No," he growled as I knew he would. "What's your mistress's name?"

"Lady Margaret. Although I think she might . . ." I scrunched up my face, like a half-wit trying to remember something. "I think she might use another name. I forget what."

The innkeeper said, "Your lady mistress runs away—"

"Not runs away—flees."

"—flees from her father's home to the Unclaimed Lands? Not likely, lad."

The other man at the table was now watching me more closely. He had as yet said nothing at all. I spoke directly to him. "Have you seen her? She's small, with brown hair and green eyes and she's very, very pretty."

There was a sudden silence among the three men. Finally the innkeeper said, "She does not travel alone."

"No." Mother Chilton had told me as much, and then had not told me whom Cecilia was with, calling me stupid for even asking.

The man with broken teeth said, "You're a fool, boy."

"I am told that often," I said with a big sunny smile. "But in her haste my lady forgot me, and my brother and I must follow her. Do you know where she went?"

They all glared at me now. I knew I had not much time. The one with broken teeth said, "She went inland, of course. Where else should one like her keeper go? She went toward Soulvine Moor, toward Hygryll. But you—"

I cried, interrupting him, "Oh, thank you! You see, I—" I knocked my pile of coins to the floor, dove under the table after it, and pulled a hair in my nose as hard as I could. When I rose again, staggering and without the coins, my eyes watered, my face had gone red, and I was sneezing violently. "Oh . . . oh, I'm afraid I . . . Help me, please, my lady fled her estate because of the plague there and my brother. . . . Help us. . . ."

The men froze. The innkeeper breathed, "Plague!" Then all three scuttled away from me.

"Help . . ." I collapsed against the table.

One man drew his sword. The other said sharply, "No! Don't go near him!"

"The coins—"

"Leave them, you idiot!"

All three left the inn, striding out into the night.

I went upstairs, collected Maggie, and we slipped away, making camp a few miles down the road in a deep thicket. First, however, I took food from the inn and another old, patched, but still serviceable blanket. It would be cold going over the mountains to Soulvine Moor.

Where my mother had died. Where Cecilia had fled, in the company of . . . whom? Where I might, at last, find the truth of both my past and my future.

"WE CANNOT GO to Soulvine Moor," Maggie said. "We *cannot*."

Morning, and Maggie and I faced each other across the embers of our campfire. Last night she had been too frightened to ask me much, but this morning she was herself again. Still afraid—if anything, she was more afraid since I had told her our destination—but since she was also Maggie, her fear led her to fight rather than cower.

I retorted, "At least you said the name. In the palace you would not even utter 'Soulvine Moor.' As if the words alone could somehow harm you."

"Not the words, you idiot! The people who might overhear them!"

That made sense. I had not known then how the palace was

riddled with spy holes, with spies, with factions. I knew now. But we were not now in the palace.

"Tell me," I said. "Tell me what Soulvine Moor is."

Despite the beautiful morning, she shuddered.

It *was* a beautiful morning. Overnight, spring had turned to the first taste of summer. Golden light lay on the half-budded trees. Hawthorne leaves unfurled with that tender yellow-green seen only once each year. Birds sang. The woods smelled fresh and expectant, spawning life.

She said, "Soulvine Moor is death."

"No riddles, Maggie. Tell me true. Who lives on Soulvine Moor?"

"The ones who never die."

"Witches?" I still wasn't sure what had happened to me at Mother Chilton's, or what I believed about it.

"No. They burn witches there, as everywhere else. But they also . . . they . . ."

"Tell me!"

She shuddered. But no one could say that Maggie did not have courage. "They don't die, because they take the life from others. They murder them and steal their souls to gain their strength to add to their own. And so they live forever."

"Nothing lives forever." I, of all people, had cause to know that! "How do they steal the souls from others?"

"I don't know. The ceremony is secret, known only to them. There are rumors . . . but no one really knows."

"Are you sure this is not just a folktale? A story meant to frighten children into being good, like the hawk-man or the monster under the mountain?"

Her temper flared. "How should I know? Do you mean,

have I ever gone to Soulvine Moor to find out? I have not, and I am not going there now. If Lady Cecilia is in the Unclaimed Lands, then I will stay with you until you find her, but not afterward. Do you hear me, Roger? Not afterward! I will not stay as a serving woman to Lady Cecilia, as you so charmingly suggested days ago. I would rather live as a scullery maid, a pig tender, even a whore! Do you understand me?"

I was shocked. Maggie, a whore? Even though I knew she didn't mean it, the words gave me a queer feeling in my heart. It was not like Maggie to be so irrational. Nothing made sense.

But I didn't dwell long on Maggie's tantrum. As I scattered the fire and we returned to trudging along the rough road, my mind roiled with what she had told me. Soulvine Moor, from whatever terrible and fearful belief, killed intruders. To "steal their souls."

My mother, Aunt Jo said, had died in Soulvine Moor.

Had she been murdered? How?

No. I could not think that. I would go mad, if I thought that. It was nothing but a folktale anyway; no one could gain immortality by taking in the souls of others. Souls could not be taken in. They could only cross over to live on in the country of the Dead, if that could be called "living." But here, in the land of the living, my Cecilia could be harmed.

"She went toward Soulvine Moor, toward Hygryll," the man with the broken teeth had said. *"Where else should one like her keeper go?"* What keeper? What did I not know about Cecilia? Lady Margaret had said there had "always been something strange about Cecilia." But to me she was like a small stream, swift and light and clear to the bottom, babbling happily along in

its little course. The man with the broken teeth had been lying, or mistaken, or cruel. Mother Chilton had not sent her to Hygryll— *"I told her to go into the unclaimed Lands but not to enter Soulvine."* Cecilia was somewhere in the Unclaimed Lands, and I would find her. I would.

And my mother—

Don't think such thoughts!

But there was only one way to stop the thoughts. I would do what I had intended to do over half a year ago, ever since Aunt Jo told me where my mother died. I would go as close to Soulvine Moor, to Hygryll, as was safe, and I would cross over. I would find my mother in the country of the Dead. Old women often talked to me there. My mother was not old, but she was there, and she would talk to me, her only child. From her, I would finally have answers.

Having a plan cheered me. It was an idiotic cheerfulness, since all difficulties still remained. But I had a plan: Find Cecilia. Enter her service, just to be around her. Then ask for a brief leave, go to the edge of Soulvine Moor, cross over, and find my mother. I could do all that. I had done so much already! And the sun shone warm, the birds trilled in the fair morning, and I was away from the palace and its ruthless, contradictory, passionate, and imprisoned queen. So my imbecilic cheerfulness sang in my blood. I whistled as we walked, something I had not done for months.

Maggie trudged beside me, head down, saying nothing.

Information was not hard to come by in the Unclaimed Lands, not once we had turned away from the sea. Along the coast were the smugglers, the wreckers, the road that carried whatever travelers there were. But as the land rose in wild ravines and desolate moors, there seemed to be only one road, sometimes dwindling to a mere cart track, sometimes lost altogether so that, cursing, I had to search to find it again. The cottages were few and mean, and their inhabitants, once they set aside their initial suspicion of strangers, were glad of travelers to break the monotonous pattern of their days. Goatherds, hunters, farmers trying to survive on a couple of poor upland acres and a fierce independence, they gave us food and shelter in exchange for a few pennies and scraps of news. Nor did they seem surprised at two young "brothers" traveling alone. Boys grew up quickly in this wild land. The food that Maggie and I were offered was scanty and sometimes almost inedible, but not once did we feel menaced as we slept among the ashes of the hearth—unless that place was already occupied by a flock of big-eyed children or by the family pig.

And nearly all of the upland folk had seen, or heard of, Cecilia.

"She be here yestreen a twelveday," they said, and their accents were the same as Bat's, the seaman off the *Frances Ormund*. "A nineday." "A threeday." We were drawing closer to her.

"How was the lady traveling?" I asked that first night. "And who was with her?"

"On a donkey, she come," an old woman told me. But when I looked closer, I saw that she was not old at all. Bent, slack-bellied, gap-toothed, she had no lines around her eyes. This woman was younger than Lady Margaret, younger than the queen, no more than thirty at the most. Her smile was sweet.

"Who was with the lady?" My stomach tightened.

"Her serving man. To take her to her cousin's manor, beyond the mountains."

Maggie was careful to not look at me. Before I could react, the woman said, "Old he seemed, for such travel. Spry enough, but old." She, who never was nor ever had a servant, shook her head over the ways of ladies, gentlemen, and their train.

Old. Who was he? And what "cousin's manor"—I had never heard of Cecilia having a relative in the Unclaimed Lands, nor that "cousin" having a manor. Although most of these mountain people had never been more than a few miles from their homes, so that "beyond the mountains" might be only their words for every place different, farther away, unknown to them.

Over the next days, at houses even poorer, in mountain dells even higher, I learned more. Cecilia and her servant had stayed one night. The lady looked tired and worn, her servant very old. No, said the next family to give us shelter, he was not her servant, he was her cousin, taking her to his farm. No, said the next, there be no "manors" in these mountains—was I a fool? Nor were there any "ladies." The woman, dressed in a plain wool gown, and her uncle were going home, farther toward the border. As he said this, the man's gaze would not meet my eyes.

"What border?"

But the man turned away and stared into the fire, scowling fiercely.

The last dwelling, the poorest yet, was far along the track from its nearest neighbor. In fact, the track seemed to end here. There was only a rough hut set in a mountain hollow, beside a high, thin, cold waterfall. A silent family, parents and four ragged children, crowded into a single drafty room. No one would answer my questions at all. When I repeated them, the man told me to hold my tongue. Maggie and I slept that night in the goat shed.

In the morning, a child brought us two small loaves of bread. In the Unclaimed Lands, hospitality was practically law, and even unwelcome, too-inquisitive guests must be fed. The bread was hard and sour, the child ragged and barefoot. Some sort of fungus grew on one of his calloused feet, between the toes and over them. It was that hand I caught hold of. His bony wrist.

"I have something for you."

"Unhand Jee!"

"Jee, I have something nice for you." With my free hand I drew from my pocket a carved willow whistle. I had made it one night at a campfire by a small creek, where willows grew. I blew on it softly, and a single sweet note sounded.

Jee stared. It was clear he had never seen such a thing. He wanted it, badly. I said, "You can have it if you answer my questions. What is the border?"

For a long moment I thought he wouldn't answer. His little face twisted horribly, he reached down to scratch at the fungus on his foot, but his gaze stayed on the whistle. Greed triumphed over fear. He croaked, "To the cursed land."

Soulvine. "Where is the border?"

"Be due east."

"How far?"

"A day's walk."

"And the lady . . . I mean, woman . . ."

"Hemfree be taking Cecilia home."

A gasp from the prone figure on the straw; Maggie was awake and had heard. In my astonishment, I let go of Jee's wrist. He snatched the whistle from my hand.

"*Hemfree be taking Cecilia home.*" The child knew their names, knew who they were. How many others of the householders had also known, and withheld the information from the outlanders, the strangers from The Queendom? Who was Hemfree? And "home"—

"They maun travel hard," the boy said. "Soldiers be coming after them."

Queen Caroline's soldiers. She had sent men to find Cecilia, who had ruined all of the queen's plans. Was that why Hemfree had brought Cecilia so close to Soulvine Moor— because pursuers were close on their trail? How close?

I seized Jee's arm. "How do you know that soldiers are after the lady?"

"I see them. From a tree."

Maggie looked from the boy to me. She said slowly, "'Home.' Lady Cecilia is from the Unclaimed Lands. No, she couldn't be—the way she talked, moved . . . she is . . . is it possible she came from . . ."

"Yes," I said, "she did."

When Cecilia had sent me to Mother Chilton for the milady posset, I had not thought it strange. After all, even Maggie had recognized the name and known the old woman as a healer. But Mother Chilton had done so much more for Cecilia. She had sheltered her when Cecilia fled the queen's wrath. She had sent Cecilia home, with the unknown "Hemfree" to escort her. And Mother Chilton had said something else on my last anguished visit to her, something about the queen. . . .

"*Caroline studied the soul arts but she has no talent. Still, it is why the queen recognized you.*" And, I realized with sickness in my belly, why the queen had brought Cecilia to court as a child. Caroline hoped that Cecilia would develop that "talent" that the queen lacked. She had not. But evidently there existed an underground web of these women, a web that spread gossamer threads from The Queendom to Soulvine Moor. Cecilia, Mother Chilton, Queen Caroline. Perhaps that web was why Queen Eleanor had refused to turn The Queendom over to her daughter. She knew that Caroline waded in dangerous waters. And now Cecilia, pursued by Greens, was being driven back to Soulvine Moor.

I don't know how long I sat there on the reeking straw of the goat shed, blind and dumb from my inner terror. Finally Maggie said softly, "Roger?"

"Yes." My voice did not sound like my own.

"Is Cecilia on Soulvine Moor?"

"I think so. Yes."

"Does she . . . Is she . . ."

"I don't know what she is."

But the moment I said it, I knew it was not true. I knew what Cecilia was. She was exactly as I had always known her: childish, heedless, sweet-natured, lovely, adorable. She was the "pretty little kitten" that Mother Chilton had called her. No more, but no less. She had no "talent"—that was why Mother Chilton had hoped that she could "find some goatherd or scrub farmer to marry her." That was why this unknown Hemfree had been sent to take care of her. Cecilia needed taking care of. That was why I, too, was here. To find and take care of Cecilia, my sweet kitten, my love.

Maggie said, "Who is 'Hemfree'?"

"Some relative or friend of Mother Chilton." And perhaps of Cecilia, as well. Someone who knew the country and the people and, perhaps even knew Soulvine Moor itself. Someone who Mother Chilton could order about, as the queen ordered Lord Robert. A man who lived in the shadow of female power. Like me.

"Roger, what are you going to do?"

"If Cecilia has gone onto Soulvine Moor, I must go after her."

"Please do not." Her voice was reasonable, but reason barely holding back a storm of emotion.

"I must."

"Why? To find a silly girl who doesn't care three pennies about you?"

"I have to go, Maggie."

The storm broke. "*Why*?" she yelled. "To be killed? To have your soul taken? Why?"

"That's a folktale. No one can take souls from the Dead."

"You don't know that!"

"Yes," I said slowly. "I do."

"It isn't—"

"Maggie," I said, taking both her hands in mine. "I'm going. If you don't want to go, then stay in the Unclaimed Lands. Go back to that farm three days' walk from here, they will take you, you're a hard worker. Here, take this." I fished out two of my remaining silver coins and held them out to her.

She threw the coins into the straw. "Keep your filthy money! But you can't go into Soulvine!"

"I can. I will."

"I won't be—"

I lost all patience. "No one asked you to be anything! Go back to that last farm! Go back to The Queendom! I don't care!"

She put her head into her hands and wept.

It was a gale of tears such as I had not imagined was in her, a deluge, nothing like the silent tears I had seen her shed for her slain brother. She wailed and sobbed—sensible, sharp tongued Maggie! I didn't put my arms around her. I sat, sullen, until the storm was over and she had grown quiet, and then I again laid the two silvers on her knee and left the goat shed. I headed east, toward the border, toward Soulvine Moor, and Cecilia.

25

A DAY'S WALK, and the land smoothed out. It didn't drop, but the ravines and hollows and mountains flattened to a vast upland plain. Nothing marked the border, but I knew I had crossed it. This was a moor, Soulvine Moor.

Almost treeless, the moor nonetheless had its own beauty. I don't know what I had expected—bare and blasted heath, maybe—but the ground was spongy, covered with moss between clumps of low, deep purple flowers. Occasionally huge outcroppings of rock thrust up from the springy peat. These outcroppings bore green moss, reminding me of the boulder in the village of Stonegreen. But there were no villages here, no cattle grazing on rich grass, no chickens or harvest faires or pretty, doomed girls like Cat Starling.

Something caught my eyes: a bit of cloth snagged on a

gorse bush. I seized it. Embroidered green silk. She had been here! I broke into a run.

A shape grew in the far distance. At first I thought it was a trick of the clear, high light. But as I drew closer, I saw it was a low hill, far off, and that smoke rose up from it. It could be a town. It could be Hygryll.

But dusk was falling, and the smoke was still far off. A cool wind began to rise. Running had exhausted me, and I could go no farther without rest. I built a small fire, to keep away beasts, in the shelter of an outcropping of stone. The peat burned with its own peculiar smoke, acrid and earthy. There was no moon, and a million stars blazed in a black sky. I had no food, but a little water was left in my water bag. I drank it, wrapped myself in my fur-lined cloak, and fell asleep.

I dreamed of my mother. *She sat in her lavender gown with a child on her lap. I was both the watcher and the child, safe and warm in my mother's arms. She sang to me softly, a tune that I heard at first without words. Then the words became clear, and Roger the Watcher's blood froze: "Die, my baby, die die, my little one, die die . . ." But Roger the child listened to the monstrous song and nestled closer, a smile on his small face and the pretty tune in his ears. "Die, my baby, die die, my little one, die die . . ."*

Hands jerked me away from her. But they were real hands, neither in the country of dreams nor the country of the Dead, and they were pulling me away from the safe warmth of the campfire. Torches sputtered and flared in the night. Men surrounded me, pulling me with rough hands, turning my face to the flickering light.

Someone gasped.

I thought it was me, so terrible did the men look. And yet there was nothing inhuman about them. They were just men, heavily bearded, dressed in tunics and boots of tanned leather. They carried small knives with handles of carved wood. And the gasp had not come from me. It came from the man holding my arm, when he gazed deep into my eyes.

"Another one!" he said. His accent was like the householders in the Unclaimed Lands, like Bat's.

"Let me see," said another voice. I struggled to be free, but the first man slipped deftly behind me and closed his arm across my neck, while twisting mine up behind me. I could not move.

"Who are you?" I said. "Do you have Lady Cecilia?"

No one answered. A much older man came forward. Between his white beard and horned hat, only his eyes showed. They were green, the startling green of new leaves. As green as Cecilia's. He studied my face for a long time, and under his gaze, strange sensations flowed through me. Not thoughts, not even emotions. It was as if a current moved in a hidden river in my mind, and all at once I remembered something non-sensical: Mrs. Humphries, in the country of the Dead, totally absorbed in watching the white stones shift shape under the flowing water of the slow river.

Finally the old man said, "No. Not another one. He has never been here before."

"But he is—"

"Yes," the old man said. "Oh, yes."

The first man let me go. And then, there in the eerie light on the ground of peat and stone, the men of Soulvine knelt to me, Roger the Fool, and bowed their heads.

❖ ❖ ❖ ❖

The Dead can sit insensible for days, years, centuries. Not so the living. I was aware of every sight, every sound, every prick of sensation on my skin as the men escorted me to Hygryll.

They talked little, and they would not answer my questions about Cecilia. They seemed to know completely who I was (which was more than I knew), so completely that it was a matter beyond discussion, as accepted as air to breathe. I was weak with hunger but afraid to ask for food. If I gave any sign of weakness, would they change from kneeling before me to killing me? Maggie had said they murdered people here to "take their souls." The belief might be folklore but the murder would be real, and I had no wish to dwell permanently in the country of the Dead. Not yet. So I walked as swiftly as they, grateful that the pace was not too quick, because of the old man. And with each step, I felt the peat springy beneath my boots, saw the torches bobbing ahead of me, smelled the sweet night air, experienced all the sensations that meant I was still alive.

Was Cecilia? Was she somewhere just ahead, in that town faint on the horizon?

And so we came to Hygryll. It lay in starlight among a group of hillocks, odd hills that were both wide and low. Then I realized that Hygryll actually lay *in* the hillocks. Each was a large round building made of, or covered with, earth and peat. A leather flap covered the doorway of the closest one. The old man pushed it aside and we entered.

I stood in a low, windowless round room of stone. A fire burned in the center, the smoke going up through a hole in the roof. The men set their torches in holders on the walls, and I saw stone benches heaped with fur blankets ringing the central space. Baskets rested under each bench. The only other furnishing was a large drum. One of my captors took the drum and went back outside. The others tossed fur blankets on the floor beside the fire.

"Sit down, *hisaf*," the old man said.

I sat. I didn't know what a *hisaf* was, or what they thought I was. I dug the nails of one hand into the palm of the other to steady myself. Outside the drum began to beat, a slow rhythm but not monotonous, a message I could not begin to decode.

One by one, men and women came into the round stone room. None was young, although none seemed as old as the green-eyed leader. I looked eagerly at each, but none was Cecilia. And yet it seemed to me that I could see something of her in this girl's chin, that youth's eyes. Each came to me, knelt, and said in their rough accents, "Welcome, *hisaf*."

More and more people, until the room was full, warm with the heat of their bodies and heavy with their silence. These were different from the people I had known all my life in The Queendom: the farmers at country faires, the innkeepers and faire folk, the soldiers and courtiers at the palace. They were different from Lord Solek's savage warriors, with their smiling and singing, their ruthless discipline. They were different even from Hartah. These sat somehow heavily, saying nothing, waiting stolidly.

They reminded me of the Dead.

When it seemed the room could hold no more, the drummer came in from outside. He put his drum on a bench and went out again. The old man stood. He spoke slowly, and despite his accent, I could understand most of his words.

"Here comes a *hisaf.* There has not been one among us for a very long time. He was not born in Soulvine, and has never been in Soulvine, but Soulvine is his home. He is welcome. Soon he will travel to—"

I didn't catch the word but, of course, he meant the country of the Dead. That was, after all, what everyone wanted from me, everywhere.

The old man finished, "But first, we will eat."

Food! My empty stomach gave a loud growl. Surely food would end my light-headedness. The stuffy room didn't help; I was shifting between a heightened, almost dizzy awareness of every detail and sudden bouts of sleepiness. In the body-packed gloom, someone threw a handful of dried leaves onto the fire and it flared. A sweet, pungent scent filled the room.

The door flap opened, letting in a brief blast of cold air. Young men and women entered, all about my age, dressed in woven white robes. Some carried big, steaming bowls, others loaves of bread. All were comely, and I looked eagerly for Cecilia. She was not among them, although the girl who came up to me had the same green eyes and brown hair. Even her smile hinted at Cecilia's. I smiled back. The young Soulviners moved around the room, offering people stew and bread. I was given only bread, and when I reached toward the stew, a girl drew my hand away gently. "You are a *hisaf.*"

That word again.

The bread tasted wonderful, sweet with honey, studded with dried fruit. The scent from the fire grew stronger as someone threw more herbs onto the coals. Drowsiness took me. Almost I dozed, but then the alert light-headedness was

back, and again everything seemed preternaturally sharp
and clear. I could have cut myself on the fur hide, the rush
torches, the very air. Dimly I realized that there was some
drug in whatever had been thrown on the fire. The young men
and women left on another blast of cold air.

It was all so strange. And if Cecilia had indeed come from
here, how much stranger the court of The Queendom must
have seemed to her! I understood a little better now her constant edge of hysteria, that urge always for more excitement,
more laughter, more dancing to banish the sense that she
would never really belong. I had never really belonged, either,
not anywhere. It made a bond between us.

Where was she? Surely they would bring her soon. . . .

The old man rose. "We are an old race, and we have drawn
strength from the souls of others. Now we will go with the
hisaf to the oldest place."

Go with me? To the country of the Dead? What did he
mean? No one could go there with me, no more than anyone
could come back with me. Or did he mean that all these men
were going to kill themselves right now?

And me, too?

Fear ran over me, banishing all drowsiness. I half stood.
But the old man stood taller than I, and the room was packed
with strong men. There was no escape. I had, as always, only
my wits. And to my drugged mind, it seemed to me that this
was a bargain: *Cross over for us, and we will give you what you ask.*

I said, "What do you wish me to learn for you in . . . in the
oldest place?"

He looked puzzled, as if my question had no meaning.
How could that be? Always those who sent me to the country

of the Dead wanted me to bring back information. Hartah, all of Hartah's desperate faire customers, Queen Caroline. But all the old man said was, "Go."

I nodded. The men closest to me drew back, as if to give me room to fall. They knew, without being told, what would happen. I drew my knife, jabbed it into my thigh, and willed myself to cross over.

Dirt in my mouth—

Worms in my eyes—

Earth imprisoning my fleshless arms and legs—

Then I was over. And not alone.

Never, never had I felt anything like this! There seemed to be a crowd of others with me, invisible but somehow *there*. They had been with me in that brief moment of death, and they were with me still, pressing like heat all around me. I screamed and ran.

A few steps, and they were gone from around me.

But now I could see them, a faint cloud of gray, like dank fog. The cloud did not move. The men of Soulvine were not present here in body, as I was. A fog could not talk to the Dead, learn from the Dead, instruct the Dead, as I had. But in some sense, the men of Soulvine were here. I had not thought such a thing possible.

But now that I was out from the midst of that fog, I could see the country of the Dead, and I saw more things I would not have thought possible.

The land that lay around me was Soulvine Moor. There were no hillock dwellings, but there was the vast, high plain dotted with outcroppings of rock, with forests and mountains in the distance. But the sky overhead flashed with lightning and crackled with thunder. The springy ground beneath my feet lurched, once so hard that I was nearly knocked over. The boulders *jiggled*, as if with energy that stone never had. And a hard wind blew, a wind that did not dissipate the patch of living fog.

Amid this chaos the Dead sat serenely, staring at a rock, a withered flower, the roiling sky. There were no drilling dead soldiers here; these men and women did not believe they were in Witchland. I had not told them so, and anyway they believed the hidden creeds of Soulvine.

Here—somewhere—was my mother.

I did not know what the people of Hygryll wanted from me. But I was here, I would take the opportunity they had handed me, and I began to search. The countryside was stretched out, as always, and the hordes of Dead scattered among the jiggling boulders. But I had time. No one could call me back to Hygryll until I chose to go. And the Dead did not wander around. I could search methodically, looking into their faces, matching them with my dim memory of my mother in her lavender gown. I began.

For what seemed like hours, I walked the plain of Soulvine Moor, struggling to stay upright on the shaking ground, ignoring the churning skies, stooping to study face after face until my knees hurt and my back ached. Still I looked. I saw old men and women, some dressed in weird clothing from long, long ago. A few of the old women looked as if they might talk to me if I roused them, but I moved on. I saw young men and women, many of the men in armor from different ages. I saw children and babies. I saw the Dead, none of whom bore signs of violence or illness, although they must have died from violence or sickness or accident or childbirth. But not, anywhere, my mother.

And then my heart stopped. I saw Cecilia.

She sat quietly, more quietly than I had ever seen her in life, amid a patch of waist-high purple flowers. Most of the flowers had withered. The wind whipped their stems and brown petals against her skin, but she didn't notice. Cecilia stared calmly at the rumbling ground.

"Cecilia!"

I stumbled over to her. She didn't look up, not even when I grabbed her, pulled her to her feet, and crushed her to me. She didn't seem to notice.

"Cecilia . . . !"

I kissed her lips, as I had longed to do for so many months. I kissed her eyes, her breast, her fragrant hair. Nothing roused her. She stood docilely, unresisting even when, in anguish and despair, I shook her hard enough to make her hair whip around her quiet face. It made no difference. She was dead.

I had failed to find her, to protect her, to keep her safe as I had once promised. Sobbing into her neck, I clutched her as she stood unknowing, all life and joy and playfulness gone. But when I finally led her forward by the hand, she walked after me, looking at nothing, or else looking at whatever the Dead see in their long trance. "Cecilia . . . I will find a way to rouse you. I *will!*"

She said nothing.

"I'm going to take you to . . . to somewhere else. Maybe once you're away from Soulvine—!"

That made no sense. The Dead of Soulvine were the same as the Dead of everywhere else. But I was beyond sense. The only thing I could think to do was to get Cecilia away from here, back to the Unclaimed Lands, back to The Queendom, where I had known her before. It was a stupid, insane idea, but because it was the only thing I could think of to do, I started to do it. I led Cecilia forward, by her limp hand.

We threaded our way among the uncaring Dead, over the quivering ground, against the strong and unearthly wind. Her hair blew loose in wild tendrils. I stumbled, and when I stumbled, Cecilia went down, too. Then I hauled her up and we kept going.

The border was not far; I had walked it just last night, with the men of Soulvine. Just before I reached it, I tripped over another stone and fell heavily on top of one of the Dead.

"Alghhh! Leave me be!"

It was an old woman. I had roused her with a sharp elbow jab to her chest. She glared at me with indignation and fury.

"I'm sorry—"

She looked closer. "What be you doing, boy? Oh! You be . . . Oh! A *hisaf*!"

She knew what I was. The next moment she looked around. Her old face, already a mass of deep wrinkles, wrinkled even more. "I . . . be dead?"

"Yes," I said. I had scrambled off her and now sat on the ground, Cecilia standing docilely above us, gazing at nothing. The old woman said, "But I cannot die."

I snapped, "Everyone dies!"

"No. I drew the strength from other souls."

All at once she, this dead woman of Soulvine, was everything that had happened to me since I entered both Soulvine Moors, the living and the dead. She was my capture by the men, she was the smoky windowless room covered with earth, as if the feasters were already in a grave. She was whatever drug had been thrown on the fire to alter my mind, sending it between drowsiness and painful sharpness. She was the green-eyed old man who made me cross over, and she was the insane beliefs that had killed Cecilia. I looked at this old woman, and hatred for all of it tore through me, bright and terrible as the lightning flashes splitting the sky. I seized her slight body and shook it like a dog with a rat.

"You 'drew no strength' from anything, you evil old woman! There is no strength to be drawn from murdering others, and there is no living forever! You are dead, dead, dead, just like all the others here! You and all the other murderers in Soulvine killed foreigners for nothing! You killed Cecilia, didn't you? And all for a stupid and pointless ceremony that gained you nothing! Nothing! Nothing! There is no way to gain anything from the souls of the Dead!"

She gazed at me without fear. She said simply, "You be wrong, boy. We can gain the strength. From the souls of the outborn. From the betrayers who left."

She moved her gaze from me to Cecilia.

"Strength from her."

26

I HAD THOUGHT I knew what horror
was. I was wrong.

The girl with the bowl of food, she of the green eyes, offering me only bread but the others stew—

I couldn't speak. Revulsion held me. But I could kill, and
I beat on the old woman with both my fists, kicked her with
my hard-toed boots, slammed her head again and again to the
ground. She looked at me with bewilderment and then with
anger, but without either pain or fear. I couldn't hurt her. She
felt alive under my hands, but she was not.

"Leave off, boy!" the old woman finally spat at me, got to
her feet, and stalked off. A few feet away she sat on a rock and
lapsed into the serene trance of the Dead.

"Cecilia," I said, seizing her hands in mine, "What they
did—I didn't get there in time to save you from—*Cecilia*—"

She could not hear me.

"They take the souls of the dead" Maggie had said to me, all those months ago, but she had not said how. And I had not believed her anyway. I was a fool. I was a hundred times a fool, and I had failed Cecilia, whom I had vowed to keep safe.

I had to get out of Soulvine Moor. I could not stay to search for my mother, I could not stay for anything, I could not stay one more second. The need to leave, *now*, was the only thing that saved me. It was something, at any rate. It was action, motion of legs and lungs and back. I grabbed Cecilia's hand and dragged her forward, both of us stumbling on the quivering ground as the lightning flashed overhead, until I was out of breath. Gasping, panting, I ran on.

But even then, I knew I could not outrun Soulvine Moor.

After I could run no longer, I walked. I walked for long, insane hours. I grew bruised from falls, dirty and sweaty and weak. Cecilia stayed unscratched, clean and unresisting, her hair fragrant as rainwater. She would walk as long as I led her, and not know she was doing it.

I kept trying to rouse her, doing everything I could. I kissed her, I shook her, and once, in frustration too great to bear, I threw her to the ground. She did not rouse. Overhead, the storm continued to threaten without ever breaking. The ground shook without ever shattering. The wind blew without ever bringing rain. And Cecilia and I walked north until I recognized the hollow and the high, sparse waterfall where Jee's hut stood in the country of the living. The cabin was not there, of course, and the hollow was littered with the usual Dead.

But it was across the border. We were out of Soulvine Moor and into the Unclaimed Lands.

Somewhere around here, in the country of the living was Maggie. Unless she had gone back to The Queendom.

I'd had an insane hope that once off Soulvine Moor, Cecilia might rouse. She did not. I was so exhausted I could barely see her. "My lady, I must sleep."

No answer.

I found us shelter from the wind beneath a stand of pine trees. Cecilia sat where I placed her. I lay on the cold and shaking ground and slept, something I had never done before in the country of the Dead. As I slipped into darkness, I was afraid that I would not wake. If you slept while here, did you die? Was the little death of sleep a passageway to the final sleep?

Almost I hoped it was. If I died, I would become like the Dead, unremembering of what had happened in Soulvine. I saw then what I had not seen before: that the lack of memory among the Dead might not be a curse but a blessing.

However, sleep didn't kill me. Eventually I woke, crying out and clutching for Cecilia. She was where I had left her. I was dizzy when I stood up.

I needed more than rest. My body here was a real body, and so was my body there. Days might have passed since I crossed over. Never had I stayed here so long, and I was weak from lack of food. The body I had left in the round, windowless room on Soulvine Moor—how long could it last without food or water? What might the men and women of Soulvine do to it if I did not return soon?

I could not rouse Cecilia, but I could talk to her, desperate talk for a desperate situation. "My lady, I have a plan."

She stared at the ground, her face expressionless.

"I am going to take you back to The Queendom. We will find a place, somewhere beautiful and far away from here. By the river, maybe, or the sea. Somewhere peaceful and sweet."

But was there anyplace like that, in this changed country of the Dead that I myself had caused to change? So much I had done wrong, so much I had failed at. But there must be someplace less damaged than the rest, some peaceful haven somewhere, and I would find it for Cecilia.

"But first," I told her, "I must leave you here and cross back over. I'm getting weak here and there. After I cross over, I'll be back at . . . at . . ." I couldn't say it aloud: *Soulvine Moor.* "Back *there*. But as soon as I can, I will leave, go to where I have left you, and cross back again. And then—"

And then what? Cecilia would still be dead. But I couldn't think about that, any more than I could think, after my sleep, about what had been done in Hygryll. There are things the mind refuses. I understood now why Maggie and the other servants would not even name Soulvine Moor.

Cecilia stared calmly at the bed of pine needles beneath us.

I couldn't leave her, not yet. So I stayed for hours more in that same mountain hollow by the little waterfall, within sight of Jee's family's Dead. I was too weak to walk. I pulled Cecilia down to me and lay with her in my arms, and I talked to her. I sang to her. I fed the pathetic illusion that she knew I was there. If I hadn't done those things, I don't think I could have gone on at all.

Finally I kissed her unresponsive lips, bit hard on my tongue, and found myself in the stone room in Hygryll.

All the men and women remained in the stone hut. For a crazy moment I thought they had all died: They sat in the unresisting trance of the Dead. But as I struggled to sit up, my head spinning, people stirred. I remembered, then, the gray fog of not-persons that had crossed over with me, and that had remained in that other Hygryll when I had fled. These monstrous people had somehow, in some thin and weird form, crossed over with me. Now they were returning to themselves, even as I was.

I loathed them. If I could have, I would have murdered them all, tortured them as Queen Caroline had once threatened to torture me.

The old man said humbly, "Thank you, *hisaf.*"

It took every ounce of strength I had left, but I staggered to my feet, made my way among the weary bodies, and pushed aside the door flap.

Spring afternoon on the moor. Sunshine washed the air with gold. The small purple flowers bloomed and birds sang and the moss was springy—and not shaking—beneath my feet. I sat, too weak to go farther, and ordered myself to not cry. *No tears.*

A girl, the same girl with green eyes and brown hair, brought me a goatskin of water and another loaf of bread. I ate it all. Then I lay facedown on the peat and slept.

For the rest of the day and all the next day, plus two nights, I did not move. The girl brought me food and water. At night someone tucked furs around me. No one tried to talk to me. The nights were sharp and cold, and someone built a fire beside me and tended it all night. I slept, and I ate, and it was the great mercy of my life—its only mercy, it seemed to me—that I did not dream.

On the third day, at dawn, I sat up, stiff in my limbs. The fire burned brightly. Beside it the old man sat on a rug of fur. He said simply, "You go now."

"Yes." I could barely get out the syllable, so great was my hatred.

"Thank you, *hisaf.*"

I swore an oath I had learned from Lord Solek, in the language I knew that the old man could not understand. Even in that, I was a coward. Was he going to try to stop me from going?

He was not. He watched as I gathered up the latest offering of bread, took the water bag, shook out my fur-lined cloak and hung it over my arm.

He said, "So it is with a *hisaf.* So it was with your father."

I whirled around so fast my boot heels tore the sod. "What do you know of my father?"

"Nothing. But he be *hisaf.* Or you could not be."

My aunt Jo had never spoken of my father. For this inhuman monster to do so was obscene. I raised my arm, but some part of my mind whispered, *If you kill him, they may not let you go. And it looks now as if they will.*

I stalked off, and no one tried to stop me. No one stopped me. I was a *hisaf,* and apparently a law unto myself.

Hah!

I trudged to the border, and over it, and through a day's walk north until in late afternoon I came again to the cabin in the hollow by the waterfall, where Cecilia waited in the country of the Dead.

And Maggie in the country of the living, furious as only Maggie could be.

"You're still here," I said stupidly.

"Where should I go?" She straightened from her task, digging spring flunter roots in a patch of sunshine, and glared at me. Jee's cabin lay beyond, looking deserted except for a thin rope of smoke coiling up against the sky. Maggie looked thinner, dirtier, but somehow less a boy in her trousers and tunic. It was her hair; it had begun to grow back in springy fair curls around her face. That face changed as she looked at me, from fury to something like fear.

"Roger?"

"Did they take you in here, then? Are you well treated?"

"Yes. Roger—what happened?"

I could only shake my head. My legs gave way suddenly and I sat abruptly on the ground. Instantly Maggie knelt beside me. "Oh—are you hurt? Wounded again? Sick?"

Wounded in my soul, sick at my heart. I could not say so. Maggie's hand on my forehead was gritty with dirt, cool of skin. She said, "You have no fever."

"No."

A long silence. Then she said, in her kind-Maggie voice, "Tell me what happened. Did you . . . did you find Cecilia?"

I heard how hard it was for her to ask that, but I had no compassion to spare for Maggie. Nor could I bring myself to tell her what had happened. I said only (and that hard enough to say), "Cecilia is dead."

"Oh!"

She was too honest to say she was sorry, and again we sat in prolonged silence. I forced myself to go on. "She was from . . . from Soulvine Moor originally—or her kin were, or something. She returned there and they killed her."

Maggie put her arms around me. I let her, but there was no comfort in her embrace. There would be no comfort for me ever again.

She seemed to know that I had said all I would say, or could. She began to talk in a low, soothing voice of earthly things, and slowly I felt her matter-of-fact voice pull me back to this world and ground me here. Did she know what she was doing? It didn't matter; the effect was the same.

"The family here took me in, yes, but as a servant rather than a guest. I help gather food, care for the babies, cook, and—I was going to say 'clean' but there is no cleaning here. Still, there's more food than you might imagine, since Tob is a good hunter. Yesterday he brought home two rabbits, and today he hunts again, hoping for a deer. Of course, in The Queendom it's illegal to shoot deer while they are in fawn, but here the law does not exist. They don't say much, any of them, and they work me much harder than is right, but I can't say they are unkind. Jee is the best of them, a curious little boy, and he will ask me questions if no one else is around. He has learned to play the willow whistle you made him, and wonderfully well. If you are hungry right now, Roger, I can bring you some of the rabbit I made today. It's flavored with wild onion and there's not much in it except rabbit and flunter, but it's hearty. There's no ale, but the water is clean and cold."

"Thank you. Rabbit would be good."

She brought it from the cabin, and Jee came back with her.

He squatted on his haunches and stared at me from wary eyes. The willow whistle hung on a strip of cloth around his neck. Some sort of paste covered the fungus on his foot—Maggie's doing, perhaps.

Jee said, "Ye went into Soulvine, despite. And saw."

"Get him away!" I screamed. "Get him away from me!"

"Jee, go into the house. Now!"

The child obeyed her, although sulkily. All at once I didn't want Maggie talking to him again. I didn't want her learning what Jee meant, didn't want her knowing what had happened to Cecilia. Let her know only that Cecilia was dead. I couldn't bear her knowing the rest.

"We're going, Maggie. Now."

"Going? Where?"

"Back to The Queendom. Or . . . or somewhere. Come." I stood, unsteady but determined, and took her hand. She must not talk to Jee, not even a word. Suddenly that seemed the most important thing in the world. In this world.

Maggie said, "I must get my cloak and the water bag."

"Leave it. The weather's warming. You can share my cloak."

Pleasure flushed her face pink, but Maggie was Maggie. "No, I should have mine. I'll just be a moment."

"No! I'll get it!" I stalked off.

The hut was dim and reeking; too many unwashed bodies had dwelt here too long. The woman sat on a rough-hewn chair, her gown open to give a baby the breast. Two smaller children played in a corner with some sticks and pebbles. Jee sat moodily poking the fire; he did not look at me as I snatched Maggie's cloak and our water bag from a hook on the wall. The cloak, too, smelled bad, and I doubted that she had been the one sleeping in it. No one spoke. I took the cloak back to Maggie, who stood uncertainly, flunter roots in her hand.

"Leave those," I said. "I have some coins left." And Maggie, too, must have the two silvers I had left her.

But it was not in Maggie's nature to leave behind anything useful, and she tucked the flunter roots into her cloak. We started back toward the cabin, and then down the rough track that seemed to be the Unclaimed Land's only road. Under the pine trees by the little waterfall, I halted.

"Roger—why, you're trembling!" Maggie said

Cecilia was here. I couldn't sense her, but she was here, in the country of the Dead that lay invisible all around us. A deep shudder ran through me. This time, however, when I felt Maggie's hand on me, I shook it off.

"I'm all right, Maggie. Just weak. We'll go another few miles and make camp, off the trail. Can you sleep without a fire tonight?"

"Of course," she said. "I have my cloak."

Maggie was never one to let pass a chance to be right.

We walked until dusk, then found a hidden thicket to stay the night. There was nothing to eat; the flunter roots could not be boiled without a fire. Stomachs alive with hunger, we rolled early into our cloaks. When I heard Maggie breathe deep and even, I crept from our thicket and made my way back up the track to the pine grove by the waterfall. There was a waxing moon and the stars shone bright in a clear sky.

In the deep shadows under the pines, I cut my arm with my little knife, and crossed over.

Cecilia sat where I had left her, gazing serenely at the same half-withered flower, oblivious of the ground shaking under her, the lightning flashing above, the stinging wind. I took her in my arms. "Cecilia, my love."

She neither resisted nor responded. A faint smile curved her rosy lips, but it was not for me. It was for whatever unknowable thoughts—if they were thoughts at all—lit the minds of the Dead. I sat there, holding my lost love, for too long. Then I stood, pulled her up with me, and began to walk.

Wherever I went in the land of the living, Cecilia must be led along the same route in the country of the Dead. That was the only way I could be sure of not losing her. I had to keep her with me, separated from me by only the dirt-and-grave-clogged passageway between my two worlds. I had to do that. I *had* to.

I'm not sure I was quite sane.

We walked for long hours through the hills and around the steep ravines of the country of the Dead, over the shaking ground and under the stormy sky. I left her in a place I would be sure to recognize even in this trackless place where countryside stretched and distorted; it was on a hilltop, beside a swift-running mountain stream. There were other Dead there, men and women dressed in strange clothing, in stranger armor, a whole crowd of motionless Dead. Once, much must have happened in the counterpart of the hilltop, on the other side. All of the Dead sat or stood or lay peacefully, and there would be no difficulty in recognizing them when I returned.

I crossed back. Then I plodded uphill, short of breath, weak with hunger, and fell asleep beside Maggie just as the sky began to lighten into dawn.

※　※　※　※

"Roger. *Roger.* We should be going."

I could not move. "Sleep," I muttered. "More sleep."

"You can't," Maggie's voice said. I hated that voice. "Someone might come after me. Or after you. We have to go."

"Can't."

"What's wrong? Are you sick?"

"Tired."

She said nothing. I opened one eye to her bleak face, and it was that bleakness that gave me strength to sit, to stand. I had brought Maggie into this. I had to get her out.

None of that was true, Maggie had brought herself into this, and I had been willing enough to abandon her to go onto Soulvine Moor, looking for Cecilia. Yet it was also true that I now felt responsible for her. Or was it? I didn't know what was true anymore. I stumbled forward.

I don't know how I kept going that morning, on no food and almost no sleep. But there came a moment when I could go no farther. The strength built up in the two days of eating outside the Soulviners' round ceremony chamber—all that strength was already gone. I sat down on the track, and I could not move.

"Roger?" Maggie said.

"I . . . can't."

"It's all right. Lean on me. Just a little farther, there you go, just get off the track into these trees . . . See, we're almost there. . . ." Encouraging, cajoling, patting me with her free hand, Maggie got me into a little copse and laid me onto the weedy ground. All morning it had been clouding, and now a light drizzle began to fall. I was glad of the rain; it hid my tears. I was at the very end of my strength and wits, the latter never much to start with. Exhausted in body and spirit, I fell asleep.

And when I woke in the evening, the rain had stopped. There was a fire. Food cooked over it. The goatskin bag swelled with water. And there was Jee, blowing softly on the whistle I had made for him.

"He brought the food," Maggie said before I could say anything, "and the ropes for snares, to catch small game. He told me it was all right to make a fire because Tob has not yet returned from his long hunt."

"Jee can't come with us."

"He says he won't go back."

"Maggie . . . consider all the . . . *no*."

Jee stared at us both, expressionless, the whistle held halfway to his lips. He cupped his other hand protectively over it.

Maggie said, all in a low rush, "I lied before, Roger. I didn't want you to know. His father beats Jee. He beats Jee's mother, too, and he would have beaten me except that he hoped I would lie with him. He stole the two silvers you left me. I was only going to wait for you another day because that's how long I thought I could hold him off, and then I was going to go and take Jee with me. He's too good for that life." Before I could answer, she raced on. "He says he won't go back. He says he'll follow us. He says he'll do that even if you beat him, too. He says . . ."

"Can't he say anything for himself?"

Jee blinked and said something. His voice was so thick, from accent or fear, that I couldn't understand the words. But they made no difference anyway.

"Maggie, his father will come after him. Maybe even after you."

"I told you, he went on a long hunt yesterday, just before you appeared. Jee says it will be at least three more days before he returns. By that time we'll be far away, if we move faster. Here, eat this, and you will feel better."

If we move faster. The only way we could move faster was if I didn't spend most of the night moving Cecilia to match our daylight travels. But Cecilia was now a night's worth of road ahead of us, and if we traveled for two days before I moved her again

"Eat!" Maggie commanded, and I ate.

"What would we *do* with Jee? Later?"

"What will we do with ourselves?" she said. To which there was no answer. But Maggie was not the girl for no answers. "How much money do you have left?"

"Why?" I countered.

"Because we could maybe start a cookshop in some village at the edge of The Queendom, where Solek's soldiers don't go. He hasn't got all that many soldiers, you know, not to post over the whole Queendom. If you have enough money left to rent some poor cottage and buy just a few vegetables to start, I could cook. Jee can hunt the meat, and we could sleep in the cottage at night. Later on, if we save money hard enough, we can add ale. Come on, Roger—*eat.*"

I ate. Her plan could work, maybe; we could survive with a small, poor cookshop far on a remote edge of The Queendom. I found I hated the idea. But why?

I didn't know. A year ago, running a cookshop in a quiet village—away from Hartah, away from danger, away from having to cross over—would have seemed the best thing that ever happened to me. But not now. Things were different. I was different.

Different how? I didn't know the answer to that, either. *"You've grown, lad. You're nearly a man,"* Mother Chilton had said. But it was not that. All boys became men. All boys—

"What is the month and day?" I asked Maggie. She was efficiently stripping the rest of the rabbit meat from the bones and wrapping it in a clean cloth. She didn't even have to ponder in order to answer me.

"Month of Sacter, tenth day."

A month before the summer solstice. Today was my birthday. I was fifteen.

For two days we walked, camping nights as the moon again waxed toward full. Once, from the crest of a wooded hill, I glimpsed soldiers in the valley below. Looking for Cecilia? They would not find her now. The thought brought no comfort.

Jee said little, but without him we would have needed to buy food at houses or inns, both giving away our presence and depleting my coins. Jee, the child, was the only one of us who could hunt, and the snares he set each night produced a steady stream of rabbits. They were spring rabbits, without much meat on their bones, but Maggie roasted them with wild roots and newly budded herbs that she picked as we walked, and by the third day, I had strength enough to go back for Cecilia. When the others slept, I crossed over.

It was a long, weary walk to the windy hilltop where I had

left Cecilia. She followed, unresisting, as I led her down the mountains. It was much more difficult here than in the land of the living because the ground shook so. Once it even *shifted*, an abrupt sideways jerk that threw us from our feet into a thicket of thorns. I rose bleeding and bruised. Cecilia rose with her green gown clean as ever, her creamy skin unscratched, her eyes blank. Above us the wind would not stop blowing, and thunder rumbled in streaky clouds.

I could not rouse Cecilia but I had roused the country of the Dead, turned it monstrous and deformed. This, too, was my fault

The next night, I walked Cecilia past the place where Maggie and Jee lay asleep. Not much farther on, the land abruptly descended. From this point on the track, I could see for miles and miles, even under the gray dimness of these thick clouds. On the horizon lay a deeper gray that, I was fairly certain, was the sea.

There was no time to lie with Cecilia in my arms, barely time for a quick embrace. I kissed her cold cheek, sat her down, and crossed back over.

Full sunlight struck my eyes, which had become accustomed to the dimness of that other country. Jee's whistle played, stopping abruptly as I rose from my bedding. And Maggie stood looking down at me with accusing eyes.

"So you're back," she said.

"I was asleep—"

She gave out a single oath, one so filthy that even Hartah had used it only rarely. Jee's whistling stopped. Maggie said without looking at him, "Go find water, Jee. *Now*. Fill the bag."

The child went, eyes wide with fear.

Maggie said, "Nothing I did could rouse you. What you . . . what you . . ." All at once her voice dropped to a whisper, and the sudden terror on her face dwarfed Jee's. "What you told me in the kitchen. It's true. Isn't it?"

I could not see anything to be gained by lying. Not anymore. Besides, she would not believe me. When Maggie made up her mind, not all of Solek's army could change it.

"Yes. It's true."

"You can . . . you can cross over to the country of the Dead."

"Yes."

"You're a witch."

"No," I said irritably. "There is no such thing as a witch. I am"—I knew only one word for it—"a *hisaf.*" *So it was with your father,* the old man's voice whispered in memory, *or you could not be.*

Maggie said, "What's a '*hisaf*'?"

"Someone who can cross over. Maggie, I did not choose this. I was born this way. But I am not a witch, and I swear to you on my mother's soul that I am no threat or danger to you. To anyone."

She considered this, her face still twisted with fear, but nonetheless considering. At that moment, fair-haired Maggie reminded me oddly of Queen Caroline, at least in expression.

"You go to her at night," she said. "You go to Lady Cecilia. That's where you went last night, isn't it? I couldn't wake you this morning but it was not illness, not even exhaustion, it was as if you . . . weren't here. Because you were not. You were with her."

"Yes." Relief washed through me. Maggie understood, she

accepted. I could stop hiding and running from her, because now at last there existed one human being who knew what I was but—unlike Hartah, unlike the queen—would not seek to use my "gift" for their own ends. Relief lightened my mind and, despite everything, I nearly laughed aloud. We were free of lies, Maggie and I, and everything from this point on would be so much simpler.

"I hate you!" Maggie screamed, and threw a roasted rabbit at me. Still warm, it burned my cheek and then fell onto the grass, a wet meaty slab. Maggie put her head in her hands and cried as if she would never stop.

"Maggie, what—what—"

"Don't touch me!" she screamed, although I hadn't tried to. "You don't understand anything! You're the stupidest man I ever met, and the most evil, and the—How can you go to her? She's dead! Dead, dead, dead, and even when she was alive, she was silly and vain and stupid—even stupider than you are! And I followed you and cooked for you and risked everything for you—don't touch me!"

"I'm not! Maggie—"

"Go! Get away from me! Or stay here with your dead and rotting whore—I don't care! I'm going!" She ran down the uneven track.

Even without much sleep, I caught her easily and pinned her arms to her sides as she tried to hit me. Her face was streaked with dirt and tears, she smelled of days of travel, and she bucked in my arms like a captured boar. Then, all at once, the bucking stopped. She threw her body against mine and kissed me hard.

So at last I knew. The suspicion I had had on the island,

the suspicion I had worked so hard to dispel, was true.

"Maggie," I gasped, when I could tear my mouth free of hers, "Maggie, no. I—"

She let me go.

We stood there for a long time, not looking at each other, under a warm noon sun. I had no idea what to say, what to do. A few moments ago I had held Cecilia in my arms—Cecilia, cool and unresponsive and unliving. Cecilia, my lady and my love. And yet I stood there on the mountain track, the land sloping away from me toward the distant sea and spring blooming all around, and my body responded to Maggie's nearness. Confusion swaddled me like dense fog.

Maggie did not seem confused. She never hesitated. Keeping her face turned away from me, she started down the track. When I ran to catch up with her, she pushed me away, hard.

I caught up with her a third time, grabbed her hand, and pressed into it three of the six silver coins I had left. Again she pushed me away. When I got back to my feet, she had marched ahead. But the coins were not among the weeds on the track; I looked. She had kept them.

Well, she had earned them.

I watched her until she was out of sight. But I didn't follow her. I couldn't—I was too weary from my night in the country of the Dead. I had to sleep now, to keep my strength up. For Cecilia.

I found a hidden thicket alive with tender green-yellow leaves, crawled under it, and fell asleep in the sweet warm sunshine.

When I woke, at dusk, I crossed over again. Jee had not returned to me, either, which did not surprise me. It was Maggie whom the child had followed, Maggie who had shown him the only real kindness the poor little rat had ever known. Maggie, who loved me, and whose love I could not return.

Why not? something whispered inside me. I silenced it. Then, still in my thicket, I crossed over. But this time, I had a desperate, hopeful, insane plan.

27

IT WAS THE PLACE I had left Cecilia
that had started me thinking. She was still there, where the
mountainside abruptly descended and the land lay spread to
the gaze for miles and miles. I had recognized part of that landscape, far below me and above the sea cliffs. It was the clearing
where the old queen's Blues had hung the yellow-haired youth,
and the second noose had dangled, awaiting me. Below the
cliff at the clearing's end was the little beach where Hartah and
his cohorts had wrecked the *Frances Ormund*.

I took Cecilia by the hand and led her toward that distant
clearing. Each time I could go no farther, I left her and returned
to my tranced body in some thicket or sheltered ditch. I slept,
bought food as I could, and grew so haggard and filthy that
farmwives began giving me bread, from pity. The moon again
passed full and began to wane. Each time, I stayed in the land

of the living only until my strength had returned, strength that I used only to walk forward to where I had left Cecilia, cross over, and journey with her again. No moon here, only the gray sky shot with flashes of lightning, the storm that never broke, the rumbling earth. Always Cecilia and I moved lower in the mountains, toward the valley where The Queendom lay.

What can I say of those days of walking with Cecilia in that country that had no days, nor any nights? The ground trembled, the sky rumbled, and she did not really know I was there. Yet that time held a wild sweetness for me. Each time I took Cecilia's hand, put my arm around her slim waist, drew her to lie next to me on the withered ground, feelings surged through me, and none of the feelings fit with any other. I could never have held this woman, a lady, in my arms under any other circumstance. I loved her. And in the round stone house on Soulvine Moor they had—

Whenever that memory assaulted me, I babbled. "Cecilia, I'm so sorry, I didn't reach you in time, I promised to keep you safe and I failed—I'll make it right for you, for us, I promise, I *promise*—" And I pressed her to me, and smelled the light flowery scent of her hair, which never changed, and a kind of despairing joy came over me, gone the next moment in a wash of black guilt.

And yet what I remember is the joy.

I don't know how many days passed this way, but eventually we reached, each in our own country, the cliff above that rocky beach.

In the land of the living, the cabin still stood, deserted and infested with spiders and mice. The yellow-haired youth's body had disappeared over the winter and spring, probably eaten by crows, but the frayed remains of the noose still swung from the oak tree. I could see the whole horrific scene as if it were not memory but solid reality before me now: Mistress Conyers in her sodden gown, torn between horror and justice. Enfield, the soldier of the Blues, itching to hang me from the same oak tree. And earlier, Hartah on the beach, his arms waving in the driving rain as the *Frances Ormund* struck the rocks and the terrified sailors staggered ashore into the wrecker's knives. My aunt Jo, shouting to me over the storm, her features blurred by flying water: *Roger! Go! Go now!* The one thing I could not see was myself, the sniveling boy who clutched at the hem of Mistress Conyers's gown and begged for his life. That boy would not come clear in my eyes, my mind, my muscles. I was no longer him.

I crossed over.

It was strange to leave a calm spring afternoon in the land of the living and arrive in storm in the country of the Dead. Always before, it had been the other way around. Now the sky here was as wild, the sea as high, the wind as howling as on the night of the wreck on the other side. The only differences were that no rain fell, and underfoot the ground shook as if it, like the *Frances Ormund*, were about to come apart.

Bat remained where I had left him all those months ago, sitting on a tree stump beside the track from cabin to cliff. He jumped up as soon as he saw me. He looked the same: flat head, big nose, greasy hair, slurred voice. A child in the tattered clothing of a shipwrecked sailor, the knife handle carved like an openmouthed fish still in his huge hand.

"Sir Witch!"

"Yes, Bat."

"Ye come for Bat!"

"Yes. Are you well?"

The simple question confused him, not unreasonably. What did "well" mean—either in Witchland or the country of the Dead? Bat said nothing. He eyed me with a mixture of fear, respect, and hope. I had no idea what time had meant to him, waiting here on his stump. Nor did I think too deeply about the matter. I was too busy pushing away pity for what I was about to do to him.

It was Bat who first showed me that the Dead do not always know they are dead. It was Bat who first showed me that, lacking this essential knowledge, a dead man could will himself to fly up the cliff face. That was what I had later used to save Cat Starling from the Blues intent on burning her. Instead I had sent her to flying away through the air, and so further convincing the soldiers that they were in Witchland. It was with Bat that I had first devised that stratagem, and it was with Bat that I was now going to test a further idea. I could not risk Cecilia for the experiment; she was too precious. First would have to come Bat.

I said, "Why do you not kneel to me, Bat? I am, after all, a lord of Witchland!"

Hastily he got down on his knees, muttering apologies I could not understand.

"I am going to release you from Witchland," I said. "Come closer."

On his knees the sailor inched toward me, until I could see the flaking white part in his greasy hair. I stepped closer, too, and our bodies touched.

"Stay completely still, Bat."

"Aye, sir." His voice trembled, but he obeyed.

I put my hands under his armpits and pulled him to me, like a child or a lover. I held him as close as possible. Then I crossed over.

Dirt in my mouth—

Worms in my eyes—

Earth imprisoning my fleshless arms and legs—

But this time it went on and on. I was trapped between, buried in the earth forever and ever and the other rotting skeleton buried with me, screaming in my nonexistent mind. . . . It went on and on and ON—

And then I was through, gasping on the fresh spring grass, and Bat sprawled at my feet, howling and terrified and alive.

It took me a long time to recover my breathing, and Bat even longer. Gasping, wheezing, the only thing I could think of was Hygryll. The men and women in the round stone room covered with earth, who had followed me—the *hisaf*—in a gray fog to the country of the Dead. They had existed in the country of the Dead only as wisps, but then, they had not actually been dead. Bat, on the other hand, had been fully in the country of the Dead, and he was now fully here.

But was he?

As soon as I had recovered enough breath and wits—*dirt in my mouth, worms in my eyes, earth imprisoning my fleshless arms and legs*—I examined Bat. He had jumped up and stood gazing wildly around, panting in great sobs, waving his knife as he looked for something to attack. I said imperiously, "It's all right, Bat. I have brought you back from Witchland. Kneel!"

He did, looking glad to have a clear order. Orders were something he could understand. Nothing else was. On his knees, he raised his face to mine. "Bat be saved from Witchland?"

"Yes. *Yes.*"

What convinced me was his smell, so strong that I had to back away. In the country of the Dead, odors were not strong. I'd had to hold Cecilia in my arms before I could catch the fragrance of her hair. But now Bat reeked of sweat, of piss, of dirt, of the sea salt dried on his tattered clothes. He was solidly *here*, embodied in the land of the living. He was alive, and he stunk to the sky.

All at once my legs gave way and I had to sit on the ground. *Bat was alive.* And I had done this. I, Roger, the *hisaf.*

"*So it is with a* hisaf. *So it was with your father. Or you could not be.*"

Could my father have done this? Perhaps this was what Soulviners meant by "living forever"—that the Dead could be brought back to life. If my father had not left us before she died, could he have brought back my mother? And if he could have done so, and had chosen not to . . .

Hatred exploded in me for this unknown man, and it was the hatred that finished me. Too much, too fast. Maggie, Bat, Cecilia . . . I burst into uncontrollable tears. Shamed, I rolled over, hid my face, and sobbed like the six-year-old I had been when my mother died. I cried and I could not stop crying.

Bat tended me. Murmuring nonwords, he covered me with my own cloak. He found water somewhere and fetched me a few drops in a young leaf. He sat beside me, a huge and stinking man, and patted my shoulder until the paroxysm passed.

"All right, Bat. All right. I am fine."

"Sir Witch," he slurred. "Ye fine?"

"I'm fine."

"Ye fine?"

"I'm *fine*. Thank you, Bat." Now another problem occurred to me—what was I going to do with him? "Do you
know where you are?"

He gestured toward the beach and said simply, "Sea."

Of course. He was a sailor. Wherever the sea was, Bat was
at home. He would accompany me to where the coastline flattened, find a ship to sign on to, and resume the life that Hartah had stolen from him—and all without ever realizing that
same life had ever been extinguished. If he spoke of Witchland, mumbled of it in his feebleminded slur, no one would
believe him.

Suddenly I wanted him gone. I wanted to be alone, to cross
over and bring back Cecilia. Nothing else mattered, nothing
else filled my mind. . . .

Why did *hisafs* not always bring back their beloved Dead?

The question needled me, and would not go away. One
possible answer: *Perhaps they did*. But if so, why had my father
not retrieved my mother? That brought me back to my oldest
questions: Why had he left her in the first place, and what had
happened in Hygryll to cause her death? If I had found her in
the country of the Dead on Soulvine Moor, I could have asked
her these questions. But I had not found her, and I was not
returning to Soulvine Moor just now. I had to bring Cecilia
back over.

But first I had to rest. Everything in me had gone weak,
used up with unnatural effort. From my pocket I fished out

six pennies and gave them to Bat. "Here, find a cottage—or someplace—and buy bread and cheese. Bring it here." Almost before the words were out, I was asleep, lying there on the track between the cliff and the clearing where the yellow-haired youth had died kicking the empty air. I must have slept around the clock, because when I woke, it was once again afternoon, the sun blazing through the half-unfurled leaves, and Bat was gone.

A loaf of bread, already crawling with ants, lay on the ground beside me. The mountain water bag was full. Bat had thought of my needs before running away from Sir Witch, who might at any moment send him back to Witchland. I didn't blame him. I brushed the ants off the bread and ate half, forcing myself to save the rest.

Next I found a stream, bathed, and washed my clothes, longing for the strong soap in Joan Campford's laundry. The stream, racing down from the mountains, was so cold that I yelled when I first ducked into it and the icy water hit my privates. Nonetheless, I scrubbed myself with gravel until my skin was red. I wanted to be clean for Cecilia.

When I and my clothes had been dried by the bright sun, I ran my fingers through my hair to comb it and shaved my face with my little knife, a business that resulted in blood I then had to stanch. When all this was done, I picked a bouquet of spring flowers and a clutch of wild strawberries, made my way back to the cabin in the clearing, and crossed over.

For a long, terrible moment, I thought I was back at the wreck of the *Frances Ormund*.

Rain lashed my face, so hard and thick that I could barely see. Rain, in the country of the Dead! The storm blew me sideways, off my feet. I picked myself up and groped my way across the clearing, calling, "Cecilia! Cecilia!"

A tree crashed to the ground, barely missing me. *I couldn't find her.* The howling wind whipped my cries away as soon as I uttered them—and why was I calling her anyway? She could not hear me, could not respond. . . . Where was she? What if the country had stretched, as it so often did, so that the clearing was not here but miles away . . . in all this pelting rain. . . . *Crack!* Lightning hit the ground a league away, deafening me.

But this storm, like those on the other side, waxed and waned. During a lull, when the wind and rain abated a little and the lightning moved off, I could see better. The Dead were still here, sitting or lying on the trembling ground, serene amid the chaos. I stumbled over an old man, who roused enough to snap something at me in an unknown tongue before returning to his eerie calm. *There, ahead* . . . But no, it was another girl in green, sitting beside a small child. . . .

Then I saw her.

Cecilia sat tranquilly at the very edge of the cliff above the sea. She could not have moved, so the cliff must have. Her green dress was as sodden as Mistress Conyers's had once been, as sodden as if Cecilia herself had been in a shipwreck. Her rich hair whipped in the wind, long tendrils writhing like snakes. I lurched forward and snatched her back from the cliff edge.

The sea below boiled. The rocks were hidden by surf and spray and rain. If there were figures on the beach below—

Hartah, Captain James Conyers, my aunt Jo—I could not see them. I did not want to see them. I clamped my teeth hard enough on my tongue to bring blood, and with Cecilia in my arms, I crossed back over.

Another crossing that seemed to go on and on, with dirt filling my mouth and the sockets of my eyes, so that I could not see the soft body I clung to so ferociously. But it was not soft, it had turned as skeletal and bony as my own, both of us were trapped here forever in the grave—

Then I was over, and she was with me.

We lay at the top of the cliff above the beach, in a tangle of spring meadow. Cecilia went very still in my arms. Her green eyes blinked: once, twice. A puzzled expression settled on her features like mist on glass. Then she jumped up, looked around, and began to scream.

"Cecilia, no! It's all right, it's all right! Cecilia!"

She stopped screaming but backed away from me, clutching her wet skirts, her eyes wide and terrified. "Roger! Where am I? What have you done?"

And then I saw the moment that memory returned in full. What was she seeing? The round stone house in Hygryll—or had her murder happened somewhere else? How had they killed her? Had she—

Cecilia's eyes rolled back in her head and she crumpled to the ground.

I wasn't in time to catch her. She fell facedown, and for a long terrible moment I thought I had lost her again. But she breathed. I rolled her over, laid her head on my lap, and rubbed her cheeks. She opened her eyes.

"Roger?" she said, so softly that I barely heard her. And then, "I died."

I couldn't bear the look in her eyes. Pain, bewilderment—she was like a small animal that cruel boys had hurt for sport, a kitten mewling and beseeching *Make it stop, oh please make it stop.* . . .

I lied to her. "It was a dream, my lady. You had a bad dream."

For just a moment some hardness flashed over her face, some glint of a Cecilia I had never seen. Then she seized what I had offered her.

"Yes, of course, a dream! A silly, bad dream—silly me! And we're here because we . . . because we . . ." Frantically she glanced around the clearing. "A picnic! Yes, of course, I remember now, a picnic—a bad dream—really, Roger, what are you doing? You must not hold me like that! Bad Roger!" She sprang up and took a few steps away from me, hysteria and flirtation mixed horribly on her face.

"Cecilia—"

"You must remember who you are!" She wagged a finger at me, stopped the gesture halfway. Again panic twisted her face, and again she drove it away. With coquettishness, with silliness, with sheer granite will. "You must remember who I am! Even on a picnic, it is not fit for you to touch me, you know!"

An enchanting smile, covering terror.

"My lady—"

"I think I want to go on now, Roger. Oh, flowers! Are those for me? Oh, you naughty boy—you shouldn't! But so pretty . . ."

She snatched up the bouquet I had picked for her and held them to the sodden bosom of her gown, smiling at me like a desperate child.

A thought came to me, unbidden and unwelcome: *Maggie would have had the courage to face the truth.*

But Maggie had never died, had never gone to that other country. And if Cecilia was a child, she was still as enchanting as ever. It was easy—so easy!—to slip back into being the humble servant I had been with her at the palace. I knelt and said, "The flowers are nowhere near as lovely as you, my lady."

She laughed. "Oh, you do overstep yourself! What a courtier you are becoming, Roger. . . . I think perhaps I am hungry, after all. What a lovely spot for a picnic, here above that sweet sea!"

I gave her what I had: stale bread and wild strawberries. I spread my cloak for her on the grass. I passed her the water bag. She prattled on, covering the strangeness of the situation with silly chatter, the only defense she had. I saw that she would never speak of what had happened to her on Soulvine Moor, nor of the weirdness of finding herself alone in the far reaches of The Queendom with me. Whatever poverty or hardship we endured, she would laugh and prattle and say nothing and rely on me utterly to take care of her, pretending that this was normal because anything else was too terrible to think about.

A child.

When the lovely spring afternoon faded, I led her—without taking her hand this time—away from the cliff. The sun had dried both our clothes. We slept in the clearing, she wrapped without comment in my cloak, I shivering on the bare ground. The cloak would have held two, but to Cecilia that was not possible. My dreams in that cursed place were terrible, but I didn't mention them. Not then, not ever. Cecilia would not have known how to comfort me—even if comfort were possible, for one who had done, seen, been such as I.

28

IT IS ONE THING to love a child in a palace, surrounded by comfort. It is another to travel with a child through rough country, trying desperately to think where to go next.

I had three silvers and seventeen pennies left of Mother Chilton's coins. Maggie's scheme of renting a cottage for a cookhouse might still be possible if I could earn just a little more money. However, I had trouble visualizing Cecilia as a serving maid. And then I had to spend two silvers on a donkey, because Cecilia could not walk very far or very long. I had to leave her hidden in a grove of trees to find somewhere to buy this donkey, and the balky animal cost me more time and money than I had expected. By the time I returned, Cecilia was curled into a quivering ball of terror in my cloak. It took me hours to soothe her.

Not that she complained. She never did that. But she was so weak, so helpless, that I spent most of my last coins on better food, on a few nights' lodgings in an inn, on an enameled comb for her hair and on a cup so that she would not have to drink from the water bag. Now there was not enough money left to rent any cottage, anywhere.

We had come to the edge of The Queendom, where the seacoast began to turn flatter and fishing villages appeared. Perhaps I could find work here? But I knew nothing about fishing, and how would I explain Cecilia? If she would just stay quiet, I might have passed her off as my sister, or even my wife. But Cecilia never stayed quiet. A constant, desperate chatter was how she kept memory outside the fortifications of her mind, and her chatter marked her every second as court bred.

"My lady," I said, "who was Hemfree?"

An expression of complete terror crossed her face, quick as lightning before it vanished. Had I, in fact, seen that expression at all? Her words came too swiftly and too loud. "I don't remember that name."

I believed her. Her memory had immediately discarded what she could not bear to remember. I tried something easier.

"When did you first come to the palace?"

"Oh, very young, a little girl! The queen herself sent for me. She knew my mother." But then something must have threatened to breach her mind, because she threw me a roguish, desperate smile and laughed. "Why, Roger, are you questioning my age? Don't you know that you must never ask a lady how old she is? Shame on you, naughty fool!"

If she had had a fan, she would have rapped me with it. But

I was no longer a fool. I turned away, but then she surprised me.

"I could get work as a lady's maid, I think," she said.

I jerked my head around to gaze at her. "A lady's maid . . . but, my lady, there are no courtiers here!"

"Oh, not here, not in a fishing village!" She laughed. "Somewhere nicer . . . or, at least, I think I could, somewhere there is a need for . . ." A puzzled expression crossed her face. Memory, or at least realization, was very close. She pushed it away.

"Oh, silly me! Of course I couldn't do that! Really . . . you shouldn't let me prattle on so, you naughty boy!"

I said quietly, "I am not a boy, Lady Cecilia."

And she was not a lady. Not here, in this place. I could not take her anywhere that she could be a lady, because Queen Caroline would have her arrested, tortured, killed, even though Lord Solek still held the power at court; I had learned as much from overheard scraps of conversations as I bought Cecilia her comb, her food, her cup, her lodging, her donkey.

Probably Cecilia and I shouldn't even stay in these remote fishing villages for very long. Fishing villages brought travelers, both by sea and land, and travelers carried news to and fro. Inevitably, someone would notice the presence of a woman as beautiful and out of place as Cecilia. That traveler would mention it elsewhere, and the news would make its slow way to the queen.

So what was I going to do with my lady, my love? How were we going to live?

If we went farther inland, not toward Glory but rather to remote villages where the chance of recognition was less and the old ways were stronger, I could do as Hartah had done. I could sell my services as a visitor to the Dead, bringing false comfort at the summer faires that would soon begin. My flesh writhed at the very idea. However, I could come up with no other. The money was gone, all but a few pennies. We had to eat.

Moodily I walked along the rocky beach, watching the boats set out in the early morning for a day of fishing. I had left Cecilia asleep in the village's only inn, a snug wooden structure with a taproom below and two tiny bedchambers above, both smelling of fish. Cecilia and I shared one of the chambers, she on the bed and I on the floor. The innkeeper's wife, who ran the place while he fished, was much younger than he, and frankly curious about Cecilia and me. But she asked nothing, and she ran her little establishment with a tolerant competence that reminded me of Maggie.

The fishing boats disappeared over the horizon. A dazzling yellow sun broke into view. I skipped a few desultory stones over the calm water, then went back to the inn and paid a precious penny for a mug of ale in the taproom. It was too early for ale, but I needed it. The innkeeper's wife served me and then sat, unbidden, at the trestle table opposite me and rested her rough-skinned elbows on the table.

"Where do ye come from, friend?"

"Many places," I said wearily. I was in no mood for conversation.

"And where do ye go?"

I didn't answer.

She studied me. Not pretty, she nonetheless had a healthy vitality, like a strong, young animal. A lively intelligence glittered in her small brown eyes. "I ask because we don't be having many visitors here, this early in the year. No, not many visitors."

"I imagine not." *Go away.*

"I wonder if ye knew the one here but two days ago."

"No."

"That's too bad. I maun return his things to somebody."

I sipped my ale, looking pointedly away. I had had enough of chattering women.

"Lookee, I show ye." She jumped up, opened a chest in a corner of the room, and pulled out a pile of rags. On top of them lay a knife with a curved blade and a wooden handle carved like an openmouthed fish.

Bat's knife.

"Ah, I see ye know him, after all," the woman said.

"Maybe. What . . . what happened to him?"

She shrugged. "No one knows. He took a room upstairs— the room ye be having now—waiting for the fleet to put back in. Out several days, they was that time. And he din't come down. I finally unlocked the door and he be gone, with his clothes on the bed and his knife under the pillow."

"His . . . clothes?"

"Aye. His only clothes, and naught else be stolen. The door was still barred on the *inside*, but he was just gone. Somebody still owes me his reckoning. But—how did he leave all naked, and for where?"

How indeed? All at once the taproom seemed cold, the ale tasteless. My stomach clenched. Bat would not have fitted through the upstairs chamber's one window. The woman had just said the door was barred from the inside. So how—

If Bat had somehow gone back to the country of the Dead,

or had been—what?—snatched back there?—then his clothes and knife would have gone with him. The Dead did not cross over naked.

No, the whole story was a lie, a ruse to get a stranger to pay what Bat owed her. My stomach unknotted and I said, "I knew the man only in passing. I owe you nothing." But I stood, my ale unfinished, and climbed the stairs to the bedchamber.

Cecilia still lay asleep. I stared at the tiny window, the thick door. *Two days ago*, the woman had said. Bat would then have been back in the land of the living for . . . how many days? I had lost track of time.

Maggie would have known.

But it didn't really matter. I sat in the chamber's one chair and watched Cecilia. She had washed her hair last night, a laborsome business involving cans of hot water that I had lugged up the stairs, and now her tresses spilled clean and shining over the rough cotton pillow. The lids of her eyes fluttered, translucent, faintly blue. Her strong young throat lay exposed, and the top of one small breast above her shift. I had never touched that breast, never would touch it. Cecilia looked more beautiful than I had ever seen her, and completely desirable. But I felt no desire.

What am I going to do with you?

I watched her for a long time. Then I woke her; I had no money to pay for this chamber for another night. I could barely pay for breakfast. She didn't grumble, but her lovely face was sullen. I went to the stable yard and watered and hitched the donkey, who did grumble. After a silent, meager breakfast, I helped Cecilia mount and we started inland, traveling on a track overgrown with weeds, toward what the innkeeper's wife said was the nearest farm village, several leagues to the northwest. The village was called Ablington. They were having a faire.

"Roger, you're not listening to me!"

I was not. But I was thinking of her, and also of Bat. I believed the barmaid had been lying, but her story would not leave my mind. I had crossed over with Cecilia the day after I had brought Bat back. Was that significant? What *had* happened to Bat?

"You're not listening!"

"I'm sorry, my lady."

I plodded on, toward the spring faire. Where I would set Cecilia in some cool grove on the far length on some village green, and I would try to do what I had vowed to never do again. To be what Hartah had made me: a liar and cheater in two countries, here and there.

But Cecilia and I never reached Ablington. We never reached anywhere at all.

It happened at dusk of the next day, beside a campfire over which I toasted the last of our bread, wishing instead for one of Jee's rabbits. Cecilia sat combing her hair with the enameled comb I had bought her. The hair rippled and shone in the firelight, glinting in a hundred shades of honey, cinnamon, gold, bronze, amber, copper, chestnut. The dusk deepened her green eyes to the color of emeralds.

"Why are you looking at me that way?" A tiny half smile at the corners of her mouth.

"Because you are the most beautiful thing I have ever seen, Cecilia."

"You should call me 'my lady.' Don't become so familiar, Roger!"

She was not teasing. Firelight flickered over the enameled comb that I could not afford, the bread of which I would give her more than half although my stomach rumbled with hunger, my fur-lined cloak that she sat upon. There rose in me an anger I had not known I felt, had not known I could feel. Not toward her.

I said, my voice low and careful, "Perhaps the circumstances justify my familiarity."

"No," she said with sweet certainty. "No, that cannot be, Roger. You know that. I am a lady, and you are the queen's fool."

"Out here there is no queen, and no fool." *And you are alive only because of me.* Made alive, kept alive.

"But they exist, nonetheless." She shook her head at me playfully, and her beautiful hair shimmered and danced.

"But things can change."

"Why should they? Anyway, *that* doesn't change."

"Why not? Why are differences in rank never to change, when all else has changed in The Queendom, in the world? Why is that one thing the same?"

"It just is." She smiled at me. The smile of a lady toward a fool. She resumed her combing.

I said, "No."

"No what?"

"No, *Cecilia*."

Her smile disappeared. She said coldly, "You are impertinent, Roger. Apologize at once."

I got to my feet. Why? I had no idea. But I stood looking down at her in the firelight: Cecilia, beautiful and dirty, exasperating and desired, enchanting and stupid. I said, "I will not apologize."

Her face began to break up. For the briefest part of a moment I thought my words had caused it, thought that her features were merely sliding into anger. Not so.

"Cecilia!"

The skin softened on her face, even as her mouth opened in a silent scream. Her nose, mouth, cheeks turned black—*rotting*. Her body slumped sideways as the bones crumbled. A terrible stink rose on the night air. Her eyes melted, staring at me—and then, just like that, nothing remained but a heap of clothing.

"Cecilia! My lady!" I threw myself on the ground, rooting through her cloak and her gown and even her shoes as though I could find some trace of her. There was nothing, not even a strand of her hair. Not even a fingernail. All gone with her— *where?*

I howled like an animal but I didn't hesitate. The fire was nearest; I used the fire. Thrusting my left hand into the embers, still crying her name, I crossed over.

She was not there.

The sky snapped and growled and poured rain in the country of the Dead; the ground shook; the Dead sat tranquilly amid the chaos. But I could not find Cecilia. I roused old women and shook them, demanding information. I tripped over rocks and bushes and bodies, searching in the windy storm. I looked in thickets, in groves, behind boulders, in ravines where the rock walls threatened to tumble down and crush me. She was not there.

Not in the land of the living, not in the country of the Dead.

"He was just gone," the innkeeper's wife had said of Bat.

I threw back my head and howled at the stormy sky. I beat my hands on a boulder. To have brought her back, to have come so close to saving her! And now—

You could not cheat death. Not for more than a few weeks, which was no time at all. Death always won.

It was morning in The Queendom when I finally crossed back over, a morning fresh with birdsong and golden dawn. The fire was long since out. I sat beside it, too anguished to tend my burned hand, too anguished even to sob.

Cecilia was gone. She no longer existed, not anywhere, in any form. Whatever the serene Dead were waiting for, there in that other country, Cecilia would never find it. This, then, was why *hisafs* did not cross over with their beloved Dead. By bringing my lady over, I had killed her more completely than the people of Soulvine Moor ever did. I, Roger Kilbourne, *hisaf.*

Roger Kilbourne, the fool to end all fools.

29

I HAD NOT KNOWN before that there are fates worse than dying, or places worse than the country of the Dead. I knew it now.

It's hard for me to remember what I did that morning of despair, or that afternoon, or that evening. I know I didn't eat, because there was no food. I know I didn't tend to my burned hand because my charred fingers blackened and blistered. The blisters burst, spilling pus and blood. Did I sit beside the dead fire, numb for all those long hours? Did I scream or cry? I don't know, and may never know. Those hours are as lost to me as was Cecilia, gone to the same dark place of anguish and utter hopelessness.

I had killed her. I must die for it.

That was the thought that brought me back to life, if life it could be called. I seized on the thought as if it would save me. I could die, and then in the country of the Dead I would come to oblivion. I would be like the rest of the Dead, serene and mindless and free of pain, sitting tranquilly on the tranquil land—

Except that the country of the Dead was no longer tranquil. And not all the Dead waited in mindless serenity. The soldiers of the Blues. Cat Starling. They had not believed they were dead, and so retained their former selves. And I, too, knew that death was not final, that it was possible to move and think and live on the far side of the grave. So would I, a *hisaf*, remain aware—perhaps for all eternity?

An eternity of remembering what I had done to Cecilia. Remembering here, or remembering there. No difference.

Death was not a way out. Not for me.

Nonetheless, I think I might have done it, just to do something, *anything*, to bring change to the despair that felt unendurable. My bowels and liver crawled in my body, seeking to get away from me. My eyes burned, hating that they must live in my head. My hands, burned and unburned, clenched into fists and yearned to beat my body into unconsciousness. I could not hold together, could not live with myself, could not endure another moment of this horror—

But the moment existed.

Then another moment.

And another—

"Roger!"

And another—

"Roger! Stop!"

And another. I attacked my enemy, who was myself. I flailed at him, charged him with deadly accuracy—

A kick to my burned hand sent me yowling in pain. My other hand dropped the knife. It was snatched from the ashes of the fire. A smell, another kick, and then a voice, young and high and frightened—

"Roger! Stop! What be ye doing?"

Jee. His skinny form emerged from the evening gloom—how had it become evening again?—at a wary distance. When I went motionless, he crept closer.

"What be ye doing? Stop that!"

"Jee—"

"Aye. I could hear ye a mile off."

"Joe."

"Aye! Yer hand—"

All at once my burned hand seemed on fire. The pain was unendurable, and I think it was the pain that brought me back to myself. There was no room for anything but the searing pain, and for what Jee said next.

He squatted beside me, peering into my face, his own in the same anguish as mine. I had not known before that the anguish of others can push away our own. Not completely—never that—but enough to survive. Jee was in that kind of anguish. Had he not been, I doubt he could have reached me at all.

"It be Maggie," he said. "Soldiers took her."

"Took her? What soldiers? Took her where?"

"Rough, big soldiers," the child said, and began to cry. "With green clothes and feathers. They took her."

The queen's soldiers.

"They be looking for you," Jee sobbed. "They asked Maggie about *you*. They took her to the whore-queen!"

Me. Maggie had been taken because the queen was looking for Roger Kilbourne, or Lord Solek was, but I guessed it was Her Grace. A desperate Queen Caroline had discovered that I had left the capital with Maggie, and the queen needed me back to use in whatever was her latest desperate bid for power. And once the queen decided she needed something, nothing stopped her from getting it. If Maggie didn't tell the queen where she had last seen me, Queen Caroline would torture it out of her. Even if Maggie did tell, she might be tortured for anything else she might know.

Maggie, in those instruments of pain I had heard existed but had never allowed myself to imagine before. I imagined them now. The rack, the nails, the red-hot pincers . . .

Slowly I sat up. Maggie, who had always been a better friend to me than I deserved. I would not fail yet another person. "Stop crying," I ordered Jee, more harshly than one should speak to a grieving child. "Stop it right now. We have to go after Maggie."

The child, raised with a brutal father in the wild Un-claimed Lands, stopped crying at once. His eyes grew huge in his tear-tracked face. "G-go after Maggie? We uns?"

"Yes," I said grimly. "We uns." Everything that had happened in the last months shifted in my mind, assuming different shapes. Like stones seen under water, shifting with the changing light.

"H-how?"

"Leave that to me."

Jee would not have been Jee if he had done that. "Ye have a plan?"

"Yes," I said, astonished to realize that yes, I did have a

plan. And I was willing to bring down two realms to carry it out.

I washed and bandaged my hand. Jee had brought food, and we ate it for strength. We traveled by night, both of us on Cecilia's donkey, Jee's slight body adding nearly nothing to the weight the beast had to carry. Still, the donkey, being a donkey, protested and refused to move. I beat it with a stick, whacking it across the nose so hard that it startled and then trotted forward. I had never beaten an animal before in my life

We traveled all night. The moon waned, but the stars were clear and high. Because I didn't know this countryside, I was forced to backtrack to the fishing village where I had heard about Bat and then take the coastal road toward the mouth of the River Thymar. In this flatter, softer countryside, the road was well marked. The donkey plodded on, hour after hour. Jee clung to my waist, saying nothing. Perhaps he was asleep. So long as he did not fall off, I looked no closer.

My burned hand sent shards of pain through me. The pain formed its own rhythm, out of time with the clopping of the donkey, and both a dissonance with the images that flashed through my brain, one at a time, with all the power and brilliance and horror of lightning that strikes and chars living flesh.

Cecilia, combing her hair in the firelight just before—

Maggie, kneading bread and smiling at me in the servants' kitchen—

My mother in her lavender gown—

Cecilia—

Maggie—

Slowly something happened to my pain. My pain, my grief, my guilt. They stopped sending me images and instead shrank inside me, growing hard and sharp, until they settled in my chest like the spiked metal ball at the end of a soldier's mace. I knew that spiked ball would be there forever. But the shrinking let me go on, and I had a battle to wage.

We traveled by night, hid and slept by day, pushed the poor donkey to its full protesting endurance. On this well-traveled road we didn't dare risk a fire, but nights were warmer now. Without Jee, I could not have done this. There was no time to stop and snare rabbits that we couldn't have cooked anyway, but he knew how to spot buried nuts, spring berries, edible roots. I was always hungry. But finally I was here, in a grove of trees just downriver from the capital. I could see the tower where I had stood with the queen, where I had been locked out all night after my "fit."

"Maggie be there?" Jee said.

"Yes."

"In that high place?"

"No." Maggie would be below, in the dungeons I had never seen, the dungeons where advisors and captains loyal to the old queen had been put to death. Or would Queen Caroline keep Maggie with her in her apartments, trying to beguile her into cooperation, as she had once beguiled me? That's what I was hoping: that Maggie was still alive, and whole. That if Queen Caroline had tried wiles and sweet promises instead of torture, Maggie would know enough to play along.

Jee slipped his grimy little hand into mine, a thing he had never done before. He must be terrified, to seek such reassurance now. He said, "Ye look and look . . ."

He was right. I had been staring at Glory as if truly ensorcelled. Sunrise, just a few minutes ago, had left long fingers of gold and pink in the eastern sky, curving around the horizon toward the island as if to embrace it. The summer morning was soft-aired, filled with fresh flowers and the trills of birds.

". . . and ye look, but we maun *do*."

"You're right, Jee. We maun do." I tore my eyes from the tower, knelt, and put both hands on his bony shoulders. "Listen to me. Listen very carefully. I am going to do things that will look strange to you, and frightening. All these things will help save Maggie. No matter what I do, you must stay where I put you. You must not run away, or scream, or do anything but stay very still. Do you understand?"

"To help save Maggie," Jee said, seizing on the only words that mattered to him.

"You *must* stay hidden, Jee. And silent."

"To help save Maggie."

He trusted me utterly—maybe because he had no other choice. I knew how that felt. I put him in a dense nest of bushes half a mile from the river, where he couldn't be seen. Then I squeezed my burned and bandaged left hand with my right, cried out, and willed myself to cross over.

The storm had, if anything, worsened. Lightning flashed over a river racing with evil-smelling rapids. The ground shook so much that it was hard to stand. Rain pelted my face, soaking through my clothing in just a few moments. I had appeared not far from a captain of the Blues, now on this side of the river.

He rushed over and cried, "The witch's captive! You're back, boy! What news?"

I nodded. It was difficult to hear over the howling wind. Through the rain I saw that the army of dead Blues had swelled to many hundreds. Had Lord Solek killed all those who tried to rebel? It seemed likely, but I had no time to ask.

"The best news," I shouted, my mouth close to the captain's ear, "we are going back to The Queendom, to fight and take back our own."

His face, streaked with rain, lit up. His lips pulled back, baring his teeth, and I almost quailed before the fierce light of hatred in his eyes.

"Aye, and in good time, boy! We have our battle plan at the ready. But something has happened to Witchland." He waved his arm to indicate the entire landscape: roiling, quaking, stormy, withered, coming apart.

He did not know that what had happened to Witchland was me. I had interfered with the order of life and death. I had convinced large numbers of dead men that they were not really dead, preventing them from lapsing into the serene, waiting trance that was their natural next state. Worse, I had brought back Bat and then Cecilia to the land of the living. A *hisaf* could make that journey, but no one else should. Taking away the subjects of the country of the Dead had torn the very fabric of that sacred place.

And now I was going to rend it far more.

"Captain, bring all your men together in"—I grasped at a military term I had heard from the queen—"in close formation. Here, now. We must act quickly!"

"You have the amulet?"

Amulet? What amulet? Then I remembered: the amulet I had invented to save Cat Starling, the amulets I had told the soldiers to make. The captain's hung from a string around his neck. Lies upon lies—and all necessary.

"Yes," I cried over the wind, "I bring you the amulet, and much more besides! Order your men!"

It took only a few shouts before several hundred men lined up in neat rows on the shaking earth. I said, "They must hold onto each other around the waists, all together."

The captain stared at me. Something flared in his eyes, anger mixed with sudden doubt. "These be soldiers, boy! They can't fight like that!"

"Not to fight. To leave Witchland. Or else they must stay here forever."

He stared at me, and for a moment I thought he would not do it. But then he turned and gave the order. His dumbfounded men glanced at each other, scowled, muttered, glared at me— and one by one, each put his arms around the men closest to him, so that the neat rows became a vast, uncomfortable mass. "You too!" I said to the captain.

"No."

I shrugged. "Then stay here."

He swore and grabbed the man closest to him. I clutched at the captain, bit my tongue so hard that blood spurted into my mouth, and willed myself to cross over, with several hundred men fastened to me like weights, or leeches.

The sky shrieked and split open. Something roared out of the rent, something bright and terrible, just as the ground gave way beneath my feet. I was falling, I was being devoured by the bright monstrosity from the sky. . . .

And then I was in the grave, that in-between place of dirt in my mouth and worms in my eyes, of being imprisoned alive in my rotted body. . . . And this time, *I could not get free.* The weight of hundreds of men pulled at me, clawing and dragging. We would all stay here forever, trapped, neither dead nor alive. An eternity of the grave, with worms in my eyes and cold on my bones—

Oh, what had I done?

And still the earth held us, the barrier between the land of the living and the country of the Dead. The grave held my rotting flesh until death—the real thing—would have been welcome. I would just give up, surrender, let myself die—

No. I must save Maggie.

With a last tremendous effort of will, I concentrated upon reaching Maggie again. *Cross over, cross over, cross over for Maggie—*

I tumbled onto the grass beside the placid blue river.

Desperately I gasped for air, the soldiers heaving and moaning beside me. Sensation returned: my arms were flesh, not rotting bones; my eyes brought vision, not maggots; my tongue could move, unchoked by fetid dirt. The weight of men no longer dragged at me. Had there been, it seemed to me now, even one more of them, I could not have made that horrendous crossing. Never again!

When I could stand, I looked for Jee, who was not there. He had stayed hidden as I'd instructed. As soon as he recovered, the captain barked orders and soon the army was in battle formation, swords drawn, shield at the ready. He spared me one glance.

"Thank you, boy. Now go."

A single look can change worlds. Before the captain's gaze returned to his men, it had gone from gratitude to distaste to dislike. I had brought him out of Witchland, but that meant I was a witch, and witches were to be feared. To be hunted. To be burned. The contradiction was more than the captain wanted to navigate. He wanted me away, so that he would not have to sail those treacherous moral seas.

I faded back into the trees until my back was at the thicket where Jee lay hidden. The Blues began to march toward the river. From below me came a sound. It might have been Jee, breathing "Roger?" It might have been the rustle of a rabbit, or a fox. Or a rat.

All these soldiers would die a second time. Like Bat's and Cecilia's, their renewed lives were illusory, temporary. In a fortnight— I had finally worked out in my mind the passage of days—they would disappear, burned horribly out of existence like wood that becomes smoke, dissipating on the very air. You could not make smoke become the oak or maple or cherry wood it had once been. And yet if I had not done this monstrous thing, what would have become of these soldiers in the country of the Dead? They did not inhabit it as the rest of the Dead did, waiting in tranced calmness. Already they were restless, bored, desperate. What would they have become in ten years' time, twenty years, a century? I had seen Dead dressed in garments much more old-fashioned than that. And meanwhile, the presence of the restless soldiers, neither dead nor alive, would have gone on destroying that peaceful countryside beyond the grave.

My doing, all my doing. But this was no worse than the rest. As the soldiers marched toward the capital, I followed.

Green archers appeared on the ramparts of the city. Then Lord Solek's warriors, each man with *gun*. I could see them clearly in the soft summer air, looking like tiny toys carved for children.

"Flank right!" the captain of the advancing Blues called. A detachment of soldiers, shields raised, moved off to the right. They would attack from the east, I guessed. The main army marched forward.

Now I could hear the iron gates to the city being lowered, loud scrapings of metal on metal in the winches. How would this army get into Glory? Not even battering rams would budge those gates. And all the soldiers were doing was marching straight forward. The Blues were locked out and outnumbered, both. And here, unlike in the country of the Dead, they could not just fly through the air.

"Boots off!" the captain called.

Boots off? Each man propped his shield on the ground in front of him and kicked off his boots. The heavy boots, I could see now, had been left unlaced.

The main section of the army broke ranks and ran, following the small section that had deflected to the east. All at once I understood the captain's plan. The east side of the city was where the laundry rooms and baths were located. These had been built out over the river, to let clean water flow in and out again, carrying soap and dirt downriver toward the sea. This was the first part of the palace I had ever seen, scrubbing myself clean after Kit Beale had brought me here. The attacking soldiers, who were from the palace and knew it as well as they knew their own bodies, would swim under the walls and take the palace from the inside. Solek had positioned his warriors and the queen's Greens on the walls, for a more conventional attack. It would take them time to reach the laundry and the baths, with their myriad rooms for each rank of palace dweller, the laundries meanwhile defended only by the unarmed women who served there.

A cry of rage from the castle, and the Green archers let fly their arrows. The warriors fired their *guns*. And a silence fell, a silence of profound astonishment, of frightened disbelief. I stopped in the act of picking up a discarded boot, my body crouched, as silent as everyone else. We had all been struck dumb.

The arrows and the *bullets* from the *guns* had all passed through the bodies of the advancing Blues as if those bodies were so much air.

My mind raced. Had Cecilia—had I ever seen her fall, seen her injured, seen her so much as stub her toe on an inn table? No. I had not. I guarded her, hovered over her, kept her safe. Her body had been solid, yes, after I brought her back, but then it had been solid in the country of the Dead, too, as she lay unknowing in my arms. The bodies of the dead Blues had been solid, and of the dead warriors, and I had seen them fight with each other and the weapons pass right through them. But that had been on the other side! Here, the Blues were alive again. . . .

No. They were still dead. They were just dead here, in The Queendom of the living.

A great shout went up from the advancing army, part fear and part amazement. Then a din, a babble. I was too far behind to hear the words, but I could see the waving arms, the spreading grins. I did catch a word, then: *witch*. And half the men turned to where I stood.

Some actually knelt—in the middle of battle, with arrows and *bullets* passing through them! *"The amulet and more,"* I had said to the Blue captain. They thought this was the "more." I had made them invincible.

Then the moment of silence, of obeisance in the midst of a lethal rain of weapons, was over. The Blues continued their dash toward the island. Some threw away their shields. Greens and warriors disappeared from the walls of the palace, presumably rushing down the stone staircases toward the east wall. I picked up a shield and followed slowly. Unlike the Blues, my body was vulnerable. I could be pierced. I could still die. By the time I reached the river, only a few Blues remained by it, as rear guards. I saw two of them running their swords through each other again and again, in wonderment that each time there was no blood, no pain, no death.

They saw me and fell to their knees. I couldn't bear to look at them. *You will be gone before the full moon.*

There were more soldiers at the river's edge across from the laundries. They, too, fell on their knees to me. I walked past them, dropped the heavy shield and the boot—why was I carrying one boot? When had I picked it up? I couldn't remember—and unlaced my own boots. These soldiers, so wrongly on their knees to the boy they wrongly perceived as their savior, either were guards or else they could not swim. I could swim. I waded into the wide, placid river and swam toward the palace.

Near the island, I swam through soap, which drifted outward in slow pools, stinging my eyes. Nearer still, and a thin river of red trickled toward me from under the palace wall. I thought at first it was dye, like the red dye on the face of Lord

Solek's singer, or the yellow dye on mine when I had been the queen's fool. Then the trickle of red spread and widened and I saw that it was blood. I thrashed through the viscous, oily water, which grew redder and soapier when I swam beneath the wall and into the washroom where once, in another life, I had been a laundress. I swam into the laundry through a pool of soap scum and blood.

Joan Campford was there, standing in a corner, three girls cowering behind her. The girls shrieked as I broke the surface of the water, but Joan recognized me, even through a coating of soapy blood.

"Roger! What . . . how . . ."

In six strides I reached her and took her by the shoulders. Around me lay the bodies of Greens and of savage warriors, slumped by the wash pots and dye vats, floating in the water, sprawled by the fire pits. One man had landed, or been thrown, halfway into a pit and the smell of burning flesh reeked through the hot air. "Joan! Where is Maggie?"

It was the only time I ever saw Joan Campford speechless.

"Maggie Hawthorne! The kitchen maid I left the palace with—I know you heard!" *Everyone always knows everything*, Maggie had said to me once. The servant-gossip spiderweb of information.

Joan said in a low voice—as if we might be overheard by the dead!—"With the queen. The queen keeps her . . ."

Not in the dungeons. Not tortured. Not yet.

I tore from the room, running through the familiar courtyards. Bodies lay everywhere, none of them Blues. All were Greens or savage warriors, and many more savages than Greens. Had many of the Greens turned traitor at the last minute, joined the Blues against the queen? It seemed possible. Many of these men on opposite sides were kin to each other, like Maggie and her late brother, Richard, and none had any love for Lord Solek.

As I neared the queen's chamber, I came on the last of the fighting. A detachment of warriors stood in the courtyard, blocking the immense, carved wooden door to the presence chamber. Among them was Lord Solek.

"For Queen Eleanor!" cried a captain of the Blues. He and his men, six strong to Solek's ten, were covered with drying soap scum. They charged forward with drawn swords. The warriors raised their *guns* and fired. The *bullets* went through the Blues and rang on the stone walls, a clear hard sound like the toll of a bell. A *bullet* bounced off the wall and past my ear, and I jumped behind the low wall of an ornamental fountain. Water spouted into the air and down on my head, washing away some of the soapy blood.

The savages fought hard. They fired their *guns*; their leather shields parried the sword thrusts; in close combat their curved short knives found the bodies of Blues again and again. Each time the knife sank into flesh and came out again, leaving no wound. The Blues grinned or yelled, and the warriors screamed back in their guttural language. The warriors landed more fatal blows, but "fatal" no longer had the same meaning. All meaning had been altered, as if the universe were no more than a tunic or gown that hadn't fit properly. One by one the savage warriors fell, pierced by a sword in the belly or eyes or neck. A Blue clubbed a twitching warrior with the butt of the man's own *gun*. Finally only Lord Solek was left alive, and I realized that the Blue captain must have planned it this way, giving his men orders to neither maim nor kill the usurper.

"My lord," the captain sneered. His six men, all uninjured, stood grouped to one side. From the rest of the palace came shouts as the invincible soldiers cut down the rest of the savage army.

Lord Solek ignored the captain. The chieftain's eyes found me, half hidden by the fountain wall. I stood. I would not cower under that contemptuous gaze.

Solek said something in his own language. Then, shockingly, he laughed. He said, "Boy . . . you win, yes? You win. Boy." Again that laugh. Quicker than the eye could follow, he raised his short knife and hurled it, without the usual spin or change in stance. The knife flew threw the air.

I had raised my right arm—why? To ward off his gaze? To strike him from a distance of twenty feet away? There was sense to the action, but my arm was already coming up as he made his quick throw, and the knife found its mark on the wrist of my right hand. My blood spurted red onto the green tiles of the queen's courtyard.

Dirt in my mouth, worms in my eyes . . . *I was crossing over*. Without will, without planning—that had not happened since my infancy. Was my mind, then, slipping backward— was I dying? *No no no no* some part of my mind shrieked. I did not want to die, not now, it was not time . . . Maggie! I wanted Maggie. More than anything in my life, I wanted to live long enough to rescue Maggie. That was my only hope for redemption.

I braced myself to land, dying, amid the shaking ground and stormy sky that I had created in the country of the Dead. Instead, I found myself in a landscape as tranquil and calm as the first time I had seen it. No storms, no earthquakes, no sky rent open by a terrible golden light that devoured . . . what? Nothing here was devoured; all was serene and unchanging, populated by the serene and unchanging Dead. The poison had been expelled from this place, the wrongness made right when the Blue army had taken away their unbelief, their in-between state of being dead without accepting death. Tranquility restored when I no longer meddled.

Why? How?

On the grass a little way from me, I saw Queen Eleanor, hands folded on her lap, sitting peacefully in the place where her throne room had been. Her blank eyes didn't see me, or anything.

Then I was back in the courtyard of the palace, falling onto the tiles even as I saw Lord Solek's body slashed to bloody ribbons by six swords at once, his blood flowing out toward the queen's door.

The Blues pounded on the door. It did not give, but the intricate green tiles with which it was decorated shattered and fell in shards. Two more Blues entered the courtyard, dragging a man I recognized: the palace steward. His keys hung from his belt.

A sword at his throat, the steward fumbled with his keys. Then his silhouette dissolved, he vanished, and I stood in the tranquil country of the Dead, but only for a moment. Again I lay in the courtyard, unable to will myself to move.

Unable to will. The savage knives, Lady Margaret had once said, were tipped with poison. Some poisons affected the mind as well as the body. Was that why I had twice been flung without volition into the country of the Dead? Even as this, my last coherent thought, came to me, my vision wavered again. Cleared, wavered, cleared one last moment.

The steward had found his key. But even before he could insert it into the lock, the door was flung open from within. Queen Caroline walked out of the chamber, her head held high. She wore the Crown of Glory, and in every line of her proud bearing was her refusal to be dragged into captivity but rather a choice to walk toward it. As she stepped over Lord Solek's body, the jewels of her great crown caught the sunlight and blazed.

And from behind her rushed Maggie, unharmed, the last thing I saw before all went dark.

30

I WOKE IN the last place I expected to be. Not in the bloody courtyard, not in the country of the Dead, not in a dungeon, not with Maggie. I woke in a small stone room I had never seen before. I was lying on a bed of straw. I was alone.

After all the killing and screaming, silence.

After dazzling spring sunlight and the bright flash of swords, pale gray light from a single tiny window in the wooden door.

After blood and torn flesh, some of it mine, poultices lay wrapped around my right hand. No pain there, only a soothing coolness. The stone room smelled of medicinal herbs and apples.

I struggled to sit up, but this was a mistake because it sent sharp pain stinging through my arm, worse when I gasped aloud. Slowly I lowered myself back onto the straw, surveying the room with only gentle, cautious turnings of my head.

The chamber was even smaller than I had thought, barely long enough for me to lie full-length, and even narrower in width. The stone floor was clean, and so was the straw I rested on, although fresh rat droppings lay against the opposite wall. The wall beside me felt cool and faintly damp; I was underground. There were no apples.

"Hello?" I called, but no one answered. I wasn't sure I wanted anyone to answer. Was this a dungeon? I decided not. Dungeons must smell of piss, of blood, of despair. These stone walls bore no stains and no marks scratched by desperate men. So, not a dungeon.

I held my left hand, the one I had burned in the campfire, close to my face and studied it. The burn was nearly healed. A patch of new skin grew pinkly amid the rougher skin around it. However, my veins and bones stood out sharply, and my wrist looked thin and weak. I had lain here for quite a while— but then why wasn't I hungry or thirsty? And where was I?

Time passed. Once or twice I called out again, but no one came.

Finally, for something to do, I unwrapped the bandages and poultices from my right hand, to see how much damage had been done by the knife Lord Solek had thrown in the last moments of his life. Poison on the blade had affected my will, I remembered that well enough, but my mind seemed all right now. What of my hand? The last of the bandages pulled free.

My hand was gone.

I stared at the stump of my wrist, where the skin had been wrapped and sewed as if I were not a man but a bolt of cloth. At the seam, my flesh puffed red and swollen, but without the black-green rot that kills. I had no fingers. No fingers, no fingernails, no palm, nothing to grasp a knife or a cup or a woman's breast, *nothing*—

I screamed, and kept on screaming until the door opened and a voice said severely, "Hush, Roger. Stop that right now."

It was Mother Chilton.

She stood filling the doorway, blocking the sudden increase of light, until she knelt beside me. The door remained open. Her young-old face bent above me, her colorless eyes reflecting all light. "You must stay quiet."

"My hand—"

"I know. I am sorry. If I hadn't cut it off, you would have died."

"*You* cut it off? But—"

"It was necessary. The black rot had set in. Lord Solek's knife was tipped with poison."

"But—my *hand*!" It came out a wail, like a six-year-old, and she frowned.

"It was only a hand," she said severely. "You have another."

The callousness and indifference of this shocked me into silence. *Only a hand?*

"Think what else you are, Roger. Now be quiet. I must go." She rose.

"No, wait! Where am I? What is happening? Maggie—"

Her face softened. "Good. You can think about someone else. I'll send Maggie to you. But be quiet until then."

"Wait!"

But she did not. Instead she said something that made no sense: "You must never seek your mother." The door closed, and I heard a key turn in the lock.

My mother? What did the witch know of my mother?

Witch. The word had come unbidden to my mind. But yes, of course, Mother Chilton was that thing I had never thought really existed: a witch. She did not have to be a witch to make a milady posset, or perhaps even to cut off my hand and drug me so that I felt no pain, but to know about my mother? And other things she had said to me, half forgotten but surely they had shown more knowledge than a natural person should possess?

"Sometimes none of us knows where we are. Or who."

"You've already caused enough disturbance in the country of the Dead."

"You know much, even more than you think, but you don't know what Cecilia truly is . . . a pretty, empty-headed tinderbox that will ignite all."

And so Cecilia had, and then had died for it. Twice. I stared at the stump of my wrist, and I waited for Maggie, and when she did not come, I went on staring at my maimed arm and silently, as quiet as instructed, I wept.

When Maggie did come, hours later, I had done weeping. Mother Chilton's drugs, whatever they were, had begun to wear off. The stump that was my wrist had begun to throb, not yet a great deal but with promise of real pain to come. I was hungry, and I needed to piss. Carefully I got myself to my feet and used a corner of the room in near darkness, covering the wetness with a little straw. The last of the light faded. I sat in complete darkness, back against the stone wall, cradling my bandaged stump in my good right hand. Finally, a lifetime later, the lock rattled. The door opened.

"Roger?"

Maggie came in with a lantern and a small sack. The lantern threw shadows on the stone wall, on the wooden door, on her. She wore a clean gown of rough blue wool. *Blue.* I had never seen her in anything but green. Her fair hair, short from its cutting when she pretended to be my brother, curled around her face. A huge bruise, turning all the colors of vegetables, swelled the left side of her face and closed her left eye.

"You're hurt!" I said, the first thing that came to me. "Were you—"

"Tortured? No. This is nothing." She set the lantern on the floor and sat beside my straw. The one gray eye that I could see studied me anxiously. "Does your hand hurt?"

"No," I said bitterly. "It can't hurt because it's not there anymore."

"Then does your wrist hurt?"

"Yes."

"I brought you some more medicine from Mother Chilton. And some food." She opened her sack.

I knocked it away, impatient with her stupidity. "I don't care about food! What happened? That cursed witch cut off my hand—"

"She's not a witch," Maggie said levelly. "Only you are."

That stopped me. Maggie stared at me with all her old disapproving severity, now decorated with fear—for this I had brought back an army from the country of the Dead? To rescue this girl, so that she could call me a witch?

"I'm not a witch. I'm a *hisaf*."

She didn't know the word, of course. The fear of me was still on her, but she continued. "Mother Chilton saved your life."

"Maybe I wish she hadn't."

"Don't talk like that. Did you . . . Roger, was it you who . . . ?"

I said simply, "Yes. To all of it."

She twisted her hands—her two good hands—together tightly in her lap, and forced herself to go on. "You brought the Blues back from Witchland? That's what the soldiers are saying. 'Witchland,' where the queen had sent them, when she made it look as if they had died. What we buried—the bodies—they were all false, sorcerous illusion. But not Richard. He was not among the Blues who returned from . . . from there." Her voice broke. "The soldiers say the queen is a witch and you are, too, but—

"You what?" I was not going to make this easy for her. She was not making it easy for me.

The hands on her lap tightened until all blood left them. "I . . . I don't think you brought them back from Witchland. I think you . . . you told me once in the kitchen, that you can . . . I think you brought them all back from the country of the Dead."

There. She had said it. I peered at her in the uneven lantern light. Bright light one place, deep shadows a few inches over. The unbruised half of Maggie's face had gone as bloodless as her hands. But she had said it. Disapproval, yes, but also courage. Maggie had always had enough courage for an entire troop of soldiers.

"Yes," I said. "I brought the Blues back from the country of the Dead."

"And . . . and Cecilia, too?"

"No." I would never tell anyone what had happened to Cecilia. The spiked metal ball twisted in my chest. Those spikes were ones that no Mother Chilton could ever cut out.

Maggie looked away from me. Abruptly she said, "Jee is safe."

I had forgotten Jee. *"You can think about someone else,"* Mother Chilton had said, but I had not thought of Jee.

Maggie continued, "He's with me in the kitchen. He sleeps under the trestle table where you used to sleep."

I said, "It was Jee who told me that the soldiers had taken you. They were looking for me?"

"Yes. The queen wanted you. I don't know why, but if you are . . . that thing that you said, the thing that can travel to the country of the Dead . . ."

"I am, yes. But I am not a witch."

She nodded, not looking at me. Her hands loosened a little in her lap. I said, "How did you get that bruise on your face?"

"A Green hit me when I tried to escape. They had orders to bring me back to the palace if they couldn't find you. The queen knew that we left together. I told her that you had left to find your mother—"

"My mother!"

"You called out for her in your sleep, several times, when we were traveling to the Unclaimed Lands."

Calling out in troubled sleep—my old problem, the thing that had brought me to Queen Caroline's attention in the first place. But that answered one question: how Mother Chilton had heard of my mother. Maggie must have told her. I wanted to believe that, just as I wanted to believe that Mother Chilton was no more than a skilled healer. I was determined to believe those things.

Maggie continued, "The queen kept me with her, trying to

make me an ally. When she saw that wasn't going to succeed, she threatened me with torture, but she hadn't yet sent me to the dungeon when your Blues arrived. I think she still had hopes of bribing me with silk dresses and green jewels." Maggie's voice turned scornful.

"Does your face hurt?"

"Not anymore. It just looks terrible." She tried to smile, and failed.

"Where is the queen now?"

"In the dungeon. The Blues hold the castle." She touched her blue gown. I saw now that it had been hastily and imperfectly dyed. Green streaks showed at the hem and neckline.

I said, "When I woke here, I thought maybe *I* was in a dungeon."

She did smile then. "You're in the dried apple cellar, Roger."

"I don't see any apples."

"It's *early summer*. The apples were all eaten over the winter. That's what you do with dried apples."

"How did I get here?"

"Joan Campford and I brought you."

"Joan? The laundress? She was there?"

"She followed you from the laundry. She and I dragged you away. Your hand . . . There was so much blood . . . anyway. A Blue captain told us to take you away and hide you. I didn't understand—I still don't. You brought back the Blues, and yet there was such hatred for you on his face!"

I understood. In a soldier, fear comes out as hatred, and debt as permission to escape.

Maggie went on. "You were covered with blood and *soap*.

Everything was chaos, with fighting in the palace and killing and shouting. . . ." She shuddered. "Anyway, Joan and I dragged you by your feet, with my petticoat wrapped bloody around your hand, to the kitchens, and then to this apple cellar. I ran for Mother Chilton."

"And the queen? They will . . ." But I already knew the answer.

"They will burn her as a witch."

"When?"

"Tomorrow at noon. Roger—is she a witch?"

"I don't know. The queen recognized . . . she could tell . . . Do you think Mother Chilton a witch?"

"No!" Maggie looked shocked. "She's a healer, is all. And she's a *good* person. Not like the queen!"

The queen was not a good person. She had poisoned her mother, murdered her enemies, threatened helpless servants like Maggie and me with torture. But I also remembered the queen's small and unnecessary kindnesses to me, remembered her desperation to protect The Queendom for little Princess Stephanie, remembered the way her dramatic beauty glowed in candlelight. She would end her life as she lived it, a riddle to all. At noon tomorrow that beauty would blacken in the fire as Cecilia had—

Don't think that.

"What is it?" Maggie's frightened voice said. "For a minute you looked so—does your hand hurt more?"

"No."

She was silent a long moment. Then she said, "Your look changed when I mentioned the queen. Did you love her so very much?"

"Love the *queen*?"

"Don't be stupid," Maggie said sharply. "The queen is a monster. I meant Lady Cecilia. Did you love her so very much?"

"Yes," I said. "Once."

"Once? You don't love her now?"

"She's dead."

"That isn't what I asked. My mother loved my father long after he died, right up until she went to her own grave. Do you love Cecilia still?"

Maggie was relentless. Moreover, she lacked experience. She didn't know that love could be overwhelmed by guilt, by anger, by childish selfishness on the part of the beloved—and yet still exist, like embers in an ash box. The embers no longer glow, no longer give off warmth. But they still smolder, and I have known them to eat through the wood of an ash box and set an entire cottage ablaze, destroying it utterly. I had not lied to Maggie. I had loved Cecilia once, and that fire was gone. But neither had I told the entire truth.

Hadn't told it, couldn't tell it. Maggie could not understand. There were only two people in the entire world who might understand. One was Mother Chilton. The other, I suspected but could not know, was my mother.

I tried again. "Maggie, I didn't bring an army here to retake the palace because of Cecilia."

Her mouth, pink beneath the huge swollen bruise on her face, frowned slightly. "You didn't?"

"No."

"I thought you wanted revenge for . . . for her. For Cecilia."

"No. I came for you. Because Jee told me you'd been taken."

Maggie went utterly still. For a moment I thought she had ceased to breathe, but then I saw her lashes, downcast, quiver. They cast shadows on the firelit skin of her unbruised cheek. When she opened her eyes, they were blurred under a sheen of tears. She leaned forward and laid her lips on mine.

The kiss was light and sweet, and it stopped time.

But when her lips pressed harder and her hand caressed my hip, I pushed her gently away. "You don't understand. I have only one hand!"

"So?"

"So," I said, bitterness rushing back into me, "I am unmanned."

Maggie gave a low, throaty chuckle, so surprising that I glared at her in indignation. Didn't she understand what it meant to lose a hand? Was she that insensitive? I was no longer an able-bodied man, no longer *whole*—

"It's not your hand I'm interested in, Roger." She laid her own hand on me, and instantly my body responded. I was shocked by how instantly, just as shocked as I was by her bawdiness—Maggie!

She wasn't careful about undressing me, or slow. When she pulled her blue gown over her head and undid the strings of her shift, I gasped. She was so beautiful in her nakedness.

The rest of the morning is both a blur and, at the same time, so sharply carved in memory that I can still see every curve of Maggie's body, can still feel every sensation in my own. We maneuvered around my bandaged stump and her bruised face, tender with each other, full of hesitation and joy. Together we went into that secret dark place of sweetness, and when it was over, we fell asleep in each other's arms, on the clean straw, in the tiny stone room that smelled of vanished apples.

I woke first. Maggie slept on, the good side of her face hidden in the good side of my arm. The lantern had gone out, but light came through the small, high window. We had slept the entire night; it was way past dawn. Bright sunlight beyond the barred window, and Maggie had said that the queen would burn at noon.

Staring at the stone ceiling above me, I realized what criti cal piece of information I did not possess.

"Maggie, wake up!"

She murmured and burrowed deeper into my side. For a moment the movement of her against my skin ignited me, but there was no time.

"Maggie! What day is this?"

Her head rose from the straw, eyes bleary, silky curls tousled on her forehead. "Day?"

"Yes! What day? How long have I been in this apple cellar?"

She looked bewildered, then affronted. "Why?"

"How long?"

"A fortnight. Mother Chilton gave you drugs, and I fed you while you raved. All nonsense syllables but it was terrible to listen to. A horrible song: 'Die, my baby. Die, die, my little one——'"

A fortnight. And I had brought the Blues back over in mid-morning. So now——

"Why was she allowed to live so long?" All those enraged soldiers I had brought back from death, eager for Her Grace's blood—

Maggie's lip curled. "The captain held her alive. He tried to force her to bring the old queen back from Witchland. But she would not, or so I was told. And then——"

"Get dressed. Right away. And help me!" I was fumbling at my tunic, my trousers. With every motion, pain throbbed in the stump of my severed wrist. My face must have frightened Maggie.

"Why? Roger—what is it?"

"Something is going to happen. Listen to me—those Greens who have rejoined the Blue army, are some of them secretly still loyal to the queen?"

Her lip curled. "Of course. Not all men are for sale, bend as they will to temporary power."

"We have to leave the palace. Leave Glory entirely, right now!"

"But . . . but why? You aren't strong enough to leave anything!"

That seemed true. The lovemaking, on top of amputation and drugs, had weakened me. It was difficult to even tug on my trousers with my good hand. But I did it.

Maggie said, "Nobody knows you're here. The fighting is over. Later, when you're stronger and the queen is dead, Joan and I can——"

"The fighting is not over!"

She stared at me, half dressed and, for Maggie, unusually slow of wits. Perhaps our love-making had affected her, too.

"*The fighting is not over,*" I repeated. "We have only a few hours to escape. When the Greens take back the throne, they will tear down every stone in the palace looking for me, who led the army that killed their queen."

"Greens take back the *throne*? Very soon the queen will be dead—"

"But Princess Stephanie will not. The Greens will seek to put her on the throne and rule through her. They—"

"Roger, the Greens left alive are not enough to defeat the Blues you brought back over!"

"I don't have time to explain—help me, Maggie! Get dressed! We must leave now, while everyone will be watching the queen's death."

"You're not making sense! The Blue army can't be defeated, can't be . . . they're . . . if what you told me . . ."

I stood shakily, my good hand braced against the wall. The ceiling of the apple cellar was so low that I had to duck my head, although Maggie, shorter than I, could stand upright. "Believe me about this, Maggie! Where in the palace are we? Below the kitchens?"

For a long moment she chewed her bottom lip, and then gave way. "We're not below the kitchens. The river comes too close there to dig underground storage rooms. We're farther inside the palace, under liveried servants' quarters. There's a passage with a door into the couriers' quarters."

One of the thrilling secret passages I had never found, except that it was not secret, and now I felt not thrills but fear. If we were caught . . .

If we were caught by Greens, torture to a slow death would surely follow. The Blues merely wanted to be rid of me, but the Greens . . . I imagined what could lie ahead for us, and a shudder convulsed my entire body. If it came to that, would I be able to escape the horrible pain by taking Maggie with me to the country of the Dead, as I had taken Cecilia out of it? But the price that Cecilia had paid . . .

We moved out of the apple cellar and along the passage. It was faced with rough-hewn stone, although the smell was of damp earth. The ceiling was even lower than the apple bin, so that I had to walk at a half crouch, and the passage was so narrow we went single file, Maggie in the lead with her lantern. I felt dizzy and my hand ached. Every few yards I leaned briefly against the damp stone to rest. Then I forced myself on.

Other doors, all closed, lined the passage. I smelled grain and wine. Then the tunnel turned, widened, and ended in a low room with a rough wooden staircase going up to a trapdoor. The room was littered with leather boots, crops, and a girl's soiled shift. Straw, nowhere near as clean as that in my apple cellar, heaped in one corner.

Maggie said over her shoulder, "The couriers and kitchen girls sometimes use this room to . . . well, you know."

I didn't ask if she had ever *you-knowed* here. I knew that she had not. I was her first, as she was mine.

"Roger, let me go ahead. To see who is about."

I nodded. She set down the lantern, climbed the steps, raised the trapdoor, and disappeared.

Alone, I collapsed onto the straw pallet. My breath came heavy and hard. The stump of my wrist began to hurt in earnest, but it was nothing compared to the panic in my mind. How could we get away? And if we escaped the palace, where could we go?

My whole life, it seemed, had consisted of desperate

attempts to escape. From Hartah, from the soldiers who had hung the yellow-haired ship wrecker, from the queen, from Lord Solek's men, from Hygryll. I longed for a place from which I did not have to escape, a place of peace and tranquility. . . .

But the only place like that was the country of the Dead.

I had just hauled myself to my feet and turned to climb the staircase when the trapdoor opened. Maggie's face loomed above me, her fair hair falling into her bruised eye. The other half of her face was white with shock.

"They are leading the queen to the fire now!" she said, "And Lord Robert rides hard on the horizon with an army!"

31

LORD ROBERT HOPEWELL.

I had forgotten him . . . and why not? The last time I had seen him had been months ago, kicking the door of the queen's privy chamber and bellowing, "Caroline!" And then the queen, barefoot and wearing nothing but a short shift, her dark hair tumbled loose around her bare shoulders, Lord Solek just gone from her bedchamber. Now Lord Robert was riding at the head of an army he had raised somehow, among farmers or outlanders or who-knows-what.

Did he love her still, love the queen's changeable and ruthless and tender beauty, even though she had betrayed him with the savage chieftain? He must still love her, to challenge the old queen's Blues for his Caroline's life.

I looked up at Maggie and said urgently, "Where are they burning the queen?"

"Just beyond the west bridge! So that the villagers can see . . . The pyre is ready. Come up quickly, there was no one around except the servant who told me, and he's gone to— come!"

But I was not able to climb the steps. Maggie had to descend and then half carry me up. She was incredibly strong. We emerged into a room crowded with pallets, saddles, items of Blue livery, bridles, and the strong odor of horsey men who lived close together. Across the chamber, a door opened onto the bright sunshine of a courtyard. I hobbled toward it, Maggie half supporting me.

"Which the quickest way out of the palace?"

"Through the kitchens."

My old route out to the city. After we left the couriers' courtyard, I recognized the route. But we couldn't follow it. All at once people filled the corridors, servants with ashen faces, even a few soldiers shouting orders. Maggie dragged me into a side passage to avoid being seen, and then into another, and all the time we were moving farther away from the kitchens. Finally we found ourselves in the courtyard outside the throne room. And there stood Mother Chilton.

"Roger," she said quietly. She looked not at all surprised to see me. "You should not be up and about."

"The Blues—" I gasped. "The battle—"

"Yes. I know. Come with me."

"I can't . . . I must . . ."

"You must get away. Yes. But not quite yet."

She walked to my other side, away from Maggie, who shrank back slightly but did not let go of my weight. However, Mother Chilton shifted most of my bulk to herself. She, too, was much stronger than she looked. Was that true of all women, then?

No. Not of Cecilia.

"Drink this," Mother Chilton said, and I did.

Its effect was immediate. Not only did my pain vanish, but strength surged through me. I stood straight, feeling my knees steady, my head lose its dizziness, my eyesight sharpen.

"It won't last long, and you will pay for it later," Mother Chilton said. "One always pays, for everything. But you already know that better than most, Roger Kilbourne, do you not? Come."

Then the great throne room doors were unlocked and open—how?—and we three walked through them. Something more had happened to my brain. Now it floated just above my head, keen-eyed but somehow unable to formulate a clear thought. I was seeing everything, understanding all, but deciding nothing. Mother Chilton decided, and I was content to obey without question, a plant turning its leaves to follow the sun. The drink . . . there had been something in the drink. . . .

Mother Chilton led us through the vast throne room, once filled with Lord Solek's men chanting his glory as he arrived in The Queendom:

Ay-la ay-la mechel ah!
Ay-la ay-la mechel ah!
Bee-la kor-so tarel ah!
Ay-la ay-la mechel ah!

It seemed as if the savage song still filled my ears, although now the huge room was silent and empty. Mother Chilton stopped at a blank expanse of wall to the left of the dais and moved her fingers quickly over sections of stone: first high, then low, then high again. The stone swung open.

Maggie gasped, but I merely smiled. It was all right. Everything was all right since I drank the potion, and of course there were secret passages in the palace, hadn't I always known so? Silly Maggie, to wonder at that. The queen had needed . . . What had the queen needed? There was something I was supposed to remember about the queen, but I could not. All I remembered was her bending over me in the candlelight of her privy chamber, more beautiful than any painting, handing me a goblet of wine. I was just back from a journey. What journey? Where? I couldn't seem to remember, and yet it was there, somewhere in my mind . . . something about the queen. . . .

"Come," Mother Chilton said.

Another staircase. But I climbed this one easily, without strain. And why not? Everything was all right, had always been all right, always would be all right. I smiled at Maggie, who glared at me, and I climbed the spiral stairs. A tower . . . we were ascending a tower. Glory had only one tower. Hadn't I climbed it before? I couldn't quite remember.

Another door, and we stood in a tiny room, smaller than even the apple cellar. Two vertical slits in the stone wall let in daylight. Mother Chilton closed the door behind her.

Maggie said fiercely, "What potion did you give him?"

"That's not for you to question, child," Mother Chilton said.

"If you knew of this secret room, then why did I have to hide him in the apple cellar? Where there was more chance of him being found?"

"This room is not secret while the queen lives."

The queen. There was something I was supposed to remember about the queen. . . .

I said lazily, "I smell smoke."

Maggie gave a cry and darted to one of the vertical slits in the wall. What could be out there? Smiling at her eagerness, I moved toward the second slit.

"Have a care, Roger," Mother Chilton said quietly. "The potion will wear off very soon."

"Oh," I said, unconcerned. I put my eye to the slit.

The tiny room looked out over one of the bridges spanning the river from palace to countryside. At first I could not understand what I was seeing. A bonfire—was it Midsummer's Eve, then? There were bonfires on Midsummer's Eve, always. But although I couldn't seem to remember the date, wasn't it too early for Midsummer's Eve? Or too late? Anyway, bonfires were for nighttime. This was full day. People, many people, were running *away* from the bonfire. Villagers and palace servants, all scattering and screaming. What a noise! Other people were trying to get close to the bonfire, and those people seemed to be soldiers, with more soldiers stopping them. . . . None of it made sense.

Why was Maggie crying like that?

Something strange was happening with the soldiers, most of whom were dressed in blue. No, only the closer ones were dressed in blue. . . . There were horsemen, too, in green, with one man on a huge black charger. He looked familiar. I could see everything sharply, more sharply than usual even at this distance, the air must be particularly clear—

The air—

The smoke—

The fighting—

"Have a care," Mother Chilton said.

The *screaming*—

Something lit up in my head, and I understood.

Queen Caroline writhed and screamed, tied to a stake in the center of the bonfire. The flames had caught her green silk gown. Her black hair, tossing wildly as she flailed, became tipped with fire. Beyond the pyre stood a ring of Blues, the Blues I had brought back from the country of the Dead, and they cut down every man who charged against them. Lord Robert's army mostly outnumbered the few hundred Blues, but the Blues could not be hurt. Swords passed through them, clubs did not crush their skulls. They didn't even bother to carry shields. The attackers, on the other hand, fell to the ground, sometimes two or three deep. Blood spouted from their arms, chests, mouths, and I could see their faces twitch in agony as they died.

The queen went on screaming, a high inhuman shriek, as her flesh began to burn.

Lord Robert's horse plunged through the fighting and somehow reached the pyre. He flung himself off his mount, which had three or four swords sticking from its poor body, just as the beast collapsed on the blood-slimed ground. Lord Robert waded into the pyre, jumped back, went again in. With his sword he slashed at the ropes that bound the burning queen.

A Blue came behind him, raised his sword, and prepared to pierce Lord Robert's back.

Maggie cried out. But I did not—*could* not. The scene

before me wavered, and if it hadn't been for Mother Chilton, I might have fallen. But she held me up, pushing me against the stone wall, and so I saw what happened next. What I had known would happen, ever since Maggie had told me in the apple cellar what day it was.

The Blue soldier attacking Lord Robert disappeared. It happened quickly. His flesh melted and ran; I could see the grotesque mask his face became, but only for a moment because it lasted only a moment. His body turned to bones and the bones to dust, and then all that was left was a pile of blue clothing and tarnished armor, the soldier gone.

And so was all the rest of the army I had brought back from death.

Lord Robert's army—what was left of it—fell on their knees and covered their eyes. Some cried out, words made unintelligible by fear and distance. The din was terrific. But missing from the shouts and prayers and exclamations was one sound.

The queen no longer screamed.

I sagged in Mother Chilton's arms and she lowered me to the floor. Standing over me, her old face was calm. She said, "Caroline is dead."

"Yes," I managed to say, despite the weakness that suddenly pressed on every part of my body, as if it were covered with heavy stones. But it was not weakness, it was sleep. I held it off long enough to make one more effort of will, one more biting of my raw tongue, to cross over for the last time.

All was serenity in the country of the Dead. The broad river flowed placidly, the sky shone with its featureless gray light, the Dead sat and stared at nothing. I saw many of Lord Solek's men, in their shaggy furs, sitting calmly on the ground, their faces blank and their *guns* stilled. I saw many, many Greens, as well. Some had died at the first battle with the dead Blues, the one that began in the laundries and raged through the palace a fortnight ago. Others had switched sides, as some men will always do, and had perished in the battle at the pyre, defending the queen to whom they had felt no loyalty in the first place. Interspersed among them sat the newly slain soldiers of Lord Robert's army, equally tranquil. Up close, I could see how many of them were boys or old men. The desperate Lord Robert had taken what soldiers he could put, by force or brib ery or—it was possible—loyalty to Queen Caroline.

There were no Blues among the Dead. I was the one who had seen to that.

In all that vast peaceful landscape, only one figure moved. She rushed toward me, her beautiful face twisted with fury and grief. "Roger! Where am I?"

"You're dead, Your Grace."

Memory took her. "Yes. I was . . . I was burned as a witch."

"Yes." And then I said the most futile words of my life— the most futile words of anyone's life, ever—and those words both were and were not true.

"I'm sorry, Your Grace."

Her fury focused. "You did this. *You.*"

"Yes."

"You took my queendom. You *burned* me—"

"No, Your Grace. I did much, but not those things. You did them to yourself."

Queen Caroline shrieked and launched herself at me. But she was no soldier, and she carried no weapons. I caught her flailing body in my arms. And then, a moment later, I was back in the secret room overlooking the west drawbridge, sliding into sleep. Mother Chilton had gone. All that remained of my last journey was the feel of Queen Caroline's body against mine, that body calming, going quiet and still.

"Good-bye, Your Grace," I had whispered to her just before my return, but I don't think she even heard me. She had already been claimed by the eerie tranquility of the Dead.

32

WE WERE NOT SEEN, Maggie and
I, as we left the palace. Maggie led the way, following instructions she had been given by Mother Chilton. Secret passageways took us to an inner wall, where a low entrance gave way
to Mother Chilton's tent. The tent was completely empty. Gone
were the potions, the feathers, the cloth bags of herbs and the
poles they had hung upon, the brazier and the single chair. The
entrance from palace to tent was so low that Maggie and I had
to crawl through on hands and knees. After we did, the stone
snapped shut, and nothing we did could open it again.

That must have been how Mother Chilton had helped
Cecilia escape from the palace. It must have been, too, how
Mother Chilton had come and gone from the palace whenever the queen summoned her. There had been some tie between them, something I did not understand and did not want

to understand. *"Caroline studied the soul arts but she has no talent,"* Mother Chilton had said to me once. Which was why the queen had sought to use my talent.

Maggie and I stayed in the deserted tent a few days, me resting while she went out to gather food and information. The food was not, at first, easy to come by. This was not because we had no money; Mother Chilton had once more left me a pile of coins, silvers and one gold piece. I did not understand why Mother Chilton helped me. She was as much a riddle as the queen, and like the queen, took her own hidden gambles. But there was no food because there was no one to buy it from. The villagers, along with most of the servants, had fled the capital after the Blue soldiers died a second time. *Witchcraft!* people cried. *Sorcery! Run! Run! Save yourselves!*

But there was nothing to save themselves from. No more witchery, no more fighting. The remnants of Lord Robert's ragtag army, plus whatever was left of the queen's Greens, were all the soldiers that remained. They were not witches and they were not fighting. They also needed to eat. One by one, the shopkeepers returned to the city, found it safe, and told others, who also returned.

Lord Robert had the good sense to take away and quietly bury the queen's burned body. Few knew where the "witch-queen" lay.

He crowned Princess Stephanie, looking small and frightened in the many-colored jewels of the Crown of Glory. Lord Robert rules as regent until the princess comes of age.

When I could travel again, Maggie and I left the city. I was disguised as a farmer who had drunk too much, but I was so thin and sick, with such a bristly untrimmed beard that had quite suddenly sprouted in place of my former downy fuzz, that no disguise might even have been necessary. I now looked older than my fifteen years. Besides, no one was looking for me. The rumor was that I, who brought the Blue army back from death, had disappeared into oblivion when they did. It is possible Mother Chilton had something to do with such rumors. It is possible she did not.

The last thing I saw, as I twisted around on the back of our donkey for a final look, was the palace's lone tower rising in the mist. Princess Stephanie's purple banner flew lonely and distant against a foggy, gray sky.

We live now in a village called Applebridge. It's far upriver, west of the capital, past where the flat valley has turned to hills, and almost as far as where the hills turn to mountains. Somewhere over those mountains is the realm of Lord Solek's savage people. The River Thymar is swift and shallow here, and barges or ferries cannot navigate the wild waters. But there is an ancient stone bridge connecting the west bank to the east, and so local farmers from all around come to Applebridge as a market town. Besides apples, the area grows corn and some other fruits, which also brings custom to the alehouse Maggie and I bought with Mother Chilton's money. The alehouse isn't much to look at: a rough taproom, a kitchen, a storeroom where I sleep, and three tiny chambers above, one for Maggie and two to house travelers. Most of our money went to buy the cottage, which despite its plainness is sound and snug. With the rest of Mother Chilton's coins, we bought a good stock of ale, which Maggie serves along with the meals she prepares. She is an excellent cook, a hardworking business partner, a saving manager.

When these nights of late summer are soft and warm and the tiny drops of moisture form on Maggie's full breasts and on her forehead under the springy fair curls, I am amazed all over again that I live in this snug village where there is peace and enough to eat, and no life-shattering surprises. Everything, in fact, that I once wanted when I lived with Hartah.

"Peter," Jee says in his high child's voice, "Maggie says ye maun come to sup now."

"Tell her I'm coming," I say, and Jee runs off. I pick up the bucket with my one good hand. I have learned to live with one hand: to keep the cottage in repair, to pour ale. The village children call me "Peter One-Hand." That is the name I use now, "Peter Forest," chosen at random. It is as Peter One-Hand that I throw the slops to the pig we have recently bought and watch it root eagerly in its wooden pen for something more than what it knows is in the slops.

Something more than what it knows.

Only once have we had a visitor from my old life. One night long ago, as I closed and shuttered the taproom for the night, she appeared in the doorway. I had not heard, not seen her approach. In the gloom, lit only by rushlights in their holders against the wall, her face was in shadow. But I knew immediately who she was.

"Mother Chilton."

"Hello, Roger."

"How did you come here without—"

"It doesn't matter." She walked in unbidden, and just as

she had done a year ago, took my face in her hand and looked into my eyes.

"You have given it up, then."

I didn't know how she knew. I had never understood her, no more than I'd understood the queen. But I was aware of what she meant. "Yes," I said, "I have given it up. I no longer cross over."

"Not even to find your mother?"

I pictured her again, my mother in her lavender gown with lavender ribbons in her hair, felt again the remembered tenderness of her arms around me. But all I said was, "No. It would do no good."

Mother Chilton nodded, as if satisfied. "You're right, Roger. You could not rouse her even if you found her. But know this—she is at peace now, even as are the country of the Dead and The Queendom."

"And Soulvine Moor?"

She looked away, shadows from the rushlights changing the planes of her face, like stones shifting shape under water. "The Moor will never be at peace while they seek what no one can have. There is no living forever, Roger. But I have come here to set your mind at ease about one thing, at least."

Despite myself, and even after all that had happened, hope surged through me. *Cecilia* . . .

"No, not she," Mother Chilton said. "That cannot be undone, as you well know. But now that you've seen what happens at Soulvine Moor, I want to tell you this: What happened to Cecilia did not happen to your mother. Hers was a natural death, and you can stop dreaming about her now."

"How did you know I—"

But Mother Chilton was gone. It seemed that the room dimmed for a moment, and when I could see it more clearly, she was no longer there. I ran outside; I saw nothing unusual.

"Peter!" Maggie called from above. "Is the taproom shuttered?"

"Yes," I said, closing and barring the door. Where had she gone? How?

"I thought I heard voices."

"No," I said. "There is no one here but us." I took the rushlight from the wall and lighted my way up the narrow stairs. At the twist of the stairwell was a small, barred window, flooded by moonlight. Silhouetted against the full moon flew a black swan, at a time of night when swans do not fly, higher than any swan ever flew. It beat its wings in a great powerful swoop, and then it was gone into the darkness.

ACKNOWLEDGMENTS

Much gratitude to my editor, Sharyn November, for her valuable contributions to this book, and to my agents, Ralph Vicinanza and Chris Schelling, for theirs.

ANNA KENDALL was born in Ireland and emigrated with her parents to the United States at age twelve. For several years she taught fourth grade. Anna lives in Seattle, where she plays a lot of chess. This is her first novel.